# AWE AND WONDER . . . MYSTERY AND POWER

"Smith was one of the greatest writers ever to work in the genre."
**—Gardner Dozois**

"Cordwainer Smith was one of the great ones."
**—Spider Robinson**

"His repute only grows with time."
**—Gregory Benford**

"Smith's Instrumentality is the most complex and lyrical of all future histories. . . . Lush, strange, unique, a treasure."
**—Stephen Baxter**

". . . the unmatchable, unthinkable Cordwainer Smith. All [his stories] are magnificently weird, most are plain magnificent, and one or two are the nearest thing to perfection that you or I will ever chance upon in our little lives."
**—John Clute**

"Better than any writer we've yet seen, Smith represents the sense of awe and wonder that is the heart of science fiction."
**—Scott Edelman**

"No one, in or out of science fiction, wrote like [Smith]; his work retains its mystery and power decades later. . . ."
**—Barry Malzberg**

"No one ever wrote quite like Smith, with his special blend of myth-making and rich invention."
***—Publishers Weekly***

"Smith is one of science fiction's most lyrical and most influential authors, and indisputably its most imaginative."
**—Cynthia Ward**, Sci-Fi.com

**Baen Books by
Cordwainer Smith**

*We the Underpeople*
*When the People Fell*

# We the Underpeople

## Cordwainer Smith

林

白

樂

### selected by
### Hank Davis

WE THE UNDERPEOPLE

This is a work of fiction. All the characters and events portrayed in this book are fictional, and any resemblance to real people or incidents is purely coincidental.

A Baen Book

Baen Publishing Enterprises
P.O. Box 1403
Riverdale, NY 10471
www.baen.com

ISBN 10: 1-4165-5567-6
ISBN 13: 978-1-4165-5567-4

Cover art by Bob Eggleton

First Baen paperback printing, August 2008

Library of Congress Control Number: 2006023133

Distributed by Simon & Schuster
1230 Avenue of the Americas
New York, NY 10020

Pages by Joy Freeman (www.pagesbyjoy.com)
Printed in the United States of America

# ∽ CONTENTS ∽

# INTRODUCTION

He erupted into our midst without warning, a little over half a century ago, with one of the strangest science-fiction stories ever published. The magazine it appeared in was pretty strange, too: a crudely printed semi-pro affair called *Fantasy Book*, emanating from Los Angeles in such tiny quantities that each issue became a collector's item almost as soon as it appeared.

The publisher of *Fantasy Book* was William L. Crawford, an old-time science-fiction enthusiast whose s-f publishing career went back to the early 1930s, when he brought out two little magazines called *Marvel Tales* and *Unusual Stories*, setting the type for them himself. No more than a thousand copies of each issue were printed, though they ran outstanding stories by the likes of H.P. Lovecraft, Clifford D. Simak, and Robert E. Howard. *Fantasy Book*, which had a wobbly eight-issue existence between 1947 and 1951, was as amateurish-looking as its Crawford predecessors—no two issues had quite the same format, and even within a single issue several typefaces usually were employed—but it, too, managed to run some valuable fiction, by A.E. van Vogt, Andre Norton, L. Ron Hubbard, Isaac Asimov in collaboration with

Frederik Pohl, and Murray Leinster. But the one story that ensures this scruffy magazine's immortality in the history of science fiction was the third item in its (undated) sixth issue, released in January of 1950: "Scanners Live in Vain" by an unknown writer with the strange name of Cordwainer Smith.

How that story came into the hands of Bill Crawford of *Fantasy Book* is something I can't tell you. John J. Pierce, a pioneer in the arcane field of Cordwainer Smith studies reported in a piece first published in 1993 that "Smith" wrote the story in 1945 and submitted it to the pre-eminent science-fiction editor of the day, John W. Campbell of *Astounding Science Fiction,* who rejected it as "too extreme." In those days stories rejected by Campbell had few other possibilities for publication—the only markets were two fairly juvenile pulp magazines called *Startling Stories* and *Thrilling Wonder Stories,* which had the same editor, and a third and even more juvenile pulp called *Planet Stories.* The remaining two magazines, *Amazing Stories* and *Fantastic Adventures,* were entirely staff-written and did not welcome unsolicited submissions.

So once a story had been to Campbell and to the editors of the *Startling-Thrilling Wonder* duo and *Planet,* there was essentially no place to publish it except some amateur magazine, and "Smith," who must have been a devoted science-fiction reader, somehow discovered *Fantasy Book* and sent his story to Bill Crawford. And that was how my teenage self happened to read, in the spring of 1950, a story that began with this startling, jarring passage:

"Martel was angry. He did not even adjust his blood away from anger. He stamped across the room by judgment, not by sight. When he saw the table hit the floor, and could tell by the expression on Luci's face that the table must have made a loud crash, he looked down to see if his leg was broken. It was not. Scanner to the core, he had to scan himself. The action was reflex: and automatic. The inventory included his legs, abdomen, Chestbox of instruments, hands, arms, face and back with the Mirror. Only then did Martel go back to being angry. He talked with his voice, even though he knew that his wife hated its blare and preferred to have him write.

"'I tell you, I must cranch. I have to cranch. It's my worry. isn't it?'"

Nobody—with the possible exception of A.E. van Vogt, whose dreamlike, surreal *The World of Null-A* was first published around the time Cordwainer Smith was writing "Scanners"—wrote science fiction that sounded like that. The lucid, unadorned prose setting forth the immeasurably strange—it was a new kind of voice.

I read on and on. One bizarre term after another tumbled forth: Scanners, the Up-and-Out, the habermans, the Cranching Wire. In time, it all made sense. By the end of the story, forty pages later, I knew that some incomparable master of science fiction had taken me to an invented world like none that had ever been portrayed before.

But who was this Cordwainer Smith?

Suddenly, everybody in the little inner world of

science fiction—there couldn't have been more than a few hundred who really cared about it in any more than a casual way—was asking that question. But no answers came forth. William Crawford let it be known that the name was a pseudonym—but for whom? Van Vogt? Hardly. If he had written it, he would have been proud to publish it under his own name. The prolific Henry Kuttner, famous for his innumerable pseudonyms? Heinlein? Sturgeon? None of the theories seemed to add up. The name itself provided no clue. ("Cordwainer" is an archaic term meaning "leather-worker" or "shoemaker.")

The hubbub died down within a few months, and the unknown Mr. Smith and his remarkable story receded into obscurity and might have remained there forever but for Frederik Pohl, not only a writer but an editor of s-f anthologies. Pohl knew about "Scanners" because he had had a story in that same issue of *Fantasy Book,* and he republished it in 1952 in a paperback called *Beyond the End of Time,* a fine fat collection that also included work by Bradbury, Asimov, van Vogt, and Heinlein. Science-fiction paperbacks were few and far between back then, and everybody who liked s-f pounced on the Pohl anthology. Thousands of readers who had never so much as heard of *Fantasy Book* now discovered Cordwainer Smith and clamored for more of his work.

They would have to wait a few years. Nothing more was heard of the mysterious Cordwainer Smith until the autumn of 1955, when *Galaxy Science Fiction,* one of the leading s-f magazines of the day, offered the second Smith story: the eccentric, powerful little tale, "The Game of Rat and Dragon." Very likely Fred Pohl had some involvement in this, too, for he was a close friend of Horace Gold, *Galaxy's* editor, and probably facilitated contact between the writer and Smith.

And then, beginning in 1957, a torrent of Cordwainer Smith stories came forth, each of them told in the same startlingly individual way as the first two, and—as gradually became apparent—each set in the same astonishingly original future Universe. There was one in 1957, two in 1958, four in 1959, one in 1960. and, between 1961 and 1965, sixteen more, most of them meaty novellas. They appeared in a wide range of science-fiction magazines, from the most minor (the short-lived *Saturn*) to the top of the line (*Galaxy* and *Fantasy and Science Fiction*). Pohl, who had replaced Horace Gold as editor of *Galaxy* in 1961, published most of the major ones, such instantly hailed masterpieces as "The Ballad of Lost C'Mell," "Think Blue, Count Two," and "The Dead Lady of Clown Town." It was obvious by now to everyone involved with science fiction that a major writer was at work in our midst.

A little information about him was beginning to leak out, too. Some time in 1963 word emerged that "Smith" was a pseudonym for one Paul Linebarger, who lived in the vicinity of Washington, D.C., and had some sort of involvement with the national military or espionage establishment. When the World Science Fiction Convention was held in Washington that year, Linebarger was not among those present, but Fred Pohl arranged for a small group of writers—I was not among them, alas—to visit him at his house. It was the only time, I believe, that he had any personal contact with the world of professional science-fiction publishing.

The extent to which the details of Paul Linebarger's life remained unknown even after that can be seen from the review I wrote in 1964 of the first Cordwainer Smith novel, *The Planet Buyer* (which was actually a section of the larger work later published as *Norstrilia*):

"Rumor has it that the author of the stories appearing under the byline of 'Cordwainer Smith' is a military man who has spent much of his life in the Orient and who now holds a high position in the Pentagon. However, I have a theory of my own.

"I think that Cordwainer Smith is a visitor from some remote period of the future, living among us perhaps as an exile from his own era or perhaps just as a tourist, and amusing himself by casting some of his knowledge of historical events into the form of science fiction. . . .

"The evidence is partly stylistic. Cordwainer Smith writes a strange, eerie prose, which though grammatical does not appear to be ordinary in any manner. Astonishingly flat declarative statements alternate with wildly soaring prose; syntax is odd and often distorted; in every way, there seems to be an alien mind putting the words together.

"The structure of the stories, too, is unconventional. Most science fiction writers go to some length to explain what is happening in their stories, and what the background details mean. Smith does a little of this, but only enough to make his work intelligible. The rest he takes for granted, as though it is *so* tiresomely familiar to him that he does not see the need to spell out the details.

"The *most* revealing thing, though, is the fact that every Cordwainer Smith story fits into a common framework—from the first one, published in 1950, on. Aside from this novel, there are about a dozen longish novelettes and a good many short stories in the Smith *oeuvre* so far, and this entire voluminous output hangs together. Smith hops across a span of perhaps fifteen thousand years, zigzagging to tell in detail a story that he has encapsulated in a sentence or two of an earlier story, but his work is always consistent. One can examine his first story or his second, or his third, and see the seeds of the tenth or twentieth. Nor is any story really complete in itself; it refers back and forth to the others, each a segment out of a vast and bewildering whole.

"It is frightening and a little implausible to think that Cordwainer Smith, circa 1948, was able to visualize an imaginary universe with such detail that he could spend the next decade and a half inventing internally consistent and externally consistent stories about it. I prefer to believe that Smith is merely making use of historical or mythical material that he learned from childhood on—spinning out for us the equivalents of the *Illiad* or the courtship of Miles Standish.

"The book at hand, which appeared in shorter form last year in *Galaxy,* is typical of his output. Maddeningly oblique, stunningly evocative, it teases and taunts, giving us an incomplete story with little hint of the real nature of the events. Though it defies coherent summary, it fascinates and compels. Rod McBan, a Parsifal-like innocent from the planet known as Old North Australia, where every man is a millionaire, escapes execution as a mental defective through some maneuver not readily intelligible to the reader. Then a computer induces him to execute a coup in futures of stroon, the immortality drug that is the source of Old North Australia's wealth, and he ends up so rich that he buys the planet Earth, again for uncertain motivations. He comes to Earth and is spirited away by the cat girl C'mell, one of Smith's most enchanting creations. Here the book ends, with a clear promise of more to come.

"The man is not just a science-fiction writer. He is a wanderer out of the future, I have no doubt. It scares me to contemplate his work or his presence among us."

I was not, of course, serious about my notion in that book review of four decades ago that Smith was a time-traveler masquerading as a science-fiction writer. The bit of legitimate biographical information I provided about him was accurate enough, but very much on the sketchy side, as we discovered in 1966 when news came of the author's death.

He was only 53, and had packed several lifetimes worth of experience into that short span. At last it was revealed that Paul M.A. Linebarger, born in Milwaukee in 1913, was the son of an American judge who had helped to finance the Chinese revolution of 1911 and was the legal advisor to its leader, Sun Yat-sen. The younger Linebarger had grown up in

China, Japan, Germany, and France, and by the age of 21 had earned a doctorate in political science at Johns Hopkins University. (Some of the strangeness of his fictional technique, apparently, was derived from his knowledge of the Chinese language and classical Chinese methods of storytelling.) Between 1930 and 1936 he had been a legal consultant to the Chinese government under Chiang Kai-shek, and during World War II, still based in China, he served as a lieutenant colonel in U.S. Army Intelligence. (This was the Pentagon connection about which we had heard.) After the war he became a professor of Asian politics at Johns Hopkins, but also found time to serve as an advisor to the British forces in Malaya and to the U.S. Eighth Army in Korea, and to write a definitive textbook on psychological warfare, several espionage thrillers, and the science-fiction works for which he will always be remembered by connoisseurs of the field.

Researchers have discovered that Linebarger had been writing science fiction from boyhood on, his first known story, "War No. 81-Q," appeared in his high-school magazine in 1928, when he was fifteen. Evidently he went on writing fantasy and science fiction stories in great abundance throughout the 1930s and 1940s, though none of them has ever been published and they can be presumed to be lost—and then, in 1945, came "Scanners Live in Vain," which would so spectacularly launch his career as a writer five years later.

A brilliant man, an extraordinary writer, Death took him much too soon, just as he was reaching his creative peak, and we will never know what glories of the imagination he would have given us if he had been granted another fifteen or twenty years. But at least we have the thirty or so science-fiction stories and the one novel that he did manage to produce in his short, busy life.

I was instrumental in arranging for the publication of the very first Cordwainer Smith short-story collection in 1963, a book to which the publisher gave the title *You Will Never Be the Same*. It is as apt a description of the effect Cordwainer Smith's fiction has on its readers as has ever been coined.

—Robert Silverberg
July 2002

# The Dead Lady of Clown Town

## ∽ 1 ∽

You already know the end—the immense drama of the Lord Jestocost, seventh of his line, and how the cat-girl C'mell initiated the vast conspiracy. But you do not know the beginning, how the first Lord Jestocost got his name, because of the terror and inspiration which his mother, Lady Goroke, obtained from the famous real-life drama of the dog-girl D'joan. It is even less likely that you know the other story—the one behind D'joan. This story is sometimes mentioned as the matter of the "nameless witch," which is absurd, because she really had a name. The name was "Elaine," an ancient and forbidden one.

Elaine was a mistake. Her birth, her life, her career were all mistakes. The ruby was wrong. How could that have happened?

Go back to An-fang, the Peace Square at An-fang, the Beginning Place at An-fang, where all things start. Bright it was. Red Square, dead square, clear square, under a yellow sun.

This was Earth Original, Manhome itself, where

Earthport thrusts its way up through hurricane clouds that are higher than the mountains.

An-fang was near a city, the only living city with a pre-atomic name. The lovely meaningless name was Meeya Meefla, where the lines of ancient roadways, untouched by a wheel for thousands of years, forever paralleled the warm, bright, clear beaches of the Old South East.

The headquarters of the People Programmer was at An-fang, and there the mistake happened:

A ruby trembled. Two tourmaline nets failed to rectify the laser beam. A diamond noted the error. Both the error and the correction went into the general computer.

The error assigned, on the general account of births for Fomalhaut III, the profession of "lay therapist, female, intuitive capacity for correction of human physiology with local resources." On some of the early ships they used to call these people *witch-women,* because they worked unaccountable cures. For pioneer parties, these lay therapists were invaluable; in settled post-Riesmannian societies, they became an awful nuisance. Sickness disappeared with good conditions, accidents dwindled down to nothing, medical work became institutional.

Who wants a witch, even a good witch, when a thousand-bed hospital is waiting with its staff eager for clinical experience . . . and only seven out of its thousand beds filled with real people? (The remaining beds were filled with lifelike robots on which the staff could practice, lest they lose their morale. They could, of course, have worked on underpeople—animals in the shape of human beings, who did the heavy and the weary work which remained as the *caput mortuum* of a really perfected economy—but it was against the law for animals, even when they were underpeople, to go to a human hospital. When underpeople got sick, the Instrumentality took care of them—in slaughter-houses. It was easier to breed new underpeople for the jobs than it was to repair sick ones. Furthermore, the tender, loving care of a hospital might give them ideas. Such as the idea that they were people. This would have been bad, from the prevailing point of view. Therefore the human hospitals remained almost empty while an underperson who sneezed four times or who vomited once was taken away, never to be ill again. The empty beds kept on with the robot patients, who went through endless repetitions of the human patterns of injury or disease.) This left no work for witches, bred and trained.

Yet the ruby had trembled; the program had indeed made a mistake; the birth-number for a "lay therapist, general, female, immediate use" had been ordered for Fomalhaut III.

Much later, when the story was all done down to its last historic detail, there was an investigation into the origins of Elaine. When the laser had trembled, both the original order and the correction were fed simultaneously into the machine. The machine recognized the contradiction and promptly referred both papers to the human supervisor, an actual man who had been working on the job for seven years.

He was studying music, and he was bored. He was so close to the end of his term that he was already counting the days to his own release. Meanwhile he was rearranging two popular songs. One was *The Big*

*Bamboo,* a primitive piece which tried to evoke the original magic of man. The other was about a girl, *Elaine, Elaine,* whom the song asked to refrain from giving pain to her loving swain. Neither of the songs was important; but between them they influenced history, first a little bit and then very much.

The musician had plenty of time to practice. He had not had to meet a real emergency in all his seven years. From time to time the machine made reports to him, but the musician just told the machine to correct its own errors, and it infallibly did so.

On the day that the accident of Elaine happened, he was trying to perfect his finger work on the guitar, a very old instrument believed to date from the pre-space period. He was playing *The Big Bamboo* for the hundredth time.

The machine announced its mistake with an initial musical chime. The supervisor had long since forgotten all the instructions which he had so worrisomely memorized seven long years ago. The alert did not really and truly matter, because the machine invariably corrected its own mistakes whether the supervisor was on duty or not.

The machine, not having its chime answered, moved into a second-stage alarm. From a loudspeaker set in the wall of the room, it shrieked in a high, clear human voice, the voice of some employee who had died thousands of years earlier:

"Alert, alert! Emergency. Correction needed. Correction needed!"

The answer was one which the machine had never heard before, old though it was. The musician's fingers ran madly, gladly over the guitar strings and he sang clearly, wildly back to the machine a message strange beyond any machine's belief:

> *Beat, beat the Big Bamboo!*
> *Beat, beat, beat the Big Bamboo for me . . . !*

Hastily the machine set its memory banks and computers to work, looking for the code reference to "bamboo," trying to make that word fit the present context. There was no reference at all. The machine pestered the man some more.

"Instructions unclear. Instructions unclear. Please correct."

"Shut up," said the man.

"Cannot comply," stated the machine. "Please state and repeat, please state and repeat, please state and repeat."

"Do shut up," said the man, but he knew the machine would not obey this. Without thinking, he turned to his other tune and sang the first two lines twice over:

> *Elaine, Elaine,*
> *go cure the pain!*
> *Elaine, Elaine,*
> *go cure the pain!*

Repetition had been inserted as a safeguard into the machine, on the assumption that no real man would repeat an error. The name "Elaine" was not correct number code, but the fourfold emphasis seemed to confirm the need for a "lay therapist, female." The machine itself noted that a genuine man had

corrected the situation card presented as a matter
of emergency.

"Accepted," said the machine.

This word, too late, jolted the supervisor away
from his music.

"Accepted what?" he asked.

There was no answering voice. There was no sound
at all except for the whisper of slightly-moistened
warm air through the ventilators.

The supervisor looked out the window. He could
see a little of the blood-black red color of the Peace
Square of An-fang; beyond lay the ocean, endlessly
beautiful and endlessly tedious.

The supervisor sighed hopefully. He was young.
"Guess it doesn't matter," he thought, picking up his
guitar.

(Thirty-seven years later, he found out that it did
matter. The Lady Goroke herself, one of the Chiefs
of the Instrumentality, sent a Subchief of the Instrumentality to find out who had caused D'joan. When
the man found that the witch Elaine was the source
of the trouble, she sent him on to find out how
Elaine had gotten into a well-ordered universe. The
supervisor was found. He was still a musician. He
remembered nothing of the story. He was hypnotized.
He still remembered nothing. The subchief invoked
an emergency and Police Drug Four ("clear memory")
was administered to the musician. He immediately
remembered the whole silly scene, but insisted that it
did not matter. The case was referred to Lady Goroke,
who instructed the authorities that the musician be
told the whole horrible, beautiful story of D'joan at
Fomalhaut—the very story which you are now being

told—and he wept. He was not punished otherwise, but the Lady Goroke commanded that those memories be left in his mind for so long as he might live.)

The man picked up his guitar, but the machine went on about its work.

It selected a fertilized human embryo, tagged it with the freakish name "Elaine," irradiated the genetic code with strong aptitudes for witchcraft, and then marked the person's card for training in medicine, transportation by sail-ship to Fomalhaut III, and release for service on the planet.

Elaine was born without being needed, without being wanted, without having a skill which could help or hurt any existing human being. She went into life doomed and useless.

It is not remarkable that she was misbegotten. Errors do happen. Remarkable was the fact that she managed to survive without being altered, corrected, or killed by the safety devices which mankind has installed in society for its own protection.

Unwanted, unused, she wandered through the tedious months and useless years of her own existence. She was well fed, richly clothed, variously housed. She had machines and robots to serve her, underpeople to obey her, people to protect her against others or against herself, should the need arise. But she could never find work; without work, she had no time for love; without work or love, she had no hope at all.

If she had only stumbled into the right experts or the right authorities, they would have altered or re-trained her. This would have made her into an acceptable woman; but she did not find the police, nor did they find her. She was helpless to correct her own programming, utterly helpless. It had been imposed on her at An-fang, way back at An-fang, where all things begin.

The ruby had trembled, the tourmaline failed, the diamond passed unsupported. Thus, a woman was born doomed.


## ∽ 2 ∾


Much later, when people made songs about the strange case of the dog-girl D'joan, the minstrels and singers had tried to imagine what Elaine felt like, and they had made up *The Song of Elaine* for her. It is not authentic, but it shows how Elaine looked at her own life before the strange case of D'joan began to flow from Elaine's own actions:

> *Other women hate me.*
> *Men never touch me.*
> *I am too much me.*
> 　　*I'll be a witch!*
>
> *Mama never towelled me.*
> *Daddy never growled me.*
> *Little kiddies grate me.*
> 　　*I'll be a bitch!*
>
> *People never named me.*
> *Dogs never shamed me.*
> *Oh, I am a such me!*
> 　　*I'll be a witch.*

*I'll make them shun me.*
*They'll never run me.*
*Could they even stun me?*
   *I'll be a witch.*

*Let them all attack me.*
*They can only rack me.*
*Me—I can hack me.*
   *I'll be a witch.*

*Other women hate me.*
*Men never touch me.*
*I am too much me.*
   *I'll be a witch.*

The song overstates the case. Women did not hate Elaine; they did not look at her. Men did not shun Elaine; they did not notice her either. There were no places on Fomalhaut III where she could have met human children, for the nurseries were far underground because of chancy radiation and fierce weather. The song pretends that Elaine began with the thought that she was not human, but underpeople, and had herself been born a dog. This did not happen at the beginning of the case, but only at the very end, when the story of D'joan was already being carried between the stars and developing with all the new twists of folklore and legend. She never went mad.

("Madness" is a rare condition, consisting of a human mind which does not engage its environment correctly. Elaine approached it before she met D'joan. Elaine was not the only case, but she was a rare and genuine one. Her life, thrust back from all attempts

at growth, had turned back on itself and her mind
had spiraled inward to the only safety she could really
know, psychosis. Madness is always better than X, and
X to each patient is individual, personal, secret, and
overwhelmingly important. Elaine had gone normally
mad; her imprinted and destined career was the
wrong one. "Lay therapists, female" were coded to
work decisively, autonomously, on their own authority, and with great rapidity. These working conditions
were needed on new planets. They were not coded
to consult other people; most places, there would be
no one to consult. Elaine did what was set for her at
An-fang, all the way down to the individual chemical
conditions of her spinal fluid. She was herself the
wrong and she never knew it. Madness was much
kinder than the realization that she was not herself,
should not have lived, and amounted at the most to
a mistake committed between a trembling ruby and
a young, careless man with a guitar.)

She found D'joan and the worlds reeled.

Their meeting occurred at a place nicknamed "the
edge of the world," where the undercity met daylight.
This was itself unusual; but Fomalhaut III was an
unusual and uncomfortable planet, where wild weather
and men's caprice drove architects to furious design
and grotesque execution.

Elaine walked through the city, secretly mad, looking for sick people whom she could help. She had
been stamped, imprinted, designed, born, bred, and
trained for this task. There was no task.

She was an intelligent woman. Bright brains serve
madness as well as they serve sanity—namely, very well
indeed. It never occurred to her to give up her mission.

The people of Fomalhaut III, like the people of Manhome Earth itself, are almost uniformly handsome; it is only in the far-out, half-unreachable worlds that the human stock, strained by the sheer effort to survive, becomes ugly, weary, or varied. She did not look much different from the other intelligent, handsome people who flocked the streets. Her hair was black, and she was tall. Her arms and legs were long, the trunk of her body short. She wore her hair brushed straight back from a high, narrow, square forehead. Her eyes were an odd, deep blue. Her mouth might have been pretty, but it never smiled, so that no one could really tell whether it was beautiful or not. She stood erect and proud: but so did everyone else. Her mouth was strange in its very lack of communicativeness and her eyes swept back and forth, back and forth like ancient radar, looking for the sick, the needy, and stricken, whom she had a passion to serve.

How could she be unhappy? She had never had time to be happy. It was easy for her to think that happiness was something which disappeared at the end of childhood. Now and then, here and there, perhaps when a fountain murmured in sunlight or when leaves exploded in the startling Fomalhautian spring, she wondered that other people—people as responsible as herself by the doom of age, grade, sex, training, and career number—should be happy when she alone seemed to have no time for happiness. But she always dismissed the thought and walked the ramps and streets until her arches ached, looking for work which did not yet exist.

Human flesh, older than history, more dogged than culture, has its own wisdom. The bodies of people are marked with the archaic ruses of survival, so that on Fomalhaut III, Elaine herself preserved the skills of ancestors she never even thought about—those ancestors who, in the incredible and remote past, had mastered terrible Earth itself. Elaine was mad. But there was a part of her which suspected that she was mad.

Perhaps this wisdom seized her as she walked from Waterrocky Road toward the bright esplanades of the Shopping Bar. She saw a forgotten door. The robots could clean near it but, because of the old, odd architectural shape, they could not sweep and polish right at the bottom line of the door. A thin hard line of old dust and caked polish lay like a sealant at the base of the doorline. It was obvious that no one had gone through for a long, long time.

The civilized rule was that prohibited areas were marked both telepathically and with symbols. The most dangerous of all had robot or underpeople guards. But everything which was not prohibited, was permitted. Thus Elaine had no right to open the door, but she had no obligation not to do so. She opened it—

By sheer caprice.

Or so she thought.

This was a far cry from the "I'll be a witch" motif attributed to her in the later ballad. She was not yet frantic, not yet desperate, she was not yet even noble.

That opening of a door changed her own world and changed life on thousands of planets for generations to come, but the opening was not itself strange. It was the tired caprice of a thoroughly frustrated and mildly unhappy woman. Nothing more. All the other descriptions of it have been improvements, embellishments, falsifications.

She did get a shock when she opened the door, but not for the reasons attributed backwards to her by balladists and historians.

She was shocked because the door opened on steps and the steps led down to landscape and sunlight—truly an unexpected sight on any world. She was looking from the New City to the Old City. The New City rose on its shell out over the Old City, and when she looked "indoors" she saw the sunset in the city below. She gasped at the beauty and the unexpectedness of it.

There, the open door—*with another world beyond it*. Here, the old familiar street, clean, handsome, quiet, useless, where her own useless self had worked a thousand times.

There—something. Here, the world she knew. She did not know the words "fairyland" or "magic place," but if she had known them, she would have used them.

She glanced to the right, to the left.

The passersby noticed neither her nor the door. The sunset was just beginning to show in the upper city. In the lower city it was already blood-red with streamers of gold like enormous frozen flame. Elaine did not know that she sniffed the air; she did not know that she trembled on the edge of tears; she did not know that a tender smile, the first smile in years, relaxed her mouth and turned her tired tense face into a passing loveliness. She was too intent on looking around.

People walked about their business. Down the road, an underpeople type—female, possibly cat—detoured far around a true human who was walking at a slower pace. Far away, a police ornithopter flapped slowly around one of the towers; unless the robots used a telescope on her or unless they had one of the rare hawk-undermen who were sometimes used as police, they could not see her.

She stepped through the doorway and pulled the door itself back into the closed position.

She did not know it, but therewith unborn futures reeled out of existence, rebellion flamed into coming centuries, people and underpeople died in strange causes, mothers changed the names of unborn lords, and starships whispered back from places which men had not even imagined before. Space³, which had always been there, waiting for men's notice, would come the sooner—because of her, because of the door, because of her next few steps, what she would say, and the child she would meet. (The ballad-writers told the whole story later on, but they told it backwards, from their own knowledge of D'joan and what Elaine had done to set the worlds afire. The simple truth is the fact that a lonely woman went through a mysterious door. That is all. Everything else happened later.)

At the top of the steps she stood, door closed behind her, the sunset gold of the unknown city streaming out in front of her. She could see where the great shell of the New City of Kalma arched out toward the sky; she could see that the buildings here were older, less harmonious than the ones she had left. She did not know the concept "picturesque," or she would have called it that. She knew no concept to describe the scene which lay peacefully at her feet.

There was not a person in sight.

Far in the distance, a fire-detector throbbed back and forth on top of an old tower. Outside of that there was nothing but the yellow-gold city beneath her, and a bird—was it a bird, or a large storm-swept leaf?—in the middle distance.

Filled with fear, hope, expectation, and the surmisal of strange appetites, she walked downward with quiet, unknown purpose.

❧ 3 ❧

At the foot of the stairs, nine flights of them there had been, a child waited—a girl, about five. The child had a bright blue smock, wavy red-brown hair, and the daintiest hands which Elaine had ever seen.

Elaine's heart went out to her. The child looked up at her and shrank away. Elaine knew the meaning of those handsome brown eyes, of that muscular supplication of trust, that recoil from people. It was not a child at all—just some animal in the shape of a person, a dog perhaps, which would later be taught to speak, to work, to perform useful services.

The little girl rose, standing as though she were about to run. Elaine had the feeling that the little dog-girl had not decided whether to run toward her or from her. She did not wish to get involved with an underperson—what woman would?—but neither did she wish to frighten the little thing. After all, it was small, very young.

The two confronted each other for a moment, the little thing uncertain, Elaine relaxed. Then the little animal-girl spoke.

"Ask her," she said, and it was a command.

Elaine was surprised. Since when did animals command?

"Ask her!" repeated the little thing. She pointed at a window which had the words TRAVELER'S AID above it. Then the girl ran. A flash of blue from her dress, a twinkle of white from her running sandals, and she was gone.

Elaine stood quiet and puzzled in the forlorn and empty city.

The window spoke to her, "You might as well come on over. You will, you know."

It was the wise mature voice of an experienced woman—a voice with a bubble of laughter underneath its phonic edge, with a hint of sympathy and enthusiasm in its tone. The command was not merely a command. It was, even at its beginning, a happy private joke between two wise women.

Elaine was not surprised when a machine spoke to her. Recordings had been telling her things all her life. She was not sure of this situation, however.

"Is there somebody there?" she said.

"Yes and no," said the voice. "I'm 'Travelers' Aid' and I help everybody who comes through this way. You're lost or you wouldn't be here. Put your hand in my window."

"What I mean is," said Elaine, "are you a person or are you a machine?"

"Depends," said the voice. "I'm a machine, but I used to be a person, long, long ago. A lady, in fact, and one of the Instrumentality. But my time came and they said to me, 'Would you mind if we made a machine print of your whole personality? It would be very helpful for the information booths.' So of course I said yes, and they made this copy, and I died, and they shot my body into space with all the usual honors, but here I was. It felt pretty odd inside this contraption, me looking at things and talking to people and giving good advice and staying busy, until they built the new city. So what do you say? Am I me or aren't I?"

"I don't know, ma'am." Elaine stood back.

The warm voice lost its humor and became commanding. "Give me your hand, then, so I can identify you and tell you what to do."

"I think," said Elaine, "that I'll go back upstairs and go through the door into the upper city."

"And cheat me," said the voice in the window, "out of my first conversation with a real person in four years?" There was demand in the voice, but there was still the warmth and the humor; there was loneliness too. The loneliness decided Elaine. She stepped up to the window and put her hand flat on the ledge.

"You're Elaine," cried the window. "You're *Elaine!* The worlds wait for you. You're from An-fang, where all things begin, the Peace Square at An-fang, on Old Earth itself!"

"Yes," said Elaine.

The voice bubbled over with enthusiasm. "He is waiting for you. Oh, he has waited for you a long, long time. And the little girl you met. *That was D'joan herself.* The story has begun. The world's great age begins anew. And I can die when it is over. So sorry, my dear. I don't mean to confuse you. I am the Lady Panc Ashash. You're Elaine. Your number originally ended 783 and you shouldn't even be on this planet.

All the important people here end with the number 5 and 6. You're a lay therapist and you're in the wrong place, but your lover is already on his way, and you've never been in love yet, and it's all too exciting."

Elaine looked quickly around her. The old lower town was turning more red and less gold as the sunset progressed. The steps behind her seemed terribly high as she looked back, the door at the top very small. Perhaps it had locked on her when she closed it. Maybe she wouldn't ever be able to leave the old lower city.

The window must have been watching her in some way, because the voice of the Lady Panc Ashash became tender,

"Sit down, my dear," said the voice from the window. "When I was me, I used to be much more polite. I haven't been me for a long, long time. I'm a machine, and still I feel like myself. Do sit down, and do forgive me."

Elaine looked around. There was the roadside marble bench behind her. She sat on it obediently. The happiness which had been in her at the top of the stairs bubbled forth anew. If this wise old machine knew so much about her, perhaps it could tell her what to do. What did the voice mean by "wrong planet"? By "lover"? By "he is coming for you now," or was that what the voice had actually said?

"Take a breath, my dear," said the voice of the Lady Panc Ashash. She might have been dead for hundreds or thousands of years, but still spoke with the authority and kindness of a great lady.

Elaine breathed deep. She saw a huge red cloud, like a pregnant whale, getting ready to butt the rim of the upper city, far above her and far out over the sea. She wondered if clouds could possibly have feelings.

The voice was speaking again. What had it said?

Apparently the question was repeated. "Did you know you were coming?" said the voice from the window.

"Of course not." Elaine shrugged. "There was just this door, and I didn't have anything special to do, so I opened it. And here was a whole new world inside a house. It looked strange and rather pretty, so I came down. Wouldn't you have done the same thing?"

"I don't know," said the voice candidly. "I'm really a machine. I haven't been me for a long, long time. Perhaps I would have, when I was alive. I don't know that, but I know about things. Maybe I can see the future, or perhaps the machine part of me computes such good probabilities that it just seems like it. I know who you are and what is going to happen to you. You had better brush your hair."

"Whatever for?" said Elaine.

"He is coming," said the happy old voice of the Lady Panc Ashash.

"*Who* is coming?" said Elaine, almost irritably.

"Do you have a mirror? I wish you would look at your hair. It could be prettier, not that it isn't pretty right now. You want to look your best. Your lover, that's who is coming, of course."

"I haven't got a lover," said Elaine. "I haven't been authorized one, not till I've done some of my lifework, and I haven't even found my lifework yet. I'm not the kind of girl who would go ask a subchief for the dreamies, not when I'm not entitled to the real thing.

I may not be much of a person, but I have some self-respect." Elaine got so mad that she shifted her position on the bench and sat with her face turned away from the all-watching window.

The next words gave her gooseflesh down her arms, they were uttered with such real earnestness, such driving sincerity. *"Elaine, Elaine, do you really have no idea of who you are?"*

Elaine pivoted on the bench so that she looked toward the window. Her face was caught redly by the rays of the setting sun. She could only gasp.

"I don't know what you mean. . . ."

The inexorable voice went on. "Think, Elaine, think. Does the name 'D'joan' mean nothing to you?"

"I suppose it's an underperson, a dog. That's what the D is for, isn't it?"

"That was the little girl you met," said the Lady Panc Ashash, as though the statement were something tremendous.

"Yes," said Elaine dutifully. She was a courteous woman, and never quarreled with strangers.

"Wait a minute," said the Lady Panc Ashash. "I'm going to get my body out. God knows when I wore it last, but it'll make you feel more at easy terms with me. Forgive the clothes. They're old stuff, but I think the body will work all right. This is the beginning of the story of D'joan, and I want that hair of yours brushed even if I have to brush it myself. Just wait right there, girl, wait right there. I'll just take a minute."

The clouds were turning from dark red to liver-black. What could Elaine do? She stayed on the bench. She kicked her shoe against the walk. She jumped a little

when the old-fashioned street lights of the lower city
went on with sharp geometrical suddenness; they did
not have the subtle shading of the newer lights in the
other city upstairs, where day phased into the bright
clear night with no sudden shift in color.

The door beside the little window creaked open.
Ancient plastic crumbled to the walk.

Elaine was astonished.

Elaine knew she must have been unconsciously
expecting a monster, but this was a charming woman
of about her own height, wearing weird, old-fashioned
clothes. The strange woman had glossy black hair,
no evidence of recent or current illness, no signs of
severe lesions in the past, no impairment evident of
sight, gait, reach, or eyesight. (There was no way she
could check on smell or taste right off, but this was
the medical check-up she had had built into her from
birth on—the checklist which she had run through
with every adult person she had ever met. She had
been designed as a "lay therapist, female" and she
was a good one, even when there was no one at all
to treat.)

Truly, the body was a rich one. It must have cost
the landing charges of forty or fifty planetfalls. The
human shape was perfectly rendered. The mouth
moved over genuine teeth; the words were formed
by throat, palate, tongue, teeth, and lips, and not
just by a microphone mounted in the head. The
body was really a museum piece. It was probably a
copy of the Lady Panc Ashash herself in time of life.
When the face smiled, the effect was indescribably
winning. The lady wore the costume of a bygone
age—a stately frontal dress of heavy blue material,

embroidered with a square pattern of gold at hem, waist, and bodice. She had a matching cloak of dark, faded gold, embroidered in blue with the same pattern of squares. Her hair was upswept and set with jeweled combs. It seemed perfectly natural, but there was dust on one side of it.

The robot smiled, "I'm out of date. It's been a long time since I was me. But I thought, my dear, that you would find this old body easier to talk to than the window over there . . ."

Elaine nodded mutely.

"You know this is not me?" said the body, sharply.

Elaine shook her head. She didn't know; she felt that she didn't know anything at all.

The Lady Panc Ashash looked at her earnestly. "This is not me. It's a robot body. You looked at it as though it were a real person. And I'm not me, either. It hurts sometimes. Did you know a machine could hurt? I can. But—I'm not *me*."

"Who are you?" said Elaine to the pretty old woman.

"Before I died, I was the Lady Panc Ashash. Just as I told you. Now I am a machine, and a part of your destiny. We will help each other to change the destiny of worlds, perhaps even to bring mankind back to humanity."

Elaine stared at her in bewilderment. This was no common robot. It seemed like a real person and spoke with such warm authority. And this thing, whatever it was, this thing seemed to know so much about her. Nobody else had ever cared. The nurse-mothers at the Childhouse on Earth had said, "Another witch-child, and pretty too, they're not much trouble," and had let her life go by.

At last Elaine could face the face which was not really a face. The charm, the humor, the expressiveness were still there.

"What—what," stammered Elaine, "do I do now?"

"Nothing," said the long-dead Lady Panc Ashash, "except to meet your destiny."

"You mean my lover?"

"So impatient!" laughed the dead woman's record in a very human way. "Such a hurry. Lover first and destiny later. I was like that myself when I was a girl."

"But what do I do?" persisted Elaine.

The night was now complete above them. The street lights glared on the empty and unswept streets. A few doorways, not one of them less than a full street-crossing away, were illuminated with rectangles of light or shadow—light if they were far from the street lights, so that their own interior lights shone brightly, shadow if they were so close under the big lights that they cut off the glare from overhead.

"Go through this door," said the old nice woman.

But she pointed at the undistinguished white of an uninterrupted wall. There was no door at all in that place.

"But there's no door there," said Elaine.

"If there were a door," said the Lady Panc Ashash, "you wouldn't need me to tell you to go through it. And you do need me."

"Why?" said Elaine.

"Because I've waited for you hundreds of years, that's why."

"That's no answer!" snapped Elaine.

"It is so an answer," smiled the woman, and her lack of hostility was not robotlike at all. It was the kindliness and composure of a mature human being. She looked up into Elaine's eyes and spoke emphatically and softly. "I know because I do know. Not because I'm a dead person—that doesn't matter any more—but because I am now a very old machine. You will go into the Brown and Yellow Corridor and you will think of your lover, and you will do your work, and men will hunt you. But you will come out happily in the end. Do you understand this?"

"No," said Elaine, "no, I don't." But she reached out her hand to the sweet old woman. The lady took her hand. The touch was warm and very human.

"You don't have to understand it. Just do it. And I know you will. So since you are going, go."

Elaine tried to smile at her, but she was troubled, more consciously worried than ever before in her life. Something real was happening to her, to her own individual self, at a very long last. "How will I get through the door?"

"I'll open it," smiled the lady, releasing Elaine's hand, "and you'll know your lover when he sings you the poem."

"Which poem?" said Elaine, stalling for time and frightened by a door which did not even exist.

"It starts, 'I knew you and loved you, and won you, in Kalma...' You'll know it. Go on in. It'll be bothersome at first, but when you meet the Hunter, it will all seem different."

"Have you ever been in there, yourself?"

"Of course not," said the dear old lady. "I'm a machine. That whole place is thoughtproof. Nobody can see, hear, think, or talk in or out of it. It's a shelter left over from the ancient wars, when the slightest sign of a thought would have brought destruction on the whole place. That's why the Lord Englok built it, long before my time. But you can go in. And you will. Here's the door."

The old robot lady waited no longer. She gave Elaine a strange friendly crooked smile, half proud and half apologetic. She took Elaine with firm fingertips holding Elaine's left elbow. They walked a few steps down toward the wall.

"Here, now," said the Lady Panc Ashash, and pushed.

Elaine flinched as she was thrust toward the wall. Before she knew it, she was through. Smells hit her like a roar of battle. The air was hot. The light was dim. It looked like a picture of the Pain Planet, hidden somewhere in space. Poets later tried to describe Elaine at the door with a verse which begins,

> *There were brown ones and blue ones*
> *And white ones and whiter,*
>   *In the hidden and forbidden*
>   *Downtown of Clown Town.*
> *There were horrid ones and horrider*
> *In the brown and yellow corridor.*

The truth was much simpler.

Trained witch, born witch that she was, she perceived the truth immediately. All these people, all she could see, at least, were sick. They needed help. They needed herself.

But the joke was on her, for she could not help a single one of them. Not one of them was a real person. They were just animals, things in the shape of man. Underpeople. Dirt.

And she was conditioned to the bone never to help *them*.

She did not know why the muscles of her legs made her walk forward, but they did.

There are many pictures of that scene.

The Lady Panc Ashash, only a few moments in her past, seemed very remote. And the city of Kalma itself, the New City, ten stories above her, almost seemed as though it had never existed at all. This, this was real.

She stared at the underpeople.

And this time, for the first time in her life, they stared right back at her. She had never seen anything like this before.

They did not frighten her; they surprised her. The fright, Elaine felt, was to come later. Soon, perhaps, but not here, not now.

## ∞ 4 ∞

Something which looked like a middle-aged woman walked right up to her and snapped at her.

"Are you death?"

Elaine stared. "Death? What do you mean? I'm Elaine."

"Be damned to that!" said the woman-thing. "Are you death?"

Elaine did not know the word "damned" but she was pretty sure that "death," even to these things, meant simply "termination of life."

"Of course not," said Elaine. "I'm just a person. A witch woman, ordinary people would call me. We don't have anything to do with you underpeople. Nothing at all." Elaine could see that the woman-thing had an enormous coiffure of soft brown sloppy hair, a sweat-reddened face, and crooked teeth which showed when she grinned.

"They all say that. They never know that they're death. How do you think we die, if you people don't send contaminated robots in with diseases? We all die off when you do that, and then some more underpeople find this place again later on and make a shelter of it and live in it for a few generations until the death machines, things like you, come sweeping through the city and kill us off again. This is Clown Town, the underpeople place. Haven't you heard of it?"

Elaine tried to walk past the woman-thing, but she found her arm grabbed. This couldn't have happened before, not in the history of the world—an underperson seizing a real person!

"Let go!" she yelled.

The woman-thing let her arm go and faced toward the others. Her voice had changed. It was no longer shrill and excited, but low and puzzled instead. "I can't tell. Maybe it is a real person. Isn't that a joke? Lost, in here with us. Or maybe she *is* death. I can't tell. What do you think, Charley-is-my-darling?"

The man she spoke to stepped forward. Elaine thought, in another time, in some other place, that underperson might pass for an attractive human being. His face was illuminated by intelligence and alertness. He looked directly at Elaine as though he had never seen her before, which indeed he had not, but he continued looking with so sharp, so strange a stare that she became uneasy. His voice, when he spoke, was brisk, high, clear, friendly; set in this tragic place, it was the caricature of a voice, as though the animal had been programmed for speech from the habits of a human, persuader by profession, whom one saw in the storyboxes telling people messages which were neither good nor important, but merely clever. The handsomeness was itself deformity. Elaine wondered if he had come from goat stock.

"Welcome, young lady," said Charley-is-my-darling. "Now that you are here, how are you going to get out? If we turned her head around, Mabel," said he to the underwoman who had first greeted Elaine, "turned it around eight or ten times, it would come off. Then we could live a few weeks or months longer before our lords and creators found us and put us all to death. What do you say, young lady? Should we kill you?"

"Kill? You mean, terminate life? You cannot. It is against the law. Even the Instrumentality does not have the right to do that without trial. You can't. You're just underpeople."

"But we will die," said Charley-is-my-darling, flashing his quick intelligent smile, "if you go back out of that door. The police will read about the Brown and Yellow Corridor in your mind and they will flush us out with poison or they will spray disease in here so that we and our children will die."

Elaine stared at him.

The passionate anger did not disturb his smile or his persuasive tones, but the muscles of his eyesockets and forehead showed the terrible strain. The result was an expression which Elaine had never seen before, a sort of self-control reaching out beyond the limits of insanity.

He stared back at her.

She was not really afraid of him. Underpeople could not twist the heads of real persons; it was contrary to all regulations.

A thought struck her. Perhaps regulations did not apply in a place like this, where illegal animals waited perpetually for sudden death. The being which faced her was strong enough to turn her head around ten times clockwise or counterclockwise. From her anatomy lessons, she was pretty sure that the head would come off somewhere during that process. She looked at him with interest. Animal-type fear had been conditioned out of her, but she had, she found, an extreme distaste for the termination of life under random circumstances. Perhaps her "witch" training would help. She tried to pretend that he was in fact a man. The diagnosis "hypertension: chronic aggression, now frustrated, leading to overstimulation and neurosis: poor nutritional record: hormone disorder probable" leapt into her mind.

She tried to speak in a new voice.

"I am smaller than you," she said, "and you can 'kill' me just as well later as now. We might as well get acquainted. I'm Elaine, assigned here from Manhome Earth."

The effect was spectacular.

Charley-is-my-darling stepped back. Mabel's mouth dropped open. The others gaped at her. One or two, more quick-witted than the rest, began whispering to their neighbors.

At last Charley-is-my-darling spoke to her. "Welcome, my lady. Can I call you my lady? I guess not. Welcome, Elaine. We are your people. We will do whatever you say. Of course you got in. The Lady Panc Ashash sent you. She has been telling us for a hundred years that somebody would come from Earth, a real person with an animal name, not a number, and that we should have a child named D'joan ready to take up the threads of destiny. Please, please sit down. Will you have a drink of water? We have no clean vessel here. We are all underpeople here and we have used everything in the place, so that it is contaminated for a real person." A thought struck him. "Baby-baby, do you have a new cup in the kiln?" Apparently he saw someone nod, because he went right on talking. "Get it out then, for our guest, with tongs. New tongs. Do not touch it. Fill it with water from the top of the little waterfall. That way our guest can have an uncontaminated drink. A clean drink." He beamed with a hospitality which was as ridiculous as it was genuine.

Elaine did not have the heart to say she did not want a drink of water.

She waited. They waited.

By now, her eyes had become accustomed to the darkness. She could see that the main corridor was painted a yellow, faded and stained, and a contrasting light brown. She wondered what possible human mind could have selected so ugly a combination. Cross-corridors seemed to open into it; at any rate, she saw illuminated archways further down and people walking out of them briskly. No one can walk briskly and naturally out of a shallow alcove, so she was pretty sure that the archways led to something.

The underpeople, too, she could see. They looked very much like people. Here and there, individuals reverted to the animal type—a horse-man whose muzzle had regrown to its ancestral size, a rat-woman with normal human features except for nylon-like white whiskers, twelve or fourteen on each side of her face, reaching twenty centimeters to either side. One looked very much like a person indeed—a beautiful young woman seated on a bench some eight or ten meters down the corridor, and paying no attention to the crowd, to Mabel, to Charley-is-my-darling, or to herself.

"Who is that?" said Elaine, pointing with a nod at the beautiful young woman.

Mabel, relieved from the tension which had seized her when she had asked if Elaine were "death," babbled with a sociability which was outré in this environment, "That's Crawlie."

"What does she do?" asked Elaine.

"She has her pride," said Mabel, her grotesque red face now jolly and eager, her slack mouth spraying spittle as she spoke.

"But doesn't she *do* anything?" said Elaine.

Charley-is-my-darling intervened. "Nobody has to do anything here, Lady Elaine—"

"It's illegal to call me 'Lady,'" said Elaine.

"I'm sorry, human being Elaine. Nobody *has* to do anything at all here. The whole bunch of us are completely illegal. This corridor is a thought-shelter, so that no thoughts can escape or enter it. Wait a bit! Watch the ceiling . . . Now!"

A red glow moved across the ceiling and was gone.

"The ceiling glows," said Charley-is-my-darling, "whenever anything *thinks* against it. The whole tunnel registers 'sewage tank: organic waste' to the outside, so that dim perceptions of life which may escape here are not considered too unaccountable. People built it for their own use, a million years ago."

"They weren't here on Fomalhaut III a million years ago," snapped Elaine. Why, she wondered, did she snap at him? He wasn't a person, just a talking animal who had missed being dropped down the nearest incinerator.

"I'm sorry, Elaine," said Charley-is-my-darling. "I should have said, a long time ago. We underpeople don't get much chance to study real history. But we use this corridor. Somebody with a morbid sense of humor named this place Clown Town. We live along for ten or twenty or a hundred years, and then people or robots find us and kill us all. That's why Mabel was upset. She thought you were death for this time. But you're not. You're *Elaine*. That's wonderful, wonderful." His sly, too-clever face beamed with transparent sincerity. It must have been quite a shock to him to be honest.

"You were going to tell me what the undergirl is for," said Elaine.

"That's Crawlie," said he. "She doesn't do anything. None of us really have to. We're all doomed anyhow. She's a little more honest than the rest of us. She has her pride. She scorns the rest of us. She puts us in our place. She makes everybody feel inferior. We think she is a valuable member of the group. We all have our pride, which is hopeless anyway, but Crawlie has her pride all by herself, without doing anything whatever about it. She sort of reminds us. If we leave her alone, she leaves us alone."

Elaine thought, You're funny things, so much like people, but so inexpert about it, as though you all had to "die" before you really learned what it is to be alive. Aloud, she could only say, "I never met anybody like that."

Crawlie must have sensed that they were talking about her, because she looked at Elaine with a short quick stare of blazing hatred. Crawlie's pretty face locked itself into a glare of concentrated hostility and scorn; then her eyes wandered and Elaine felt that she, Elaine, no longer existed in the thing's mind, except as a rebuke which had been administered and forgotten. She had never seen privacy as impenetrable as Crawlie's. And yet the being, whatever she might have been made from, was very lovely in human terms.

A fierce old hag, covered with mouse-gray fur, rushed up to Elaine. The mouse-woman was the Baby-baby who had been sent on the errand. She held a ceramic cup in a pair of long tongs. Water was in it.

Elaine took the cup.

Sixty to seventy underpeople, including the little girl in the blue dress whom she had seen outside, watched her as she sipped. The water was good. She drank it all. There was a universal exhalation, as though everyone in the corridor had waited for this moment. Elaine started to put the cup down but the old mouse-woman was too quick for her. She took the cup from Elaine, stopping her in mid-gesture and using the tongs, so that the cup would not be contaminated by the touch of an underperson.

"That's right, Baby-baby," said Charley-is-my-darling, "we can talk. It is our custom not to talk with a newcomer until we have offered our hospitality. Let me be frank. We may have to kill you, if this whole business turns out to be a mistake, but let me assure you that if I do kill you, I will do it nicely and without the least bit of malice. Right?"

Elaine did not know what was so right about it,

and said so. She visualized her head being twisted off. Apart from the pain and the degradation, it seemed so terribly messy—to terminate life in a sewer with things which did not even have a right to exist.

He gave her no chance to argue, but just went on explaining, "Suppose things turn out just right. Suppose that you are the Esther-Elaine-or-Eleanor that we have all been waiting for—the person who will do something to D'joan and bring us all help and deliverance—give us life, in short, *real life*—then what do we do?"

"I don't know where you get all these ideas about me. Why am I Esther-Elaine-or-Eleanor? What do I do to D'joan? Why me?"

Charley-is-my-darling stared at her as though he could not believe her question. Mabel frowned as though she could not think of the right words to put forth her opinions. Baby-baby, who had glided back to the group with swift mouselike suddenness, looked around as though she expected someone from the rear to speak. She was right. Crawlie turned her face toward Elaine and said, with infinite condescension:

"I did not know that real people were ill-informed or stupid. You seem to be both. We have all our information from the Lady Panc Ashash. Since she is dead, she has no prejudices against us underpeople. Since she has not had much of anything to do, she has run through billions and billions of probabilities for us. All of us know what most probabilities come to—sudden death by disease or gas, or maybe being hauled off to the slaughterhouses in big police ornithopters. But Lady Panc Ashash found that perhaps a person with a name like yours would come, a human being with an

old name and not a number name, that that person
would meet the Hunter, that she and the Hunter
would teach the underchild D'joan a message, and
that the message would change the worlds. We have
kept one child after another named D'joan, waiting
for a hundred years. Now you show up. Maybe you
are the one. You don't look very competent to me.
What are you good for?"

"I'm a witch," said Elaine.

Crawlie could not keep the surprise from showing
in her face. "A witch? Really?"

"Yes," said Elaine, rather humbly.

"I wouldn't be one," said Crawlie. "I have my pride."
She turned her face away and locked her features in
their expression of perennial hurt and disdain.

Charley-is-my-darling whispered to the group nearby,
not caring whether Elaine heard his words or not,
"That's wonderful, wonderful. She is a witch. A human
witch. Perhaps the great day is here! Elaine," said he
humbly, "will you please look at us?"

Elaine looked. When she stopped to think about
where she was, it was incredible that the empty old
lower city of Kalma should be just outside, just beyond
the wall, and the busy new city a mere thirty-five
meters higher. This corridor was a world to itself. It
felt like a world, with the ugly yellows and browns,
the dim old lights, the stenches of man and animal
mixed under intolerably bad ventilation. Baby-baby,
Crawlie, Mabel, and Charley-is-my-darling were part
of this world. They were real; but they were outside,
outside, so far as Elaine herself was concerned.

"Let me go," she said. "I'll come back some day."

Charley-is-my-darling, who was so plainly the leader,

spoke as if in a trance: "You don't understand, Elaine. The only 'going' you are going to go is death. There is no other direction. We can't let the old you go out of this door, not when the Lady Panc Ashash has thrust you in to us. Either you go forward to your destiny, to our destiny too, either you do that, and all works out all right, so that you love us, and we love you," he added dreamily, "or else I kill you with my own hands. Right here. Right now. I could give you another clean drink of water first. But that is all. There isn't much choice for you, human being Elaine. What do you think would happen if you went outside?"

"Nothing, I hope," said Elaine.

"Nothing!" snorted Mabel, her face regaining its original indignation. "The police would come flapping by in their ornithopter—"

"And they'd pick your brains," said Baby-baby.

"And they'd know about us," said a tall pale man who had not spoken before.

"And we," said Crawlie from her chair, "would all of us die within an hour or two at the longest. Would that matter to you, Ma'am and Elaine?"

"And," added Charley-is-my-darling, "they would disconnect the Lady Panc Ashash, so that even the recording of that dear dead lady would be gone at last, and there would be no mercy at all left upon this world."

"What is 'mercy'?" asked Elaine.

"It's obvious you never heard of it," said Crawlie.

The old mouse-hag Baby-baby came close to Elaine. She looked up at her and whispered through yellow teeth, "Don't let them frighten you, girl. Death doesn't matter all that much, not even to you true humans with your four hundred years or to us animals with the slaughterhouse around the corner. Death is a *when,* not a *what.* It's the same for all of us. Don't be scared. Go straight ahead and you may find mercy and love. They're much richer than death, if you can only find them. Once you do find them, death won't be very important."

"I still don't know *mercy,*" said Elaine, "but I thought I knew what *love* was, and I don't expect to find my lover in a dirty old corridor full of underpeople."

"I don't mean that kind of love," laughed Baby-baby, brushing aside Mabel's attempted interruption with a wave of her hand-paw. The old mouse face was on fire with sheer expressiveness. Elaine could suddenly imagine what Baby-baby had looked like to a mouse-underman when she was young and sleek and gray. Enthusiasm flushed the old features with youth as Baby-baby went on, "I don't mean love for a lover, girl. I mean love for yourself. Love for life. Love for all things living. Love even for me. Your love for me. Can you imagine that?"

Elaine swam through fatigue but she tried to answer the question. She looked in the dim light at the wrinkled old mouse-hag with her filthy clothes and her little red eyes. The fleeting image of the beautiful young mouse-woman had faded away; there was only this cheap, useless old thing, with her inhuman demands and her senseless pleading. People never loved underpeople. They used them, like chairs or doorhandles. Since when did a doorhandle demand the Charter of Ancient Rights?

"No," said Elaine calmly and evenly, "I can't imagine ever loving you."

"I knew it," said Crawlie from her chair. There was triumph in the voice.

Charley-is-my-darling shook his head as if to clear his sight. "Don't you even know who controls Fomalhaut III?"

"The Instrumentality," said Elaine. "But do we have to go on talking? Let me go or kill me or something. This doesn't make sense. I was tired when I got here, and I'm a million years tireder now."

Mabel said, "Take her along."

"All right," said Charley-is-my-darling. "Is the Hunter there?"

The child D'joan spoke. She had stood at the back of the group. "He came in the other way when she came in the front."

Elaine said to Charley-is-my-darling, "You lied to me. You said there was only one way."

"I did not lie," said he. "There is only one way for you or me or for the friends of the Lady Panc Ashash. The way you came. The other way is death."

"What do you mean?"

"I mean," he said, "that it leads straight into the slaughterhouses of the men you do not know. The Lords of the Instrumentality who are here on Fomalhaut III. There is the Lord Femtiosex, who is just and without pity. There is the Lord Limaono, who thinks that underpeople are a potential danger and should not have been started in the first place. There is the Lady Goroke, who does not know how to pray, but who tries to ponder the mystery of life and who has shown kindnesses to underpeople, as long as the kindnesses were lawful ones. And there is the Lady Arabella Underwood, whose justice no man can understand. Nor underpeople either," he added with a chuckle.

"Who is she? I mean, where did she get the funny

name? It doesn't have a number in it. It's as bad as
your names. Or my own," said Elaine.

"She's from Old North Australia, the stroon world,
on loan to the Instrumentality, and she follows the
laws she was born to. The Hunter can go through the
rooms and the slaughterhouses of the Instrumentality,
but could you? Could I?"

"No," said Elaine.

"Then forward," said Charley-is-my-darling, "to
your death or to great wonders. May I lead the way,
Elaine?"

Elaine nodded wordlessly.

The mouse-hag Baby-baby patted Elaine's sleeve,
her eyes alive with strange hope. As Elaine passed
Crawlie's chair, the proud, beautiful girl looked straight
at her, expressionless, deadly, and severe. The dog-girl
D'joan followed the little procession as if she had
been invited.

They walked down and down and down. Actually,
it could not have been a full half-kilometer. But with
the endless browns and yellows, the strange shapes of
the lawless and untended underpeople, the stenches
and the thick heavy air, Elaine felt as if she were
leaving all known worlds behind.

In fact, she was doing precisely that, but it did not
occur to her that her own suspicion might be true.

$\sim$ **5** $\sim$

At the end of the corridor there was a round gate
with a door of gold or brass.

Charley-is-my-darling stopped.

"I can't go further," he said. "You and D'joan will have to go on. This is the forgotten antechamber between the tunnel and the upper palace. The Hunter is there. Go on. You're a person. It is safe. Underpeople usually die in there. Go on." He nudged her elbow and pulled the sliding door apart.

"But the little girl," said Elaine.

"She's not a girl," said Charley-is-my-darling. "She's just a dog—as I'm not a man, just a goat brightened and cut and trimmed to look like a man. If you come back, Elaine, I will love you like God or I will kill you. It depends."

"Depends on what?" asked Elaine. "And what is 'God'?"

Charley-is-my-darling smiled the quick tricky smile which was wholly insincere and completely friendly, both at the same time. It was probably the trademark of his personality in ordinary times. "You'll find out about God somewhere else, if you do. Not from us. And the depending is something you'll know for yourself. You won't have to wait for me to tell you. Go along now. The whole thing will be over in the next few minutes."

"But D'joan?" persisted Elaine.

"If it doesn't work," said Charley-is-my-darling, "we can always raise another D'joan and wait for another you. The Lady Panc Ashash had promised us that. Go on in!"

He pushed her roughly, so that she stumbled through. Bright light dazzled her and the clean air tasted as good as fresh water on her first day out of the spaceship pod.

The little dog-girl had trotted in beside her.

The door, gold or brass, clanged to behind them.

Elaine and D'joan stood still, side by side, looking forward and upward.

There are many famous paintings of that scene. Most of the paintings show Elaine in rags with the distorted, suffering face of a witch. This is strictly unhistorical. She was wearing her everyday culottes, blouse, and twin over-the-shoulder purses when she went in the other end of Clown Town. This was the usual dress on Fomalhaut III at that time. She had done nothing at all to spoil her clothes, so she must have looked the same when she came out. And D'joan—well, everyone knows what D'joan looked like.

The Hunter met them.

The Hunter met them, and new worlds began.

He was a shortish man, with black curly hair, black eyes that danced with laughter, broad shoulders, and long legs. He walked with a quick sure step. He kept his hands quiet at his side, but the hands did not look tough and calloused, as though they had been terminating lives, even the lives of animals.

"Come up and sit down," he greeted them. "I've been waiting for you both."

Elaine stumbled upward and forward. "Waiting?" she gasped.

"Nothing mysterious," he said. "I had the viewscreen on. The one into the tunnel. Its connections are shielded, so the police could not have peeped it."

Elaine stopped dead still. The little dog-girl, one step behind her, stopped too. She tried to draw herself up to her full height. She was about the same tallness that he was. It was difficult, since he stood four or five steps above them. She managed to keep her voice even when she said:

"You know, then?"

"What?"

"All those things they said."

"Sure I know them," he smiled. "Why not?"

"But," stammered Elaine, "about you and me being lovers? That too?"

"That too." He smiled again. "I've been hearing it half my life. Come on up, sit down, and have something to eat. We have a lot of things to do tonight, if history is to be fulfilled through us. What do you eat, little girl?" said he kindly to D'joan. "Raw meat or people food?"

"I'm a finished girl," said D'joan, "so I prefer chocolate cake with vanilla ice cream."

"That you shall have," said the Hunter. "Come, both of you, and sit down."

They had topped the steps. A luxurious table, already set, was waiting for them. There were three couches around it. Elaine looked for the third person who would join them. Only as she sat down did she realize that he meant to invite the dog-child.

He saw her surprise, but did not comment on it directly.

Instead, he spoke to D'joan.

"You know me, girl, don't you?"

The child smiled and relaxed for the first time since Elaine had seen her. The dog-girl was really strikingly beautiful when the tension went out of her. The wariness, the quietness, the potential disquiet—these were dog qualities. Now the child seemed wholly human and mature far beyond her years. Her white face had dark, dark brown eyes.

"I've seen you lots of times, Hunter. And you've told me what would happen if I turned out to be *the* D'joan. How I would spread the word and meet great trials. How I might die and might not, but people and underpeople would remember my name for thousands of years. You've told me almost everything I know—except the things that I can't talk to you about. You know them too, but you won't talk, will you?" said the little girl imploringly.

"I know you've been to Earth," said the Hunter.

"Don't say it! Please don't say it!" pleaded the girl.

"Earth! Manhome itself?" cried Elaine. "How, by the stars, did you get there?"

The Hunter intervened. "Don't press her, Elaine. It's a big secret, and she wants to keep it. You'll find out more tonight than mortal woman was ever told before."

"What does 'mortal' mean?" asked Elaine, who disliked antique words.

"It just means having a termination of life."

"That's foolish," said Elaine. "Everything terminates. Look at those poor messy people who went on beyond the legal four hundred years." She looked around. Rich black-and-red curtains hung from ceiling to floor. On one side of the room there was a piece of furniture she had never seen before. It was like a table, but it had little broad flat doors on the front, reaching from side to side; it was richly ornamented with unfamiliar woods and metals. Nevertheless, she had more important things to talk about than furniture.

She looked directly at the Hunter (no organic disease; wounded in left arm at an earlier period; somewhat excessive exposure to sunlight; might need correction for near vision) and demanded of him:

"Am I captured by you, too?"

"Captured?"

"You're a Hunter. You hunt things. To kill them, I suppose. That underman back there, the goat who calls himself Charley-is-my-darling—"

"He never does!" cried the dog-girl, D'joan, interrupting.

"Never does what?" said Elaine, cross at being interrupted.

"He never calls himself that. Other people, underpeople I mean, call him that. His name is Balthasar, but nobody uses it."

"What does it matter, little girl?" said Elaine. "I'm talking about my life. Your friend said he would take my life from me if something did not happen."

Neither D'joan nor the Hunter said anything.

Elaine heard a frantic edge go into her voice. "You heard it!" She turned to the Hunter. "You saw it on the viewscreen."

The Hunter's voice was serenity and assurance: "We three have things to do before this night is out. We won't get them done if you are frightened or worried. I know the underpeople, but I know the Lords of the Instrumentality as well—all four of them, right here. The Lords Limaono and Femtiosex and the Lady Goroke. And the Norstrilian, too. They will protect you. Charley-is-my-darling might want to take your life from you because he is worried, afraid that the tunnel of Englok, where you just were, will be discovered. I have ways of protecting him and yourself as well. Have confidence in me for a while. That's not so hard, is it?"

"But," protested Elaine, "the man—or the goat—or

whatever he was, Charley-is-my-darling, he said it would all happen right away, as soon as I came up here with you."

"How can anything happen," said little D'joan, "if you keep talking all the time?"

The Hunter smiled.

"That's right," he said. "We've talked enough. Now we must become lovers."

Elaine jumped to her feet. "Not with me, you don't. Not with her here. Not when I haven't found my work to do. I'm a witch. I'm supposed to do something, but I've never really found out what it was."

"Look at this," said the Hunter calmly, walking over to the wall, and pointing with his finger at an intricate circular design.

Elaine and D'joan both looked at it.

The Hunter spoke again, his voice urgent. "Do you see it, D'joan? Do you really see it? The ages turn, waiting for this moment, little child. Do you see it? Do you see yourself in it?"

Elaine looked at the little dog-girl. D'joan had almost stopped breathing. She stared at the curious symmetrical pattern as though it were a window into enchanting worlds.

The Hunter roared, at the top of his voice, "D'joan! Joan! Joanie!"

The child made no response.

The Hunter stepped over to the child, slapped her gently on the cheek, shouted again. D'joan continued to stare at the intricate design.

"Now," said the Hunter, "you and I make love. The child is absent in a world of happy dreams. That design is a mandala, something left over from the unimaginable past. It locks the human consciousness in place. D'joan will not see us or hear us. We cannot help her go toward her destiny unless you and I make love first."

Elaine, her hand to her mouth, tried to inventory symptoms as a means of keeping her familiar thoughts in balance. It did not work. A relaxation spread over her, a happiness and quiet that she had not once felt since her childhood.

"Did you think," said the Hunter, "that I hunted with my body and killed with my hands? Didn't anyone ever tell you that the game comes to me rejoicing, that the animals die while they scream with pleasure? I'm a telepath, and I work under license. And I have my license now from the dead Lady Panc Ashash."

Elaine knew that they had come to the end of the talking. Trembling, happy, frightened, she fell into his arms and let him lead her over to the couch at the side of the black-and-gold room.

A thousand years later, she was kissing his ear and murmuring loving words at him, words that she did not even realize she knew. She must, she thought, have picked up more from the storyboxes than she ever realized.

"You're my love," she said, "my only one, my darling. Never, never leave me; never throw me away. Oh, Hunter, I love you so!"

"We part," he said, "before tomorrow is gone, but shall meet again. Do you realize that all this has only been a little more than an hour?"

Elaine blushed. "And I," she stammered, "I—I'm hungry."

"Natural enough," said the Hunter. "Pretty soon we can waken the little girl and eat together. And then history will happen, unless somebody walks in and stops us."

"But, darling," said Elaine, "can't we go on—at least for a while? A year? A month? A day? Put the little girl back in the tunnel for a while."

"Not really," said the Hunter, "but I'll sing you the song that came into my mind about you and me. I've been thinking bits of it for a long time, but now it has really happened. Listen."

He held her two hands in his two hands, looked easily and frankly into her eyes. There was no hint in him of telepathic power.

He sang to her the song which we know as *I Loved You and Lost You.*

> *I knew you, and loved you,*
> *    and won you, in Kalma.*
> *I loved you, and won you,*
> *    and lost you, my darling!*
> *The dark skies of Waterrock*
> *    swept down against us.*
> *Lightning-lit only*
> *    by our own love, my lovely!*
>
> *Our time was a short time,*
> *    a sharp hour of glory—*
> *We tasted delight*
> *    and we suffer denial.*
> *The tale of us two*
> *    is a bittersweet story,*
> *Short as a shot*
> *    but as long as death.*

*We met and we loved,*
   *and vainly we plotted*
*To rescue beauty*
   *from a smothering war.*
*Time had no time for us,*
   *the minutes, no mercy.*
*We have loved and lost,*
   *and the world goes on.*

*We have lost and have kissed,*
   *and have parted, my darling!*
*All that we have,*
   *we must save in our hearts, love.*
*The memory of beauty*
   *and the beauty of memory . . .*
*I've loved you, and won you,*
   *and lost you, in Kalma.*

His fingers, moving in the air, produced a soft
organ-like music in the room. She had noticed music-
beams before, but she had never had one played for
herself.

By the time he was through singing, she was sobbing.
It was all so true, so wonderful, so heartbreaking.

He had kept her right hand in his left hand. Now
he released her suddenly. He stood up.

"Let's work first. Eat later. Someone is near us."

He walked briskly over to the little dog-girl, who
was still seated on the chair looking at the mandala
with open, sleeping eyes. He took her head firmly and
gently between his two hands and turned her eyes away
from the design. She struggled momentarily against
his hands and then seemed to wake up fully.

She smiled. "That was nice. I rested. How long was it—five minutes?"

"More than that," said the Hunter gently. "I want you to take Elaine's hand."

A few hours ago, and Elaine would have protested at the grotesquerie of holding hands with an underperson. This time, she said nothing, but obeyed: she looked with much love toward the Hunter.

"You two don't have to know much," said the Hunter. "You, D'joan, are going to get everything that is in our minds and in our memories. You will become us, both of us. Forevermore. You will meet your glorious fate."

The little girl shivered. "Is this really the day?"

"It is," said the Hunter. "Future ages will remember this night."

"And you, Elaine," said he to her, "have nothing to do but to love me and to stand very still. Do you understand? You will see tremendous things, some of them frightening. But they won't be real. Just stand still."

Elaine nodded wordlessly.

"In the name," said the Hunter, "of The First Forgotten One, in the name of the Second Forgotten One, in the name of the Third Forgotten One. For the love of people, that will give them life. For the love that will give them a clean death and true . . ." His words were clear but Elaine could not understand them.

The day of days was here.

She knew it.

She did not know how she knew it, but she did.

The Lady Panc Ashash crawled up through the solid floor, wearing her friendly robot body. She came near to Elaine and murmured:

"Have no fear, no fear."

Fear? thought Elaine. This is no time for fear. It is much too interesting.

As if to answer Elaine, a clear, strong, masculine voice spoke out of nowhere:

*This is the time for the daring sharing.*

When these words were spoken, it was as if a bubble had been pricked. Elaine felt her personality and D'joan's mingling. With ordinary telepathy, it would have been frightening. But this was not communication. It was being.

She had become Joan. She felt the clean little body in its tidy clothes. She became aware of the girl-shape again. It was oddly pleasant and familiar, in terribly faraway kinds of feeling, to remember that she had had that shape once—the smooth, innocent flat chest; the uncomplicated groin; the fingers which still felt as though they were separate and alive in extending from the palm of the hand. But the mind—*that* child's mind! It was like an enormous museum illuminated by rich stained-glass windows, cluttered with variegated heaps of beauty and treasure, scented by strange incense which moved slowly in unpropelled air. D'joan had a mind which reached all the way back to the color and glory of man's antiquity. D'joan had been a Lord of the Instrumentality, a monkey-man riding the ships of space, a friend of the dear dead Lady Panc Ashash, and Panc Ashash herself.

No wonder the child was rich and strange: she had been made the heir of all the ages.

*This is the time for the glaring top of the truth at the wearing sharing,* said the nameless, clear, loud voice in her mind. *This is the time for you and him.*

Elaine realized that she was responding to hypnotic

suggestions which the I
the mind of the little d
triggered into full pote
of them came into tel

For a fraction of a
but astonishment with
herself—every detail,
feeling and contour o
of how her breasts hu
her belly-muscles holding her female backbone straight
and erect—

Female backbone?

Why had she thought that she had a female backbone?

And then she knew.

She was following the Hunter's mind as his awareness
rushed through her body, drank it up, enjoyed it, loved
it all over again, this time from the inside out.

She knew somehow that the little dog-girl watched
everything quietly, wordlessly, drinking in from them
both the full nuance of being truly human.

Even with the delirium, she sensed embarrassment.
It might be a dream, but it was still too much. She
began to close her mind and the thought had come
to her that she should take her hands away from the
hands of Hunter and the dog-child.

But then fire came . . .

## ∽ 6 ∽

Fire came up from the floor, burning about them
intangibly. Elaine felt nothing . . . but she could sense
the touch of the little girl's hand.

*We the*
*Flames around th*
*voice from nowhe*
*Fire around*
*Hot is wha*
*Sudden*
52
*not the*
*and*

*dames, games,* said an idiot
.e.

*he pyre, sire,* said another.

*t we got, tot,* said a third.

...y Elaine remembered Earth, but it was
Earth she knew. She was herself D'joan,
...ot D'joan. She was a tall, strong monkey-man,
...stinguishable from a true human being. She/he had
tremendous alertness in her/his heart as she/he walked
across the Peace Square at An-fang, the Old Square
at An-fang, where all things begin. She/he noticed a
discrepancy. Some of the buildings were not there.

The real Elaine thought to herself, "So that's what
they did with the child—printed her with the memories
of other underpeople. Other ones, who dared things
and went places."

The fire stopped.

Elaine saw the black-and-gold room clean and
untroubled for a moment before the green white-
topped ocean rushed in. The water poured over the
three of them without getting them wet in the least.
The greenness washed around them without pressure,
without suffocation.

Elaine was the Hunter. Enormous dragons floated in
the sky above Fomalhaut III. She felt herself wander-
ing across a hill, singing with love and yearning. She
had the Hunter's own mind, his own memory. The
dragon sensed him, and flew down. The enormous
reptilian wings were more beautiful than a sunset,
more delicate than orchids. Their beat in the air was
as gentle as the breath of a baby. She was not only
Hunter but dragon too; she felt the minds meeting
and the dragon dying in bliss, in joy.

Somehow the water was gone. So too were D'joan and the Hunter. She was not in the room. She was taut, tired, worried Elaine, looking down a nameless street for hopeless destinations. She had to do things which could never be done. The wrong me, the wrong time, the wrong place—and I'm alone, I'm alone, I'm alone, her mind screamed. The room was back again; so too were the hands of the Hunter and the little girl.

Mist began rising—

Another dream? thought Elaine. Aren't we done?

But there was another voice somewhere, a voice which grated like the rasp of a saw cutting through bone, like the grind of a broken machine still working at ruinous top speed. It was an evil voice, a terror-filling voice.

Perhaps this really was the "death" which the tunnel underpeople had mistaken her for.

The Hunter's hand released hers. She let go of D'joan.

There was a strange woman in the room. She wore the baldric of authority and the leotards of a traveler.

Elaine stared at her.

"You'll be punished," said the terrible voice, which now was coming out of the woman.

"Wh—wh—what?" stammered Elaine.

"You're conditioning an underperson without authority. I don't know who you are, but the Hunter should know better. The animal will have to die, of course," said the woman, looking at little D'joan.

Hunter muttered, half in greeting to the stranger, half in explanation to Elaine, as though he did not know what else to say:

"Lady Arabella Underwood."

Elaine could not bow to her, though she wanted to. The surprise came from the little dog girl.

*I am your sister Joan,* she said, *and no animal to you.*

The Lady Arabella seemed to have trouble hearing. (Elaine herself could not tell whether she was hearing spoken words or taking the message with her mind.)

*I am Joan and I love you.*

The Lady Arabella shook herself as though water had splashed on her. "Of course you're Joan. You love me. And I love you."

*People and underpeople meet on the terms of love.*

"Love. Love, of course. You're a good little girl. And so right." *You will forget me,* said Joan, *until we meet and love again.*

"Yes, darling. Good-by for now."

At last D'joan did use words. She spoke to the Hunter and Elaine, saying, "It is finished. I know who I am and what I must do. Elaine had better come with me. We will see you soon, Hunter—if we live."

Elaine looked at the Lady Arabella, who stood stock still, staring like a blind woman. The Hunter nodded at Elaine with his wise, kind, rueful smile.

The little girl led Elaine down, down, down to the door which led back to the tunnel of Englok. Just as they went through the brass door, Elaine heard the voice of the Lady Arabella say to the Hunter:

"What are you doing here all by yourself? The room smells funny. Have you had animals here? Have you killed something?"

"Yes, Ma'am," said the Hunter as D'joan and Elaine stepped through the door.

"What?" cried the Lady Arabella.

Hunter must have raised his voice to a point of

penetrating emphasis because he wanted the other two to hear him, too:

"I have killed, Ma'am," he said, "as always—with love. This time it was a system."

They slipped through the door while the Lady Arabella's protesting voice, heavy with authority and inquiry, was still sweeping against the Hunter.

Joan led. Her body was the body of a pretty child, but her personality was the full awakening of all the underpeople who had been imprinted on her. Elaine could not understand it, because Joan was still the little dog-girl, but Joan was now also Elaine, also Hunter. There was no doubt about their movement; the child, no longer an undergirl, led the way and Elaine, human or not, followed.

The door closed behind them. They were back in the Brown and Yellow Corridor. Most of the underpeople were awaiting them. Dozens stared at them. The heavy animal-human smells of the old tunnel rolled against them like thick, slow waves. Elaine felt the beginning of a headache at her temples, but she was much too alert to care.

For a moment, D'joan and Elaine confronted the underpeople.

Most of you have seen paintings or theatricals based upon this scene. The most famous of all is, beyond doubt, the fantastic "one-line drawing" of San Shigonanda—the board of the background almost uniformly gray, with a hint of brown and yellow on the left, a hint of black and red on the right, and in the center the strange white line, almost a smear of paint, which somehow suggests the bewildered girl Elaine and the doom-blessed child Joan.

Charley-is-my-darling was, of course, the first to find his voice. (Elaine did not notice him as a goat-man any more. He seemed an earnest, friendly man of middle age, fighting poor health and an uncertain life with great courage. She now found his smile persuasive and charming. Why, thought Elaine, didn't I see him that way before? Have I changed?)

Charley-is-my-darling had spoken before Elaine found her wits. "He did it. Are you D'joan?"

"Am I D'joan?" said the child, asking the crowd of deformed, weird people in the tunnel. "Do you think I am D'joan?"

"No! No! You are the lady who was promised—you are the bridge-to-man," cried a tall yellow-haired old woman, whom Elaine could not remember seeing before. The woman flung herself to her knees in front of the child, and tried to get D'joan's hand. The child held her hands away, quietly, but firmly, so the woman buried her face in the child's skirt and wept.

"I am Joan," said the child, "and I am dog no more. You are people now, people, and if you die with me, you will die men. Isn't that better than it has ever been before? And you, Ruthie," said she to the woman at her feet, "stand up and stop crying. Be glad. These are the days that I shall be with you. I know your children were all taken away and killed, Ruthie, and I am sorry. I cannot bring them back. But I give you womanhood. I have even made a person out of Elaine."

"Who are you?" said Charley-is-my-darling. "Who are you?"

"I'm the little girl you put out to live or die an hour ago. But now I am Joan, not D'joan, and I bring you a weapon. You are women. You are men. You are people. You can use the weapon."

"What weapon?" The voice was Crawlie's, from about the third row of spectators.

"Life and life-with," said the child Joan.

"Don't be a fool," said Crawlie. "What's the weapon? Don't give us words. We've had words and death ever since the world of underpeople began. That's what *people* give us—good words, fine principles, and cold murder, year after year, generation after generation. Don't tell me I'm a person—I'm not. I'm a bison and I know it. An animal fixed up to look like a person. Give me a something to kill with. Let me die fighting."

Little Joan looked incongruous in her young body and short stature, still wearing the little blue smock in which Elaine had first seen her. She commanded the room. She lifted her hand and the buzz of low voices, which had started while Crawlie was yelling, dropped off to silence again.

"Crawlie," she said, in a voice that carried all the way down the hall, "peace be with you in the everlasting now."

Crawlie scowled. She did have the grace to look puzzled at Joan's message to her, but she did not speak.

"Don't talk to me, dear people," said little Joan. "Get used to me first. I bring you life-with. It's more than love. Love's a hard, sad, dirty word, a cold word, an old word. It says too much and it promises too little. I bring you something much bigger than love. If you're alive, you're alive. If you're alive-with, then you know the other life is there too—both of you, any of you, all of you. Don't do anything. Don't grab, don't clench, don't possess. Just *be*. That's the weapon. There's not a flame or a gun or a poison that can stop it."

"I want to believe you," said Mabel, "but I don't know how to."

"Don't believe me," said little Joan. "Just wait and let things happen. Let me through, good people. I have to sleep for a while. Elaine will watch me while I sleep and when I get up, I will tell you why you are underpeople no longer."

Joan started to move forward—

A wild ululating screech split the corridor.

Everyone looked around to see where it came from.

It was almost like the shriek of a fighting bird, but the sound came from among them.

Elaine saw it first.

Crawlie had a knife and just as the cry ended, she flung herself on Joan.

Child and woman fell on the floor, their dresses a tangle. The large hand rose up twice with the knife, and the second time it came up red.

From the hot shocking burn in her side, Elaine knew that she must herself have taken one of the stabs. She could not tell whether Joan was still living.

The undermen pulled Crawlie off the child.

Crawlie was white with rage. "Words, words, words. She'll kill us all with her words."

A large, fat man, with the muzzle of a bear on the front of an otherwise human-looking head and body, stepped around the man who held Crawlie. He gave her one tremendous slap. She dropped to the floor unconscious. The knife, stained with blood, fell on the old worn carpet. (Elaine thought automatically: restorative for her later; check neck vertebrae; no problem of bleeding.)

For the first time in her life, Elaine functioned as a wholly efficient witch. She helped the people pull the clothing from little Joan. The tiny body, with the heavy purple-dark blood pumping out from just below the rib-cage, looked hurt and fragile. Elaine reached in her left handbag. She had a surgical radar pen. She held it to her eye and looked through the flesh, up and down the wound. The peritoneum was punctured, the liver cut, the upper folds of the large intestine were perforated in two places. When she saw this, she knew what to do. She brushed the bystanders aside and got to work.

First she glued the cuts from the inside out, starting with the damage to the liver. Each touch of the organic adhesive was preceded by a tiny spray of re-coding powder, designed to reinforce the capacity of the injured organ to restore itself. The probing, pressing, squeezing took eleven minutes. Before it was finished, Joan had awakened, and was murmuring:

"Am I dying?"

"Not at all," said Elaine, "unless these human medicines poison your dog blood."

"Who did it?"

"Crawlie?"

"Why?" said the child. "Why? Is she hurt too? Where is she?"

"Not as hurt as she is going to be," said the goat-man, Charley-is-my-darling. "If she lives, we'll fix her up and try her and put her to death."

"No, you won't," said Joan. "You're going to love her. You must."

The goat-man looked bewildered.

He turned in his perplexity to Elaine. "Better have a look at Crawlie," said he. "Maybe Orson killed her with that slap. He's a bear, you know."

"So I saw," said Elaine, drily. What did the man think that thing looked like, a hummingbird?

She walked over to the body of Crawlie. As soon as she touched the shoulders, she knew that she was in for trouble. The outer appearances were human, but the musculature beneath was not. She suspected that the laboratories had left Crawlie terribly strong, keeping the buffalo strength and obstinacy for some remote industrial reason of their own. She took out a brainlink, a close-range telepathic hookup which worked only briefly and slightly, to see if the mind still functioned. As she reached for Crawlie's head to attach it, the unconscious girl sprang suddenly to life, jumped to her feet, and said:

"No, you don't! You don't peep me, you dirty human!"

"Crawlie, stand still."

"Don't boss me, you monster!"

"Crawlie, that's a bad thing to say." It was eerie to hear such a commanding voice coming from the throat and mouth of a small child. Small she might have been, but Joan commanded the scene.

"I don't care what I say. You all hate me."

"That's not true, Crawlie."

"You're a dog and now you're a person. You're born a traitor. Dogs have always sided with people. You hated me even before you went into that room and changed into something else. Now you are going to kill us all."

"We may die, Crawlie, but I won't do it."

"Well, you hate me, anyhow. You've always hated me."

"You may not believe it," said Joan, "but I've always loved you. You were the prettiest woman in our whole corridor."

Crawlie laughed. The sound gave Elaine gooseflesh. "Suppose I believed it. How could I live if I thought that people loved me? If I believed you, I would have to tear myself to pieces, to break my brains on the wall, to do—" The laughter changed to sobs, but Crawlie managed to resume talking: "You things are so stupid that you don't even know that you're monsters. You're not people. You never will be people. I'm one of you myself. I'm honest enough to admit what I am. We're dirt, we're nothing, we're things that are less than machines. We hide in the earth like dirt and when people kill us they do not weep. At least we were hiding. Now you come along, you and your tame human woman"—Crawlie glared briefly at Elaine—"and you try to change even that. I'll kill you again if I can, you dirt, you slut, you dog! What are you doing with that child's body? We don't even know who you are now. Can you tell us?"

The bear-man had moved up close to Crawlie, unnoticed by her, and was ready to slap her down again if she moved against little Joan.

Joan looked straight at him and with a mere movement of her eyes she commanded him not to strike.

"I'm tired," she said, "I'm tired, Crawlie. I'm a thousand years old when I am not even five. And I am Elaine now, and I am Hunter too, and I am the Lady Panc Ashash, and I know a great many more things than I thought I would ever know. I have work to do,

Crawlie, because I love you, and I think I will die soon. But please, good people, first let me rest."

The bear-man was on Crawlie's right. On her left, there had moved up a snake-woman. The face was pretty and human, except for the thin forked tongue which ran in and out of the mouth like a dying flame. She had good shoulders and hips but no breasts at all. She wore empty golden brassiere cups which swung against her chest. Her hands looked as though they might be stronger than steel. Crawlie started to move toward Joan, and the snake-woman hissed.

It was the snake hiss of Old Earth.

For a second, every animal-person in the corridor stopped breathing. They all stared at the snake-woman. She hissed again, looking straight at Crawlie. The sound was an abomination in that narrow space. Elaine saw that Joan tightened up like a little dog, Charley-is-my-darling looked as though he was ready to leap twenty meters in one jump, and Elaine herself felt an impulse to strike, to kill, to destroy. The hiss was a challenge to them all.

The snake-woman looked around calmly, fully aware of the attention she had obtained.

"Don't worry, dear people. See, I'm using Joan's name for all of us. I'm not going to hurt Crawlie, not unless she hurts Joan. But if she hurts Joan, if anybody hurts Joan, they will have me to deal with. You have a good idea who I am. We S-people have great strength, high intelligence, and no fear at all. You know we cannot breed. People have to make us one by one, out of ordinary snakes. Do not cross me, dear people. I want to learn about this new love which Joan is bringing, and nobody is going to hurt Joan while I am here. Do you

hear me, people? Nobody. Try it, and you die. I think
I could kill almost all of you before I died, even if you
all attacked me at once. Do you hear me, people? *Leave
Joan alone.* That goes for you, too, you soft human
woman. I am not afraid of you either. You there," said
she to the bear-man, "pick little Joan up and carry her
to a quiet bed. She must rest. She must be quiet for
a while. You be quiet too, all you people, or you will
meet me. Me." Her black eyes roved across their faces.
The snake-woman moved forward and they parted in
front of her, as though she were the only solid being
in a throng of ghosts.

Her eyes rested a moment on Elaine. Elaine met
the gaze, but it was an uncomfortable thing to do.
The black eyes with neither eyebrows nor lashes
seemed full of intelligence and devoid of emotion.
Orson, the bear-man, followed obediently behind. He
carried little Joan.

As the child passed Elaine she tried to stay awake.
She murmured, "Make me bigger. Please make me
bigger. Right away."

"I don't know how . . ." said Elaine.

The child struggled to full awakening. "I'll have work
to do. Work . . . and maybe my death to die. It will all
be wasted if I am this little. Make me bigger."

"But—" protested Elaine again.

"If you don't know, ask the lady."

"What lady?"

The S-woman had paused, listening to the conversation. She cut in.

"The Lady Panc Ashash, of course. The dead one.
Do you think that a living Lady of the Instrumentality
would do anything but kill us all?"

As the snake-woman and Orson carried Joan away, Charley-is-my-darling came up to Elaine and said, "Do you want to go?"

"Where?"

"To the Lady Panc Ashash, of course."

"Me?" said Elaine. "Now?" said Elaine, even more emphatically. "Of course not," said Elaine, pronouncing each word as though it were a law. "What do you think I am? A few hours ago I did not even know that you existed. I wasn't sure about the word 'death.' I just assumed that everything terminated at four hundred years, the way it should. It's been hours of danger, and everybody has been threatening everybody else for all that time. I'm tired and I'm sleepy and I'm dirty, and I've got to take care of myself, and besides—"

She stopped suddenly and bit her lip. She had started to say, *and besides, my body is all worn out with that dreamlike love-making which the Hunter and I had together.* That was not the business of Charley-is-my-darling: he was goat enough as he was. His mind was goatish and would not see the dignity of it all.

The goat-man said, very gently, "You are making history, Elaine, and when you make history you cannot always take care of all the little things too. Are you happier and more important than you ever were before? Yes? Aren't you a different you from the person who met Balthasar just a few hours ago?"

Elaine was taken aback by the seriousness. She nodded.

"Stay hungry and tired. Stay dirty. Just a little longer. Time must not be wasted. You can talk to the Lady Panc Ashash. Find out what we must do about little

Joan. When you come back with further instructions, I will take care of you myself. This tunnel is not as bad a town as it looks. We will have everything you could need, in the Room of Englok. Englok himself built it, long ago. Work just a little longer, and then you can eat and rest. We have everything here. 'I am the citizen of no mean city.' But first you must help Joan. You love Joan, don't you?"

"Oh, yes, I do," she said.

"Then help us just a little bit more."

With death? she thought. With murder? With violation of law? But—but it was all for Joan.

It was thus that Elaine went to the camouflaged door, went out under the open sky again, saw the great saucer of Upper Kalma reaching out over the Old Lower City. She talked to the voice of the Lady Panc Ashash, and obtained certain instructions, together with other messages. Later, she was able to repeat them, but she was too tired to make out their real sense.

She staggered back to the place in the wall where she thought the door to be, leaned against it, and nothing happened.

"Further down, Elaine, further down. Hurry! When I used to be me, I too got tired," came the strong whisper of the Lady Panc Ashash, "but do hurry!"

Elaine stepped away from the wall, looking at it.

A beam of light struck her.

The Instrumentality had found her.

She rushed wildly at the wall.

The door gaped briefly. The strong welcome hand of Charley-is-my-darling helped her in.

"The light! The light!" cried Elaine. "I've killed us all. They saw me."

"Not yet," smiled the goat-man, with his quick crooked intelligent smile. "I may not be educated, but I am pretty smart."

He reached toward the inner gate, glanced back at Elaine appraisingly, and then shoved a man-sized robot through the door.

"There it goes, a sweeper about your size. No memory bank. A worn-out brain. Just simple motivations. If they come down to see what they thought they saw, they will see this instead. We keep a bunch of these at the door. We don't go out much, but when we do, it's handy to have these to cover up with."

He took her by the arm. "While you eat, you can tell me. Can we make her bigger . . . ?"

"Who?"

"Joan, of course. Our Joan. That's what you went to find out for us."

Elaine had to inventory her own mind to see what the Lady Panc Ashash had said on that subject. In a moment she remembered.

"You need a pod. And a jelly bath. And narcotics, because it will hurt. Four hours."

"Wonderful," said Charley-is-my-darling, leading her deeper and deeper into the tunnel.

"But what's the use of it," said Elaine, "if I've ruined us all? The Instrumentality saw me coming in. They will follow. They will kill all of you, even Joan. Where is the Hunter? Shouldn't I sleep first?" She felt her lips go thick with fatigue; she had not rested or eaten since she took that chance on the strange little door between Waterrocky Road and the Shopping Bar.

"You're safe, Elaine, you're safe," said Charley-is-

my-darling, his sly smile very warm and his smooth
voice carrying the ring of sincere conviction. For
himself, he did not believe a word of it. He thought
they were all in danger, but there was no point in
terrifying Elaine. Elaine was the only real person on
their side, except for the Hunter, who was a strange
one, almost like an animal himself, and for the Lady
Panc Ashash, who was very benign, but who was, after
all, a dead person. He was frightened himself, but he
was afraid of fear. Perhaps they were all doomed.

In a way, he was right.

## ∽ 7 ∽

The Lady Arabella Underwood had called the Lady
Goroke.

"Something has tampered with my mind."

The Lady Goroke felt very shocked. She threw
back the inquiry. *Put a probe on it.*

"I did. Nothing."

Nothing?

More shock for the Lady Goroke. *Sound the alert,
then.*

"Oh, no. Oh, no, no. It was a friendly, nice tampering." The Lady Arabella Underwood, being an
Old North Australian, was rather formal: she always
thought full words at her friends, even in telepathic
contact. She never sent mere raw ideas.

*But that's utterly unlawful. You're part of the Instru-
mentality. It's a crime!* thought the Lady Goroke.

She got a giggle for reply.

*You laugh . . . ?* she inquired.

"I just thought a new Lord might be here. From the Instrumentality. Having a look at me."

The Lady Goroke was very proper and easily shocked. *We wouldn't do that!*

The Lady Arabella thought to herself but did not transmit, "Not to you, my dear. You're a blooming prude." To the other she transmitted, "Forget it then."

Puzzled and worried, the Lady Goroke thought: *Well, all right. Break?*

"Right-ho. Break."

The Lady Goroke frowned to herself. She slapped her wall. *Planet Central,* she thought at it.

A mere man sat at a desk.

"I am the Lady Goroke," she said.

"Of course, my Lady," he replied.

"Police fever, one degree. One degree only. Till rescinded. Clear?"

"Clear, my Lady. The entire planet?"

"Yes," she said.

"Do you wish to give a reason?" His voice was respectful and routine.

"Must I?"

"Of course not, my Lady."

"None given, then. Close."

He saluted and his image faded from the wall.

She raised her mind to the level of a light clear call. *Instrumentality Only—Instrumentality Only. I have raised the police fever level one degree by command. Reason, personal disquiet. You know my voice. You know me. Goroke.*

Far across the city—a police ornithopter flapped slowly down the street.

The police robot was photographing a sweeper,

the most elaborately malfunctioning sweeper he had ever seen.

The sweeper raced down the road at unlawful speeds, approaching three hundred kilometers an hour, stopped with a sizzle of plastic on stone, and began picking dust-motes off the pavement.

When the ornithopter reached it, the sweeper took off again, rounded two or three corners at tremendous speed, and then settled down to its idiot job.

The third time this happened, the robot in the ornithopter put a disabling slug through it, flew down, and picked it up with the claws of his machine.

He saw it in close view.

"Birdbrain. Old model. Birdbrain. Good they don't use those any more. The thing could have hurt a Man. Now, I'm printed from a mouse, a real mouse with lots and lots of brains."

He flew toward the central junkyard with the wornout sweeper. The sweeper, crippled but still conscious, was trying to pick dust off the iron claws which held it.

Below them, the Old City twisted out of sight with its odd geometrical lights. The New City, bathed in its soft perpetual glow, shone out against the night of Fomalhaut III. Beyond them, the everlasting ocean boiled in its private storms.

On the actual stage the actors cannot do much with the scene of the interlude, where Joan was cooked in a single night from the size of a child five years old to the tallness of a miss of fifteen or sixteen. The biological machine did work well, though at the risk of her life. It made her into a vital, robust young person, without changing her mind at all. This is hard for any actress to portray. The storyboxes have the advantage. They can show the machine with all sorts of improvements—flashing lights, bits of lightning, mysterious rays. Actually, it looked like a bathtub full of boiling brown jelly, completely covering Joan.

Elaine, meanwhile, ate hungrily in the palatial room of Englok himself. The food was very, very old, and she had doubts, as a witch, about its nutritional value, but it stilled her hunger. The denizens of Clown Town had declared this room "off limits" to themselves, for reasons which Charley-is-my-darling could not make plain. He stood in the doorway and told her what to do to find food, to activate the bed out of the floor, to open the bathroom. Everything was very old-fashioned and nothing responded to a simple thought or to a mere slap.

A curious thing happened.

Elaine had washed her hands, had eaten, and was preparing for her bath. She had taken most of her clothes off, thinking only that Charley-is-my-darling was an animal, not a man, so that it did not matter.

Suddenly she knew it did matter.

He might be an underperson but he was a man to her. Blushing deeply all the way down to her neck, she ran into the bathroom and called back to him:

"Go away. I will bathe and then sleep. Wake me when you have to, not before."

"Yes, Elaine."

"And—and—"

"Yes?"

"Thank you," she said. "Thank you very much. Do you know, I never said 'thank you' to an underperson before."

"That's all right," said Charley-is-my-darling with a smile. "Most real people don't. Sleep well, my dear Elaine. When you awaken, be ready for great things. We shall take a star out of the skies and shall set thousands of worlds on fire . . ."

"What's that?" she said, putting her head around the corner of the bathroom.

"Just a figure of speech," he smiled. "Just meaning that you won't have much time. Rest well. Don't forget to put your clothes in the ladysmaid machine. The ones in Clown Town are all worn out. But since we haven't used this room, yours ought to work."

"Which is it?" she said.

"The red lid with the gold handle. Just lift it." On that domestic note he left her to rest, while he went off and plotted the destiny of a hundred billion lives.

They told her it was mid-morning when she came out of the room of Englok. How could she have known it? The brown-and-yellow corridor, with its gloomy old yellow lights, was just as dim and stench-ridden as ever.

The people all seemed to have changed.

Baby-baby was no longer a mouse-hag, but a woman of considerable force and much tenderness. Crawlie was as dangerous as a human enemy, staring at Elaine, her beautiful face gone bland with hidden hate. Charley-is-my-darling was gay, friendly, and persuasive. She thought she could read expressions on the faces of Orson and the S-woman, odd though their features were.

After she had gotten through some singularly polite greetings, she demanded, "What's happening now?"

A new voice spoke up—a voice she knew and did not know.

Elaine glanced over at a niche in the wall.

The Lady Panc Ashash! And who was that with her?

Even as she asked herself the question, Elaine knew the answer. It was Joan, grown, only half a head less tall than the Lady Panc Ashash or herself. It was a new Joan, powerful, happy, and quiet; but it was all the dear little old D'joan too.

"Welcome," said the Lady Panc Ashash, "to our revolution."

"What's a revolution?" asked Elaine. "And I thought you couldn't come in here with all the thought shielding?"

The Lady Panc Ashash lifted a wire which trailed back from her robot body. "I rigged this up so that I could use the body. Precautions are no use any more. It's the other side which will need the precautions now. A revolution is a way of changing systems and people. This is one. You go first, Elaine. This way."

"To die? Is that what you mean?"

The Lady Panc Ashash laughed warmly. "You know me by now. You know my friends here. You know what your own life has been down to now, a useless witch in a world which did not want you. We may die, but it's what we do before we die that counts. This is Joan going to meet her destiny. You lead as far as the Upper City. Then Joan will lead. And then we shall see."

"You mean, all these people are going too?" Elaine looked at the ranks of the underpeople, who were beginning to form into two queues down the corridor. The queues bulged wherever mothers led their children by the hand or carried small ones in their arms. Here and there the line was punctuated by a giant underperson.

They have been nothing, thought Elaine, and I was nothing too. Now we are all going to do something, even though we may be terminated for it. "May be," thought she: "shall be" is the word. But it is worth it if Joan can change the worlds, even a little bit, even for other people.

Joan spoke up. Her voice had grown with her body, but it was the same dear voice which the little dog-girl had had sixteen hours (they seem sixteen years, thought Elaine) ago, when Elaine first met her at the door to the tunnel of Englok.

Joan said, "Love is not something special, reserved for men alone.

"Love is not proud. Love has no real name. Love is for life itself, and we have life.

"We cannot win by fighting. People outnumber us, outgun us, outrun us, outfight us. But people did not create us. Whatever made people, made us too. You all know that, but will we say the name?"

There was a murmur of *no* and *never* from the crowd.

"You have waited for me. I have waited too. It is time to die, perhaps, but we will die the way people did in the beginning, before things became easy and cruel for them. They live in a stupor and they die in a dream. It is not a good dream and if they awaken, they will know that we are people too. Are you with me?" They murmured *yes*. "Do you love me?" Again they murmured agreement. "Shall we go out and meet the day?" They shouted their acclaim.

Joan turned to the Lady Panc Ashash. "Is everything as you wished and ordered?"

"Yes," said the dear dead woman in the robot body.

"Joan first, to lead you. Elaine preceding her, to drive away robots or ordinary underpeople. When you meet real people, you will love them. That is all. You will love them. If they kill you, you will love them. Joan will show you how. Pay no further attention to me. Ready?"

Joan lifted her right hand and said words to herself. The people bowed their heads before her, faces and muzzles and snouts of all sizes and colors. A baby of some kind mewed in a tiny falsetto to the rear.

Just before she turned to lead the procession, Joan turned back to the people and said, "Crawlie, where are you?"

"Here, in the middle," said a clear, calm voice far back.

"Do you love me now, Crawlie?"

"No, D'joan. I like you less than when you were a little dog. But these are my people too, as well as yours. I am brave. I can walk. I won't make trouble."

"Crawlie," said Joan, "will you love people if we meet them?"

All faces turned toward the beautiful bison-girl. Elaine could just see her, way down the murky corridor. Elaine could see that the girl's face had turned utter, dead white with emotion. Whether rage or fear, she could not tell.

At last Crawlie spoke, "No, I won't love people. And I won't love you. I have my pride."

Softly, softly, like death itself at a quiet bedside, Joan spoke. "You *can* stay behind, Crawlie. You can stay here. It isn't much of a chance, but it's a chance."

Crawlie looked at her. "Bad luck to you, dog-woman, and bad luck to the rotten human being up there beside you."

Elaine stood on tiptoe to see what would happen. Crawlie's face suddenly disappeared, dropping downward.

The snake woman elbowed her way to the front, stood close to Joan where the others could see her, and sang out in a voice as clear as metal itself:

"Sing 'poor, poor, Crawlie,' dear people. Sing 'I love Crawlie,' dear people. She is dead. I just killed her so that we would all be full of love. I love you too," said the S-woman, on whose reptilian features no sign of love or hate could be seen.

Joan spoke up, apparently prompted by the Lady Panc Ashash. "We do love Crawlie, dear people. Think of her and then let us move forward."

Charley-is-my-darling gave Elaine a little shove. "Here, you lead."

In a dream, in a bewilderment, Elaine led.

She felt warm, happy, brave when she passed close to the strange Joan, so tall and yet so familiar. Joan gave her a full smile and whispered, "Tell me I'm doing well, human woman. I'm a dog and dogs have lived a million years for the praise of man."

"You're right, Joan, you're completely right! I'm with you. Shall I go now?" responded Elaine.

Joan nodded, her eyes brimming with tears.

Elaine led.

Joan and the Lady Panc Ashash followed, dog and dead woman championing the procession.

The rest of the underpeople followed them in turn, in a double line.

When they made the secret door open, daylight flooded the corridor. Elaine could almost feel the stale odor-ridden air pouring out with them. When she glanced back into the tunnel for the last time, she saw the body of Crawlie lying all alone on the floor.

Elaine herself turned to the steps and began going up them.

No one had yet noticed the procession.

Elaine could hear the wire of the Lady Panc Ashash dragging on the stone and metal of the steps as they climbed.

When she reached the top door, Elaine had a moment of indecision and panic. "This is my life, my life," she thought. "I have no other. What have I done? Oh, Hunter, Hunter, where are you? Have you betrayed me?"

Said Joan softly behind her, "Go on! Go on. This is a war of love. Keep going."

Elaine opened the door to the upper street. The roadway was full of people. Three police ornithopters flapped slowly overhead. This was an unusual number. Elaine stopped again.

"Keep walking," said Joan, "and warn the robots off."

Elaine advanced and the revolution began.

### ∾ 8 ∾

The revolution lasted six minutes and covered one hundred and twelve meters.

The police flew over as soon as the underpeople began pouring out of the doorway.

The first one glided in like a big bird, his voice asking, "Identify! Who are you?"

Elaine said, "Go away. That is a command."

"Identify yourself," said the bird-like machine,

banking steeply with the lens-eyed robot peering at Elaine out of its middle.

"Go away," said Elaine. "I am a true human and I command."

The first police ornithopter apparently called to the others by radio. Together they flapped their way down the corridor between the big buildings.

A lot of people had stopped. Most of their faces were blank, a few showing animation or amusement or horror at the sight of so many underpeople all crowded in one place.

Joan's voice sang out, in the clearest possible enunciation of the Old Common Tongue:

"Dear people, we are people. We love you. We love you."

The underpeople began to chant *love, love, love* in a weird plainsong full of sharps and halftones. The true humans shrank back. Joan herself set the example by embracing a young woman of about her own height. Charley-is-my-darling took a human man by the shoulders and shouted at him:

"I love you, my dear fellow! Believe me, I do love you. It's wonderful meeting you." The human man was startled by the contact and even more startled by the glowing warmth of the goat-man's voice. He stood mouth slack and body relaxed with sheer, utter, and accepted surprise.

Somewhere to the rear a person screamed.

A police ornithopter came flapping back. Elaine could not tell if it was one of the three she had sent away, or a new one altogether. She waited for it to get close enough to hail, so that she could tell it to go away. For the first time, she wondered about the actual physical character of danger. Could the police machine put a slug through her? Or shoot flame at her? Or lift her screaming, carrying her away with its iron claws to some place where she would be pretty and clean and never herself again? "Oh, Hunter, Hunter, where are you now? Have you forgotten me? Have you betrayed me?"

The underpeople were still surging forward and mingling with the real people, clutching them by their hands or their garments, and repeating in the queer medley of voices:

"I love you. Oh, please, I love you! We are people. We are your sisters and brothers . . ."

The snake-woman wasn't making much progress. She had seized a human man with her more-than-iron hand. Elaine hadn't seen her saying anything, but the man had fainted dead away. The snake-woman had him draped over her arm like an empty overcoat and was looking for somebody else to love.

Behind Elaine a low voice said, "He's coming soon."

"Who?" said Elaine to the Lady Panc Ashash, knowing perfectly well whom she meant, but not wanting to admit it, and busy with watching the circling ornithopter at the same time.

"The Hunter, of course," said the robot with the dear dead lady's voice. "He'll come for you. You'll be all right. I'm at the end of my wire. Look away, my dear. They are about to kill me again and I am afraid that the sight would distress you."

Fourteen robots, foot models, marched with military decision into the crowd. The true humans took heart from this and some of them began to slip away into doorways. Most of the real people were still so surprised that they stood around with the under-people pawing at them, babbling the accents of love over and over again, the animal origin of their voices showing plainly.

The robot sergeant took no note of this. He approached the Lady Panc Ashash only to find Elaine standing in his way.

"I command you," she said, with all the passion of a working witch, "I *command* you to leave this place."

His eye-lenses were like dark-blue marbles floating in milk. They seemed swimmy and poorly focused as he looked her over. He did not reply but stepped around her, faster than her own body could intercept him. He made for the dear, dead Lady Panc Ashash.

Elaine, bewildered, realized that the Lady's robot body seemed more human than ever. The robot-sergeant confronted her.

This is the scene which we all remember, the first authentic picture tape of the entire incident:

The gold and black sergeant, his milky eyes staring at the Lady Panc Ashash.

The Lady herself, in the pleasant old robot body, lifting a commanding hand.

Elaine, distraught, half-turning as though she would grab the robot by his right arm. Her head is moving so rapidly that her black hair swings as she turns.

Charley-is-my-darling shouting, "I love, love, love!" at a small handsome man with mouse-colored hair. The man is gulping and saying nothing.

All this we know.

Then comes the unbelievable, which we now believe, the event for which the stars and worlds were unprepared.

Mutiny.

Robot mutiny.

Disobedience in open daylight.

The words are hard to hear on the tape, but we can still make them out. The recording device on the police ornithopter had gotten a square fix on the face of the Lady Panc Ashash. Lip-readers can see the words plainly; non-lip-readers can hear the words the third or fourth time the tape is run through the eyebox.

Said the Lady, "Overridden."

Said the sergeant, "No, you're a robot."

"See for yourself. Read my brain. I am a robot. I am also a woman. You cannot disobey people. I am people. I love you. Furthermore, you are people. You think. We love each other. Try. Try to attack."

"I—I cannot," said the robot sergeant, his milky eyes seeming to spin with excitement. "You love me? You mean I'm *alive*? I *exist*?"

"With love, you do," said the Lady Panc Ashash. "Look at her," said the Lady, pointing to Joan, "because she has brought you love."

The robot looked and disobeyed the law. His squad looked with him.

He turned back to the Lady and bowed to her: "Then you know what we must do, if we cannot obey you and cannot disobey the others."

"Do it," she said sadly, "but know what you are doing. You are not really escaping two human commands. You are making a choice. You. That makes you men."

The sergeant turned to his squad of man-sized robots: "You hear that? She says we are *men*. I believe her. Do you believe her?"

"We do," they cried almost unanimously.

This is where the picture-tape ends, but we can imagine how the scene was concluded. Elaine had stopped short, just behind the sergeant-robot. The other robots had come up behind her. Charley-is-my-darling had stopped talking. Joan was in the act of lifting her hands in blessing, her warm brown dog eyes gone wide with pity and understanding.

People wrote down the things that we cannot see.

Apparently the robot-sergeant said, "Our love, dear people, and good-bye. We disobey and die." He waved his hand to Joan. It is not certain whether he did or did not say, "Good-bye, our lady and our liberator." Maybe some poet made up the second saying; the first one, we are sure about. And we are sure about the next word, the one which historians and poets all agree on. He turned to his men and said,

"Destruct."

Fourteen robots, the black-and-gold sergeant and his thirteen silver-blue foot soldiers, suddenly spurted white fire in the street of Kalma. They detonated their suicide buttons, thermite caps in their own heads. They had done something with no human command at all, on an order from another robot, the body of the Lady Panc Ashash, and she in turn had no human authority, but merely the word of the little dog-girl Joan, who had been made an adult in a single night.

Fourteen white flames made people and underpeople turn their eyes aside. Into the light there dropped a special police ornithopter. Out of it came the two Ladies, Arabella Underwood and Goroke. They lifted their forearms to shield their eyes from the blazing dying robots. They did not see the Hunter, who had moved

mysteriously into an open window above the street and
who watched the scene by putting his hands over his
eyes and peeking through the slits between his fingers.
While the people still stood blinded, they felt the fierce
telepathic shock of the mind of the Lady Goroke taking command of the situation. That was her right, as a
Chief of the Instrumentality. Some of the people, but
not all of them, felt the outré countershock of Joan's
mind reaching out to meet the Lady Goroke.

"I command," thought the Lady Goroke, her mind
kept open to all beings.

"Indeed you do, but I love, I love you," thought Joan.

The first-order forces met.

They engaged.

The revolution was over. Nothing had really happened, but Joan had forced people to meet her. This
was nothing like the poem about people and underpeople getting all mixed up. The mixup came much
later, even after the time of C'mell. The poem is pretty,
but it is dead wrong, as you can see for yourself:

> You should ask me,
>   Me, me, me
> Because I know—
> I used to live
>   On the Eastern Shore.
> Men aren't men,
> And women aren't women,
> And people aren't people any more.

There is no Eastern Shore on Fomalhaut III anyhow; the people/underpeople crisis came much later
than this. The revolution had failed, but history had

reached its new turning-point, the quarrel of the two Ladies. They left their minds open out of sheer surprise. Suicidal robots and world-loving dogs were unheard-of. It was bad enough to have illegal underpeople on the prowl, but these new things—ah!

*Destroy them all,* said the Lady Goroke.

"Why?" thought the Lady Arabella Underwood.

*Malfunction,* replied Goroke.

"But they're not machines!"

*Then they're animals—underpeople. Destroy! Destroy!*

Then came the answer which has created our own time. It came from the Lady Arabella Underwood, and all Kalma heard it:

*Perhaps they are people. They must have a trial.*

The dog-girl Joan dropped to her knees. "I have succeeded. I have succeeded, I have succeeded! You can kill me, dear people, but I love, love you!"

The Lady Panc Ashash said quietly to Elaine, "I thought I would be dead by now. Really dead, at last. But I am not. I have seen the worlds turn, Elaine, and you have seen them turn with me."

The underpeople had fallen quiet as they heard the high-volume telepathic exchange between the two great Ladies.

The real soldiers dropped out of the sky, their ornithopters whistling as they hawked down to the ground. They ran up to the underpeople and began binding them with cord.

One soldier took a single look at the robot body of the Lady Panc Ashash. He touched it with his staff, and the staff turned cherry-red with heat. The robot-body, its heat suddenly drained, fell to the ground in a heap of icy crystals.

Elaine walked between the frigid rubbish and the red-hot staff. She had seen Hunter.

She missed seeing the soldier who came up to Joan, started to bind her, and then fell back weeping, babbling, "She loves me! She loves me!"

The Lord Femtiosex, who commanded the inflying soldiers, bound Joan with cord despite her talking.

Grimly he answered her: "Of course you love me. You're a good dog. You'll die soon, doggy, but till then, you'll obey."

"I'm obeying," said Joan, "but I'm a dog *and* a person. Open your mind, man, and you'll feel it."

Apparently he did open his mind and felt the ocean of love riptiding into him. It shocked him. His arm swung up and back, the edge of the hand striking at Joan's neck for the ancient kill.

"No, you don't," thought the Lady Arabella Underwood. "That child is going to get a proper trial."

He looked at her and glared. *Chief doesn't strike Chief, my Lady. Let go my arm.*

Thought the Lady Arabella at him, openly and in public: *A trial, then.*

In his anger he nodded at her. He would not think or speak to her in the presence of all the other people.

A soldier brought Elaine and Hunter before him.

"Sir and master, these are people, not underpeople. But they have dog-thoughts, cat-thoughts, goat-thoughts, and robot-ideas in their heads. Do you wish to look?"

"Why look?" said the Lord Femtiosex, who was as blond as the ancient pictures of Baldur, and oftentimes that arrogant as well. "The Lord Limaono is arriving. That's all of us. We can have the trial here and now."

Elaine felt cords bite into her wrists; she heard the Hunter murmur comforting words to her, words which she did not quite understand.

"They will not kill us," he murmured, "though we will wish they had, before this day is out. Everything is happening as she said it would, and—"

"Who is that she?" interrupted Elaine.

"She? The lady, of course. The dear dead Lady Panc Ashash, who has worked wonders after her own death, merely with the print of her personality on the machine. Who do you think told me what to do? Why did we wait for you to condition Joan to greatness? Why did the people way down in Clown Town keep on raising one D'joan after another, hoping that hope and a great wonder would occur?"

"You knew?" said Elaine. "You knew . . . before it happened?"

"Of course," said the Hunter, "not exactly, but more or less. She had had hundreds of years after death inside that computer. She had time for billions of thoughts. She saw how it would be if it had to be, and I—"

"Shut up, you people!" roared the Lord Femtiosex. "You are making the animals restless with your babble. Shut up, or I will stun you!"

Elaine fell silent.

The Lord Femtiosex glanced around at her, ashamed at having made his anger naked before another person. He added quietly:

"The trial is about to begin. The one that the tall Lady ordered."

## ∾ 9 ∾

You all know about the trial, so there is no need to linger over it. There is another picture of San Shigonanda, the one from his conventional period, which shows it very plainly.

The street had filled full of real people, crowding together to see something which would ease the boredom of perfection and time. They all had numbers or number-codes instead of names. They were handsome, well, dully happy. They even looked a great deal alike, similar in their handsomeness, their health, and their underlying boredom. Each of them had a total of four hundred years to live. None of them knew real war, even though the extreme readiness of the soldiers showed vain practice of hundreds of years. The people were beautiful, but they felt themselves useless, and they were quietly desperate without knowing it themselves. This is all clear from the painting, and from the wonderful way that San Shigonanda has of forming them in informal ranks and letting the calm blue light of day shine down on their handsome, hopeless features.

With the underpeople, the artist performs real wonders.

Joan herself is bathed in light. Her light brown hair and her doggy brown eyes express softness and tenderness. He even conveys the idea that her new body is terribly new and strong, that she is virginal and ready to die, that she is a mere girl and yet completely fearless. The posture of love shows in her legs: she stands lightly. Love shows in her hands: they are turned outward toward the judges. Love shows in her smile: it is confident.

And the judges!

The artist has them, too. The Lord Femtiosex, calm again, his narrow sharp lips expressing perpetual rage against a universe which has grown too small for him. The Lord Limaono, wise, twice-reborn, sluggardly, but alert as a snake behind the sleepy eyes and the slow smile. The Lady Arabella Underwood, the tallest true-human present, with her Norstrilian pride and the arrogance of great wealth, along with the capricious tenderness of great wealth, showing in the way that she sat, judging her fellow judges instead of the prisoners. The Lady Goroke, bewildered at last, frowning at a play of fortune which she does not understand. The artist has it all.

And you have the real view-tapes, too, if you want to go to a museum. The reality is not as dramatic as the famous painting, but it has value of its own. The voice of Joan, dead these many centuries, is still strangely moving. It is the voice of a dog-carved-into-man, but it is also the voice of a great lady. The image of the Lady Panc Ashash must have taught her that, along with what she had learned from Elaine and Hunter in the antechamber above the Brown and Yellow Corridor of Englok.

The words of the trial, they too have survived. Many of them have become famous, all across the worlds.

Joan said, during inquiry, "But it is the duty of life to find more than life, and to exchange itself for that higher goodness."

Joan commented, upon sentence, "My body is your property, but my love is not. My love is my own, and I shall love you fiercely while you kill me."

When the soldiers had killed Charley-is-my-darling and were trying to hack off the head of the S-woman until one of them thought to freeze her into crystals, Joan said:

"Should we be strange to you, we animals of Earth that you have brought to the stars? We shared the same sun, the same oceans, the same sky. We are all from Manhome. How do you know that we would not have caught up with you if we had all stayed at home together? My people were dogs. They loved you before you made a woman-shaped thing out of my mother. Should I not love you still? The miracle is not that you have made people out of us. The miracle is that it took us so long to understand it. We are people now, and so are you. You will be sorry for what you are going to do to me, but remember that I shall love your sorrow, too, because great and good things will come out of it."

The Lord Limaono slyly asked, "What is a 'miracle'?"

And her words were, "There is knowledge from Earth which you have not yet found again. There is the name of the nameless one. There are secrets hidden in time from you. Only the dead and the unborn can know them right now: I am both."

The scene is familiar, and yet we will never understand it.

We know what the Lords Femtiosex and Limaono thought they were doing. They were maintaining established order and they were putting it on tape. The minds of men can live together only if the basic ideas are communicated. Nobody has, even now, found out a way of recording telepathy directly into an instrument. We get pieces and snatches and wild jumbles, but we never get a satisfactory record of what one of the great ones was transmitting to another. The two male chiefs were trying to put on record all those things about the episode which would teach careless people not to play with the lives of the underpeople. They were even trying to make underpeople understand the rules and designs by virtue of which they had been transformed from animals into the highest servants of man. This would have been hard to do, given the bewildering events of the last few hours, even from one Chief of the Instrumentality to another; for the general public, it was almost impossible. The outpouring from the Brown and Yellow Corridor was wholly unexpected, even though the Lady Goroke had surprised D'joan; the mutiny of the robot police posed problems which would have to be discussed halfway across the galaxy. Furthermore, the dog-girl was making points which had some verbal validity. If they were left in the form of mere words without proper context, they might affect heedless or impressionable minds. A bad idea can spread like a mutated germ. If it is at all interesting, it can leap from one mind to another halfway across the universe before it has a stop put to it. Look at the ruinous fads and foolish fashions which have nuisanced mankind even in the ages of the highest orderliness. We today know that variety, flexibility, danger, and the seasoning of a little hate can make love and life bloom as they never bloomed before; we know it is better to live with the complications of thirteen thousand old languages resurrected from the dead ancient past than it is to live with the cold blind-alley perfection of the Old Common Tongue. We know a lot of things which the Lords Femtiosex and Limaono did not, and before we consider them stupid or cruel, we must remember that centuries passed before mankind finally came to grips with the problem of the underpeople and decided what "life" was within the limits of the human community.

Finally, we have the testimony of the two Lords themselves. They both lived to very advanced ages, and toward the end of their lives they were worried and annoyed to find that the episode of D'joan over-shadowed all the bad things which had not happened during their long careers—bad things which they had labored to forestall for the protection of the planet Fomalhaut III—and they were distressed to see themselves portrayed as casual, cruel men when in fact they were nothing of the sort. If they had seen that the story of Joan on Fomalhaut III would get to be what it is today—one of the great romances of mankind, along with the story of C'mell or the romance of the lady who sailed *The Soul*—they would not only have been disappointed, but they would have been justifiably angry at the fickleness of mankind as well. Their roles are clear, because they made them clear. The Lord Femtiosex accepts the responsibility for the notion of fire; the Lord Limaono agrees that he concurred in the decision. Both of them, many years later, reviewed the tapes of the scene and agreed that something which the Lady Arabella Underwood had said or thought—

Something had made them do it.

But even with the tapes to refresh and clarify their memories, they could not say what.

We have even put computers on the job of cata-loguing every word and every inflection of the whole trial, but they have not pinpointed the critical point either.

And the Lady Arabella—nobody ever questioned her. They didn't dare. She went back to her own planet of Old North Australia, surrounded by the immense treasure of the santaclara drug, and no planet is going to pay at the rate of two thousand million credits a day for the privilege of sending an investigator to talk to a lot of obstinate, simple, wealthy Norstrilian peasants who will not talk to offworlders anyhow. The Norstrilians charge that sum for the admission of any guest not selected by their own invitation; so we will never know what the Lady Arabella Underwood said or did after she went home. The Norstrilians said they did not wish to discuss the matter, and if we do not wish to go back to living a mere seventy years we had better not anger the only planet which produces stroon.

And the Lady Goroke—she, poor thing, went mad. Mad, for a period of years.

People did not know it till later, but there was no word to be gotten out of her. She performed the odd actions which we now know to be a part of the dynasty of Lords Jestocost, who forced themselves by diligence and merit upon the Instrumentality for two hundred and more years. But on the case of Joan she had nothing to say.

The trial is therefore a scene about which we know everything—and nothing.

We think that we know the physical facts of the life of D'joan who became Joan. We know about the Lady Panc Ashash who whispered endlessly to the underpeople about a justice yet to come. We know the whole life of the unfortunate Elaine and of her involvement with the case. We know that there were in those centuries, when underpeople first developed, many warrens in which illegal underpeople used their near-human wits, their animal cunning, and their gift of speech to survive even when mankind had declared them surplus. The Brown and Yellow Corridor was not by any means the only one of its kind. We even know what happened to the Hunter.

For the other underpeople—Charley-is-my-darling, Baby-baby, Mabel, the S-woman, Orson, and all the others—we have the tapes of the trial itself. They were not tried by anybody. They were put to death by the soldiers on the spot, as soon as it was plain that their testimony would not be needed. As witnesses, they could live a few minutes or an hour; as animals, they were already outside the regulations.

Ah, we know all about that now, and yet know nothing. Dying is simple, though we tend to hide it away. The *how* of dying is a minor scientific matter; the *when* of dying is a problem to each of us, whether he lives on the old-fashioned 400-year-life planets or on the radical new ones where the freedoms of disease and accident have been reintroduced; the *why* of it is still as shocking to us as it was to pre-atomic man, who used to cover farmland with the boxed bodies of his dead. These underpeople died as no animals had ever died before. Joyfully.

One mother held her children up for the soldier to kill them all.

She must have been of rat origin, because she had septuplets in closely matching form.

The tape shows us the picture of the soldier getting ready.

The rat-woman greets him with a smile and holds up her seven babies. Little blondes they are, wearing pink or blue bonnets, all of them with glowing cheeks and bright little eyes.

"Put them on the ground," said the soldier. "I'm going to kill you and them too." On the tape, we can hear the nervous peremptory edge of his voice. He added one word, as though he had already begun to think that he had to justify himself to these under-people. "Orders," he added.

"It doesn't matter if I hold them, soldier. I'm their mother. They'll feel better if they die easily with their mother near. I love you, soldier. I love all people. You are my brother, even though my blood is rat blood and yours is human. Go ahead and kill them, soldier. I can't even hurt you. Can't you understand it? *I love you, soldier.* We share a common speech, common hopes, common fears, and a common death. That is what Joan has taught us all. Death is not bad, soldier. It just comes badly, sometimes, but you will remember me after you have killed me and my babies. You will remember that I love you now—"

The soldier, we see on the tape, can stand it no longer. He clubs his weapon, knocks the woman down; the babies scatter on the ground. We see his booted heel rise up and crush down against their heads. We hear the wet popping sound of the little heads breaking, the sharp cut-off of the baby wails as they die. We get one last view of the rat-woman herself. She has stood up again by the time the seventh baby is killed. She offers her hand to the soldier to shake. Her face is dirty and bruised, a trickle of blood running down her left cheek. Even now, we know she is a rat, an underperson, a modified animal, a nothing. And yet we, even we across the centuries, feel that she has somehow become more of a person than we are—that she dies human and fulfilled. We know that she has triumphed over death: we have not.

We see the soldier looking straight at her with eerie horror, as though her simple love were some unfathomable device from an alien source.

We hear her next words on the tape:

"Soldier, I love all of you—"

His weapon could have killed her in a fraction of a second, if he had used it properly. But he didn't. He clubbed it and hit her, as though his heat-remover had been a wooden club and himself a wild man instead of part of the elite guard of Kalma.

We know what happens then.

She falls under his blows. She points. Points straight at Joan, wrapped in fire and smoke.

The rat-woman screams one last time, screams into the lens of the robot camera as though she were talking not to the soldier but to all mankind:

"You can't kill *her*. You can't kill love. I love you, soldier, love you. You can't kill *that*. Remember—"

His last blow catches her in the face.

She falls back on the pavement. He thrusts his foot, as we can see by the tape, directly on her throat. He leaps forward in an odd little jig, bringing his full weight down on her fragile neck. He swings while stamping downward, and we then see his face, full on in the camera.

It is the face of a weeping child, bewildered by hurt and shocked by the prospect of more hurt to come.

He had started to do his duty, and duty had gone wrong, all wrong.

Poor man. He must have been one of the first men in the new world who tried to use weapons against love. Love is a sour and powerful ingredient to meet in the excitement of battle.

All the underpeople died that way. Most of them died smiling, saying the word "love" or the name "Joan."

The bear-man Orson had been kept to the very end. He died very oddly. He died laughing.

The soldier lifted his pellet-thrower and aimed it straight at Orson's forehead. The pellets were 22 millimeters in diameter and had a muzzle velocity of only 125 meters per second. In that manner, they could stop recalcitrant robots or evil underpeople, without any risk of penetrating buildings and hurting the true people who might be inside, out of sight.

Orson looks, on the tape the robots made, as though he knows perfectly well what the weapon is. (He probably did. Underpeople used to live with the danger of a violent death hanging over them from birth until removal.) He shows no fear of it, in the pictures we have; he begins to laugh. His laughter is warm, generous, relaxed—like the friendly laughter of a happy foster-father who has found a guilty and embarrassed child, knowing full well that the child expects punishment but will not get it.

"Shoot, man. You can't kill me, man. I'm in your mind. I love you. Joan taught us. Listen, man. There is no death. Not for love. Ho, ho, ho, poor fellow, don't be afraid of me. Shoot! You're the unlucky one. You're going to live. And remember. And remember. And remember. I've made you human, fellow."

The soldier croaks, "What did you say?"

"I'm saving you, man. I'm turning you into a real

human being. With the power of Joan. The power of love. Poor guy! Go ahead and shoot me if it makes you uncomfortable to wait. You'll do it anyhow."

This time we do not see the soldier's face but the tightness of his back and neck betray his own internal stress.

We see the big broad bear face blossom forth in an immense splash of red as the soft heavy pellets plow into it.

Then the camera turns to something else.

A little boy, probably a fox, but very finished in his human shape.

He was bigger than a baby, but not big enough, like the larger underchildren, to have understood the deathless importance of Joan's teaching.

He was the only one of the group who behaved like an ordinary underperson. He broke and ran.

He was clever: He ran among the spectators, so that the soldier could not use pellets or heat-reducers on him without hurting an actual human being. He ran and jumped and dodged, fighting passively but desperately for his life.

At last one of the spectators—a tall man with a silver hat—tripped him up. The fox-boy fell to the pavement, skinning his palms and knees. Just as he looked up to see who might be coming at him, a bullet caught him neatly in the head. He fell a little way forward, dead.

People die. We know how they die. We have seen them die shy and quiet in the Dying Houses. We have seen others go into the 400-year-rooms, which have no door knobs and no cameras on the inside. We have seen pictures of many dying in natural disasters, where the robot crews took picture-tapes for the record and the investigation later on. Death is not uncommon, and it is very unpleasant.

But this time, death itself was different. All the fear of death—except for the one little fox-boy, too young to understand and too old to wait for death in his mother's arms—had gone out of the underpeople. They met death willingly, with love and calmness in their bodies, their voices, their demeanor. It did not matter whether they lived long enough to know what happened to Joan herself: they had perfect confidence in her, anyway.

This indeed was the new weapon, love and the good death.

Crawlie, with her pride, had missed it all.

The investigators later found the body of Crawlie in the corridor. It was possible to reconstruct who she had been and what had happened to her. The computer in which the bodiless image of the Lady Panc Ashash survived for a few days after the trial was, of course, found and disassembled. Nobody thought at the time to get her opinions and last words. A lot of historians have gnashed their teeth over that.

The details are therefore clear. The archives even preserve the long interrogation and responses concerning Elaine, when she was processed and made clear after the trial. But we do not know how the idea of "fire" came in.

Somewhere, beyond sight of the tape-scanner, the word must have been passed between the four chiefs of the Instrumentality who were conducting the trial. There is the protest of the Chief of Birds (Robot), or police chief of Kalma, a Subchief named Fisi.

The records show his appearance. He comes in at the right side of the scene, bows respectfully to the four Chiefs, and lifts his right hand in the traditional sign for "beg to interrupt," an odd twist of the elevated hand which the actors had found it very difficult to copy when they tried to put the whole story of Joan and Elaine into a single drama. (In fact, he had no more idea that future ages would be studying his casual appearance than did the others. The whole episode was characterized by haste and precipitateness, in the light of what we now know.) The Lord Limaono says:

"Interruption refused. We are making a decision."

The Chief of Birds spoke up anyhow.

"My words are for your decision, my Lords and my Ladies."

"Say it, then," commanded the Lady Goroke, "but be brief."

"Shut down the viewers. Destroy that animal. Brainwash the spectators. Get amnesia yourselves, for this one hour. This whole scene is dangerous. I am nothing but a supervisor of ornithopters, keeping perfect order, but I—"

"We have heard enough." said the Lord Femtiosex. "You manage your birds and we'll run the worlds. How do you dare to think 'like a Chief'? We have responsibilities which you can't even guess at. Stand back."

Fisi, in the pictures, stands back, his face sullen. In that particular frame of scenes, one can see some of the spectators going away. It was time for lunch and they had become hungry; they had no idea that they were going to miss the greatest atrocity in history, about which a thousand and more grand operas would be written.

Femtiosex then moved to the climax. "More knowledge, not less, is the answer to this problem. I have heard about something which is not as bad as the Planet Shayol, but which can do just as well for an exhibit on a civilized world. You there," said he to Fisi, the Chief of Birds, "bring oil and a spray. Immediately."

Joan looked at him with compassion and longing, but she said nothing. She suspected what he was going to do. As a girl, as a dog, she hated it; as a revolutionary, she welcomed it as the consummation of her mission.

The Lord Femtiosex lifted his right hand. He curled the ring finger and the little finger, putting his thumb over them. That left the first two fingers extended straight out. At that time, the sign from one Chief to another, meaning, "private channels, telepathic, immediate." It has since been adopted by underpeople as their emblem for political unity.

The four Chiefs went into a trancelike state and shared the judgment.

Joan began to sing in a soft, protesting, doglike wail, using the off-key plainsong which the underpeople had sung just before their hour of decision when they left the Brown and Yellow Corridor. Her words were nothing special, repetitions of the "people, dear people, I love you" which she had been communicating ever since she came to the surface of Kalma. But the way she did it has defied imitation across the centuries. There are thousands of lyrics and melodies which call themselves, one way and another, *The Song of Joan,* but none of them come near to the heart-wrenching pathos of the original tapes. The singing, like her own personality, was unique.

The appeal was deep. Even the real people tried to listen, shifting their eyes from the four immobile Chiefs of the Instrumentality to the brown-eyed singing girl. Some of them just could not stand it. In true human fashion, they forgot why they were there and went absent-mindedly home to lunch.

Suddenly Joan stopped.

Her voice ringing clearly across the crowd, she cried out:

"The end is near, dear people. The end is near."

Eyes all shifted to the two Lords and the two Ladies of the Instrumentality. The Lady Arabella Underwood looked grim after the telepathic conference. The Lady Goroke was haggard with wordless grief. The two Lords looked severe and resolved.

It was the Lord Femtiosex who spoke.

"We have tried you, animal. Your offense is great. You have lived illegally. For that the penalty is death. You have interfered with robots in some manner which we do not understand. For that brand-new crime, the penalty should be more than death; and I have recommended a punishment which was applied on a planet of the Violet Star. You have also said many unlawful and improper things, detracting from the happiness and security of mankind. For that the penalty is re-education, but since you have two death sentences already, this does not matter. Do you have anything to say before I pronounce sentence?"

"If you light a fire today, my Lord, it will never be put out in the hearts of men. You can destroy me. You can reject my love. You cannot destroy the goodness in yourselves, no matter how much goodness may anger you—"

"Shut up!" he roared. "I asked for a plea, not a speech. You will die by fire, here and now. What do you say to that?"

"I love you, dear people."

Femtiosex nodded to the men of the Chief of Birds, who had dragged a barrel and a spray into the street in front of Joan.

"Tie her to that post," he commanded. "Spray her. Light her. Are the tape-makers in focus? We want this to be recorded and known. If the underpeople try this again, they will see that mankind controls the worlds." He looked at Joan and his eyes seemed to go out of focus. In an unaccustomed voice he said, "I am not a bad man, little dog-girl, but you are a bad animal and we must make an example of you. Do you understand that?"

"Femtiosex," she cried, leaving out his title, "I am very sorry for you. I love you too."

With these words of hers, his face became clouded and angry again. He brought his right hand down in a chopping gesture.

Fisi copied the gesture and the men operating the barrel and spray began to squirt a hissing stream of oil on Joan. Two guards had already chained her to the lamp post, using an improvised chain of handcuffs to make sure that she stood upright and remained in plain sight of the crowd.

"Fire," said Femtiosex.

Elaine felt the Hunter's body, beside her, cramp sharply. He seemed to strain intensely. For herself, she felt the way she had felt when she was defrozen and taken out of the adiabatic pod in which she had made the trip from Earth—sick to her stomach, confused in her mind, emotions rocking back and forth inside her.

Hunter whispered to her, "I tried to reach her mind so that she would die easy. Somebody else got there first. I . . . don't know who it is."

Elaine stared.

The fire was being brought. Suddenly it touched the oil and Joan flamed up like a human torch.

## ∽ 10 ∽

The burning of D'joan at Fomalhaut took very little time, but the ages will not forget it.

Femtiosex had taken the cruelest step of all.

By telepathic invasion he had suppressed her human mind, so that only the primitive canine remained.

Joan did not stand still like a martyred queen.

She struggled against the flames which licked her and climbed her. She howled and shrieked like a dog in pain, like an animal whose brain—good though it is—cannot comprehend the senselessness of human cruelty.

The result was directly contrary to what the Lord Femtiosex had planned.

The crowd of people stirred forward, not with curiosity but because of compassion. They had avoided the broad areas of the street on which the dead underpeople lay as they had been killed, some pooled in their own blood, some broken by the hands of robots, some reduced to piles of frozen crystal. They walked over the dead to watch the dying, but their watching was not the witless boredom of people who never see a spectacle; it was the movement of living things, instinctive and deep, toward the sight of another living thing in a position of danger and ruin.

Even the guard who had held Elaine and Hunter by gripping Hunter's arm—even he moved forward a few unthinking steps. Elaine found herself in the first row of the spectators, the acrid, unfamiliar smell of burning oil making her nose twitch, the howls of the dying dog-girl tearing through her eardrums into her brain. Joan was turning and twisting in the fire now, trying to avoid the flames which wrapped her tighter than clothing. The odor of something sickening and strange reached the crowd. Few of them had ever smelled the stink of burning meat before.

Joan gasped.

In the ensuing seconds of silence, Elaine heard something she had never expected to hear before—the weeping of grown human beings. Men and women stood there sobbing and not knowing why they sobbed.

Femtiosex loomed over the crowd, obsessed by the failure of his demonstration. He did not know that the Hunter, with a thousand kills behind him, was committing the legal outrage of peeping the mind of a Chief of the Instrumentality.

The Hunter whispered to Elaine, "In a minute I'll try it. She deserves something better than that . . ."

Elaine did not ask what. She too was weeping.

The whole crowd became aware that a soldier was calling. It took them several seconds to look away from the burning, dying Joan.

The soldier was an ordinary one. Perhaps he was the one who had been unable to tie Joan with bonds a few minutes ago, when the Lords decreed that she be taken into custody.

He was shouting now, shouting frantically and wildly, shaking his fist at the Lord Femtiosex.

"You're a liar, you're a coward, you're a fool, and I challenge you—"

The Lord Femtiosex became aware of the man and of what he was yelling. He came out of his deep concentration and said, mildly for so wild a time:

"What do you mean?"

"This is a crazy show. There is no girl here. No fire. Nothing. You are hallucinating the whole lot of us for some horrible reason of your own, and I'm challenging you for it, you animal, you fool, you coward."

In normal times even a Lord had to accept a challenge or adjust the matter with clear talk.

This was no normal time.

The Lord Femtiosex said, "All this is real. I deceive no one."

"If it's real, Joan, I'm with you!" shrieked the young soldier. He jumped in front of the jet of oil before the other soldiers could turn it off and then he leapt into the fire beside Joan.

Her hair had burned away but her features were still clear. She had stopped the doglike whining shriek. Femtiosex had been interrupted. She gave the soldier, who had begun to burn as he stood voluntarily beside her, the gentlest and most feminine of smiles. Then she frowned, as though there were something which she should remember to do, despite the pain and terror which surrounded her.

"Now!" whispered the Hunter. He began to hunt the Lord Femtiosex as sharply as he had ever sought the alien, native minds of Fomalhaut III.

The crowd could not tell what had happened to the Lord Femtiosex. Had he turned coward? Had he gone mad? (Actually, the Hunter, by using every gram of the power of his mind, had momentarily taken Femtiosex courting in the skies; he and Femtiosex were both male birdlike beasts, singing wildly for the beautiful female who lay hidden in the landscape far, far below.)

Joan was free, and she knew she was free.

She sent out her message. It knocked both Hunter and Femtiosex out of thinking; it flooded Elaine; it made even Fisi, the Chief of Birds, breathe quietly. She called so loudly that within the hour messages were pouring in from the other cities to Kalma, asking what had happened. She thought a single message, not words. But in words it came to this:

"Loved ones, you kill me. This is my fate. I bring love, and love must die to live on. Love asks nothing, does nothing. Love thinks nothing. Love is knowing yourself and knowing all other people and things. Know—and rejoice. I die for all of you now, dear ones—"

She opened her eyes for a last time, opened her mouth, sucked in the raw flame, and slumped forward. The soldier, who had kept his nerve while his clothing and body burned, ran out of the fire, afire himself, toward his squad. A shot stopped him and he pitched flat forward.

The weeping of the people was audible throughout the streets. Underpeople, tame and licensed ones, stood shamelessly among them and wept too.

The Lord Femtiosex turned wearily back to his colleagues.

The face of Lady Goroke was a sculptured, frozen caricature of sorrow.

He turned to the Lady Arabella Underwood. "I seem to have done something wrong, my Lady. Take over, please."

The Lady Arabella stood up. She called to Fisi, "Put out that fire."

She looked out over the crowd. Her hard, honest Norstrilian features were unreadable. Elaine, watching her, shivered at the thought of a whole planet full of people as tough, obstinate, and clever as these.

"It's over," said the Lady Arabella. "People, go away. Robots, clean up. Underpeople, to your jobs."

She looked at Elaine and the Hunter. "I know who you are and I suspect what you have been doing. Soldiers, take them away."

The body of Joan was fire-blackened. The face did not look particularly human anymore; the last burst of fire had caught her in the nose and eyes. Her young, girlish breasts showed with heart-wrenching immodesty that she had been young and female once. Now she was dead, just dead.

The soldiers would have shoveled her into a box if she had been an underperson. Instead, they paid her the honors of war that they would have given to one of their own comrades or to an important civilian in time of disaster. They unslung a litter, put the little blackened body on it, and covered the body with their own flag. No one had told them to do so.

As their own soldier led them up the road toward the Waterrock, where the houses and offices of the

military were located, Elaine saw that he too had
been crying.

She started to ask him what he thought of it, but
Hunter stopped her with a shake of the head. He
later told her that the soldier might be punished for
talking with them.

When they got to the office, they found the Lady
Goroke already there.

The Lady Goroke already there . . . It became a
nightmare in the weeks that followed. She had gotten
over her grief and was conducting an inquiry into the
case of Elaine and D'joan.

The Lady Goroke already there . . . She was waiting
when they slept. Her image, or perhaps herself, sat in
on all the endless interrogations. She was particularly
interested in the chance meeting of the dead Lady
Panc Ashash, the misplaced witch Elaine, and the
non-adjusted man, the Hunter.

The Lady Goroke already there . . . She asked them
everything, but she told them nothing.

Except for once.

Once she burst out, violently personal after endless hours of formal, official work, "Your minds will
be cleansed when we get through, so it wouldn't
matter how much else you know. Do you know that
this has hurt me—me!—all the way to the depths of
everything I believe in?"

They shook their heads.

"I'm going to have a child, and I'm going back to
Manhome to have it. And I'm going to do the genetic
coding myself. I'm going to call him Jestocost. That's
one of the Ancient Tongues, the Paroskii one, for
'cruelty,' to remind him where he comes from, and

why. And he, or his son, or *his* son will bring justice back into the world and solve the puzzle of the underpeople. What do you think of that? On second thought, don't think. It's none of your business, and I am going to do it anyway."

They stared at her sympathetically, but they were too wound up in the problems of their own survival to extend her much sympathy or advice. The body of Joan had been pulverized and blown into the air, because the Lady Goroke was afraid that the underpeople would make a *goodplace* out of it; she felt that way herself, and she knew that if she herself were tempted, the underpeople would be even more tempted.

Elaine never knew what happened to the bodies of all the other people who had turned themselves, under Joan's leadership, from animals into mankind, and who had followed the wild, foolish march out of the Tunnel of Englok into the Upper City of Kalma. Was it really wild? Was it really foolish? If they had stayed where they were, they might have had a few days or months or years of life, but sooner or later the robots would have found them and they would have been exterminated like the vermin which they were. Perhaps the death they had chosen was better. Joan *did* say, "It's the mission of life always to look for something better than itself, and then to try to trade life itself for meaning."

At last, the Lady Goroke called them in and said, "Goodbye, you two. It's foolish, saying goodbye, when an hour from now you will remember neither me nor Joan. You've finished your work here. I've set up a lovely job for you. You won't have to live in a city. You will be weather-watchers, roaming the hills and watching for all the little changes which the machines can't interpret fast enough. You will have whole lifetimes of marching and picnicking and camping together. I've told the technicians to be very careful, because you two are very much in love with each other. When they re-route your synapses, I want that love to be there with you."

They each knelt and kissed her hand. They never wittingly saw her again. In later years they sometimes saw a fashionable ornithopter soaring gently over their camp, with an elegant woman peering out of the side of it; they had no memories to know that it was the Lady Goroke, recovered from madness, watching over them.

Their new life was their final life.

Of Joan and the Brown and Yellow Corridor, nothing remained.

They were both very sympathetic toward animals, but they might have been this way even if they had never shared in the wild political gamble of the dear dead Lady Panc Ashash.

One time a strange thing happened. An underman from an elephant was working in a small valley, creating an exquisite rock garden for some important official of the Instrumentality who might later glimpse the garden once or twice a year. Elaine was busy watching the weather, and the Hunter had forgotten that he had ever hunted, so that neither of them tried to peep the underman's mind. He was a huge fellow, right at the maximum permissible size—five times the gross stature of a man. He had smiled at them friendlily in the past.

One evening he brought them fruit. Such fruit! Rare off-world items which a year of requests would not have obtained for ordinary people like them. He smiled his big, shy elephant smile, put the fruit down, and prepared to lumber off.

"Wait a minute," cried Elaine. "Why are you giving us this? Why us?"

"For the sake of Joan," said the elephant-man.

"Who's Joan?" said the Hunter.

The elephant-man looked sympathetically at them. "That's all right. You don't remember her, but I do."

"But what did Joan do?" said Elaine.

"She loved you. She loved us all," said the elephant-man. He turned quickly, so as to say no more. With incredible deftness for so heavy a person, he climbed speedily into the fierce lovely rocks above them and was gone.

"I wish we had known her," said Elaine. "She sounds very nice."

In that year there was born the man who was to be the first Lord Jestocost.

# Under Old Earth

*I need a temporary dog*
*For a temporary job*
*On a temporary place*
*Like Earth!*

—Song from
*The Merchant of Menace*

## ∾ 1 ∾

There were the Douglas-Ouyang planets, which circled their sun in a single cluster, riding around and around the same orbit unlike any other planets known. There were the gentlemen-suicides back on Earth, who gambled their lives—even more horribly, gambled sometimes for things worse than their lives—against different kinds of geophysics which real men had never experienced. There were girls who fell in love with such men, however stark and dreadful their personal fates might be. There was the Instrumentality, with its unceasing labor to keep man man. And there were the citizens who walked in the boulevards before the Rediscovery of Man. The citizens were happy. They had to be happy. If they were found sad, they were calmed and drugged and changed until they were happy again.

This story concerns three of them: the gambler who took the name Sun-boy, who dared to go down to the Gebiet, who confronted himself before he died; the girl Santuna, who was fulfilled in a thousand ways before she died; and the Lord Sto Odin, a most ancient of days, who knew it all and never dreamed of preventing any of it.

Music runs through this story. The soft sweet music of the Earth Government and the Instrumentality, bland as honey and sickening in the end. The wild illegal pulsations of the Gebiet, where most men were forbidden to enter. Worst of all, the crazy fugues and improper melodies of the Bezirk, closed to men for fifty-seven centuries—opened by accident, found, trespassed in! And with it our story begins.

## ∾ 2 ∾

The Lady Ru had said, a few centuries before: "Scraps of knowledge have been found. In the ultimate beginning of man, even before there were aircraft, the wise man Laodz declared, 'Water does nothing but it penetrates everything. Inaction finds the road.' Later an ancient Lord said this: 'There is a music which underlies all things. We dance to the tunes all our lives, though our living ears never hear the music which guides us and moves us. Happiness can kill people as softly as shadows seen in dreams.' We must be people first and happy later, lest we live and die in vain."

The Lord Sto Odin was more direct. He declared the truth to a few private friends: "Our population is dropping on most worlds, including the Earth. People have children, but they don't want them very much. I myself have been a three-father to twelve children, a two-father to four, and a one-father, I suppose, to many others. I have had zeal for work and I have mistaken it for zeal in living. They are not the same.

"Most people want happiness. Good: we have given them happiness.

"Dreary useless centuries of happiness, in which all the unhappy were corrected or adjusted or killed. Unbearable desolate happiness without the sting of grief, the wine of rage, the hot fumes of fear. How many of us have ever tasted the acid, icy taste of old resentment? That's what people really lived for in the Ancient Days, when they pretended to be happy and were actually alive with grief, rage, fury, hate, malice, and hope! Those people bred like mad. They populated the stars while they dreamed of killing each other, secretly or openly. Their plays concerned murder or betrayal or illegal love. Now we have no murder. We cannot imagine any kind of love which is illegal. Can you imagine the Murkins with their highway net? Who can fly anywhere today without seeing that net of enormous highways? Those roads are ruined, but they're still here. You can see the abominable things quite clearly from the moon. Don't think about the roads. Think of the millions of vehicles that ran on those roads, the people filled with greed and rage and hate, rushing past each other with their engines on fire. They say that fifty thousand a year were killed on the roads alone. We would call that a war. What

people they must have been, to rush day and night
and to build things which would help other people
to rush even more! They were different from us.
They must have been wild, dirty, free. Lusting for
life, perhaps, in a way that we do not. We can easily
go a thousand times faster than they ever went, but
who, nowadays, bothers to go? Why go? It's the same
there as here, except for a few fighters or technicians."
He smiled at his friends and added, ". . . and Lords
of the Instrumentality, like ourselves. We go for the
reasons of the Instrumentality. Not ordinary people
reasons. Ordinary people don't have much reason to
do anything. They work at the jobs which we think up
for them, to keep them happy while the robots and
the underpeople do the real work. They walk. They
make love. But they are never unhappy."

*"They can't be!"*

The Lady Mmona disagreed. "Life can't be as bad
as you say. We don't just think they are happy. We
*know* they are happy. We look right into their brains
with telepathy. We monitor their emotional patterns
with robots and scanners. It's not as though we didn't
have samples. People are always turning unhappy.
We're correcting them all the time. And now and
then there are bad accidents, which even we cannot
correct. When people are very unhappy, they scream
and weep. Sometimes they even stop talking and just
die, despite everything we can do for them. You can't
say that isn't real!"

"But I do," said the Lord Sto Odin.

"You do what?" cried Mmona.

"I do say this happiness is not real," he insisted.

"How can you," she shouted at him, "in the face of

the evidence? *Our* evidence, which we of the Instrumentality decided on a long time ago. We collect it ourselves. Can we, the Instrumentality, be wrong?"

"Yes," said the Lord Sto Odin.

This time it was the entire circle who went silent.

Sto Odin pleaded with them. "Look at *my* evidence. People don't care whether they are one-fathers or one-mothers or not. They don't know which children are theirs, anyhow. Nobody dares to commit suicide. We keep them too happy. But do we spend any time keeping the talking animals, the underpeople, as happy as men? And do underpeople commit suicide?"

"Certainly," said Mmona. "They are preconditioned to commit suicide if they are hurt too badly for easy repair or if they fail in their appointed work."

"I don't mean that. Do they ever commit suicide for *their* reasons, not ours?"

"No," said the Lord Nuru-or, a wise young Lord of the Instrumentality. "They are too desperately busy doing their jobs and staying alive."

"How long does an underperson live?" said Sto Odin, with deceptive mildness.

"Who knows?" said Nuru-or. "Half a year, a hundred years, maybe several hundred years."

"What happens if he does not work?" said the Lord Sto Odin, with a friendly-crafty smile.

"We kill him," said Mmona, "or our robot-police do."

"And does the animal know it?"

"Know he will be killed if he does not work?" said Mmona. "Of course. We tell all of them the same thing. Work or die. What's that got to do with people?"

The Lord Nuru-or had fallen silent and a wise, sad smile had begun to show on his face. He had begun to suspect the shrewd, dreadful conclusion toward which the Lord Sto Odin was driving.

But Mmona did not see it and she pressed the point. "My Lord," said she, "you are insisting that people are happy. You admit they do not like to be unhappy. You seem to want to bring up a problem which has no solution. Why complain of happiness? Isn't it the best which the Instrumentality can do for mankind? That's our mission. Are you saying that we are failing in it?"

"Yes. We are failing." The Lord Sto Odin looked blindly at the room as though alone.

He was the oldest and wisest, so they waited for him to talk.

He breathed lightly and smiled at them again. "You know when I am going to die?"

"Of course," said Mmona, thinking for half a second. "Seventy-seven days from now. But you posted the time yourself. And it is not our custom, my Lord, as you well know, to bring intimate things into meetings of the Instrumentality."

"Sorry," said Sto Odin, "but I'm not violating a law. I'm making a point. We are sworn to uphold the dignity of man. Yet we are killing mankind with a bland hopeless happiness which has prohibited news, which has suppressed religion, which has made all history an official secret. I say that the evidence is that we are failing and that mankind, whom we've sworn to cherish, is failing too. Failing in vitality, strength, numbers, energy. I have a little while to live. I am going to try to find out."

The Lord Nuru-or asked with sorrowful wisdom, as though he guessed the answer: "And where will you go to find out?"

"I shall go," said the Lord Sto Odin, "down into the Gebiet."

"The Gebiet—oh, no!" cried several. And one voice added, "You're immune."

"I shall waive immunity and I shall go," said the Lord Sto Odin. "Who can do anything to a man who is already almost a thousand years old and who has chosen only seventy-seven more days to live?"

"But you can't!" said Mmona. "Some criminal might capture you and duplicate you, and then we would all of us be in peril."

"When did you last hear of a criminal among mankind?" said Sto Odin.

"There are plenty of them, here and there in the offworlds."

"But on Old Earth itself?" asked Sto Odin.

She stammered. "I don't know. There must have been a criminal once." She looked around the room. "Don't any of the rest of you know?"

There was silence.

The Lord Sto Odin stared at them all. In his eyes was the brightness and fierceness which had made whole generations of lords plead with him to live just a few more years, so that he could help them with their work. He had agreed, but within the last quarter-year he had overridden them all and had picked his day of death. He had lost none of his powers in doing this. They shrank from his stare while they waited with respect for his decision.

The Lord Sto Odin looked at the Lord Nuru-or and said, "I think you have guessed what I am going to do in the Gebiet and why I have to go there."

"The Gebiet is a preserve where no rules apply

and no punishments are inflicted. Ordinary people can do what *they* want down there, not what we think they should want. From all I hear, it is pretty nasty and pointless, the things that they find out. But you, perhaps, may sense the inwardness of these things. You may find a cure for the weary happiness of mankind."

"That is right," said Sto Odin. "And that is why I am going, after I make the appropriate official preparations."

### ∾ 3 ∾

Go he did. He used one of the most peculiar conveyances ever seen on Earth, since his own legs were too weak to carry him far. With only two-ninths of a year to live, he did not want to waste time getting his legs regrafted.

He rode in an open sedan-chair carried by two Roman legionaries.

The legionaries were actually robots, without a trace of blood or living tissue in them. They were the most compact and difficult kind to create, since their brains had to be located in their chests—several million sheets of incredibly fine laminations, imprinted with the whole life experience of an important, useful, and long-dead person. They were clothed as legionaries, down to cuirasses, swords, kilts, greaves, sandals, and shields, merely because it was the whim of the Lord Sto Odin to go behind the rim of history for his companions. Their bodies, all metal, were very strong. They could batter walls, jump chasms, crush any man or underperson with their mere fingers, or throw their swords with the accuracy of guided projectiles.

The forward legionary, Flavius, had been head of Fourteen-B in the Instrumentality—an espionage division so secret that even among Lords, few knew exactly of its location or its function. He was (or had been, till he was imprinted on a robot-mind as he lay dying) the director of historical research for the whole human race. Now he was a dull, pleasant machine carrying two poles until his master chose to bring his powerful mind into bright, furious alert by speaking the simple Latin phrase, understood by no other person living, *Summa nulla est.*

The rear legionary, Livius, had been a psychiatrist who turned into a general. He had won many battles until he chose to die, somewhat before his time, because he perceived that battle itself was a struggle for the defeat of himself.

Together, and added to the immense brainpower of the Lord Sto Odin himself, they represented an unsurpassable team.

"The Gebiet," commanded the Lord Sto Odin.

"The Gebiet," said both of them heavily, picking up the chair with its supporting poles.

"And then the Bezirk," he added.

"The Bezirk," they chimed in toneless voices.

Sto Odin felt his chair tilt back as Livius put his two ends of the poles carefully on the ground, came up beside Sto Odin, and saluted with open palm.

"May I awaken?" said Livius in an even, mechanical voice.

"*Summa nulla est,*" said the Lord Sto Odin.

Livius's face sprang into full animation. "You must

not go there, my Lord! You would have to waive immunity and meet all dangers. There is nothing there yet. Not yet. Some day they will come pouring out of that underground Hades and give you men a real fight. Now, no. They are just miserable beings, cooking away in their weird unhappiness, making love in manners which you never thought of—"

"Never mind what you think I've thought. What's your objection in real terms?"

"It's pointless, my Lord! You have only bits of a year to live. Do something noble and great for man before you die. They may turn us off. We would like to share your work before you go away."

"Is that all?" said Sto Odin.

"My Lord," said Flavius, "you have awakened me too. I say, go forward. History is being respun down there. Things are loose which you great ones of the Instrumentality have never even suspected. Go now and look, before you die. You may do nothing, but I disagree with my companion. It is as dangerous as Space$^3$ might be, if we ever were to find it, but it is *interesting*. And in this world where all things have been done, where all thoughts have been thought, it is hard to find things which still prompt the human mind with raw curiosity. I'm dead, as you perfectly well know, but even I, inside this machine brain, feel the tug of adventure, the pull of danger, the magnetism of the unknown. For one thing, they are committing crimes down there. And you Lords are overlooking them."

"We chose to overlook them. We are not stupid. We wanted to see what might happen," said the Lord Sto Odin, "and we have to give those people time before we find out just how far they might go if they are cut off from controls."

"They are having babies!" said Flavius excitedly.

"I know that."

"They have hooked in two illegal instant-message machines," shouted Flavius.

Sto Odin was calm. "So that's why the Earth's credit structure has appeared to be leaking in its balance of trade."

"They have a piece of the congohelium!" shouted Flavius.

"The congohelium!" shouted the Lord Sto Odin. "Impossible! It's unstable. They could kill themselves. They could hurt Earth! What are they doing with it?"

"Making music," said Flavius, more quietly.

"Making *what?*"

"Music. Songs. Nice noise to dance to."

The Lord Sto Odin sputtered. "Take me there right now. This is ridiculous. Having a piece of the congohelium down there is as bad as wiping out inhabited planets to play checkers."

"My Lord," said Livius.

"Yes?" said Sto Odin.

"I withdraw my objections," said Livius.

Sto Odin said, very dryly, "Thank you."

"They have something else down there. When I did not want you to go, I did not mention it. It might have aroused your curiosity. They have a god."

The Lord Sto Odin said, "If this is going to be a historical lecture, save it for another time. Go back to sleep and carry me down."

Livius did not move. "I mean what I said."

"A god? What do you call a god?"

"A person or an idea capable of starting wholly new cultural patterns in motion."

The Lord Sto Odin leaned forward. "You *know* this?"

"We both do," said Flavius and Livius.

"We saw him," said Livius. "You told us, a tenth-year ago, to walk around freely for thirty hours, so we put on ordinary robot bodies and happened to get into the Gebiet. When we sensed the congohelium operating, we had to go on down to find out what it was doing. Usually, it is employed to keep the stars in their place—"

"Don't tell me that. I know it. Was it a man?"

"A man," said Flavius, "who is re-living the life of Akhnaton."

"Who's that?" said the Lord Sto Odin, who knew history, but wanted to see how much his robots knew.

"A king, tall, long-faced, thick-lipped, who ruled the human world of Egypt long, long before atomic power. Akhnaton invented the best of the early gods. This man is re-enacting Akhnaton's life step by step. He has already made a religion out of the sun. He mocks at happiness. People listen to him. They joke about the Instrumentality."

Livius added, "We saw the girl who loves him. She herself was young, but beautiful. And I think she has powers which will make the Instrumentality promote her or destroy her some day in the future."

"They both made music," said Flavius, "with that piece of the congohelium. And this man or god—this new kind of Akhnaton, whatever you may want to call him, my Lord—he was dancing a strange kind of dance. It was like a corpse being tied with rope and dancing like a marionette. The effect on the people around him was as good as the best hypnotism you ever saw. I'm a robot now, but it bothered even me."

"Did the dance have a name?" said Sto Odin.

"I don't know the name," said Flavius, "but I memorized the song, since I have total recall. Do you wish to hear it?"

"Certainly," said the Lord Sto Odin.

Flavius stood on one leg, threw his arms out at weird, improbable angles, and began to sing in a high, insulting tenor voice which was both fascinating and repugnant:

*Jump, dear people, and I'll howl for you.*
*Jump and howl and I'll weep for you.*
    *I weep because I'm a weeping man.*
    *I'm a weeping man because I weep.*
*I weep because the day is done,*
        *Sun is gone,*
        *Home is lost,*
        *Time killed dad.*
        *I killed time.*
        *World is round.*
        *Day is run,*
        *Clouds are shot,*
        *Stars are out,*
        *Mountain's fire,*
        *Rain is hot,*
        *Hot is blue.*
        *I am done.*
        *So are you.*
*Jump, dear people, for the howling man.*
*Leap, dear people, for the weeping man.*
    *I'm a weeping man because I weep for you!*

"Enough," said the Lord Sto Odin.

Flavius saluted. His face went back to amiable stolidity. Just before he took the front ends of the shaft he glanced back and brought forth one last comment:

"The verse is skeltonic."

"Tell me nothing more of your history. Take me there."

The robots obeyed. Soon the chair was jogging comfortably down the ramps of the ancient left-over city which sprawled beneath Earthport, that miraculous tower which seemed to touch the stratocumulus clouds in the blue, clear nothingness above mankind. Sto Odin went to sleep in his strange vehicle and did not notice that the human passers-by often stared at him.

The Lord Sto Odin woke fitfully in strange places as the legionaries carried him further and further into the depths below the city, where sweet pressures and warm, sick smells made the air itself feel dirty to his nose.

"Stop!" whispered the Lord Sto Odin, and the robots stopped.

"Who am I?" he said to them.

"You have announced your will to die, my Lord," said Flavius, "seventy-seven days from now, but so far your name is still the Lord Sto Odin."

"I am alive?" the Lord asked.

"Yes," said both the robots.

"You are dead?"

"We are not dead. We are machines, printed with the minds off men who once lived. Do you wish to turn back, my Lord?"

"No. No. Now I remember. You are the robots.

Livius, the psychiatrist and general Flavius, the secret historian. You have the minds of men, and are not men?"

"That is right, my Lord," said Flavius.

"Then how can *I* be alive—I, Sto Odin?"

"You should feel it yourself, sir," said Livius, "though the mind of the old is sometimes very strange."

"How can I be alive?" asked Sto Odin, staring around the city. "How can I be alive when the people who knew me are dead? They have whipped through the corridors like wraiths of smoke, like traces of cloud; they were here, and they loved me, and they knew me, and now they are dead. Take my wife, Eileen. She was a pretty thing, a brown-eyed child who came out of her learning chamber all perfect and all young. Time touched her and she danced to the cadence of time. Her body grew full, grew old. We repaired it. But at last she cramped in death and she went to that place to which I am going. If you are dead, you ought to be able to tell me what death is like, where the bodies and minds and voices and music of men and women whip past these enormous corridors, these hardy pavements, and are then gone. How can passing ghosts like me and my kind, each with just a few dozen or a few hundred years to go before the great blind winds of time whip us away—how can phantoms like me have built this solid city, these wonderful engines, these brilliant lights which never go dim? How did we do it, when we pass so swiftly, each of us, all of us? Do you know?"

The robots did not answer. Pity had not been programmed into their systems. The Lord Sto Odin harangued them nonetheless:

"You are taking me to a wild place, a free place, an evil place, perhaps. They are dying there too, as all men die, as I shall die, so soon, so brightly and simply. I should have died a long time ago. I was the people who knew me, I was the brothers and comrades who trusted me, I was the women who comforted me, I was the children whom I loved so bitterly and so sweetly many ages ago. Now they are gone. Time touched them, and they were not. I can see everyone that I ever knew racing through these corridors, see them young as toddlers, see them proud and wise and full with business and maturity, see them old and contorted as time reached out for them and they passed hastily away. Why did they do it? How can I live on? When I am dead, will I know that I once lived? I know that some of my friends have cheated and lie in the icy sleep, hoping for something which they do not know. I've had life, and I know it. What is life? A bit of play, a bit of learning, some words well-chosen, some love, a trace of pain, more work, memories, and then dirt rushing up to meet sunlight. That's all we've made of it—we, who have conquered the stars! Where are my friends? Where is my *me* that I once was so sure of, when the people who knew me were time-swept like storm-driven rags toward darkness and oblivion? You tell me. You ought to know! You are machines and you were given the minds of men. You ought to know what we amount to, from the outside in."

"We were built," said Livius, "by men and we have whatever men put into us, nothing more. How can we answer talk like yours? It is rejected by our minds, good though our minds may be. We have no grief, no fear, no fury. We know the names of these feelings but not the feelings themselves. We hear your words but we do not know what you are talking about. Are you trying to tell us what life feels like? If so, we already know. Not much. Nothing special. Birds have life too, and so do fishes. It is you people who can talk and who can knot life into spasms and puzzles. You muss things up. Screaming never made the truth truthful, at least, not to us."

"Take me down," said Sto Odin. "Take me down to the Gebiet, where no well-mannered man has gone in many years. I am going to judge that place before I die."

They lifted the sedan-chair and resumed their gentle dog-trot down the immense ramps down toward the warm steaming secrets of the Earth itself. The human pedestrians became more scarce, but undermen—most often of gorilla or ape origin—passed them, toiling their way upward while dragging shrouded treasures which they had filched from the uncatalogued storehouses of man's most ancient past. At other times there was a wild whirl of metal wheels on stone roadway; the undermen, having offloaded their treasures at some intermediate point high above, sat on their wagons and rolled back downhill, like grotesque enlargements of the ancient human children who were once reported to have played with wagons in this way.

A command, scarcely a whisper, stopped the two legionaries again. Flavius turned. Sto Odin was indeed calling both of them. They stepped out of the shafts and came around to him, one on each side.

"I may be dying right now," he whispered, "and that would be most inconvenient at this time. Get out my manikin meee!"

"My Lord," said Flavius, "it is strictly forbidden

for us robots to touch any human manikin, and if
we do touch one, we are commanded to destroy
ourselves immediately thereafter! Do you wish us to
try, nevertheless? If so, which one of us? You have
the command, my Lord."

## ～ 4 ～

He waited so long that even the robots began to
wonder if he died amid the thick wet air and the
nearby stench of steam and oil.

The Lord Sto Odin finally roused himself and said:
"I need no help. Just put the bag with my manikin
meee on my lap."

"This one?" asked Flavius, lifting a small brown
suitcase and handling it with a very gingerly touch
indeed.

The Lord Sto Odin gave a barely perceptible nod
and whispered. "Open it carefully for me. But do not
touch the manikin, if those are your orders."

Flavius twisted at the catch of the bag. It was hard
to manage. Robots did not feel fear, but they were
intellectually attuned to the avoidance of danger;
Flavius found his mind racing with wild choices as
he tried to get the bag open. Sto Odin tried to help
him, but the ancient hand, palsied and weak, could
not even reach the top of the case. Flavius labored
on, thinking that the Gebiet and Bezirk had their
dangers, but that this meddling with manikins was
the riskiest thing which he had ever encountered
while in robot form, though in his human life he had
handled many of them, including his own. They were

"manikin, electro-encephalographic and endocrine" in model form, and they showed in miniaturized replica the entire diagnostic position of the patient for whom they were fashioned.

Sto Odin whispered to them. "There's no helping it. Turn me up. If I die, take my body back and tell the people that I misjudged my time."

Just as he spoke, the case sprang open. Inside it there lay a little naked human man, a direct copy of Sto Odin himself.

"We have it, my Lord," cried Livius, from the other side. "Let me guide your hand to it, so that you can see what to do."

Though it was forbidden for robots to touch manikins meee, it was legal for them to touch a human person with the person's consent. Livius's strong cupro-plastic fingers, with a reserve of many tons of gripping power in their human-like design, pulled the hands of the Lord Sto Odin forward until they rested on the manikin meee. Flavius, quick, smooth, agile, held the Lord's head upright on his weary old neck, so that the ancient Lord could see what the hands were doing.

"Is any part dead?" said the old Lord to the manikin, his voice clearer for the moment.

The manikin shimmered and two spots of solid black showed along the outside upper right thigh and the right buttock.

"Organic reserve?" said the Lord to his own manikin meee, and again the machine responded to his command. The whole miniature body shimmered to a violent purple and then subsided to an even pink.

"I still have some all-around strength left in this

body, prosthetics and all," said Sto Odin to the two robots. "Set me up, I tell you! Set me up."

"Are you sure, my Lord," said Livius, "that we should do a thing like that here where the three of us are alone in a deep tunnel? In less than half an hour we could take you to a real hospital, where actual doctors could examine you."

"I said," repeated the Lord Sto Odin, "set me up. I'll watch the manikin while you do it."

"Your control is in the usual place, my Lord?" asked Livius.

"How much of a turn?" asked Flavius.

"Nape of my neck, of course. The skin over it is artificial and self-sealing. One twelfth of a turn will be enough. Do you have a knife with you?"

Flavius nodded. He took a small sharp knife from his belt, probed gently around the old Lord's neck, and then brought the knife down with a quick, sure turn.

"That did it!" said Sto Odin, in a voice so hearty that both of them stepped back a little. Flavius put the knife back in his belt. Sto Odin, who had almost been comatose a moment before, now held the manikin meee in his unaided hands. "See, gentlemen!" he cried. "You may be robots, but you can still see the truth and report it."

They both looked at the manikin meee, which Sto Odin now held in front of himself, his thumb and fingertip in the armpits of the medical doll.

"Watch what it reads," he said to them with a clear, ringing voice.

"Prosthetics!" he shouted at the manikin.

The tiny body changed from its pink color to a mixture. Both legs turned the color of a deep bruised blue.

The legs, the left arm, one eye, one ear, and the skullcap stayed blue, showing the prostheses in place.

"Felt pain!" shouted Sto Odin at the manikin. The little doll returned to its light pink color. All the details were there, even to genitals, toenails, and eyelashes. There was no trace of the black color of pain in any part of the little body.

"Potential pain!" shouted Sto Odin. The doll shimmered. Most of it settled to the color of dark walnut wood, with some areas of intense brown showing more clearly then the rest.

"Potential breakdown—one day!" shouted Sto Odin. The little body went back to its normal color of pink. Small lightnings showed at the base of the brain, but nowhere else.

"I'm all right," said Sto Odin. "I can continue as I have done for the last several hundred years. Leave me set up on this high life-output. I can stand it for a few hours, and if I cannot, there's little lost." He put the manikin back in its bag, hung the bag on the doorhandle of the sedan-chair, and commanded the legionaries, "Proceed!"

The legionaries stared at him as if they could not see him.

He followed the lines of glance and saw that they were gazing rigidly at his manikin meee. It had turned black.

"Are you dead?" asked Livius, speaking as hoarsely as a robot could.

"Not dead at all!" cried Sto Odin. "I have been death in fractions of a moment, but for the time I am still life. That was just the pain-sum of my living body which showed on the manikin meee. The fire of

life still burns within me. Watch as I put the manikin
away . . ." The doll flared into a swirl of pastel orange
as the Lord Sto Odin pulled the cover down.

They looked away as though they had seen an evil
or an explosion.

"Down, men, down," he cried, calling them wrong
names as they stepped back between their carrying shafts
to take him deeper under the vitals of the earth.

## ∽ 5 ∽

He dreamed brown dreams while they trotted down
endless ramps. He woke a little to see the yellow
walls passing. He looked at his dry old hand and it
seemed to him that in this atmosphere, he had himself
become more reptilian than human.

"I am caught by the dry, drab enturtlement of
old, old age," he murmured, but the voice was weak
and the robots did not hear him. They were running
downward on a long meaningless concrete ramp which
had become filmed by a leak of ancient oil, and they
were taking care that they did not stumble and drop
their precious master.

At a deep, hidden point the downward ramp divided,
the left into a broad arena of steps which could have
seated thousands of spectators for some never-to-occur
event, and the right into a narrow ramp which bore
upward and then curved, yellow lights and all.

"Stop!" called Sto Odin. "Do you see her? Do you
hear it?"

"Hear what?" said Flavius.

"The beat and the cadence of the congohelium

rising out of the Gebiet. The whirl and the skirl of impossible music coming at us through miles of solid rock? That girl whom I can already see, waiting at a door which should never have been opened? The sound of the star-borne music, not designed for the proper human ear?" He shouted, "Can't you hear it? That cadence. The unlawful metal of congohelium so terrible far underground? Dah, dah. Dah, dah. Dah. Music which nobody has ever understood before?"

Said Flavius, "I hear nothing, saving the pulse of air in this corridor, and your own heartbeat, my Lord. And something else, a little like machinery, very far away."

"There, that!" cried Sto Odin, "which you call 'a little like machinery,' does it come in a beat of five separate sounds, each one distinct?"

"No. No, sir. Not five."

"And you, Livius, when you were a man, you were very telepathic? Is there any of that left in the robot which is you?"

"No, my Lord, nothing. I have good senses, and I am also cut into the subsurface radio of the Instrumentality. Nothing unusual."

"No five-beat? Each note separate, short of prolonged, given meaning and shape by the terrible music of the congohelium, imprisoned with us inside this much-too-solid rock? You hear nothing?"

The two robots, shaped like Roman legionaries, shook their heads.

"But I can see her, through this stone. She has breasts like ripe pears and dark brown eyes that are like the stones of fresh-cut peaches. And I can hear what they are singing, their weird silly words of a pentapaul, made into something majestic by the awful music of the congohelium. Listen to the words. When I repeat them, they sound just silly, because the dread-inspiring music does not come with them. Her name is Santuna and she stares at him. No wonder she stares. He is much more tall than most men, yet he makes this foolish song into something frightening and strange.

> *Slim Jim.*
> *Dim him.*
> *Grim.*

And his name is Yebayee, but now he is Sun-boy. He has the long face and the thick lips of the first man to talk about one god and one only: Akhnaton."

"Akhnaton the pharaoh," said Flavius. "That name was known in my office when I was a man. It was a secret. One of the first and greatest of the more-than-ancient kings. You see him, my Lord?"

"Through this rock I see him. Through this rock I hear the delirium engendered by the congohelium. I go to him." The Lord Sto Odin stepped out of the sedan chair and beat softly and weakly against the solid stone wall of the corridor. The yellow lamps gleamed. The legionaries were helpless. Here was something which their sharp swords could not pierce. Their once-human personalities, engraved on their micro-miniaturized brains, could not make sense out of the all-too-human situation of an old, old man dreaming wild dreams in a remote tunnel.

Sto Odin leaned against the wall, breathing heavily, and said to them with a sibilant rasp:

"These are no whispers which can be missed. Can't you hear the five-beat of the congohelium, making its crazy music again? Listen to the words of this one. It's another pentapaul. Silly, bony words given flesh and blood and entrails by the music which carries them. Here, listen.

*Try. Vie.*
*Cry. Die.*
*Bye.*

This one you did not hear either?"

"May I use my radio to ask the surface of Earth for advice?" said one of the robots.

"Advice! Advice! What advice do we need? This *is* the Gebiet and one more hour of running and you will be in the heart of the Bezirk."

He climbed back into the sedan chair and commanded, "Run, men, run! It can't be more than three or four kilometers somewhere in this warren of stone. I will guide you. If I stop guiding you, you may take my body back to the surface, so that I can be given a wonderful funeral and be shot with a rocket-coffin into space with an orbit of no return. You have nothing to worry about. You are machines, nothing more, are you not? Are you not?" His voice shrilled at the end.

Said Flavius, "Nothing more."

Said Livius, "Nothing more. And yet—"

"And yet what?" demanded the Lord Sto Odin.

"And yet," said Livius, "I know I am a machine, and I know that I have known feelings only when I was once a living man. I sometimes wonder if you people might go too far. Too far, with us robots. Too far, perhaps, with the underpeople too. Things were once simple, when everything that talked was a human being and everything which did not talk was not. You may be coming to an ending of the ways."

"If you had said that on the surface," said the Lord Sto Odin grimly, "your head might have been burned off by its automatic magnesium flare. You know that there you are monitored against having illegal thoughts."

"Too well do I know it," said Livius, "and I know that I must have died once as a man, if I exist here in robot form. Dying didn't seem to hurt me then and it probably won't hurt next time. But nothing really matters much when we get down this far into the Earth. When we get this far down, everything changes. I never really understood that the inside of the world was this big and this sick."

"It's not how far down we are," said the Lord crossly, "it's *where* we are. This is the Gebiet, where all laws have been lifted, and down below and over yonder is the Bezirk, where laws have never been. Carry me rapidly now. I want to look on this strange musician with the face of Akhnaton and I want to talk to the girl who worships him, Santuna. Run carefully now. Up a little, to the left a little. If I sleep, do not worry. Keep going. I will waken myself when we come anywhere near the music of the congohelium. If I can hear it now, so far away, think of what it will be like when you yourselves approach it!"

He leaned back in his seat. They picked up the shafts of the sedan-chair and ran in the direction which they had been told.

## ∾ 6 ∾

They had run for more than an hour, with occasional delays when they had tricky footwork over leaking pipes or damaged walkways, when the light became so bright that they had to reach in their pouches and put on sun-glasses, which looked very odd indeed underneath the Roman helmets of two fully armed legionaries. (It was even more odd, of course, that the eyes were not eyes at all; robot eyes were like white marbles swimming in little bowls of glittering ink, producing a grimly milky stare.) They looked at their master and he had not yet stirred, so they took a corner of his robe and twisted it firmly into a bandage to protect his eyes against the bright light.

The new light made the yellow bulbs of the corridor fade out of notice. The light was like a whole aurora borealis compressed and projected through the basement corridor of a hotel left over from long ago. Neither of the robots knew the nature of the light, but it pulsed in beats of five.

The music and the lights became obtrusive even to the two robots as they walked or trotted downward toward the center of the world. The air-forcing system must have been very strong, because the inner heat of the Earth had not reached them, even at this great depth. Flavius had no idea of how many kilometers below the surface they had come. He knew that it was not much in planetary distance, but it was very far indeed for an ordinary walk.

The Lord Sto Odin sat up in the litter quite suddenly. When the two robots slowed, he said crossly at them: "Keep going. Keep going. I am going to set myself up. I'm strong enough to do it."

He took out the manikin meee and studied it in the light of the minor aurora borealis which repeated itself in the corridor. The manikin ran through its changes of diagnoses and colors. The Lord was satisfied. With firm old fingers he put the knifetip to the back of his neck and set his output of vital energies at an even higher level.

The robots did what they had been told.

The lights had been bewildering. Sometimes they made walking itself difficult. It was hard to believe that dozens or hundreds, perhaps thousands, of human beings had found their way through these uncharted corridors in order to discover the inmost precincts of the Bezirk, where all things were allowed. Yet the robots had to believe it. They themselves had been here before and they scarcely remembered how they had found their way the other time.

And the music! It beat at them harder than ever before. It came in beats of five, ringing out the tones of the pentapaul, the five-word verse which the mad cat-minstrel C'paul had developed while playing his c'lute some centuries before. The form itself confirmed and reinforced the poignancy of cats combined with the heartbreaking intelligence of the human being. No wonder people had found their way down here.

In all the history of man, there was no act which could not be produced by any one of the three bitterest forces in the human spirit—religious faith, vengeful vainglory, or sheer vice. Here, for the sake of vice, men had found the undiscoverable deep and had put it to wild, filthy uses. The music called them on.

This was very special music. It came at Sto Odin
and his legionaries in two utterly different ways by now,
reverberating at them through solid rock and echoing,
re-echoing through the maze of corridors, carried by
the dark heavy air. The corridor lights were still yellow, but the electromagnetic illuminations, which kept
time to the music, made the ordinary lighting seem
wan. The music controlled all things, paced all time,
called all life to itself. It was song of a kind which
the two robots had not noticed with such intensity
on their previous visit.

Even the Lord Sto Odin, for all his travels and
experiences, had never heard it before.

It was all of this:

The beat and the heat and the neat repeat of the
notes which poured from the congohelium—metal
never made for music, matter and antimatter locked in
a fine magnetic grid to ward off the outermost perils
of space. Now a piece of it was deep in the body of
Old Earth, counting out strange cadences. The churn
and the burn and the hot return of music riding the
living rock, accompanying itself in an air-carried echo.
The surge and the urge of an erotic dirge which
moaned, groaned through the heavy stone.

Sto Odin woke and stared sharply forward, seeing
nothing but experiencing everything.

"Soon we shall see the gate and the girl," said he.

"You know this, man? *You* who have never been
here before?" Livius had spoken.

"I know it," said the Lord Sto Odin, "because I
know it,"

"You wear the feathers of immunity."

"I wear the feathers of immunity."

"Does that mean that we, your robots, are free too, down in this Bezirk?"

"Free as you like," said the Lord Sto Odin, "provided that you do my wishes. Otherwise I shall kill you."

"If we keep going," said Flavius, "may we sing the underpeople song? It might keep some of that terrible music out of our brains. The music has all feelings and we have none. Nevertheless it disturbs us. I do not know why."

"My radio contact with the surface has lapsed," said Livius irrelevantly. "I need to sing too."

"Go ahead, both of you," said the Lord Sto Odin. "But keep on going, or you die."

The robots lifted their voice in song:

> *I eat my rage.*
> *I swallow my grief.*
> *There's no relief*
> *From pain or age.*
>     *Our time comes.*

> *I work my life.*
> *I breathe my breath.*
> *I face my death*
> *Without a wife.*
>     *Our time comes.*

> *We undermen*
> *Shove, crush, and crash.*
> *There'll be a clash*
> *And thunder when*
>     *Our time comes.*

Though the song had the barbarous, ancient thrill of bagpipes in it, the melody could not counter or cancel the sane, wild rhythm of the congohelium beating at them, now, from all directions at once.

"Nice piece of sedition, that," said the Lord Sto Odin dryly, "but I like it better as music than I do this noise which is tearing its way through the depths of the world. Keep going. Keep going. I must meet this mystery before I die."

"We find it hard to endure that music coming at us through the rock," said Livius.

"It seems to us that it is much stronger than it was when we came here some months ago. Could it have changed?" asked Flavius.

"*That* is the mystery. We let them have the Gebiet, beyond our own jurisdiction. We gave them the Bezirk, to do with as they please. But these ordinary people have created or encountered some extraordinary power. They have brought new things into the Earth. It may be necessary for all three of us to die before we settle the matter."

"We can't die the way you do," said Livius. "We're already robots, and the people from whom we were imprinted have been dead a long time. Do you mean you would turn us off?"

"I would, perhaps, or else some other force. Would you mind?"

"Mind? You mean, have emotions about it? I don't know," said Flavius. "I used to think that I had real, full experience when you used the phrase *Summa nulla est* and brought us up to full capacity, but that music which we have been hearing has the effect of a thousand passwords all said at once. I am beginning to care about my life and I think that I am becoming what your reference explained by the word 'afraid.'"

"I too feel it," said Livius. "This is not a power which we knew to exist on Earth before. When I was a strategist someone told me about the really indescribable dangers connected with the Douglas-Ouyang planets, and it seems to me now that a danger of that kind is already with us, here inside the tunnel. Something which Earth never made. Something which man never developed. Something which no robot could out-compute. Something wild and very strong brought into being by the use of the congohelium. Look around us."

He did not need to say that. The corridor itself had become a living, pulsing rainbow.

They turned one last loop in the corridor and they were there—

The very last limit of the realm of distress.

The source of evil music.

The end of the Bezirk.

They knew it because the music blinded them, the lights deafened them, their senses ran into one another and became confused. This was the immediate presence of the congohelium.

There was a door, immensely large, carved with elaborate Gothic ornament. It was much too big for any human man to have had need of it. In the door a single figure stood, her breasts accented into vivid brights and darks by the brilliant light which poured from one side of the door only, the right.

They could see through the door, into an immense hall wherein the floor was covered by hundreds of limp bundles of ragged clothing. These were the people, unconscious. Above them and between them there danced the high figure of a male, holding a glittering something in his hands. He prowled and leaped and twisted and turned to the pulsation of the music which he himself produced.

"*Summa nulla est,*" said the Lord Sto Odin. "I want you two robots to be keyed to maximum. Are you now to top alert?"

"We are, sir," chorused Livius and Flavius.

"You have your weapons?"

"We cannot use them," said Livius, "since it is contrary to our programming, but *you* can use them, sir."

"I'm not sure," said Flavius. "I'm not at all sure. We are equipped with surface weapons. This music, these hypnotics, these lights—who knows what they may have done to us and to our weapons, which were never designed to operate this far underground?"

"No fear," said Sto Odin. "I'll take care of all of it."

He took out a small knife.

When the knife gleamed under the dancing lights, the girl in the doorway finally took notice of the Lord Sto Odin and his strange companions.

She spoke to him, and her voice rode through the heavy air with the accents of clarity and death.

≈ 7 ≈

"Who are you," she said, "that you should bring weapons to the last uttermost limits of the Bezirk?"

"This is just a small knife, lady," said the Lord Sto Odin, "and with this I can do no harm to anyone. I am an old man and I am setting my own vitality button higher."

She watched incuriously as he brought the point of the knife to the nape of his own neck and then gave it three full, deliberate turns.

Then she stared and said, "You are strange, my Lord. Perhaps you are dangerous to my friends and me."

"I am dangerous to no one." The robots looked at him, surprised, because of the fullness and the richness of his voice. He had set his vitality very high indeed, giving himself, at that rate, perhaps no more than an hour or two of life, but he had regained the physical power and the emotional force of his own prime years. They looked at the girl. She had taken Sto Odin's statement at full face value, almost as though it were an incontrovertible canon of faith.

"I wear," Sto Odin went on, "these feathers. Do you know what they signify?"

"I can see," she said, "that you are a Lord of the Instrumentality, but I do not know what the feathers mean . . ."

"Waiver of immunity. Anyone who can manage it is allowed to kill me or to hurt me without danger of punishment." He smiled, a little grimly. "Of course, I have the right to fight back, and I do know how to fight. My name is the Lord Sto Odin. Why are you here, girl?"

"I love that man in there—if he is a man any more."

She stopped and pursed her lips in bewilderment. It was strange to see those girlish lips compressed in a momentary stammer of the soul. She stood there, more nude than a newborn infant, her face covered with provocative, off-beat cosmetics. She lived for a mission of love in the depths of the nothing and nowhere: yet she remained a girl, a person, a human being capable, as she was now, of an immediate relationship to another human being.

"He *was* a man, my Lord, even when he came back from the surface with that piece of congohelium. Only a few weeks ago, those people were dancing too. Now they just lie on the ground. They do not even die. I myself held the congohelium too, and I made music with it. Now the power of the music is eating him up and he dances without resting. He won't come out to me and I do not dare go into that place with him. Perhaps I too would end up as one more heap on the floor."

A crescendo of the intolerable music made speech intolerable for her. She waited for it to pass while the room beyond blazed a pulsing violet at them.

When the music of the congohelium subsided a little, Sto Odin spoke: "How long has it been that he has danced alone with this strange power coursing through him?"

"One year. Two years. Who can tell? I came down here and lost time when I arrived. You Lords don't even let us have clocks and calendars up on the surface."

"We ourselves saw you dancing just a tenth-year ago," said Livius, interrupting.

She glanced at them, quickly, incuriously. "Are you the same two robots who were here a while back? You look very different now. You look like ancient soldiers. I can't imagine why . . . All right, maybe it was a week, maybe it was a year."

"What were you doing down here?" asked Sto Odin, gently.

"What do you think?" she said. "Why do all the other people come down here? I was running away from the timeless time, the lifeless life, the hopeless hope that you Lords apply to all mankind on the surface. You let the robots and the underpeople work, but you freeze the real people in a happiness which has no hope and no escape."

"I'm right," cried Sto Odin. "I'm right, though I die for it!"

"I don't understand you," said the girl. "Do you mean that you too, a Lord, have come down here to escape from the useless hope that wraps up all of us?"

"No, no, no," he said, as the shifting lights of the congohelium music made improbable traceries across his features. "I just meant that I told the other Lords that something like this was happening to you ordinary people on the surface. Now you are telling me exactly what I told them. Who were you, anyhow?"

The girl glanced down at her unclothed body as though she were aware, for the first time, of her nakedness. Sto Odin could see the blush pour from her face down across her neck and chest. She said, very quietly: "Don't you know? We never answer that question down here."

"You have rules?" he said. "You people have rules, even here in the Bezirk?"

She brightened up when she realized that he had not meant the indecent question as an impropriety. Eagerly she explained. "There aren't any rules. They are just understandings. Somebody told me when I left the ordinary world and crossed the line of the Gebiet. I suppose they did not tell you because you were a Lord, or because they hid from your strange war-robots."

"I met no one, coming down."

"Then they were hiding from you, my Lord."

Sto Odin looked around at his legionaries to see if they would confirm that statement but neither Flavius nor Livius said anything at all.

He turned back to the girl. "I didn't mean to pry. Can you tell me what kind of person you are? I don't need the particulars."

"When I was alive, I was a once-born," she said. "I did not live long enough to be renewed. The robots and a Subcommissioner of the Instrumentality took a look at me to see if I could be trained for the Instrumentality. More than enough brains, they said, but no character at all. I thought about that a long time. 'No character at all.' I knew I couldn't kill myself, and I didn't want to live, so I looked happy every time I thought a monitor might be scanning me and I found my way to the Gebiet. It wasn't death, and it wasn't life, but it was an escape from endless fun. I hadn't been down here long"—she pointed at the Gebiet above them—"before I met him. We loved each other very soon and he said that the Gebiet was not much improvement on the surface. He said he had already been down here, in the Bezirk, looking for a fun-death."

"A what?" said Sto Odin, as if he could not believe the words.

"A fun-death. Those were his words and his idea. I followed him around and we loved each other. I waited for him when he went to the surface to get the congohelium. I thought that his love for me would put the fun-death out of his mind."

"Are you telling me the whole truth?" said Sto Odin. "Or is this just your part of the story?"

She stammered protests but he did not ask again.

The Lord Sto Odin said nothing but he looked heavily at her.

She winced, bit her lip, and finally said, through all the music and the lights, very clearly indeed, "Stop it. You are hurting me."

The Lord Sto Odin stared at her, said innocently, "I am doing nothing," and stared on. There was much to stare at. She was a girl the color of honey. Even through these lights and shadows he could see that she had no clothing at all. Nor did she have a single hair left on her body—no head of hair, no eyebrows, probably no eyelashes, though he could not tell at that distance. She had traced golden eyebrows far up on her forehead, giving her the look of endless mocking inquiry. She had painted her mouth gold, so that when she spoke, her words cascaded from a golden source. She had painted her upper eyelids golden too, but the lower were black as carbon itself. The total effect was alien to all the previous experiences of mankind: it was lascivious grief to the thousandth power, dry wantonness perpetually unfulfilled, femaleness in the service of remote purposes, humanity enraptured by strange planets.

He stood and stared. If she were still human at all, this would sooner or later force her to take the initiative. It did.

She spoke again, "Who are you? You are living too fast, too fiercely. Why don't you go in and dance, like all the others?" She gestured past the open door, where the ragged unconscious shapes of all the people lay strewn about the floor.

"You call that dancing?" said the Lord Sto Odin. "I

do not. There is one man who dances. Those others lie on the floor. Let me ask you the same question. Why don't you dance yourself?"

"I want *him,* not the dance. I am Santuna and he seized me once in human, mortal, ordinary love. But he becomes Sun-boy, more so every day, and he dances with those people who lie on the floor—"

"You call that dancing?" snapped the Lord Sto Odin. He shook his head and added grimly, "I see no dance."

"You don't see it? You really don't see it?" she cried.

He shook his head obstinately and grimly.

She turned so that she looked into the room beyond her and she brought her high, clear penetrating wail which even cut through the five-beat pulse of the congohelium. She cried:

"Sun-boy, Sun-boy, hear me!"

There was no break in the quick escape of the feet which pattered in the figure eight, no slowing down the fingers which beat against the shimmering non-focus of the metal which was carried in the dancer's arms.

"My lover, my beloved, my man!" she cried again, her voice even more shrill and demanding than before.

There was a break in the cadence of the music and the dance. The dancer sheered toward them with a perceptible slowing down of his cadence. The lights of the inner room, the great door, and the outer hall all became more steady. Sto Odin could see the girl more clearly; she really didn't have a single hair on her body. He could see the dancer too; the young man was tall, thin beyond the ordinary suffering of man, and the metal which he carried shimmered like water reflecting a thousand lights. The dancer spoke, quickly and angrily:

"You called me. You have called me thousands of times. Come on in, if you wish. But don't call me."

As he spoke, the music faded out completely, the bundles on the floor began to stir and to groan and to awaken.

Santuna stammered hastily, "This time it wasn't me. It was these people. One of them is very strong. He cannot see the dancers."

Sun-boy turned to the Lord Sto Odin. "Come in and dance then, if you wish. You are already here. You might as well. Those machines of yours"—he nodded at the robot-legionaries—"they couldn't dance anyhow. Turn them off." The dancer started to turn away.

"I shall not dance, but I would like to see it," said Sto Odin, with enforced mildness. He did not like this young man at all—not the phosphorescence of his skin, the dangerous metal cradled in his arm, the suicidal recklessness of his prancing walk. Anyhow, there was too much light this far underground and too few explanations of what was being done.

"Man, you're a peeper. That's real nasty, for an old man like you. Or do you just want to be a *man!*"

The Lord Sto Odin felt his temper flare up. "Who are you, man, that you should call man *man* in such a tone? Aren't you still human, yourself?"

"Who knows? Who cares? I have tapped the music of the universe. I have piped all imaginable happiness into this room. I am generous. I share it with these friends of mine." Sun-boy gestured at the ragged heaps on the floor, who had begun to squirm in their misery without the music. As Sto Odin saw into the room more clearly, he could see that the bundles on the floor were young people, mostly young men, though there were a few girls among them. They all of them looked sick and weak and pale.

Sto Odin retorted, "I don't like the looks of this. I have half a mind to seize you and to take that metal."

The dancer spun on the ball of his right foot, as though to leap away in a wild prance.

The Lord Sto Odin stepped into the room after Sun-boy.

Sun-boy turned full circle, so that he faced Sto Odin once again. He pushed the Lord out of the door, marching him firmly but irresistibly three steps backward.

"Flavius, seize the metal. Livius, take the man," spat Sto Odin.

Neither robot moved.

Sto Odin, his senses and his strength set high by the severe twist upward which he had given his vitality button, stepped forward to seize the congohelium himself. Made one step and no more: he froze in the doorway, immobile.

He had not felt like that since the last time the doctors put him in a surgery machine, when they found that part of his skull had developed bone-cancer from old, old radiation in space and from the subsequent effects of sheer age. They had given him a prosthetic half-skull and for the time of the operation he had been immobilized by straps and drugs. This time there were no straps, no drugs, but the forces which Sun-boy had invoked were equally strong.

The dancer danced in an enormous figure-eight among the clothed bodies lying on the floor. He had been singing the song which the robot Flavius had repeated far up above, on the surface of the Earth—the song about the weeping man.

But Sun-boy did not weep.

His ascetic, thin face was twisted in a broad grin of mockery. When he sang about sorrow it was not sorrow which he really expressed, but derision, laughter, contempt for ordinary human sorrow. The congohelium shimmered and the aurora borealis almost blinded Sto Odin. There were two other drums in the middle of the room, one with high notes and the other with even higher ones.

The congohelium resonated: *boom—boom—doom—doom—room!*

The large ordinary drum rattled out, when Sun-boy passed it and reached out his fingers: *ritiplin, ritiplin, rataplan, ritiplin!*

The small, strange drum emitted only two notes, and it almost croaked them: *kid-nork, kid-nork, kid-nork!*

As Sun-boy danced back the Lord Sto Odin thought that he could hear the voice of the girl Santuna, calling to Sun-boy, but he could not turn his head to see if she were speaking.

Sun-boy stood in front of Sto Odin, his feet still weaving as he danced, his thumbs and his palms torturing hypnotic dissonances from the gleaming congohelium.

"Old man, you tried to trick me. You failed."

The Lord Sto Odin tried to speak, but the muscles of his mouth and throat would not respond. He wondered what force this was, which could stop all unusual effort but still leave his heart free to beat, his lungs to breathe, his brain (both natural and prosthetic) to think.

The boy danced on. He danced away a few steps, turned and danced back to Sto Odin.

"You wear the feather of immunity. I am free to kill you. If I did, the Lady Mmona and the Lord Nuru-or and your other friends would never know what happened."

If Sto Odin could have moved his eyelids that much, he would have opened his eyes in astonishment at the discovery that a superstitious dancer, far underground, knew the secret business of the Instrumentality.

"You can't believe what you are looking at, even though you see it plainly," said Sun-boy more seriously. "You think that a lunatic has found a way to work wonders with a piece of the congohelium taken far underground. Foolish old man! No ordinary lunatic would have carried this metal down here without blowing up the fragment and himself with it. No man could have done what I have done. You are thinking, If the gambler who took the name Sun-boy is not a man, what is he? What brings the power and music of the Sun so far down underground? Who makes the wretched ones of the world dream in a crazy, happy sleep while their life spills and leaks into a thousand kinds of times, a thousand kinds of worlds? Who does it, if it is not mere me? You don't have to ask. I can tell perfectly well what you are thinking. I'll dance it for you. I am a very kind man, even though you do not like me."

The dancer's feet had been moving in the same place while he spoke.

Suddenly he whirled away, leaping and vaulting over the wretched human figures on the floor.

He passed the big drum and touched it: *ritiplin, rataplan!*

Left hand brushed the little drum: *kid-nork, kid-nork!*

Both hands seized the congohelium, as though the strong wrists were going to tear it apart.

The whole room blazed with music, gleamed with thunder as the human senses interpenetrated each other. The Lord Sto Odin felt the air pass his skin like cool, wet oil. Sun-boy the dancer became transparent and through him the Lord Sto Odin could see a landscape which was not Earth and never would be.

"Fluminescent, luminescent, incandescent, fluorescent," sang the dancer. "Those are the worlds of the Douglas-Ouyang planets, seven planets in a close group, all traveling together around a single sun. Worlds of wild magnetism and perpetual dustfall, where the surfaces of the planets are changed by the forever-shifting magnetism of their erratic orbits! Strange worlds, where stars dance dances wilder than any dance ever conceived by man—planets which have a consciousness in common, but perhaps not intelligence—planets which called across all space and all time for companionship until *I*, me the gambler, came down to this cavern and found them. Where you had left them, my Lord Sto Odin, when you said to a robot:

"'I do not like the looks of those planets,' said you, Sto Odin, speaking to a robot a long time ago. 'People might get sick or crazy, just looking at them,' said you, Sto Odin, long, long ago. 'Hide the knowledge in some out of the way computer,' you commanded, Sto Odin, before I was born. But the computer was that one, that one in the corner behind you, which you cannot turn to see. I came down to this room, looking for a fun-suicide, something really unusual which would bang the noddies when they found I had gotten away. I danced here in the darkness, almost the way I am dancing now, and I had taken about twelve different kinds of drugs, so that I was wild and free and very very receptive. That computer spoke to me, Sto Odin. *Your* computer, not mine. It spoke to me, and you know what it said?

"You might as well know, Sto Odin, because you are dying. You set your vitality high in order to fight me. I have made you stand still. Could I do that if I were a mere man? Look. I will turn solid again."

With a rainbow-like scream of chords and sounds, Sun-boy twisted the congohelium again until both the inner chamber and the outer bloomed with lights of a thousand colors and the deep underground air became drenched with music which seemed psychotic, because no human mind had ever invented it. The Lord Sto Odin, imprisoned in his own body with his two legionary-robots frozen half a pace behind him, wondered if he really were dying in vain and tried to guess whether he would be blinded and deafened by this dancer before he died. The congohelium twisted and shone before him.

Sun-boy danced backward over the bodies on the floor, danced backward with an odd cadenced run which looked as though he were plunging forward in a wild, competitive foot-race when the music and his own footsteps carried him back, toward the center of the inner room. The figure jumped in an odd stance, face looking so far downward that Sun-boy might have been studying his own steps on the floor, the congohelium held above and behind his neck, legs lifting high in the cruel high-kneed prance.

The Lord Sto Odin thought he could hear the girl calling again, but he could not distinguish words.

The drums spoke again: *ritiplin, ritiplin, rataplan!* and then *kid-nork, kid-nork, kid-nork!*

The dancer spoke as the pandemonium subsided. He spoke, and his voice was high, strange, like a bad recording played on the wrong machine: .

"The something is talking to you. You can talk."

The Lord Sto Odin found that his throat and lips moved. Quietly, secretly, like an old soldier, he tried his feet and fingers: these did not move. Only his voice could be used. He spoke, and he said the obvious:

"Who are you, *something!*"

Sun-boy looked across at Sto Odin. He stood erect and calm. Only his feet moved, and they did a wild, agile little jig which did not affect the rest of his body. Apparently some kind of dance was necessary to keep the connection going between the unexplained reach of the Douglas-Ouyang planets, the piece of the congohelium, the more than human dancer, and the tortured blissful figures on the floor. The face, the face itself was quite composed and almost sad.

"I have been told," said Sun-boy, "to show you who I am."

He danced around the drums *rataplan, rataplan! kid-nork-nork, kid-nork, kid-nork-nork!*

He held the congohelium high and wrenched it so that a great moan came out. Sto Odin felt sure that a sound as wild and forlorn as that would be sure to reach the surface of the Earth many kilometers above, but his prudent judgment assured him that this was a fanciful thought gestated by his personal situation, and that any real sound strong enough to reach all the way to the surface would also be strong enough to bring the bruised and shattered rock of the ceiling pouring down upon their heads.

The congohelium ran down the colors of the spectrum until it stopped at a dark, wet liver-red, very close to black.

The Lord Sto Odin, in that momentary near silence, found that the entire story had been thrust into his mind without being strung out and articulated with words. The true history of this chamber had entered his memory sidewise, as it were. In one moment he knew nothing of it; in the next instant it was as if he had remembered the whole narrative for most of his life.

He also felt himself set free.

He stumbled backward three or four steps.

To his immense relief, his robots turned around, themselves free, and accompanied him. He let them put their hands in his armpits.

His face was suddenly covered with kisses.

His plastic cheek felt, thinly and dimly, the imprint, real and living, of female human lips. It was the odd girl—beautiful, bald, naked, and golden-lipped—who had waited and shouted from the door.

Despite physical fatigue and the sudden shock of intruded knowledge, the Lord Sto Odin knew what he had to say.

"Girl, you shouted for me."

"Yes, my Lord."

"You have had the strength to watch the congohelium and not to give in to it?"

She nodded but said nothing.

"You have been strong-willed enough not to go into that room?"

"Not strong-willed, my Lord. I just love him, my man in there."

"You have waited, girl, for many months?"

"Not all the time. I go up the corridor when I have to eat or drink or sleep or do my personals. I even have mirrors and combs and tweezers and paint there, to make myself beautiful, the way that Sun-boy might want me."

The Lord Sto Odin looked over his shoulder. The music was low and keening with some emotions other than grief. The dancer was doing a long, slow dance, full of creeping and reaches, as he passed the congohelium from one hand to the other. "Do you hear me, dancer?" called the Lord Sto Odin, the Instrumentality once more coursing through his veins.

The dancer did not speak nor seem to change his course. But *kid-nork, kid-nork* said the little drum, quite unexpectedly.

"He, and the face behind him—they will let the girl leave if she really forgets him and this place in the act of leaving. Won't you?" said Sto Odin to the dancer.

*Ritiplin, rataplan* said the big drum, which had not sounded since Sto Odin was let free.

"But I don't want to go," said the girl.

"I know you don't want to go. You will go to please me. You can come back as soon as I have done my work." She stood mute so he continued.

"One of my robots, Livius, the one imprinted by a psychiatrist general, will run with you, but I command him to forget this place and all things connected with it. *Summa nulla est.* Have you heard me, Livius? You will run with this girl and you will forget. You will run and forget. You too will run and forget, Santuna my dear, but two Earthnychthemerons from now you will remember just enough to come back here, should you wish to, should you need to. Otherwise you will go to the Lady Mmona and learn from her what you should do for the rest of your life."

"You are promising, my Lord, that in two days and nights I can come back if I even feel like it."

"Now run, my girl, run. Run to the surface. Livius, carry her if you must. But run! run! run! More than she depends upon it."

Santuna looked at him very earnestly. Her nakedness was innocence. The gold upper eyelids met the black lower eyelids as she blinked and then brushed away wet tears.

"Kiss me," she said, "and I will run."

He leaned down and kissed her.

She turned, looked back one last time at her dancer-lover, and then ran long-legged into the corridor. Livius ran after her, gracefully, untiringly. In twenty minutes they would be reaching the upper limits of the Gebiet.

"You know what I am doing?" said Sto Odin to the dancer.

This time the dancer and the force behind him did not deign to answer.

Said Sto Odin, "Water. There is water in a jug in my litter. Take me there, Flavius."

The robot-legionary took the aged and trembling Sto Odin to the litter.

## ⌒ 8 ⌒

The Lord Sto Odin then performed the trick which changed human history for many centuries to come and, in so doing, exploded an enormous cavern in the vitals of the Earth.

He used one of the most secret ruses of the Instrumentality.

He triple-thought.

Only a few very adept persons could triple-think, when they were given every possible chance of training. Fortunately for mankind, the Lord Sto Odin had been one of the successful ones.

He set three systems of thought into action. At the top level he behaved rationally as he explored the old room; at a lower level of his mind he planned a wild surprise for the dancer with the congohelium. But at the third, lowest level, he decided what he must do in the time of a single blink and trusted his autonomic nervous system to carry out the rest.

These are the commands he gave:

Flavius should be set on the wild-alert and readied for attack.

The computer should be reached and told to record the whole episode, everything which Sto Odin had learned, and should be shown how to take countermeasures while Sto Odin gave the matter no further conscious thought. The gestalt of action—the general frame of retaliation—was clear for thousandths of a second in Sto Odin's mind and then it dropped from sight.

The music rose to a roar.

White light covered Sto Odin.

"You meant me harm!" called Sun-boy from beyond the Gothic door.

"I meant you harm," Sto Odin acknowledged, "but it was a passing thought. I did nothing. You are watching me."

"I am watching you," said the dancer grimly. *Kidnork, kid-nork* went the little drum. "Do not go out of my sight. When you are ready to come through my door, call me or just think of it. I will meet you and help you in."

"Good enough," said Lord Sto Odin.

Flavius still held him. Sto Odin concentrated on the melody which Sun-boy was creating, a wild new song never before suspected in the history of the world. He wondered if he could surprise the dancer by throwing his own song back at him. At the same instant, his fingers were performing a third set of actions which Sto Odin's mind no longer had to heed. Sto Odin's hand opened a lid in the robot's chest, right into the laminated controls of the brain. The hand itself changed certain adjustments, commanding that the robot should, within the quarter-hour, kill all forms of life within reach other than the command-transmitter. Flavius did not know what had been done to him; Sto Odin did not even notice what his own hand had done.

"Take me over to the old computer," said Sto Odin to the robot Flavius. "I want to discover how the strange story which I have just learned may be true." Sto Odin kept thinking of music which would even startle the user of the congohelium.

He stood at the computer.

His hand, responding to the triple-think command which it had been given, turned the computer up and pressed the button, *Record this scene.* The computer's old relays almost grunted as they came to the alert and complied.

"Let me see the map," said Sto Odin to the computer.

Far behind him, the dancer had changed his pace into a fast jog-trot of hot suspicion.

The map appeared on the computer.

"Beautiful," said Sto Odin.

The entire labyrinth had become plain. Just above them was one of the ancient, sealed-off anti-seismic shafts—a straight, empty tubular shaft, two hundred meters wide, kilometers high. At the top, it had a lid which kept out the mud and water of the ocean floor. At the bottom, since there was no pressure other than air to worry about, it had been covered with a plastic which looked like rock, so that neither people nor robots which might be passing would try to climb into it.

"Watch what I am doing!" cried Sto Odin to the dancer.

"I am watching," said Sun-boy, and there was almost a growl of perplexity in his sung-forth response.

Sto Odin shook the computer and ran the fingers of his right hand over it and coded a very specific request. His left hand—preconditioned by the triple-think—coded the emergency panel at the side of the computer with two simple, clear engineering instructions.

Sun-boy's laughter rang out behind him. "You are asking that a piece of the congohelium be sent down to you. Stop! Stop, before you sign it with your name and your authority as a Lord of the Instrumentality. Your unsigned request will do no harm. The central computer up top will just think that it is some of the crazy people in the Bezirk making senseless demands." The voice rose to a note of urgency, "Why did the machine signal 'received and complied with' to you just now?"

The Lord Sto Odin lied blandly, "I don't know. Maybe they will send me a piece of the congohelium to match the one that you have there."

"You're lying," cried the dancer. "Come over here to the door."

Flavius led the Lord Sto Odin to the ridiculous-beautiful Gothic archway.

The dancer was leaping from foot to foot. The congohelium shone a dull alert red. The music wept as though all the anger and suspicion of mankind had been incorporated into a new unforgettable fugue, like a delirious atonal counterpoint to Johann Sebastian Bach's *Third Brandenburg Concerto.*

"I am here," the Lord Sto Odin spoke easily.

"You are dying!" cried the dancer.

"I was dying before you first noticed me. I set my vitality control to maximum after I entered the Bezirk."

"Come on in, then," said Sun-boy, "and you will never die."

Sto Odin took the edge of the door and let himself down to the stone floor. Only when he was comfortably seated did he speak:

"I am dying, that is true. But I would rather not come in. I will just watch you dance as I die."

"What are you doing? What have you done?" cried Sun-boy. He stopped dancing and walked over to the door.

"Search me if you wish," said the Lord Sto Odin.

"I am searching you," said the dancer, "but I see nothing but your desire to get a piece of the congo-helium for yourself and to out-dance me."

At this point Flavius went berserk. He ran back to the litter, leaned over, and ran toward the door. In each hand he carried an enormous solid-steel bearing.

"What's that robot doing?" cried the dancer. "I can see your mind but you are not telling him anything! He uses those steel balls to break obstructions—"

He gasped as the attack came.

Quicker than the eye could follow the movement, Flavius's sixty-ton-capacity arm whistled through the air as he flung the first steel missile directly at Sun-boy. Sun-boy, or the power within him, leapt aside with insect speed. The ball plowed through two of the rag-clothed human bodies on the floor. One body said *whoof!* as it died, but the other body let out no sound at all: the head had been torn off in first impact. Before the dancer could speak, Flavius flung the second ball.

This time the doorway caught it. The powers which had immobilized Sto Odin and his robots were back in operation. The ball sang as it plunged into the doorway, stopped in mid-air, sang again as the door flung it back at Flavius.

The returning ball missed Flavius's head but crushed his chest utterly. That was where his real brain was. There was a flicker of light as the robot went out, but even in dying Flavius seized the ball one last time

and flung it at Sun-boy. The robot terminated operation and the heavy ball, flung wild, caught the Lord
Sto Odin in the right shoulder. The Lord Sto Odin
felt pain until he dragged over his manikin meee and
turned all pain off. Then he looked at the shoulder. It
was almost totally demolished. Blood from his organic
body and hydraulic fluid from his prosthetics joined
in a slow, heavy stream as the liquids met, merged,
and poured down his side.

The dancer almost forgot to dance.

Sto Odin wondered how far the girl had gone.

The air pressure changed.

"What is happening to the air? Why did you think
about the girl? What is happening?"

"Read me," said the Lord Sto Odin.

"I will dance and get my powers first," said Sun-boy.

For a few brief minutes it seemed that the dancer
with the congohelium would cause a rock-fall.

The Lord Sto Odin, dying, closed his eyes and
found that it was restful to die. The blaze and noise
of the world around him remained interesting, but
had become unimportant.

The congohelium with a thousand shifting rainbows
and the dancer had attained near-transparency when
Sun-boy came back to read Sto Odin's mind.

"I see nothing," said Sun-boy worriedly. "Your vitality button is too high and you will die soon. Where
is all that air coming from? I seem to hear a faraway
roar. But you are not causing it. Your robot went wild.
All you do is to look at me contentedly and die. That
is very strange. You want to die your way when you
could live unimaginable lives in here with us!"

"That is right," said the Lord Sto Odin. "I am dying

my way. But dance for me, do dance for me with the congohelium, while I tell you your own story as you told it to me. It would be a pleasure to get the story straight before I die."

The dancer looked irresolute, started to dance, and then turned back to the Lord Sto Odin.

"Are you sure you want to die right away? With the power of what you call the Douglas-Ouyang planets, which I receive right here with the help of the congohelium, you could be comfortable enough while I danced and you could still die whenever you wished. Vitality buttons are much weaker than the powers which I command. I could even help to lift you across the threshold of my door . . ."

"No," said the Lord Sto Odin. "Just dance for me while I die. My way."

## 9

Thus the world turned. Millions of tons of water were rushing toward them.

Within minutes the Gebiet and the Bezirk would drown as the air whistled upward. Sto Odin noted contentedly that there was an air-shaft at the top of the dancer's room. He did not allow himself to third-think of what would happen when the matter and anti-matter of the congohelium were immersed in rushing salt water. Something like forty megatons, he supposed, with the tired feeling of a man who has thought a problem through long, long ago and remembers it briefly only after the situation has long passed.

Sun-boy was acting out religion before the age of

space. He chorused hymns, he lifted his eyes and his hands and his piece of the congohelium to the sun; he played the rattle of whirling dervishes, the temple bells of the Man on the Two Pieces of Wood, and the other temple bells of that saint who had escaped time simply by seeing it and stepping out of it. Buddha, was that his name? And he went on to the severe profanities which afflicted mankind after the Old World fell.

The music kept measure.

And the lights, too.

Whole processions of ghostly shadows followed Sun-boy as he showed how old mankind had found the gods, and the Sun, and then other gods. He pantomimed man's most ancient mystery—that man pretended to be afraid of death, when it was life that never understood it.

And as he danced, the Lord Sto Odin repeated his own story to him:

"You fled the surface, Sun-boy, because the people were stupid clods, happy and dull in their miserable happiness. You fled because you could not stand being a chicken in a poultry house, antiseptically bred, safely housed, and frozen when dead. You joined the other miserable, bright, restless people who sought freedom in the Gebiet. You learned about their drugs and their liquors and their smokes. You knew their women, and their parties, and their games. It wasn't enough. You became a gentleman-suicide, a hero seeking a fun-death which would stamp you with your individuality. You came on down to the Bezirk, the most forgotten and loathsome place of all. You found nothing. Just the old machines and the empty corridors. Here and there a few mummies or bones. Just the silent lights and the faint murmur of air through the corridors."

"I hear water now," said the dancer, still dancing, "rushing water. Don't you hear it, my dying Lord?"

"If I did hear it, I wouldn't care. Let's get on with your story. You came to this room. The weird door made it look like a good place for a fun-death, such as you poor castaways liked to seek, except that there was not much sport in dying unless other people know that you did it intentionally, and know how you did it. Anyway, it was a long climb back up into the Gebiet, where your friends were, so you slept by this computer.

"In the night, while you slept, as you dreamed, the computer sang to you:

> *I need a temporary dog*
> *For a temporary job*
> *On a temporary place*
> *Like Earth!*

When you woke up you were surprised to find that you had dreamed an entire new kind of music. Really wild music which made people shudder with its delicious evil. And with the music, you had a job. To steal a piece of the congohelium.

"You were a clever man, Sun-boy, before the trip down here. The Douglas-Ouyang planets caught you and made you a thousand times cleverer. You and your friends, this is what you told me—or what the presence behind you told me, just a half hour ago—you and your friends stole a subspace communicator console, got a fix on the Douglas-Ouyang planets, and got drunk at the sight. Iridescent, luminescent. Waterfalls uphill. All that kind of thing."

"And you did get the congohelium. The congohelium is made of matter and antimatter laminated apart by a dual magnetic grid. With that the presence of the Douglas-Ouyang planets made you independent of organic processes. You did not need food or rest or even air or drink any more. The Douglas-Ouyang planets are very old. They kept you as a link. I have no idea of what they intended to do with Earth and with mankind. If this story gets out, future generations will call you the merchant of menace, because you used the normal human appetitiousness for danger to trap other people with hypnotics and with music."

"I hear water," interrupted Sun-boy. "I *do* hear water!"

"Never mind," said the Lord Sto Odin, "your story is more important. Anyhow, what could you and I do about it? I am dying, sitting in a pool of blood and effluvium. You can't leave this room with the congohelium. Let me go on. Or perhaps the Douglas-Ouyang entity, whatever it was—"

"*Is*," said Sun-boy.

"—whatever it is, may just have been longing for sensuous companionship. Dance on, man, dance on."

Sun-boy danced and the drums talked with him, *rataplan, rataplan! kid-nork, kid-nork, nork!* while the congohelium made music scream through the solid rock.

The other sound persisted.

Sun-boy stopped and stared.

"It is water. It *is*."

"Who knows?" said the Lord Sto Odin.

"Look," screamed Sun-boy, holding the congohelium high. "Look!"

The Lord Sto Odin did not need to look. He knew full well that the first few tons of water, mud-laden and heavy, had come frothing down the corridor and into their rooms.

"But what do *I* do?" screamed the voice of Sun-boy. Sto Odin felt that it was not Sun-boy speaking, but some relay speaking from the power of the Douglas-Ouyang planets. A power which had tried to find friendship with man, but had found the wrong man and the wrong friendship.

Sun-boy took control of himself. His feet splashed in the water as he danced. The colors shone on the water as it rose. *Ritiplin, tiplin!* said the big drum. *Kid-nork, kid-nork,* said the little drum. *Boom, boom, doom, doom, room,* said the congohelium.

The Lord Sto Odin felt his old eyes blur but he could still see the blazing image of the wild dancer.

"This is a good way to die," thought he, as he died.

## ∾ 10 ∾

Far above, on the surface of the planet, Santuna felt the continent itself heave beneath her feet and saw the eastern horizon grow dark as a volcano of muddy steam shot up from the calm blue sunlit ocean.

"This must not, must *not* happen again!" she said, thinking of Sun-boy and the congohelium and the death of the Lord Sto Odin.

"Something must be done about it," she added to herself.

And she did it.

In later centuries she brought disease, risk, and misery back to increase the happiness of man. She was one of the principal architects of the Rediscovery of Man, and at her most famous she was known as the Lady Alice More.

# Mother Hitton's Littul Kittons

*Poor communications deter theft;*
*good communications promote theft;*
*perfect communications stop theft.*
— Van Braam

## ∞ 1 ∞

The moon spun. The woman watched. Twenty-one facets had been polished at the moon's equator. Her function was to arm it. She was Mother Hitton, the weapons mistress of Old North Australia.

She was a ruddy-faced, cheerful blonde of indeterminate age. Her eyes were blue, her bosom heavy, her arms strong. She looked like a mother, but the only child she had ever had died many generations ago. Now she acted as mother to a planet, not to a person; the Norstrilians slept well because they knew she was watching. The weapons slept their long, sick sleep.

This night she glanced for the two-hundredth time at the warning bank. The bank was quiet. No danger lights shone. Yet she felt an enemy out somewhere in the universe—an enemy waiting to strike at her and her world, to snatch at the immeasurable wealth of

173

the Norstrilians—and she snorted with impatience. *Come along, little man,* she thought. *Come along, little man, and die. Don't keep me waiting.*

She smiled when she recognized the absurdity of her own thought.

She waited for him.

And he did not know it.

He, the robber, was relaxed enough. He was Benjacomin Bozart, and was highly trained in the arts of relaxation.

No one at Sunvale, here on Ttiollé, could suspect that he was a senior warden of the Guild of Thieves, reared under the light of the starry-violet star. No one could smell the odor of Viola Siderea upon him. "Viola Siderea," the Lady Ru had said, "was once the most beautiful of worlds and it is now the most rotten. Its people were once models for mankind, and now they are thieves, liars, and killers. You can smell their souls in the open day." The Lady Ru had died a long time ago. She was much respected, but she was wrong. The robber did not smell to others at all. He knew it. He was no more "wrong" than a shark approaching a school of cod. Life's nature is to live, and he had been nurtured to live as he had to live—by seeking prey.

How else could he live? Viola Siderea had gone bankrupt a long time ago, when the photonic sails had disappeared from space and the planoforming ships began to whisper their way between the stars. His ancestors had been left to die on an off-trail planet. They refused to die. Their ecology shifted and they became predators upon man, adapted by time and genetics to their deadly tasks. And he, the robber, was champion of all his people—the best of their best.

He was Benjacomin Bozart.

He had sworn to rob Old North Australia or to die in the attempt, and he had no intention of dying.

The beach at Sunvale was warm and lovely. Ttiollé was a free and casual transit planet. His weapons were luck and himself: he planned to play both well.

The Norstrilians could kill.

So could he.

At this moment, in this place, he was a happy tourist at a lovely beach. Elsewhere, elsewhen, he could become a ferret among conies, a hawk among doves.

Benjacomin Bozart, thief and warden. He did not know that someone was waiting for him. Someone who did not know his name was prepared to waken death, just for him. He was still serene.

Mother Hitton was not serene. She sensed him dimly but could not yet spot him.

One of her weapons snored. She turned it over.

A thousand stars away, Benjacomin Bozart smiled as he walked toward the beach.


∽ **2** ∽


Benjacomin felt like a tourist. His tanned face was tranquil. His proud, hooded eyes were calm. His handsome mouth, even without its charming smile, kept a suggestion of pleasantness at its corners. He looked attractive without seeming odd in the least. He looked much younger than he actually was. He walked with springy, happy steps along the beach of Sunvale.

The waves rolled in, white-crested, like the breakers of Mother Earth. The Sunvale people were proud of the way their world resembled Manhome itself. Few of them had ever seen Manhome, but they had all heard a bit of history and most of them had a passing anxiety when they thought of the ancient government still wielding political power across the depth of space. They did not like the old Instrumentality of Earth, but they respected and feared it. The waves might remind them of the pretty side of Earth; they did not want to remember the not-so-pretty side.

This man was like the pretty side of old Earth. They could not sense the power within him. The Sunvale people smiled absently at him as he walked past them along the shoreline.

The atmosphere was quiet and everything around him serene. He turned his face to the sun. He closed his eyes. He let the warm sunlight beat through his eyelids, illuminating him with its comfort and its reassuring touch.

Benjacomin dreamed of the greatest theft that any man had ever planned. He dreamed of stealing a huge load of the wealth from the richest world that mankind had ever built. He thought of what would happen when he would finally bring riches back to the planet of Viola Siderea where he had been reared. Benjacomin turned his face away from the sun and languidly looked over the other people on the beach.

There were no Norstrilians in sight yet. They were easy enough to recognize. Big people with red complexions; superb athletes and yet, in their own way, innocent, young, and very tough. He had trained for this theft for two hundred years, his life prolonged for the purpose by the Guild of Thieves on Viola Siderea. He himself embodied the dreams of his own planet, a poor planet once a crossroads of commerce, now sunken to being a minor outpost for spoliation and pilferage.

He saw a Norstrilian woman come out from the hotel and go down to the beach. He waited, and he looked, and he dreamed. He had a question to ask and no adult Australian would answer it.

"Funny," thought he, "that I call them 'Australians' even now. That's the old, old Earth name for them—rich, brave, tough people. Fighting children standing on half the world . . . and now they are the tyrants of all mankind. They hold the wealth. They have the santaclara, and other people live or die depending upon the commerce they have with the Norstrilians. But I won't. And my people won't. We're men who are wolves to man."

Benjacomin waited gracefully. Tanned by the light of many suns, he looked forty though he was two hundred. He dressed casually, by the standards of a vacationer. He might have been an intercultural salesman, a senior gambler, an assistant starport manager. He might even have been a detective working along the commerce lanes. He wasn't. He was a thief. And he was so good a thief that people turned to him and put their property in his hands because he was reassuring, calm, gray-eyed, blond-haired. Benjacomin waited. The woman glanced at him, a quick glance full of open suspicion.

What she saw must have calmed her. She went on past. She called back over the dune, "Come on, Johnny, we can swim out here." A little boy, who looked eight or ten years old, came over the dune top, running toward his mother.

Benjacomin tensed like a cobra. His eyes became sharp, his eyelids narrowed.

This was the prey. Not too young, not too old. If the victim had been too young he wouldn't know the answer; if the victim were too old it was no use taking him on. Norstrilians were famed in combat; adults were mentally and physically too strong to warrant attack.

Benjacomin knew that every thief who had approached the planet of the Norstrilians—who had tried to raid the dream world of Old North Australia—had gotten out of contact with his people and had died. There was no word of any of them.

And yet he knew that hundreds of thousands of Norstrilians must know *the* secret. They now and then made jokes about it. He had heard these jokes when he was a young man, and now he was more than an old man without once coming near the answer. Life was expensive. He was well into his third lifetime and the lifetimes had been purchased honestly by his people. Good thieves all of them, paying out hard-stolen money to obtain the medicine to let their greatest thief remain living. Benjacomin didn't like violence. But when violence prepared the way to the greatest theft of all time, he was willing to use it.

The woman looked at him again. The mask of evil which had flashed across his face faded into benignity; he calmed. She caught him in that moment of relaxation. She liked him.

She smiled and, with that awkward hesitation so characteristic of the Norstrilians, she said, "Could you mind my boy a bit while I go in the water? I think we've seen each other here at the hotel."

"I don't mind," said he. "I'd be glad to. Come here, son."

Johnny walked across the sunlit dunes to his own death. He came within reach of his mother's enemy.

But the mother had already turned.

The trained hand of Benjacomin Bozart reached out. He seized the child by the shoulder. He turned the boy toward him, forcing him down. Before the child could cry out, Benjacomin had the needle into him with the truth drug.

All Johnny reacted to was pain, and then a hammer-blow inside his own skull as the powerful drug took force.

Benjacomin looked out over the water. The mother was swimming. She seemed to be looking back at them. She was obviously unworried. To her, the child seemed to be looking at something the stranger was showing him in a relaxed, easy way.

"Now, sonny," said Benjacomin, "tell me, what's the outside defense?"

The boy didn't answer.

"What is the outer defense, sonny? What is the outer defense?" repeated Benjacomin. The boy still didn't answer.

Something close to horror ran over the skin of Benjacomin Bozart as he realized that he had gambled his safety on this planet, gambled the plans themselves for a chance to break the secret of the Norstrilians.

He had been stopped by simple, easy devices. The child had already been conditioned against attack. Any attempt to force knowledge out of the child brought on a conditioned reflex of total muteness. The boy was literally unable to talk.

Sunlight gleaming on her wet hair, the mother turned around and called back, "Are you all right, Johnny?"

Benjacomin waved to her instead. "I'm showing him my pictures, ma'am. He likes 'em. Take your time." The mother hesitated and then turned back to the water and swam slowly away.

Johnny, taken by the drug, sat lightly, like an invalid, on Benjacomin's lap.

Benjacomin said, "Johnny, you're going to die now and you will hurt terribly if you don't tell me what I want to know." The boy struggled weakly against his grasp. Benjacomin repeated, "I'm going to hurt you if you don't tell me what I want to know. What are the outer defenses? What are the outer defenses?"

The child struggled and Benjacomin realized that the boy was putting up a fight to comply with the orders, not a fight to get away. He let the child slip through his hands and the boy put out a finger and began writing on the wet sand. The letters stood out.

A man's shadow loomed behind them.

Benjacomin, alert, ready to spin, kill, or run, slipped to the ground beside the child and said, "That's a jolly puzzle. That is a good one. Show me some more." He smiled up at the passing adult. The man was a stranger. The stranger gave him a very curious glance which became casual when he saw the pleasant face of Benjacomin, so tenderly and so agreeably playing with the child.

The fingers were still making the letters in the sand.

There stood the riddle in letters: MOTHER HITTON'S LITTUL KITTONS.

The woman was coming back from the sea, the mother with questions. Benjacomin stroked the sleeve of his coat and brought out his second needle, a shallow poison which it would take days or weeks of laboratory work to detect. He thrust it directly into the boy's brain, slipping the needle up behind the skin at the edge of the hairline. The hair shadowed the tiny prick. The incredibly hard needle slipped under the edge of the skull. The child was dead.

Murder was accomplished. Benjacomin casually erased the secret from the sand. The woman came nearer. He called to her, his voice full of pleasant concern, "Ma'am, you'd better come here, I think your son has fainted from the heat."

He gave the mother the body of her son. Her face changed to alarm. She looked frightened and alert. She didn't know how to meet this.

For a dreadful moment she looked into his eyes.

Two hundred years of training took effect . . . She saw nothing. The murderer did not shine with murder. The hawk was hidden beneath the dove. The heart was masked by the trained face.

Benjacomin relaxed in professional assurance. He had been prepared to kill her too, although he was not sure that he could kill an adult, female Norstrilian. Very helpfully said he, "You stay here with him. I'll run to the hotel and get help. I'll hurry."

He turned and ran. A beach attendant saw him and ran toward him. "The child's sick," he shouted. He came to the mother in time to see blunt, puzzled tragedy on her face and with it, something more than tragedy: doubt.

"He's not sick," said she. "He's dead."

"He can't be." Benjacomin looked attentive. He felt attentive. He forced the sympathy to pour out of his posture, out of all the little muscles of his face. "He can't be. I was talking to him just a minute ago. We were doing little puzzles in the sand."

The mother spoke with a hollow, broken voice that sounded as though it would never find the right chords for human speech again, but would go on forever with the ill-attuned flats of unexpected grief. "He's dead," she said. "You saw him die and I guess I saw him die, too. I can't tell what's happened. The child was full of santaclara. He had a thousand years to live but now he's dead. What's your name?"

Benjacomin said, "Eldon. Eldon the salesman, ma'am. I live here lots of times."

## ∞ 3 ∞

"Mother Hitton's littul kittons. Mother Hitton's littul kittons."

The silly phrase ran in his mind. Who was Mother Hitton? Who was she the mother of? What were *kittons*? Were they a misspelling for "kit-tens"? Little cats? Or were they something else?

Had he killed a fool to get a fool's answer?

How many more days did he have to stay there with the doubtful, staggered woman? How many days did he have to watch and wait? He wanted to get back to Viola Siderea; to take the secret, bad as it was, for his people to study. Who was Mother Hitton?

He forced himself out of his room and went downstairs.

The pleasant monotony of a big hotel was such that the other guests looked interestedly at him. He was the man who had watched while the child died on the beach.

Some lobby-living scandalmongers that stayed there had made up fantastic stories that he had killed the child. Others attacked the stories, saying they knew perfectly well who Eldon was. He was Eldon the salesman. It was ridiculous.

People hadn't changed much, even though the ships with the Go-Captains sitting at their hearts whispered between the stars, even though people shuffled between worlds—when they had the money to pay their passage back and forth—like leaves falling in soft, playful winds. Benjacomin faced a tragic dilemma. He knew very well that any attempt to decode the answer would run directly into the protective devices set up by the Norstrilians.

Old North Australia was immensely wealthy. It was known the length and breadth of all the stars that they had hired mercenaries, defensive spies, hidden agents, and alerting devices.

Even Manhome—Mother Earth herself, whom no money could buy—was bribed by the drug of life. An ounce of the santaclara drug, reduced, crystallized, and called "stroon," could give forty to sixty years of life. Stroon entered the rest of the Earths by ounces and pounds, but it was refined back on North Australia by the ton. With treasure like this, the Norstrilians owned an unimaginable world whose resources overreached all conceivable limits of money. They could buy anything. They could pay with other people's lives.

For hundreds of years they had given secret funds

to buying foreigners' services to safeguard their own security.

Benjacomin stood there in the lobby: "Mother Hitton's littul kittons."

He had all the wisdom and wealth of a thousand worlds stuck in his mind but he didn't dare ask anywhere as to what it meant.

Suddenly he brightened.

He looked like a man who had thought of a good game to play, a pleasant diversion to be welcomed, a companion to be remembered, a new food to be tasted. He had had a very happy thought.

There was one source that wouldn't talk. The library. He could at least check the obvious, simple things, and find out what there was already in the realm of public knowledge concerning the secret he had taken from the dying boy.

His own safety had not been wasted, Johnny's life had not been thrown away, if he could find any one of the four words as a key. *Mother* or *Hitton* or *Littul,* in its special meaning, or *Kitton.* He might yet break through to the loot of Norstrilia.

He swung jubilantly, turning on the ball of his right foot. He moved lightly and pleasantly toward the billiard room, beyond which lay the library. He went in.

This was a very expensive hotel and very old-fashioned. It even had books made out of paper, with genuine bindings. Benjacomin crossed the room. He saw that they had the *Galactic Encyclopedia* in two hundred volumes. He took down the volume headed "Hi-Hi." He opened it from the rear, looking for the name "Hitton," and there it was. "Hitton, Benjamin—pioneer of Old North Australia. Said to be originator of part of the defense system. Lived A.D. 10719–17213." That was all. Benjacomin moved among the books. The word "kittons" in that peculiar spelling did not occur anywhere, neither in the encyclopedia nor in any other list maintained by the library. He walked out and upstairs, back to his room.

"Littul" had not appeared at all. It was probably the boy's own childish mistake.

He took a chance. The mother, half blind with bewilderment and worry, sat in a stiff-backed chair on the edge of the porch. The other women talked to her. They knew her husband was coming. Benjacomin went up to her and tried to pay his respects. She didn't see him.

"I'm leaving now, ma'am. I'm going on to the next planet, but I'll be back in two or three subjective weeks. And if you need me for urgent questions, I'll leave my addresses with the police here."

Benjacomin left the weeping mother.

Benjacomin left the quiet hotel. He obtained a priority passage.

The easy-going Sunvale police made no resistance to his demand for a sudden departure visa. After all, he had an identity, he had his own funds, and it was not the custom of Sunvale to contradict its guests. Benjacomin went on the ship and as he moved toward the cabin in which he could rest for a few hours, a man stepped up beside him. A youngish man, hair parted in the middle, short of stature, gray of eyes.

This man was the local agent of the Norstrilian secret police.

Benjacomin, trained thief that he was, did not recognize the policeman. It never occurred to him that the library itself had been attuned and that the word "kittons" in the peculiar Norstrilian spelling was itself an alert. Looking for that spelling had set off a minor alarm. He had touched the trip-wire.

The stranger nodded. Benjacomin nodded back. "I'm a traveling man, waiting over between assignments. I haven't been doing very well. How are you making out?"

"Doesn't matter to me. I don't earn money; I'm a technician. Liverant is the name."

Benjacomin sized him up. The man was a technician all right. They shook hands perfunctorily. Liverant said, "I'll join you in the bar a little later. I think I'll rest a bit first."

They both lay down then and said very little while the momentary flash of planoform went through the ship. The flash passed. From books and lessons they knew that the ship was leaping forward in two dimensions while, somehow or other, the fury of space itself was fed into the computers—and that these in turn were managed by the Go-captain who controlled the ship.

They knew these things but they could not feel them. All they felt was the sting of a slight pain.

The sedative was in the air itself, sprayed in the ventilating system. They both expected to become a little drunk.

The thief Benjacomin Bozart was trained to resist intoxication and bewilderment. Any sign whatever that a telepath had tried to read his mind would have been met with fierce animal resistance, implanted in his unconscious during early years of training. Bozart was not trained against deception by a technician; it never occurred to the Thieves' Guild back on Viola Siderea that it would be necessary for their own people to resist deceivers. Liverant had already been in touch with Norstrilia—Norstrilia whose money reached across the stars, Norstrilia who had alerted a hundred thousand worlds against the mere thought of trespass.

Liverant began to chatter. "I wish I could go further than this trip. I wish that I could go to Olympia. You can buy anything in Olympia."

"I've heard of it," said Bozart. "It's sort of a funny trading planet with not much chance for businessmen, isn't it?"

Liverant laughed and his laughter was merry and genuine. "Trading? They don't trade. They swap. They take all the stolen loot of a thousand worlds and sell it over again and they change it and they paint it and they mark it. That's their business there. The people are blind. It's a strange world, and all you have to do is to go in there and you can have anything you want. Man," said Liverant, "what I could do in a year in that place! Everybody is blind except me and a couple of tourists. And there's all the wealth that everybody thought he's mislaid, half the wrecked ships, the forgotten colonies (they've all been cleaned out), and bang! it all goes to Olympia."

Olympia wasn't really that good and Liverant didn't know why it was his business to guide the killer there. All he knew was that he had a duty and the duty was to direct the trespasser.

Many years before either man was born the code word had been planted in directories, in books, in packing cases and invoices: *Kittons* misspelled. This was the cover name for the outer moon of Norstrilian defense. The use of the cover name brought a raging alert ready into action, with systemic nerves as hot and quick as incandescent tungsten wire.

By the time that they were ready to go to the bar and have refreshments, Benjacomin had half forgotten that it was his new acquaintance who had suggested Olympia rather than another place. He had to go to Viola Siderea to get the credits to make the flight to take the wealth, to win the world of Olympia.

∾ **4** ∾

At home on his native planet Bozart was a subject of a gentle but very sincere celebration.

The elders of the Guild of Thieves welcomed him. They congratulated him. "Who else could have done what you've done, boy? You've made the opening move in a brand new game of chess. There has never been a gambit like this before. We have a name; we have an animal. We'll try it right here." The Thieves' Council turned to their own encyclopedia. They turned through the name "Hitton" and then found the reference "kitton." None of them knew that a false lead had been planted there—by an agent in their world.

The agent, in his turn, had been seduced years before, debauched in the middle of his career, forced into temporary honesty, blackmailed and sent home. In all the years that he had waited for a dreaded countersign—a countersign which he himself never knew to be an extension of Norstrilian intelligence—he never dreamed that he could pay his debt to the outside world so simply. All they had done was to send him one page to add to the encyclopedia. He added it and then went home, weak with exhaustion. The years of fear and waiting were almost too much for the thief. He drank heavily for fear that he might otherwise kill himself. Meanwhile, the pages remained in order, including the new one, slightly altered for his colleagues. The encyclopedia indicated the change like any normal revision, though the whole entry was new and falsified:

Beneath this passage one revision ready. Dated 24th year of second issue.

The reported "Kittons" of Norstrilia are nothing more than the use of organic means to induce the disease in Earth-mutated sheep which produces a virus in its turn, refinable as the santaclara drug. The term "Kittons" enjoyed a temporary vogue as a reference term both to the disease and to the destructibility of the disease in the event of external attack. This is believed to have been connected with the career of Benjamin Hitton, one of the original pioneers of Norstrilia.

The Council of Thieves read it and the Chairman of the Council said, "I've got your papers ready. You can go try them now. Where do you want to go? Through Neuhamburg?"

"No," said Benjacomin. "I thought I'd try Olympia."

"Olympia's all right," said the chairman. "Go easy. There's only one chance in a thousand you'll fail. But if you do, we might have to pay for it."

He smiled wryly and handed Benjacomin a blank mortgage against all the labor and all the property of Viola Siderea.

The Chairman laughed with a sort of snort. "It'd be pretty rough on us if you had to borrow enough on the trading planet to force us to become honest—and then lost out anyhow."

"No fear," said Benjacomin. "I can cover that."

There are some worlds where all dreams die, but square-clouded Olympia is not one of them. The eyes of men and women are bright on Olympia, for they see nothing.

"Brightness was the color of pain," said Nachtigall, "when we could see. If thine eye offend thee, pluck thyself out, for the fault lies not in the eye but in the soul."

Such talk was common in Olympia, where the settlers went blind a long time ago and now think themselves superior to sighted people. Radar wires tickle their living brains; they can perceive radiation as well as can an animal-type man with little aquariums hung in the middle of his face. Their pictures are sharp, and they demand sharpness. Their buildings soar at impossible angles. Their blind children sing songs as the tailored climate proceeds according to the numbers, geometrical as a kaleidoscope.

There went the man, Bozart himself. Among the blind his dreams soared, and he paid money for information which no living person had ever seen.

Sharp-clouded and aqua-skied, Olympia swam past him like another man's dream. He did not mean to tarry there, because he had a rendezvous with death in the sticky, sparky space around Norstrilia.

Once in Olympia, Benjacomin went about his arrangements for the attack on Old North Australia.

On his second day on the planet he had been very lucky. He met a man named Lavender and he was sure he had heard the name before. Not a member of his own Guild of Thieves, but a daring rascal with a bad reputation among the stars.

It was no wonder that he had found Lavender. His pillow had told him Lavender's story fifteen times during his sleep in the past week. And, whenever he dreamed, he dreamed dreams which had been planted in his mind by the Norstrilian counterintelligence. They had beaten him in getting to Olympia first and they were prepared to let him have only that which he deserved. The Norstrilian police were not cruel, but they were out to defend their world. And they were also out to avenge the murder of a child.

The last interview which Benjacomin had with Lavender in striking a bargain before Lavender agreed was a dramatic one.

Lavender refused to move forward.

"I'm not going to jump off anywhere. I'm not going to raid anything. I'm not going to steal anything. I've been rough, of course I have. But I don't get myself killed and that's what you're bloody well asking for."

"Think of what we'll have. The wealth. I tell you, there's more money here than anything else anybody's ever tried."

Lavender laughed. "You think I haven't heard that before? You're a crook and I'm a crook. I don't do anything that's speculation. I want my hard cash down. I'm a fighting man and you're a thief and I'm not going to ask you what you're up to . . . but I want my money first."

"I haven't got it," said Benjacomin.

Lavender stood up.

"Then you shouldn't have talked to me. Because it's going to cost you money to keep me quiet whether you hire me or not."

The bargaining process started.

Lavender looked ugly indeed. He was a soft, ordinary man who had gone to a lot of trouble to become evil. Sin is a lot of work. The sheer effort it requires often shows in the human face.

Bozart stared him down, smiling easily, not even contemptuously.

"Cover me while I get something from my pocket," said Bozart.

Lavender did not even acknowledge the comment. He did not show a weapon. His left thumb moved slowly across the outer edge of his hand. Benjacomin recognized the sign, but did not flinch.

"See," he said. "A planetary credit."

Lavender laughed. "I've heard that, too."

"Take it," said Bozart.

The adventurer took the laminated card. His eyes widened. "It's real," he breathed. "It is real." He looked up, incalculably more friendly. "I never even saw one of these before. What are your terms?"

Meanwhile the bright, vivid Olympians walked back and forth past them, their clothing all white and black in dramatic contrast. Unbelievable geometric designs shone on their cloaks and their hats. The two bargainers ignored the natives. They concentrated on their own negotiations.

Benjacomin felt fairly safe. He placed a pledge of one year's service of the entire planet of Viola Siderea in exchange for the full and unqualified services of Captain Lavender, once of the Imperial Marines Internal Space Patrol. He handed over the mortgage. The year's guarantee was written in. Even on Olympia there were accounting machines which relayed the bargain back to Earth itself, making the mortgage a valid and binding commitment against the whole planet of thieves.

"This," thought Lavender, "was the first step of revenge." After the killer had disappeared his people would have to pay with sheer honesty. Lavender looked at Benjacomin with a clinical sort of concern.

Benjacomin mistook his look for friendliness and Benjacomin smiled his slow, charming, easy smile. Momentarily happy, he reached out his right hand to give Lavender a brotherly solemnification of the bargain. The men shook hands, and Bozart never knew with what he shook hands.

## ∽ 5 ∽

"Gray lay the land oh. Gray grass from sky to sky. Not near the weir, dear. Not a mountain, low or high—only hills and gray gray. Watch the dappled, dimpled twinkles blooming on the star bar.

"That is Norstrilia.

"All the muddy gubbery is gone—all the work and the waiting and the pain.

"Beige-brown sheep lie on blue-gray grass while the clouds rush past, low overhead, like iron pipes ceilinging the world.

"Take your pick of sick sheep, man, it's the sick that pays. Sneeze me a planet, man, or cough me up a spot of immortality. If it's barmy there, where the noddies and the trolls like you live, it's too right here.

"That's the book, boy.

"If you haven't seen Norstrilia, you haven't seen it. If you did see it, you wouldn't believe it.

"Charts call it Old North Australia."

Here in the heart of the world was the farm which guarded the world. This was the Hitton place.

Towers surrounded it, and wires hung between the towers, some of them drooping crazily and some gleaming with the sheen not shown by any other metal made by men from Earth. Within the towers there was open land. And within the open land there were twelve thousand hectares of concrete. Radar reached down to within millimeter smoothness of the surface of the concrete and the other radar threw patterns back and forth, down through molecular thinness. The farm went on. In its center there was a group of buildings. That was where Katherine Hitton worked on the task which her family had accepted for the defense of her world.

No germ came in, no germ went out. All the food came in by space transmitter. Within this, there lived animals. The animals depended on her alone. Were she to die suddenly, by mischance or as a result of an attack by one of the animals, the authorities of her world had complete facsimiles of herself with which to train new animal tenders under hypnosis.

This was a place where the gray wind leapt forward released from the hills, where it raced across the gray concrete, where it blew past the radar towers. The polished, faceted, captive moon always hung due overhead. The wind hit the buildings, themselves gray, with the impact of a blow, before it raced over the open concrete beyond and whistled away into the hills.

Outside the buildings, the valley had not needed much camouflage. It looked like the rest of Norstrilia. The concrete itself was tinted very slightly to give the impression of poor, starved, natural soil. This was the farm, and this the woman. Together they were the outer defense of the richest world mankind had ever built.

Katherine Hitton looked out the window and thought to herself, "Forty-two days before I go to market and it's a welcome day that I get there and hear the jig of a music."

> *Oh, to walk on market day,*
> *And see my people proud and gay!*

She breathed deeply of the air. She loved the gray hills—though in her youth she had seen many other worlds. And then she turned back into the building to the animals and the duties which awaited her. She was the only Mother Hitton and these were her littul kittons.

She moved among them. She and her father had bred them from Earth mink, from the fiercest, smallest, craziest little minks that had ever been shipped out from Manhome. Out of these minks they had made their lives to keep away other predators who might bother the sheep on whom the stroon grew. But these minks were born mad.

Generations of them had been bred psychotic to the bone. They lived only to die and they died so that they could stay alive. These were the kittons of Norstrilia. Animals in whom fear, rage, hunger, and sex were utterly intermixed; who could eat themselves or each other; who could eat their young, or people, or anything organic; animals who screamed with murder-lust when they felt love; animals born to loathe themselves with a fierce and livid hate and who survived only because their waking moments were spent on couches, strapped tight, claw by claw, so that they could not hurt each other or themselves. Mother Hitton let them waken only a few moments in each lifetime. They bred and killed. She wakened them only two at a time.

All that afternoon she moved from cage to cage. The sleeping animals slept well. The nourishment ran into their blood streams; they lived sometimes for years without awaking. She bred them when the males were only partly awakened and the females aroused only enough to accept her veterinary treatments. She herself had to pluck the young away from their mothers as the sleeping mothers begot them. Then she nourished the young through a few happy weeks of kittonhood, until their adult natures began to take, their eyes ran red with madness and heat, and their emotions sounded in the sharp, hideous, little cries they uttered through the building; and the twisting of their neat, furry faces, the rolling of their crazy, bright eyes, and the tightening of their sharp, sharp claws.

She woke none of them this time. Instead, she tightened them in their straps. She removed the nutrients. She gave them delayed stimulus medicine which would, when they were awakened, bring them suddenly full waking with no lulled stupor first.

Finally, she gave herself a heavy sedative, leaned back in a chair, and waited for the call which would come.

When the shock came and the call came through,

she would have to do what she had done thousands of times before.

She would ring an intolerable noise through the whole laboratory.

Hundreds of the mutated minks would awaken. In awakening, they would plunge into life with hunger, with hate, with rage, and with sex; plunge against their straps; strive to kill each other, their young, themselves, her. They would fight everything and everywhere, and do everything they could to keep going.

She knew this.

In the middle of the room there was a tuner. The tuner was a direct, empathic relay, capable of picking up the simpler range of telepathic communications. Into this tuner went the concentrated emotions of Mother Hitton's littul kittons.

The rage, the hate, the hunger, the sex were all carried far beyond the limits of the tolerable, and then all were thereupon amplified. And then the waveband on which this telepathic control went out was amplified, right there beyond the studio, on the high towers that swept the mountain ridge, up and beyond the valley in which the laboratory lay. And Mother Hitton's moon, spinning geometrically, bounced the relay into a hollow englobement

From the faceted moon, it went to the satellites—sixteen of them, apparently part of the weather control system. These blanketed not only space, but nearby subspace. The Norstrilians had thought of everything.

The short shocks of an alert came from Mother Hitton's transmitter bank.

A call came. Her thumb went numb.

The noise shrieked.

The mink awakened.

Immediately, the room was full of chattering, scraping, hissing, growling, and howling.

Under the sound of the animal voices, there was the other sound: a scratchy, snapping sound like hail falling on a frozen lake. It was the individual claws of hundreds of mink trying to tear their way through metal panels.

Mother Hitton heard a gurgle. One of the minks had succeeded in tearing its paw loose and had obviously started to work on its own throat. She recognized the tearing fur, the ripping of veins.

She listened for the cessation of that individual voice, but she couldn't be sure. The others were making too much noise. One mink less.

Where she sat, she was partly shielded from the telepathic relay, but not altogether. She herself, old as she was, felt queer wild dreams go through her. She thrilled with hate as she thought of beings suffering out beyond her—suffering terribly, since they were not masked by the built-in defenses of the Norstrilian communications system.

She felt the wild throb of long-forgotten lust.

She hungered for things she had not known she remembered. She went through the spasms of fear that the hundreds of animals expressed.

Underneath this, her sane mind kept asking. "How much longer can I take it? How much longer must I take it? Lord God, be good to your people here on this world! Be good to poor old me."

The green light went on.

She pressed a button on the other side of her chair. The gas hissed in. As she passed into unconsciousness, she knew that her kittons passed into instant unconsciousness too.

She would waken before they did and then her duties would begin: checking the living ones, taking out the one that had clawed out its own throat, taking out those who had died of heart attacks, re-arranging them, dressing their wounds, treating them alive and asleep—asleep and happy—breeding, living in their sleep—until the next call should come to waken them for the defense of the treasures which blessed and cursed her native world.

## ∞ 6 ∞

Everything had gone exactly right. Lavender had found an illegal planoform ship. This was no inconsequential accomplishment, since planoform ships were very strictly licensed and obtaining an illegal one was a chore on which a planet full of crooks could easily have worked a lifetime.

Lavender had been lavished with money— Benjacomin's money.

The honest wealth of the thieves' planet had gone in and had paid the falsifications and great debts, imaginary transactions that were fed to the computers for ships and cargoes and passengers that would be almost untraceably commingled in the commerce of ten thousand worlds.

"Let him pay for it," said Lavender, to one of his confederates, an apparent criminal who was also a Norstrilian agent. "This is paying good money for bad. You better spend a lot of it."

Just before Benjacomin took off Lavender sent on an additional message.

He sent it directly through the Go-Captain, who usually did not carry messages. The Go-Captain was a relay commander of the Norstrilian fleet, but he had been carefully ordered not to look like it.

The message concerned the planoform license—another twenty-odd tablets of stroon which could mortgage Viola Siderea for hundreds upon hundreds of years. The captain said: "I don't have to send that through. The answer is yes."

Benjacomin came into the control room. This was contrary to regulations, but he had hired the ship to violate regulations.

The Captain looked at him sharply. "You're a passenger. Get out."

Benjacomin said: "You have my little yacht on board. I am the only man here outside of your people."

"Get out. There's a fine if you're caught here."

"It does not matter," Benjacomin said. "I'll pay it."

"You will, will you?" said the Captain. "You would not be paying twenty tablets of stroon. That's ridiculous. Nobody could get that much stroon."

Benjacomin laughed, thinking of the thousands of tablets he would soon have. All he had to do was to leave the planoform ship behind, strike once, go past the kittons and come back.

His power and his wealth came from the fact that he knew he could now reach it. The mortgage of twenty tablets of stroon against this planet was a low price to pay if it would pay off at thousands to one. The Captain replied: "It's not worth it, it just is not worth risking twenty tablets for your being here. But I can tell you how to get inside the Norstrilian communications net if that is worth twenty-seven tablets."

Benjacomin went tense.

For a moment he thought he might die. All this work, all this training—the dead boy on the beach, the gamble with the credit; and now this unsuspected antagonist!

He decided to face it out. "What do you know?" said Benjacomin.

"Nothing," said the Captain.

"You said 'Norstrilia.'"

"That I did," said the Captain.

"If you said Norstrilia, you must have guessed it. Who told you?"

"Where else would a man go if you look for infinite riches? If you get away with it. Twenty tablets is nothing to a man like you."

"It's two hundred years' worth of work from three hundred thousand people," said Benjacomin grimly.

"When you get away with it, you will have more than twenty tablets, and so will your people."

And Benjacomin thought of the thousands and thousands of tablets. "Yes, that I know."

"If you don't get away with it, you've got the card."

"That's right. All right. Get me inside the net. I'll pay the twenty-seven tablets."

"Give me the card."

Benjacomin refused. He was a trained thief, and he was alert to thievery. Then he thought again. This was the crisis of his life. He had to gamble a little on somebody.

He had to wager the card. "I'll mark it and then I'll give it back to you." Such was his excitement that

Benjacomin did not notice that the card went into a duplicator, that the transaction was recorded, that the message went back to Olympia Center, that the loss and the mortgage against the planet of Viola Siderea should be credited to certain commercial agencies in Earth for three hundred years to come.

Benjacomin got the card back. He felt like an honest thief.

If he did die, the card would be lost and his people would not have to pay. If he won, he could pay that little bit out of his own pocket.

Benjacomin sat down. The Go-captain signaled to his pinlighters. The ship lurched.

For half a subjective hour they moved, the Captain wearing a helmet of space upon his head, sensing and grasping and guessing his way, stepping stone to stepping stone, right back to his home. He had to fumble the passage, or else Benjacomin might guess that he was in the hands of double agents.

But the captain was well trained. Just as well trained as Benjacomin.

Agents and thieves, they rode together.

They planoformed inside the communications net. Benjacomin shook hands with them. "You are allowed to materialize as soon as I call."

"Good luck, Sir," said the Captain.

"Good luck to me," said Benjacomin.

He climbed into his space yacht. For less than a second in real space, the gray expanse of Norstrilia loomed up. The ship which looked like a simple warehouse disappeared into planoform, and the yacht was on its own.

The yacht dropped.

As it dropped, Benjacomin had a hideous moment of confusion and terror.

He never knew the woman down below but she sensed him plainly as he received the wrath of the much-amplified kittons. His conscious mind quivered under the blow. With a prolongation of subjective experience which made one or two seconds seem like months of hurt drunken bewilderment, Benjacomin Bozart swept beneath the tide of his own personality. The moon relay threw minkish minds against him. The synapses of his brain re-formed to conjure up might-have-beens, terrible things that never happened to any man. Then his knowing mind whited out in an overload of stress.

His subcortical personality lived on a little longer.

His body fought for several minutes. Mad with lust and hunger, the body arched in the pilot's seat, the mouth bit deep into his own arm. Driven by lust, the left hand tore at his face, ripping out his left eyeball. He screeched with animal lust as he tried to devour himself . . . not entirely without success.

The overwhelming telepathic message of Mother Hitton's littul kittons ground into his brain.

The mutated minks were fully awake.

The relay satellites had poisoned all the space around him with the craziness to which the minks were bred.

Bozart's body did not live long. After a few minutes, the arteries were open, the head slumped forward, and the yacht was dropping helplessly toward the warehouses which it had meant to raid. Norstrilian police picked it up.

The police themselves were ill. All of them were

ill. All of them were white-faced. Some of them had vomited. They had gone through the edge of the mink defense. They had passed through the telepathic band at its thinnest and weakest point. This was enough to hurt them badly.

They did not want to know.

They wanted to forget.

One of the younger policemen looked at the body and said, "What on earth could do that to a man?"

"He picked the wrong job," said the police captain.

The young policeman said: "What's the wrong job?"

"The wrong job is trying to rob us, boy. We are defended, and we don't want to know how."

The young policeman, humiliated and on the verge of anger, looked almost as if he would defy his superior, while keeping his eyes away from the body of Benjacomin Bozart.

The older man said: "It's all right. He did not take long to die and this is the man who killed the boy Johnny, not very long ago."

"Oh, him? So soon?"

"We brought him." The old police officer nodded. "We let him find his death. That's how we live. Tough, isn't it?"

The ventilators whispered softly, gently. The animals slept again. A jet of air poured down on Mother Hitton. The telepathic relay was still on. She could feel herself, the sheds, the faceted moon, the little satellites. Of the robber there was no sign.

She stumbled to her feet. Her raiment was moist with perspiration. She needed a shower and fresh clothes . . .

Back at Manhome, the Commercial Credit Circuit called shrilly for human attention. A junior subchief of the Instrumentality walked over to the machine and held out his hand.

The machine dropped a card neatly into his fingers.

He looked at the card.

"Debit Viola Siderea—credit Earth Contingency—subcredit Norstrilian account—four hundred million man megayears."

Though all alone, he whistled to himself in the empty room. "We'll all be dead, stroon or no stroon, before they finish paying that!" He went off to tell his friends the odd news.

The machine, not getting its card back, made another one.

# Alpha Ralpha Boulevard

We were drunk with happiness in those early years. Everybody was, especially the young people. These were the first years of the Rediscovery of Man, when the Instrumentality dug deep in the treasury, reconstructing the old cultures, the old languages, and even the old troubles. The nightmare of perfection had taken our forefathers to the edge of suicide. Now under the leadership of the Lord Jestocost and the Lady Alice More, the ancient civilizations were rising like great land masses out of the sea of the past.

I myself was the first man to put a postage stamp on a letter, after fourteen thousand years. I took Virginia to hear the first piano recital. We watched at the eye-machine when cholera was released in Tasmania, and we saw the Tasmanians dancing in the streets, now that they did not have to be protected any more. Everywhere, things became exciting. Everywhere, men and women worked with a wild will to build a more imperfect world.

I myself went into a hospital and came out French. Of course I remembered my early life; I remembered it, but it did not matter. Virginia was French, too, and we had the years of our future lying ahead of us like ripe fruit hanging in an orchard of perpetual summers. We had no idea when we would die. Formerly, I would be able to go to bed and think, "The government has given me four hundred years. Three hundred and seventy-four years from now, they will stop the stroon injections and I will then die." Now I knew anything could happen. The safety devices had been turned off. The diseases ran free. With luck, and hope, and love, I might live a thousand years. Or I might die tomorrow. I was free.

We revelled in every moment of the day.

Virginia and I bought the first French newspaper to appear since the Most Ancient World fell. We found delight in the news, even in the advertisements. Some parts of the culture were hard to reconstruct. It was difficult to talk about foods of which only the names survived, but the homunculi and the machines, working tirelessly in Downdeep-downdeep, kept the surface of the world filled with enough novelties to fill anyone's heart with hope. We knew that all of this was make-believe, and yet it was not. We knew that when the diseases had killed the statistically correct number of people, they would be turned off; when the accident rate rose too high, it would stop without our knowing why. We knew that over us all, the Instrumentality watched. We had confidence that the Lord Jestocost and the Lady Alice More would play with us as friends and not use us as victims of a game.

Take, for example, Virginia. She had been called Menerima, which represented the coded sounds of her birth number. She was small, verging on chubby; she was compact; her head was covered with tight brown curls; her eyes were a brown so deep and so rich that it took sunlight, with her squinting against it, to bring forth the treasures of her irises. I had known her well, but never known her. I had seen her often, but never seen her with my heart, until we met just outside the hospital, after becoming French.

I was pleased to see an old friend and started to speak in the Old Common Tongue, but the words jammed, and as I tried to speak it was not Menerima any longer, but someone of ancient beauty, rare and strange—someone who had wandered into these latter days from the treasure worlds of time past. All I could do was to stammer:

"What do you call yourself now?" And I said it in ancient French.

She answered in the same language, *"Je m'appelle Virginie."*

Looking at her and falling in love was a single process. There was something strong, something wild in her, wrapped and hidden by the tenderness and youth of her girlish body. It was as though destiny spoke to me out of the certain brown eyes, eyes which questioned me surely and wonderingly, just as we both questioned the fresh new world which lay about us.

"May I?" said I, offering her my arm, as I had learned in the hours of hypnopedia. She took my arm and we walked away from the hospital.

I hummed a tune which had come into my mind, along with the ancient French language.

She tugged gently on my arm, and smiled up at me.

"What is it," she asked, "or don't you know?"

The words came soft and unbidden to my lips and I sang it very quietly, muting my voice in her curly hair, half-singing half-whispering the popular song which

had poured into my mind with all the other things
which the Rediscovery of Man had given me:

> *She wasn't the woman I went to seek.*
> *I met her by the merest chance.*
> *She did not speak the French of France,*
> *But the surdèd French of Martinique.*
>
> *She wasn't rich. She wasn't chic.*
> *She had a most entrancing glance,*
> *And that was all. . . .*

Suddenly I ran out of words. "I seem to have forgotten the rest of it. It's called 'Macouba' and it has
something to do with a wonderful island which the
ancient French called Martinique."

"I know where that is," she cried. She had been
given the same memories that I had. "You can see it
from Earthport!"

This was a sudden return to the world we had
known. Earthport stood on its single pedestal, twelve
miles high, at the eastern edge of the small continent.
At the top of it, the Lords worked amid machines
which had no meaning any more. There the ships
whispered their way in from the stars. I had seen
pictures of it, but I had never been there. As a
matter of fact, I had never known anyone who had
actually been up Earthport. Why should we have
gone? We might not have been welcome, and we
could always see it just as well through the pictures on the eye-machine. For Menerima—familiar,
dully pleasant, dear little Menerima—to have gone
there was uncanny. It made me think that in the

Old Perfect World things had not been as plain or forthright as they seemed.

Virginia, the new Menerima, tried to speak in the Old Common Tongue, but she gave up and used French instead:

"My aunt," she said, meaning a kindred lady, since no one had had aunts for thousands of years, "was a Believer. She took me to the Abba-dingo. To get holiness and luck."

The old me was a little shocked; the French me was disquieted by the fact that this girl had done something unusual even before mankind itself turned to the unusual. The Abba-dingo was a long-obsolete computer set part way up the column of Earthport. The homunculi treated it as a god, and occasionally people went to it. To do so was tedious and vulgar.

Or had been. Till all things became new again.

Keeping the annoyance out of my voice, I asked her: "What was it like?"

She laughed lightly, yet there was a trill to her laughter which gave me a shiver. If the old Menerima had had secrets, what might the new Virginia do? I almost hated the fate which made me love her, which made me feel that the touch of her hand on my arm was a link between me and time-forever.

She smiled at me instead of answering my question. The surfaceway was under repair; we followed a ramp down to the level of the top underground, where it was legal for true persons and hominids and homunculi to walk.

I did not like the feeling; I had never gone more than twenty minutes' trip from my birthplace. This ramp looked safe enough. There were few hominids around these days, men from the stars who (though of true human stock) had been changed to fit the conditions of a thousand worlds. The homunculi were morally repulsive, though many of them looked like very handsome people; bred from animals into the shape of men, they took over the tedious chores of working with machines where no real man would wish to go. It was whispered that some of them had even bred with actual people, and I would not want my Virginia to be exposed to the presence of such a creature.

She had been holding my arm. When we walked down the ramp to the busy passage, I slipped my arm free and put it over her shoulders, drawing her closer to me. It was light enough, bright enough to be clearer than the daylight which we had left behind, but it was strange and full of danger. In the old days, I would have turned around and gone home rather than expose myself to the presence of such dreadful beings. At this time, in this moment, I could not bear to part from my new-found love, and I was afraid that if I went back to my own apartment in the tower, she might go to hers. Anyhow, being French gave a spice to danger.

Actually, the people in the traffic looked commonplace enough. There were many busy machines, some in human form and some not. I did not see a single hominid. Other people, whom I knew to be homunculi because they yielded the right of way to us, looked no different from the real human beings on the surface. A brilliantly beautiful girl gave me a look which I did not like—saucy, intelligent, provocative beyond all limits of flirtation. I suspected her of being a dog by origin. Among the homunculi, d'persons are the ones most apt to take liberties. They even have a dog-man philosopher who once produced a tape arguing that since dogs are the most ancient of men's allies, they have the right to be closer to man than any other form of life. When I saw the tape, I thought it amusing that a dog should be bred into the form of a Socrates; here, in the top underground, I was not so sure at all. What would I do if one of them became insolent? Kill him? That meant a brush with the law and a talk with the Subcommissioners of the Instrumentality.

Virginia noticed none of this.

She had not answered my question, but was asking me questions about the top underground instead. I had been there only once before, when I was small, but it was flattering to have her wondering, husky voice murmuring in my ear.

Then it happened.

At first I thought he was a man, foreshortened by some trick of the underground light. When he came closer, I saw that he was not. He must have been five feet across the shoulders. Ugly red scars on his forehead showed where the horns had been dug out of his skull. He was a homunculus, obviously derived from cattle stock. Frankly, I had never known that they left them that ill-formed.

And he was drunk.

As he came closer I could pick up the buzz of his mind. . . . *they're not people, they're not hominids, and they're not Us—what are they doing here? The words they think confuse me.* He had never telepathed French before.

This was bad. For him to talk was common enough,

but only a few of the homunculi were telepathic—those with special jobs, such as in the Downdeep-downdeep, where only telepathy could relay instructions.

Virginia clung to me.

Thought I, in clear Common Tongue: *True men are we. You must let us pass.*

There was no answer but a roar. I do not know where he got drunk, or on what, but he did not get my message.

I could see his thoughts forming up into panic, helplessness, hate. Then he charged, almost dancing toward us, as though he could crush our bodies.

My mind focused and I threw the stop order at him.

It did not work.

Horror-stricken, I realized that I had thought French at him.

Virginia screamed.

The bull-man was upon us.

At the last moment he swerved, passed us blindly, and let out a roar which filled the enormous passage. He had raced beyond us.

Still holding Virginia, I turned around to see what had made him pass us.

What I beheld was odd in the extreme.

Our figures ran down the corridor away from us—my black-purple cloak flying in the still air as my image ran, Virginia's golden dress swimming out behind her as she ran with me. The images were perfect and the bull-man pursued them.

I stared around in bewilderment. We had been told that the safeguards no longer protected us.

A girl stood quietly next to the wall. I had almost mistaken her for a statue. Then she spoke,

"Come no closer. I am a cat. It was easy enough to fool him. You had better get back to the surface."

"Thank you," I said, "thank you. What is your name?"

"Does it matter?" said the girl. "I'm not a person."

A little offended, I insisted, "I just wanted to thank you." As I spoke to her I saw that she was as beautiful and as bright as a flame. Her skin was clear, the color of cream, and her hair—finer than any human hair could possibly be—was the wild golden orange of a Persian cat.

"I'm C'mell," said the girl, "and I work at Earthport."

That stopped both Virginia and me. Cat-people were below us, and should be shunned, but Earthport was above us, and had to be respected. Which was C'mell?

She smiled, and her smile was better suited for my eyes than for Virginia's. It spoke a whole world of voluptuous knowledge. I knew she wasn't trying to do anything to me; the rest of her manner showed that. Perhaps it was the only smile she knew.

"Don't worry," she said, "about the formalities. You'd better take these steps here. I hear him coming back."

I spun around, looking for the drunken bull-man. He was not to be seen.

"Go up here," urged C'mell. "They are emergency steps and you will be back on the surface. I can keep him from following. Was that French you were speaking?"

"Yes," said I. "How did you—?"

"Get along," she said. "Sorry I asked. Hurry!"

I entered the small door. A spiral staircase went to the surface. It was below our dignity as true people to use steps, but with C'mell urging me, there was nothing else I could do. I nodded goodbye to C'mell and drew Virginia after me up the stairs.

At the surface we stopped.

Virginia gasped, "Wasn't it horrible?"

"We're safe now," said I.

"It's not safety," she said. "It's the dirtiness of it. Imagine having to talk to her!"

Virginia meant that C'mell was worse than the drunken bull-man. She sensed my reserve because she said,

"The sad thing is, you'll see her again . . ."

"What! How do you know that?"

"I don't know it," said Virginia. "I guess it. But I guess good, very good. After all, I went to the Abba-dingo."

"I asked you, darling, to tell me what happened there."

She shook her head mutely and began walking down the streetway. I had no choice but to follow her. It made me a little irritable.

I asked again, more crossly, "What was it like?"

With hurt girlish dignity she said, "Nothing, nothing. It was a long climb. The old woman made me go with her. It turned out that the machine was not talking that day, anyhow, so we got permission to drop down a shaft and to come back on the rolling road. It was just a wasted day."

She had been talking straight ahead, not to me, as though the memory were a little ugly.

Then she turned her face to me. The brown eyes looked into my eyes as though she were searching for my soul. (Soul. There's a word we have in French, and there is nothing quite like it in the Old Common Tongue.) She brightened and pleaded with me:

"Let's not be dull on the new day. Let's be good to the new us, Paul. Let's do something really French, if that's what we are to be.

"A café," I cried. "We need a café. And I know where one is."

"Where?"

"Two undergrounds over. Where the machines come out and where they permit the homunculi to peer in the window." The thought of homunculi peering at us struck the new me as amusing, though the old me had taken them as much for granted as windows or tables. The old me never met any, but knew that they weren't exactly people, since they were bred from animals, but they looked just like people, and they could talk. It took a Frenchman like the new me to realize that they could be ugly, or beautiful, or picturesque. More than picturesque: romantic.

Evidently Virginia now thought the same, for she said, "But they're *nette*, just adorable. What is the café called?"

"The Greasy Cat," said I.

The Greasy Cat. How was I to know that this led to a nightmare between high waters, and to the winds which cried? How was I to suppose that this had anything to do with Alpha Ralpha Boulevard?

No force in the world could have taken me there, if I had known.

Other new-French people had gotten to the café before us.

A waiter with a big brown moustache took our

order. I looked closely at him to see if he might be a
licensed homunculus, allowed to work among people
because his services were indispensable; but he was
not. He was pure machine, though his voice rang out
with old-Parisian heartiness, and the designers had
even built into him the nervous habit of mopping the
back of his hand against his big moustache, and had
fixed him so that little beads of sweat showed high
up on his brow, just below the hairline.

"Mamselle? M'sieu? Beer? Coffee? Red wine next
month. The sun will shine in the quarter after the
hour and after the half-hour. At twenty minutes to
the hour it will rain for five minutes so that you can
enjoy these umbrellas. I am a native of Alsace. You
may speak French or German to me."

"Anything," said Virginia. "You decide, Paul."

"Beer, please," said I. "Blonde beer for both of us."

"But certainly, M'sieu," said the waiter.

He left, waving his cloth wildly over his arm.

Virginia puckered up her eyes against the sun and
said, "I wish it would rain now. I've never seen real rain."

"Be patient, honey."

She turned earnestly to me. "What is 'German,'
Paul?"

"Another language, another culture. I read they
will bring it to life next year. But don't you like being
French?"

"I like it fine," she said. "Much better than being
a number. But, Paul—" And then she stopped, her
eyes blurred with perplexity.

"Yes, darling?"

"Paul," she said, and the statement of my name was a
cry of hope from some depth of her mind beyond new

me, beyond old me, beyond even the contrivances of the Lords who moulded us. I reached for her hand.

Said I, "You can tell me, darling."

"Paul," she said, and it was almost weeping, "Paul, why does it all happen so fast? This is our first day, and we both feel that we may spend the rest of our lives together. There's something about marriage, whatever that is, and we're supposed to find a priest, and I don't understand that, either. Paul, Paul, Paul, why does it happen so fast? I want to love you. I do love you. But I don't want to be *made* to love you. I want it to be the real me," and as she spoke, tears poured from her eyes though her voice remained steady enough.

Then it was that I said the wrong thing.

"You don't have to worry, honey. I'm sure that the Lords of the Instrumentality have programmed everything well."

At that, she burst into tears, loudly and uncontrollably. I had never seen an adult weep before. It was strange and frightening.

A man from the next table came over and stood beside me, but I did not so much as glance at him.

"Darling," said I, reasonably, "darling, we can work it out—"

"Paul, let me leave you, so that I may be yours. Let me go away for a few days or a few weeks or a few years. Then, if—if—if I *do* come back, you'll know it's me and not some program ordered by a machine. For God's sake, Paul—for God's sake!" In a different voice she said, "What is God, Paul? They gave us the words to speak, but I do not know what they mean."

The man beside me spoke. "I can take you to God," he said.

"Who are you?" said I. "And who asked you to interfere?" This was not the kind of language that we had ever used when speaking the Old Commón Tongue—when they had given us a new language they had built in temperament as well.

The stranger kept his politeness—he was as French as we but he kept his temper well.

"My name," he said, "is Maximilien Macht, and I used to be a Believer."

Virginia's eyes lit up. She wiped her face absent-mindedly while staring at the man. He was tall, lean, sunburned. (How could he have gotten sunburned so soon?) He had reddish hair and a moustache almost like that of the robot waiter.

"You asked about God, Mamselle," said the stranger. "God is where he has always been—around us, near us, in us."

This was strange talk from a man who looked worldly. I rose to my feet to bid him goodbye. Virginia guessed what I was doing and she said:

"That's nice of you, Paul. Give him a chair."

There was warmth in her voice.

The machine waiter came back with two conical beakers made of glass. They had a golden fluid in them with a cap of foam on top. I had never seen or heard of beer before, but I knew exactly how it would taste. I put imaginary money on the tray, received imaginary change, paid the waiter an imaginary tip. The Instrumentality had not yet figured out how to have separate kinds of money for all the new cultures, and of course you could not use real money to pay for food or drink. Food and drink are free.

The machine wiped his moustache, used his serviette

(checked red and white) to dab the sweat off his brow, and then looked inquiringly at Monsieur Macht.

"M'sieu, you will sit here?"

"Indeed," said Macht.

"Shall I serve you here?"

"But why not?" said Macht. "If these good people permit."

"Very well," said the machine, wiping his moustache with the back of his hand. He fled to the dark recesses of the bar.

All this time Virginia had not taken her eyes off Macht.

"You are a Believer?" she asked. "You are still a Believer, when you have been made French like us? How do you know you're you? Why do I love Paul? Are the Lords and their machines controlling everything in us? I want to be *me*. Do you know how to be *me*?"

"Not you, Mamselle," said Macht. "That would be too great an honor. But I am learning how to be myself. You see," he added, turning to me, "I have been French for two weeks now, and I know how much of me is myself, and how much has been added by this new process of giving us language and danger again."

The waiter came back with a small beaker. It stood on a stem, so that it looked like an evil little miniature of Earthport. The fluid it contained was milky white.

Macht lifted his glass to us. "Your health!"

Virginia stared at him as if she were going to cry again. When he and I sipped, she blew her nose and put her handkerchief away. It was the first time I had ever seen a person perform that act of blowing the nose, but it seemed to go well with our new culture.

Macht smiled at both of us, as if he were going to begin a speech. The sun came out, right on time. It gave him a halo, and made him look like a devil or a saint.

But it was Virginia who spoke first.

"You have been there?"

Macht raised his eyebrows a little, frowned, and said, "Yes," very quietly.

"Did you get a word?" she persisted.

"Yes." He looked glum, and a little troubled.

"What did it say?"

For answer, he shook his head at her, as if there were things which should never be mentioned in public.

I wanted to break in, to find out what this was all about.

Virginia went on, heeding me not at all: "But it did say something!"

"Yes," said Macht.

"Was it important?"

"Mamselle, let us not talk about it."

"We must," she cried. "It's life or death." Her hands were clenched so tightly together that her knuckles showed white. Her beer stood in front of her, untouched, growing warm in the sunlight.

"Very well," said Macht, "you may ask . . . I cannot guarantee to answer."

I controlled myself no longer. "What's all this about?"

Virginia looked at me with scorn, but even her scorn was the scorn of a lover, not the cold remoteness of the past. "Please, Paul, you wouldn't know. Wait a while. What did it say to you, M'sieu Macht?"

"That I, Maximilien Macht, would live or die with a brown-haired girl who was already betrothed." He smiled wryly. "And I do not even quite know what 'betrothed' means."

"We'll find out," said Virginia. "When did it say this?"

"Who is 'it'?" I shouted at them. "For God's sake, what is this all about?"

Macht looked at me and dropped his voice when he spoke: "The Abba-dingo." To her he said, "Last week."

Virginia turned white. "So it does work, it does, it does. Paul darling, it said nothing to me. But it said to my aunt something which I can't ever forget!"

I held her arm firmly and tenderly and tried to look into her eyes, but she looked away. Said I, "What did it say?"

"Paul and Virginia."

"So what?" said I.

I scarcely knew her. Her lips were tense and compressed. She was not angry. It was something different, worse. She was in the grip of tension. I suppose we had not seen that for thousands of years, either. "Paul, seize this simple fact, if you can grasp it. The machine gave that woman our names—but it gave them to her twelve years ago."

Macht stood up so suddenly that his chair fell over, and the waiter began running toward us.

"That settles it," he said. "We're all going back."

"Going where?" I said.

"To the Abba-dingo."

"But why now?" said I; and, "Will it work?" said Virginia, both at the same time.

"It always works," said Macht, "if you go on the northern side."

"How do you get there?" said Virginia.

Macht frowned sadly. "There's only one way. By Alpha Ralpha Boulevard." Virginia stood up. And so did I.

Then, as I rose, I remembered. Alpha Ralpha Boulevard. It was a ruined street hanging in the sky, faint as a vapor trail. It had been a processional highway once, where conquerors came down and tribute went up. But it was ruined, lost in the clouds, closed to mankind for a hundred centuries.

"I know it," said I. "It's ruined."

Macht said nothing, but he stared at me as if I were an outsider . . .

Virginia, very quiet and white of countenance, said, "Come along."

"But why," said I. "Why?"

"You fool," she said, "if we don't have a God, at least we have a machine. This is the only thing left on or off the world which the Instrumentality doesn't understand. Maybe it tells the future. Maybe it's an unmachine. It certainly comes from a different time. Can't you use it, darling? If it says we're us, we're *us*."

"And if it doesn't?"

"Then we're not." Her face was sullen with grief.

"What do you mean?"

"If we're not us," she said, "we're just toys, dolls, puppets that the Lords have written on. You're not you and I'm not me. But if the Abba-dingo, which knew the names Paul and Virginia twelve years before it happened—if the Abba-dingo says that we are us, I don't care if it's a predicting machine or a god or a devil or a what. I don't care, but I'll have the truth."

What could I have answered to that? Macht led, she followed, and I walked third in single file. We left the sunlight of The Greasy Cat; just as we left, a light rain began to fall. The waiter, looking momentarily like the machine that he was, stared straight ahead. We crossed the lip of the underground and went down to the fast expressway.

When we came out, we were in a region of fine homes. All were in ruins. The trees had thrust their way into the buildings. Flowers rioted across the lawn, through the open doors, and blazed in the roofless rooms. Who needed a house in the open, when the population of Earth had dropped so that the cities were commodious and empty?

Once I thought I saw a family of homunculi, including little ones, peering at me as we trudged along the soft gravel road. Maybe the faces I had seen at the edge of the house were fantasies.

Macht said nothing.

Virginia and I held hands as we walked beside him. I could have been happy at this odd excursion, but her hand was tightly clenched in mine. She bit her lower lip from time to time. I knew it mattered to her—she was on a pilgrimage. (A pilgrimage was an ancient walk to some powerful place, very good for body and soul.) I didn't mind going along. In fact, they could not have kept me from coming, once she and Macht decided to leave the café. But I didn't have to take it seriously. Did I?

What did Macht want?

Who was Macht? What thoughts had that mind learned in two short weeks? How had he preceded us into a new world of danger and adventure? I did not trust him. For the first time in my life I felt alone. Always, always, up to now, I had only to think about the Instrumentality and some protector leaped fully armed into my mind. Telepathy guarded against all dangers, healed all hurts, carried each of us forward to the one hundred and forty-six thousand and ninety-seven days which had been allotted us. Now it was different. I did not know this man, and it was on him that I relied, not on the powers which had shielded and protected us.

We turned from the ruined road into an immense boulevard. The pavement was so smooth and unbroken that nothing grew on it, save where the wind and dust had deposited random little pockets of earth.

Macht stopped.

"This is it," he said. "Alpha Ralpha Boulevard."

We fell silent and looked at the causeway of forgotten empires.

To our left the boulevard disappeared in a gentle curve. It led far north of the city in which I had been reared. I knew that there was another city to the north, but I had forgotten its name. Why should I have remembered it? It was sure to be just like my own.

But to the right—

To the right the boulevard rose sharply, like a ramp. It disappeared into the clouds. Just at the edge of the cloud-line there was a hint of disaster. I could not see for sure, but it looked to me as though the whole boulevard had been sheared off by unimaginable forces. Somewhere beyond the clouds there stood the Abba-dingo, the place where all questions were answered . . .

Or so they thought.

Virginia cuddled close to me.

"Let's turn back," said I. "We are city people. We don't know anything about ruins."

"You can if you want to," said Macht. "I was just trying to do you a favor."

We both looked at Virginia.

She looked up at me with those brown eyes. From the eyes there came a plea older than woman or man, older than the human race. I knew what she was going to say before she said it. She was going to say that she *had* to know.

Macht was idly crushing some soft rocks near his foot.

At last Virginia spoke up: "Paul, I don't want danger for its own sake. But I meant what I said back there. Isn't there a chance that we were *told* to love each other? What sort of a life would it be if our happiness, our own selves, depended on a thread in a machine or on a mechanical voice which spoke to us when we were asleep and learning French? It may be fun to go back to the old world. I guess it is. I know that you give me a kind of happiness which I never even suspected before this day. If it's really us, we have something wonderful, and we ought to know it. But if it isn't—" She burst into sobs.

I wanted to say, "If it isn't, it will seem just the same," but the ominous sulky face of Macht looked at me over Virginia's shoulder as I drew her to me. There was nothing to say.

I held her close.

From beneath Macht's foot there flowed a trickle of blood. The dust drank it up.

"Macht," said I, "are you hurt?"

Virginia turned around, too.

Macht raised his eyebrows at me and said with unconcern, "No. Why?"

"The blood. At your feet."

He glanced down. "Oh, those," he said, "they're nothing. Just the eggs of some kind of an un-bird which does not even fly."

"Stop it!" I shouted telepathically, using the Old Common Tongue. I did not even try to think in our new-learned French.

He stepped back a pace in surprise.

Out of nothing there came to me a message: *thankyou thankyou goodgreat gohomeplease thankyou goodgreat goaway manbad manbad manbad . . .* Somewhere an animal or bird was warning me against Macht. I thought a casual *thanks* to it and turned my attention to Macht.

He and I stared at each other. Was this what *culture* was? Were we now men? Did freedom always include the freedom to mistrust, to fear, to hate?

I liked him not at all. The words of forgotten crimes came into my mind: *assassination, murder, abduction, insanity, rape, robbery . . .*

We had known none of these things and yet I felt them all.

He spoke evenly to me. We had both been careful to guard our minds against being read telepathically, so that our only means of communication were empathy and French. "It's your idea," he said, most untruthfully, "or at least your lady's . . ."

"Has lying already come into the world," said I, "so that we walk into the clouds for no reason at all?"

"There is a reason," said Macht.

I pushed Virginia gently aside and capped my mind so tightly that the anti-telepathy felt like a headache.

"Macht," said I, and I myself could hear the snarl of an animal in my own voice, "tell me why you have brought us here or I will kill you."

He did not retreat. He faced me, ready for a fight. He said, "Kill? You mean, to make me dead?" but his words did not carry conviction. Neither one of us knew how to fight, but he readied for defense and I for attack.

Underneath my thought shield an animal thought crept in: *goodman goodman take him by the neck no-air he-aaah no-air he-aaah like broken egg . . .*

I took the advice without worrying where it came from. It was simple. I walked over to Macht, reached my hands around his throat, and squeezed. He tried to push my hands away. Then he tried to kick me. All I did was hang on to his throat. If I had been a Lord or a Go-captain, I might have known about fighting. But I did not, and neither did he.

It ended when a sudden weight dragged at my hands.

Out of surprise, I let go.

Macht had become unconscious. Was that *dead*?

It could not have been, because he sat up. Virginia ran to him. He rubbed his throat and said with a rough voice:

"You should not have done that."

This gave me courage. "Tell me," I spat at him,

"tell me why you wanted us to come, or I will do it again."

Macht grinned weakly. He leaned his head against Virginia's arm. "It's fear," he said. "Fear."

"Fear?" I knew the word—*peur*—but not the meaning. Was it some kind of disquiet or animal alarm?

I had been thinking with my mind open; he thought back *yes*.

"But why do you like it?" I asked.

*It is delicious*, he thought. *It makes me sick and thrilly and alive. It is like strong medicine, almost as good as stroon. I went there before. High up, I had much fear. It was wonderful and bad and good, all at the same time. I lived a thousand years in a single hour. I wanted more of it, but I thought it would be even more exciting with other people.*

"Now I will kill you," said I in French. "You are very—very . . ." I had to look for the word. "You are very evil."

"No," said Virginia, "let him talk."

He thought at me, not bothering with words. *This is what the Lords of the Instrumentality never let us have. Fear. Reality. We were born in a stupor and we died in a dream. Even the underpeople, the animals, had more life than we did. The machines did not have fear. That's what we were. Machines who thought they were men. And now we are free.*

He saw the edge of raw, red anger in my mind, and he changed the subject. *I did not lie to you. This is the way to the Abba-dingo. I have been there. It works. On this side, it always works.*

"It works," cried Virginia. "You see he says so. It works! He is telling the truth. Oh, Paul, do let's go on!"

"All right," said I, "we'll go."

I helped him rise. He looked embarrassed, like a man who has shown something of which he is ashamed.

We walked onto the surface of the indestructible boulevard. It was comfortable to the feet.

At the bottom of my mind the little unseen bird or animal babbled its thoughts at me: *goodman goodman make him dead take water take water . . .*

I paid no attention as I walked forward with her and him, Virginia between us. I paid no attention.

I wish I had.

We walked for a long time.

The process was new to us. There was something exhilarating in knowing that no one guarded us, that the air was free air, moving without benefit of weather machines. We saw many birds, and when I thought at them I found their minds startled and opaque; they were natural birds, the like of which I had never seen before. Virginia asked me their names, and I outrageously applied all the bird-names which we had learned in French without knowing whether they were historically right or not.

Maximilien Macht cheered up, too, and he even sang us a song, rather off key, to the effect that we would take the high road and he the low one, but that he would be in Scotland before us. It did not make sense, but the lilt was pleasant. Whenever he got a certain distance ahead of Virginia and me, I made up variations on "Macouba" and sang-whispered the phrases into her pretty ear:

*She wasn't the woman I went to seek.*
*I met her by the merest chance.*
*She did not speak the French of France,*
*But the surded French of Martinique.*

We were happy in adventure and freedom, until we became hungry. Then our troubles began.

Virginia stepped up to a lamp-post, struck it lightly with her fist, and said, "Feed me." The post should either have opened, serving us a dinner, or else told us where, within the next few hundred yards, food was to be had. It did neither. It did nothing. It must have been broken.

With that, we began to make a game of hitting every single post.

Alpha Ralpha Boulevard had risen about half a kilometer above the surrounding countryside. The wild birds wheeled below us. There was less dust on the pavement, and fewer patches of weeds. The immense road, with no pylons below it, curved like an unsupported ribbon into the clouds.

We wearied of beating posts and there was neither food nor water.

Virginia became fretful: "It won't do any good to go back now. Food is even farther the other way. I do wish you'd brought something."

How should I have thought to carry food? Who ever carries food? Why would they carry it, when it is everywhere? My darling was unreasonable, but she was my darling and I loved her all the more for the sweet imperfections of her temper.

Macht kept tapping pillars, partly to keep out of our fight, and obtained an unexpected result.

At one moment I saw him leaning over to give the pillar of a large lamp the usual hearty but guarded *whop*—in the next instant he yelped like a dog and was sliding uphill at a high rate of speed. I heard him shout something, but could not make out the words, before he disappeared into the clouds ahead.

Virginia looked at me. "Do you want to go back now? Macht is gone. We can say that I got tired."

"Are you serious?"

"Of course, darling."

I laughed, a little angrily. She had insisted that we come, and now she was ready to turn around and give it up, just to please me.

"Never mind," said I. "It can't be far now. Let's go on."

"Paul . . ." She stood close to me. Her brown eyes were troubled, as though she were trying to see all the way into my mind through my eyes. I thought to her, *Do you want to talk this way?*

"No," said she, in French. "I want to say things one at a time. Paul, I do want to go to the Abba-dingo. I need to go. It's the biggest need in my life. But at the same time, I don't want to go. There is something wrong up there. I would rather have you on the wrong terms than not have you at all. Something could happen."

Edgily, I demanded, "Are you getting this 'fear' that Macht was talking about?"

"Oh, no, Paul, not at all. This feeling isn't exciting. It feels like something broken in a machine—"

"Listen!" I interrupted her.

From far ahead, from within the clouds, there came a sound like an animal wailing. There were words in it. It must have been Macht. I thought I heard "take care." When I sought him with my mind, the distance made circles and I got dizzy.

"Let's follow, darling," said I.

"Yes, Paul," said she, and in her voice there was an unfathomable mixture of happiness, resignation, and despair . . .

Before we moved on, I looked carefully at her. She *was* my girl. The sky had turned yellow and the lights were not yet on. In the yellow rich sky her brown curls were tinted with gold, her brown eyes approached the black in their irises, her young and fate-haunted face seemed more meaningful than any other human face I had ever seen.

"You *are* mine," I said.

"Yes, Paul," she answered me and then smiled brightly. "*You* said it! That is doubly nice."

A bird on the railing looked sharply at us and then left. Perhaps he did not approve of human nonsense, so flung himself downward into dark air. I saw him catch himself, far below, and ride lazily on his wings.

"We're not as free as birds, darling," I told Virginia, "but we are freer than people have been for a hundred centuries."

For answer she hugged my arm and smiled at me.

"And now," I added, "to follow Macht. Put your arms around me and hold me tight. I'll try hitting that post. If we don't get dinner we may get a ride."

I felt her take hold tightly and then I struck the post.

Which post? An instant later the posts were sailing by us in a blur. The ground beneath our feet seemed steady, but we were moving at a fast rate. Even in the service underground I had never seen a roadway as fast as this. Virginia's dress was blowing so hard that it made snapping sounds like the snap of fingers. In no time at all we were in the cloud and out of it again.

A new world surrounded us. The clouds lay below and above. Here and there blue sky shone through. We were steady. The ancient engineers must have devised the walkway cleverly. We rode up, up, up without getting dizzy.

Another cloud.

Then things happened so fast that the telling of them takes longer than the event.

Something dark rushed at me from up ahead. A violent blow hit me in the chest. Only much later did I realize that this was Macht's arm trying to grab me before we went over the edge. Then we went into another cloud. Before I could even speak to Virginia a second blow struck me. The pain was terrible. I had never felt anything like that in all my life. For some reason, Virginia had fallen over me and beyond me. She was pulling at my hands.

I tried to tell her to stop pulling me, because it hurt, but I had no breath. Rather than argue, I tried to do what she wanted. I struggled toward her. Only then did I realize that there was nothing below my feet—no bridge, no jetway, nothing.

I was on the edge of the boulevard, the broken edge of the upper side. There was nothing below me except for some looped cables, and, far underneath them, a tiny ribbon which was either a river or a road.

We had jumped blindly across the great gap and I had fallen just far enough to catch the upper edge of the roadway on my chest.

It did not matter, the pain.

In a moment the doctor-robot would be there to repair me.

A look at Virginia's face reminded me there was no doctor-robot, no world, no Instrumentality, nothing but wind and pain. She was crying. It took a moment for me to hear what she was saying.

"I did it, I did it, darling, are you dead?"

Neither one of us was sure what "dead" meant, because people always went away at their appointed time, but we knew that it meant a cessation of life. I tried to tell her that I was living, but she fluttered over me and kept dragging me farther from the edge of the drop.

I used my hands to push myself into a sitting position.

She knelt beside me and covered my face with kisses.

At last I was able to gasp, "Where's Macht?"

She looked back. "I don't see him."

I tried to look too. Rather than have me struggle, she said, "You stay quiet. I'll look again."

Bravely she walked to the edge of the sheared-off boulevard. She looked over toward the lower side of the gap, peering through the clouds which drifted past us as rapidly as smoke sucked by a ventilator. Then she cried out:

"I see him. He looks so funny. Like an insect in the museum. He is crawling across on the cables."

Struggling to my hands and knees, I neared her and looked too. There he was, a dot moving along a thread, with the birds soaring by beneath him. It looked very unsafe. Perhaps he was getting all the "fear" that he needed to keep himself happy. I did not want that "fear," whatever it was. I wanted food, water, and a doctor-robot.

None of these were here.

I struggled to my feet. Virginia tried to help me but I was standing before she could do more than touch my sleeve.

"Let's go on."

"On?" she said.

"On to the Abba-dingo. There may be friendly machines up there. Here there is nothing but cold and wind, and the lights have not yet gone on."

She frowned. "But Macht . . . ?"

"It will be hours before he gets here. We can come back."

She obeyed.

Once again we went to the left of the boulevard. I told her to squeeze my waist while I struck the pillars, one by one. Surely there must have been a reactivating device for the passengers on the road.

The fourth time, it worked.

Once again the wind whipped our clothing as we raced upward on Alpha Ralpha Boulevard.

We almost fell as the road veered to the left. I caught my balance, only to have it veer the other way.

And then we stopped.

This was the Abba-dingo.

A walkway littered with white objects—knobs and rods and imperfectly formed balls about the size of my head.

Virginia stood beside me, silent.

*About the size of my head?* I kicked one of the objects aside and then knew, knew for sure, what it was. It was people. The inside parts. I had never seen such things before. And that, that on the ground, must once have been a hand. There were hundreds of such things along the wall.

"Come, Virginia," said I, keeping my voice even, and my thoughts hidden.

She followed without saying a word. She was curious about the things on the ground, but she did not seem to recognize them.

For my part. I was watching the wall.

At last I found them—the little doors of Abba-dingo. One said METEOROLOGICAL. It was not Old Common Tongue, nor was it French, but it was so close that I knew it had something to do with the behavior of air. I put my hand against the panel of the door. The panel became translucent and ancient writing showed through. There were numbers which meant nothing, words which meant nothing, and then:

*Typhoon coming.*

My French had not taught me what a "coming" was, but "typhoon" was plainly *typhon*, a major air disturbance. Thought I, *let the weather machines take care of the matter.* It had nothing to do with us.

"That's no help," said I.

"What does it mean?" she said.

"The air will be disturbed."

"Oh," said she. "That couldn't matter to us, could it?"

"Of course not."

I tried the next panel, which said FOOD. When my hand touched the little door, there was an aching creak inside the wall, as though the whole tower retched. The door opened a little bit and a horrible odor came out of it. Then the door closed again.

The third door said HELP and when I touched it
nothing happened. Perhaps it was some kind of tax-
collecting device from the ancient days. It yielded
nothing to my touch. The fourth door was larger and
already partly open at the bottom. At the top, the name
of the door was PREDICTIONS. Plain enough, that one
was, to anyone who knew Old French. The name at
the bottom was more mysterious: PUT PAPER HERE
it said, and I could not guess what it meant.

I tried telepathy. Nothing happened. The wind
whistled past us. Some of the calcium balls and knobs
rolled on the pavement. I tried again, trying my utmost
for the imprint of long-departed thoughts. A scream
entered my mind, a thin long scream which did not
sound much like people. That was all.

Perhaps it did upset me. I did not feel "fear," but
I was worried about Virginia.

She was staring at the ground.

"Paul," she said, "isn't that a man's coat on the
ground among those funny things?"

Once I had seen an ancient X-ray in the museum,
so I knew that the coat still surrounded the material
which had provided the inner structure of the man.
There was no ball there, so that I was quite sure he
was *dead*. How could that have happened in the old
days? Why did the Instrumentality let it happen? But
then, the Instrumentality had always forbidden this side
of the tower. Perhaps the violators had met their own
punishment in some way I could not fathom.

"Look, Paul," said Virginia. "I can put my hand in."

Before I could stop her, she had thrust her hand
into the flat open slot which said PUT PAPER HERE.

She screamed.

Her hand was caught.

I tried to pull at her arm, but it did not move. She began gasping with pain. Suddenly her hand came free.

Clear words were cut into the living skin. I tore my cloak off and wrapped her hand.

As she sobbed beside me I unbandaged her hand. As I did so she saw the words on her skin.

The words said, in clear French: *You will love Paul all your life.*

Virginia let me bandage her hand with my clòak and then she lifted her face to be kissed. "It was worth it," she said; "it was worth all the trouble, Paul. Let's see if we can get down. Now I know."

I kissed her again and said, reassuringly, "You do know, don't you?"

"Of course," she smiled through her tears. "The Instrumentality could not have contrived this. What a clever old machine! Is it a god or a devil, Paul?"

I had not studied those words at that time, so I patted her instead of answering. We turned to leave.

At the last minute I realized that I had not tried PREDICTIONS myself.

"Just a moment, darling. Let me tear a little piece off the bandage."

She waited patiently. I tore a piece the size of my hand, and then I picked up one of the ex-person units on the ground. It may have been the front of an arm. I returned to push the cloth into the slot, but when I turned to the door, an enormous bird was sitting there.

I used my hand to push the bird aside, and he cawed at me. He even seemed to threaten me with his cries and his sharp beak. I could not dislodge him.

Then I tried telepathy. *I am a true man. Go away!*

The bird's dim mind flashed back at me nothing but *no-no-no-no-no!*

With that I struck him so hard with my fist that he fluttered to the ground. He righted himself amid the white litter on the pavement and then, opening his wings, he let the wind carry him away.

I pushed in the scrap of cloth, counted to twenty in my mind, and pulled the scrap out.

The words were plain, but they meant nothing: *You will love Virginia twenty-one more minutes.*

Her happy voice, reassured by the prediction but still unsteady from the pain in her written-on hand, came to me as though it were far away. "What does it say, darling?"

Accidentally on purpose, I let the wind take the scrap. It fluttered away like a bird. Virginia saw it go.

"Oh," she cried disappointedly. "We've lost it! What did it say?"

"Just what yours did."

"But what words, Paul? How did it say it?"

With love and heartbreak and perhaps a little "fear," I lied to her and whispered gently,

"It said, 'Paul will always love Virginia.'"

She smiled at me radiantly. Her stocky, full figure stood firmly and happily against the wind. Once again she was the chubby, pretty Menerima whom I had noticed in our block when we both were children. And she was more than that. She was my new-found love in our new-found world. She was my mademoiselle from Martinique. The message was foolish. We had seen from the food-slot that the machine was broken.

"There's no food or water here," said I. Actually,

there was a puddle of water near the railing, but it had been blown over the human structural elements on the ground, and I had no heart to drink it.

Virginia was so happy that, despite her wounded hand, her lack of water, and her lack of food, she walked vigorously and cheerfully.

Thought I to myself, *Twenty-one minutes. About six hours have passed. If we stay here we face unknown dangers.*

Vigorously we walked downward, down Alpha Ralpha Boulevard. We had met the Abba-dingo and were still "alive." I did not think that I was "dead," but the words had been meaningless so long that it was hard to think them.

The ramp was so steep going down that we pranced like horses. The wind blew into our faces with incredible force. That's what it was, wind, but I looked up the word *vent* only after it was all over.

We never did see the whole tower—just the wall at which the ancient jetway had deposited us. The rest of the tower was hidden by clouds which fluttered like torn rags as they raced past the heavy material.

The sky was red on one side and a dirty yellow on the other.

Big drops of water began to strike at us.

"The weather machines are broken," I shouted to Virginia.

She tried to shout back to me but the wind carried her words away. I repeated what I had said about the weather machines. She nodded happily and warmly, though the wind was by now whipping her hair past her face and the pieces of water which fell from up above were spotting her flame-golden gown. It did not matter. She clung to my arm. Her happy face smiled at me as we stamped downward, bracing ourselves against the decline in the ramp. Her brown eyes were full of confidence and life. She saw me looking at her and she kissed me on the upper arm without losing step. She was my own girl forever, and she knew it.

The water-from-above, which I later knew was actual "rain," came in increasing volume. Suddenly it included birds. A large bird flapped his way vigorously against the whistling air and managed to stand still in front of my face, though his air speed was many leagues per hour. He cawed in my face and then was carried away by the wind. No sooner had that one gone than another bird struck me in the body. I looked down at it but it too was carried away by the racing current of air. All I got was a telepathic echo from its bright blank mind: *no-no-no-no!*

*Now what?* thought I. A bird's advice is not much to go upon.

Virginia grabbed my arm and stopped.

I too stopped.

The broken edge of Alpha Ralpha Boulevard was just ahead. Ugly yellow clouds swam through the break like poisonous fish hastening on an inexplicable errand.

Virginia was shouting.

I could not hear her, so I leaned down. That way her mouth could almost touch my ear.

"Where is Macht?" she shouted.

Carefully I took her to the left side of the road, where the railing gave us some protection against the heavy racing air, and against the water commingled with it. By now neither of us could see very far. I made her drop to her knees. I got down beside her. The falling water pelted our backs. The light around us had turned to a dark dirty yellow.

We could still see, but we could not see much.

I was willing to sit in the shelter of the railing, but she nudged me. She wanted us to do something about Macht. What anyone could do, that was beyond me. If he had found shelter, he was safe, but if he was out on those cables, the wild pushing air would soon carry him off and then there would be no more Maximilien Macht. He would be "dead" and his interior parts would bleach somewhere on the open ground.

Virginia insisted.

We crept to the edge.

A bird swept in, true as a bullet, aiming for my face. I flinched. A wing touched me. It stung against my cheek like fire. I did not know that feathers were so tough. The birds must all have damaged mental mechanisms, thought I, if they hit people on Alpha Ralpha. That is not the right way to behave toward true people.

At last we reached the edge, crawling on our bellies. I tried to dig the fingernails of my left hand into the stone like material of the railing, but it was flat, and there was nothing much to hold to, save for the ornamental fluting. My right arm was around Virginia. It hurt me badly to crawl forward that way, because my body was still damaged from the blow against the edge of the road, on the way coming up. When I hesitated, Virginia thrust herself forward.

We saw nothing.

The gloom was around us.

The wind and the water beat at us like fists.

Her gown pulled at her like a dog worrying its master. I wanted to get her back into the shelter of the railing, where we could wait for the air disturbance to end.

Abruptly, the light shone all around us. It was wild electricity, which the ancients called *lightning*. Later I found that it occurs quite frequently in the areas beyond the reach of the weather machines.

The bright quick light showed us a white face staring at us. He hung on the cables below us. His mouth was open, so he must have been shouting. I shall never know whether the expression on his face showed "fear" or great happiness. It was full of excitement. The bright light went out and I thought that I heard the echo of a call. I reached for his mind telepathically and there was nothing there. Just some dim obstinate bird thinking at me, *no-no-no-no-no!*

Virginia tightened in my arms. She squirmed around. I shouted at her in French. She could not hear.

Then I called with my mind.

Someone else was there.

Virginia's mind blazed at me, full of revulsion, *The cat girl. She is going to touch me!*

She twisted. My right arm was suddenly empty. I saw the gleam of a golden gown flash over the edge, even in the dim light. I reached with my mind, and I caught her cry:

"Paul, Paul, I love you. Paul . . . help me!"

The thoughts faded as her body dropped.

The someone else was C'mell, whom we had first met in the corridor.

*I came to get you both,* she thought at me, *not that the birds cared about her.*

*What have the birds got to do with it?*

*You saved them. You saved their young, when the red-topped man was killing them all. All of us have been worried about what you true people would do to us when you were free. We found out. Some of you are bad and kill other kinds of life. Others of you are good and protect life.*

Thought I, is that all there is to *good* and *bad*?

Perhaps I should not have left myself off guard. People did not have to understand fighting, but the homunculi did. They were bred amidst battle and they served through troubles. C'mell, cat-girl that she was, caught me on the chin with a pistonlike fist. She had no anesthesia and the only way—cat or no cat—that she could carry me across the cables in the "typhoon" was to have me unconscious and relaxed.

I awakened in my own room. I felt very well indeed. The robot-doctor was there. Said he:

"You've had a shock. I've already reached the Subcommissioner of the Instrumentality, and I can erase the memories of the last full day, if you want me to."

His expression was pleasant.

Where was the racing wind? The air falling like stone around us? The water driving where no weather machines controlled it? Where was the golden gown and the wild fear-hungry face of Maximilien Macht?

I thought these things, but the robot-doctor, not being telepathic, caught none of it. I stared hard at him.

"Where," I cried, "is my own true love?"

Robots cannot sneer, but this one attempted to do so. "The naked cat-girl with the blazing hair? She left to get some clothing."

I stared at him.

His fuddy-duddy little machine mind cooked up its own nasty little thoughts, "I must say, sir, you 'free people' change very fast indeed . . ."

Who argues with a machine? It wasn't worth answering him.

But that other machine? Twenty-one minutes. How could that work out? How could it have known? I did not want to argue with that other machine either. It must have been a very powerful left-over machine—perhaps something used in ancient wars. I had no intention of finding out. Some people might call it a god. I call it nothing. I do not need "fear" and I do not propose to go back to Alpha Ralpha Boulevard again.

But hear, oh heart of mine!—how can you ever visit the café again?

C'mell came in and the robot-doctor left.

# The Ballad of Lost C'mell

*She got the which of the what-she-did,*
*Hid the bell with a blot, she did,*
*But she fell in love with a hominid.*
*Where is the which of the what-she-did?*

from *THE BALLAD OF LOST C'MELL*

She was a girlygirl and they were true men, the
lords of creation, but she pitted her wits against
them and she won. It had never happened before,
and it is sure never to happen again, but she did
win. She was not even of human extraction. She was
cat-derived, though human in outward shape, which
explains the C in front of her name. Her father's name
was C'mackintosh and her name C'mell. She won her
tricks against the lawful and assembled Lords of the
Instrumentality.

It all happened at Earthport, greatest of buildings,
smallest of cities, standing twenty-five kilometers high
at the western edge of the Smaller Sea of Earth.

Jestocost had an office outside the fourth valve.

249

## ∾ 1 ∾

Jestocost liked the morning sunshine, while most of the other Lords of the Instrumentality did not, so that he had no trouble in keeping the office and the apartments which he had selected. His main office was ninety meters deep, twenty meters high, twenty meters broad. Behind it was the "fourth valve," almost a thousand hectares in extent. It was shaped helically, like an enormous snail. Jestocost's apartment, big as it was, was merely one of the pigeonholes in the muffler of the rim of Earthport. Earthport stood like an enormous wineglass, reaching from the magma to the high atmosphere.

Earthport had been built during mankind's biggest mechanical splurge. Though men had had nuclear rockets since the beginning of consecutive history, they had used chemical rockets to load the interplanetary ion-drive and nuclear-drive vehicles or to assemble the photonic sail-ships for interstellar cruises. Impatient with the troubles of taking things bit by bit into the sky, they had worked out a billion-ton rocket, only to find that it ruined whatever countryside it touched in landing. The Daimoni—people of Earth extraction, who came back from somewhere beyond the stars—had helped men build it of weatherproof, rustproof, timeproof, stressproof material. Then they had gone away and had never come back.

Jestocost often looked around his apartment and wondered what it might have been like when white-hot gas, muted to a whisper, surged out of the valve into his own chamber and the sixty-three other chambers like it. Now he had a back wall of heavy timber, and the valve itself was a great hollow cave where a few wild things lived. Nobody needed that much space any more. The chambers were useful, but the valve did nothing. Planoforming ships whispered in from the stars; they landed at Earthport as a matter of legal convenience, but they made no noise and they certainly had no hot gases.

Jestocost looked at the high clouds far below him and talked to himself, "Nice day. Good air. No trouble. Better eat."

Jestocost often talked like that to himself. He was an individual, almost an eccentric. One of the top council of mankind, he had problems, but they were not personal problems. He had a Rembrandt hanging above his bed—the only Rembrandt known in the world, just as he was possibly the only person who could appreciate a Rembrandt. He had the tapestries of a forgotten empire hanging from his back wall. Every morning the sun played a grand opera for him, muting and lighting and shifting the colors so that he could almost imagine that the old days of quarrel, murder, and high drama had come back to Earth again. He had a copy of Shakespeare, a copy of Colegrove, and two pages of the Book of Ecclesiastes in a locked box beside his bed. Only forty-two people in the universe could read Ancient English, and he was one of them. He drank wine, which he had made by his own robots in his own vineyards on the Sunset Coast. He was a man, in short, who had arranged his own life to live comfortably, selfishly, and well on the personal side, so that he could give generously and impartially of his talents on the official side.

When he awoke on this particular morning, he had no idea that a beautiful girl was about to fall hopelessly in love with him—that he would find, after a hundred years and more of experience in government, another government on Earth just as strong and almost as ancient as his own—that he would willingly fling himself into conspiracy and danger for a cause which he only half understood. All these things were mercifully hidden from him by time, so that his only question on arising was, should he or should he not have a small cup of white wine with his breakfast. On the one hundred seventy-third day of each year, he always made a point of eating eggs. They were a rare treat, and he did not want to spoil himself by having too many, nor to deprive himself and forget a treat by having none at all. He puttered around the room, muttering, "White wine? White wine?"

C'mell was coming into his life, but he did not know it. She was fated to win; that part, she herself did not know.

Ever since mankind had gone through the Rediscovery of Man, bringing back governments, money, newspapers, national languages, sickness, and occasional death, there had been the problem of the underpeople—people who were not human, but merely humanly shaped from the stock of Earth animals. They could speak, sing, read, write, work, love, and die; but they were not covered by human law, which simply defined them as "homunculi" and gave them a legal status close to animals or robots. Real people from off-world were always called "hominids."

Most of the underpeople did their jobs and accepted their half-slave status without question. Some became famous—C'mackintosh had been the first Earth-being to·manage a fifty-meter broad-jump under normal gravity. His picture was seen in a thousand worlds. His daughter, C'mell, was a girlygirl, earning her living by welcoming human beings and hominids from the outworlds and making them feel at home when they reached Earth. She had the privilege of working at Earthport, but she had the duty of working very hard for a living which did not pay well. Human beings and hominids had lived so long in an affluent society that they did not know what it meant to be poor. But the Lords of the Instrumentality had decreed that underpeople—derived from animal stock—should live under the economics of the Ancient World; they had to have their own kind of money to pay for their rooms, their food, their possessions, and the education of their children. If they became bankrupt, they went to the Poorhouse, where they were killed painlessly by means of gas.

It was evident that humanity, having settled all of its own basic problems, was not quite ready to let Earth animals, no matter how much they might be changed, assume a full equality with man.

The Lord Jestocost, seventh of that name, opposed the policy. He was a man who had little love, no fear, freedom from ambition, and a dedication to his job: but there are passions of government as deep and challenging as the emotions of love. Two hundred years of thinking himself right and of being outvoted had instilled in Jestocost a furious desire to get things done his own way.

Jestocost was one of the few true men who believed in the rights of the underpeople. He did not think that mankind would ever get around to correcting ancient wrongs unless the underpeople themselves had some of the tools of power—weapons, conspiracy, wealth, and (above all) organization with which to challenge man. He was not afraid of revolt, but he thirsted for justice with an obsessive yearning which overrode all other considerations.

When the Lords of the Instrumentality heard that there was the rumor of a conspiracy among the underpeople, they left it to the robot police to ferret it out.

Jestocost did not.

He set up his own police, using underpeople themselves for the purpose, hoping to recruit enemies who would realize that he was a friendly enemy and who would in course of time bring him into touch with the leaders of the underpeople.

If those leaders existed, they were clever. What sign did a girlygirl like C'mell ever give that she was the spearhead of a crisscross of agents who had penetrated Earthport itself? They must, if they existed, be very, very careful. The telepathic monitors, both robotic and human, kept every thought-band under surveillance by random sampling. Even the computers showed nothing more significant than improbable amounts of happiness in minds which had no objective reason for being happy.

The death of her father, the most famous cat-athlete which the underpeople had ever produced, gave Jestocost his first definite clue.

He went to the funeral himself, where the body was packed in an ice-rocket to be shot into space. The mourners were thoroughly mixed with the curiosity-seekers. Sport is international, inter-race, inter-world, inter-species. Hominids were there: true men, one hundred percent human, they looked weird and horrible because they or their ancestors had undergone bodily modifications to meet the life conditions of a thousand worlds.

Underpeople, the animal-derived "homunculi," were there, most of them in their work clothes, and they looked more human than did the human beings from the outer worlds. None were allowed to grow up if they were less than half the size of man, or more than six times the size of man. They all had to have human features and acceptable human voices. The punishment for failure in their elementary schools was death. Jestocost looked over the crowd and wondered to himself, "We have set up the standards of the toughest kind of survival for these people and we give them the most terrible incentive, life itself, as the condition of absolute progress. What fools we are to think that they will not overtake us!" The true people in the group did not seem to think as he did. They tapped the underpeople peremptorily with their canes, even though this was an underperson's funeral, and the bear-men, bull-men, cat-men, and others yielded immediately and with a babble of apology.

C'mell was close to her father's icy coffin.

Jestocost not only watched her; she was pretty to watch. He committed an act which was an indecency in an ordinary citizen but lawful for a Lord of the Instrumentality: he peeped her mind.

And then he found something which he did not expect.

As the coffin left, she cried, "Ee-telly-kelly, help me! help me!"

She had thought phonetically, not in script, and he had only the raw sound on which to base a search.

Jestocost had not become a Lord of the Instrumentality without applying daring. His mind was quick, too quick to be deeply intelligent. He thought by gestalt, not by logic. He determined to force his friendship on the girl.

He decided to await a propitious occasion, and then changed his mind about the time.

As she went home from the funeral, he intruded upon the circle of her grim-faced friends, underpeople who were trying to shield her from the condolences of ill-mannered but well-meaning sports enthusiasts.

She recognized him, and showed him the proper respect.

"My Lord, I did not expect you here. You knew my father?"

He nodded gravely and addressed sonorous words of consolation and sorrow, words which brought a murmur of approval from humans and underpeople alike.

But with his left hand hanging slack at his side, he made the perpetual signal of *alarm! alarm!* used with the Earthport staff—a repeated tapping of the thumb against the third finger—when they had to set one another on guard without alerting the offworld transients.

She was so upset that she almost spoiled it all. While he was still doing his pious doubletalk, she cried in a loud clear voice:

"You mean *me?*"

And he went on with his condolences: ". . . and I do mean *you*, C'mell, to be the worthiest carrier of your father's name. *You* are the one to whom we turn in this time of common sorrow. *Who could I mean but you* if

I say that C'mackintosh never did things by halves, and died young as a result of his own zealous conscience? Good-bye, C'mell, I go back to my office."

She arrived forty minutes after he did.

## ∽ 2 ∾

He faced her straightaway, studying her face.

"This is an important day in your life."

"Yes, my Lord, a sad one."

"I do not," he said, "mean your father's death and burial. I speak of the future to which we all must turn. Right now, it's you and me."

Her eyes widened. She had not thought that he was that kind of man at all. He was an official who moved freely around Earthport, often greeting important offworld visitors and keeping an eye on the bureau of ceremonies. She was a part of the reception team, when a girlygirl was needed to calm down a frustrated arrival or to postpone a quarrel. Like the geisha of ancient Japan, she had an honorable profession; she was not a bad girl but a professionally flirtatious hostess. She stared at the Lord Jestocost. He did not *look* as though he meant anything improperly personal. But, thought she, you can never tell about men.

"You know men," he said, passing the initiative to her.

"I guess so," she said. Her face looked odd. She started to give him smile No. 3 (extremely adhesive) which she had learned in the girlygirl school. Realizing it was wrong, she tried to give him an ordinary smile. She felt she had made a face at him.

"Look at me," he said, "and see if you can trust me. I am going to take both our lives in my hands."

She looked at him. What imaginable subject could involve him, a Lord of the Instrumentality, with herself, an undergirl? They never had anything in common. They never would.

But she stared at him.

"I want to help the underpeople."

He made her blink. That was a crude approach, usually followed by a very raw kind of pass indeed. But his face was illuminated by seriousness. She waited.

"Your people do not have enough political power even to talk to us. I will not commit treason to the true human race, but I am willing to give your side an advantage. If you bargain better with us, it will make all forms of life safer in the long run."

C'mell stared at the floor, her red hair soft as the fur of a Persian cat. It made her head seem bathed in flames. Her eyes looked human, except that they had the capacity of reflecting when light struck them; the irises were the rich green of the ancient cat. When she looked right at him, looking up from the floor, her glance had the impact of a blow. "What do you want from me?"

He stared right back. "Watch me. Look at my face. Are you sure, *sure* that I want nothing from you personally?"

She looked bewildered. "What else is there to want from me except personal things? I am a girlygirl. I'm not a person of any importance at all, and I do not have much of an education. You know more, sir, than I will ever know."

"Possibly," he said, watching her.

She stopped feeling like a girlygirl and felt like a citizen. It made her uncomfortable.

"Who," he said, in a voice of great solemnity, "is your own leader?"

"Commissioner Teadrinker, sir. He's in charge of all outworld visitors." She watched Jestocost carefully; he still did not look as if he were playing tricks.

He looked a little cross. "I don't mean him. He's part of my own staff. Who's your leader among the underpeople?"

"My father was, but he died."

Jestocost said, "Forgive me. Please have a seat. But I don't mean that."

She was so tired that she sat down into the chair with an innocent voluptuousness which would have disorganized any ordinary man's day. She wore girlygirl clothes, which were close enough to the everyday fashion to seem agreeably modish when she stood up. In line with her profession, her clothes were designed to be unexpectedly and provocatively revealing when she sat down—not revealing enough to shock the man with their brazenness, but so slit, tripped, and cut that he got far more visual stimulation than he expected.

"I must ask you to pull your clothing together a little," said Jestocost in a clinical turn of voice. "I am a man, even if I am an official, and this interview is more important to you and to me than any distraction would be."

She was a little frightened by his tone. She had meant no challenge. With the funeral that day, she meant nothing at all; these clothes were the only kind she had.

He read all this in her face.

Relentlessly, he pursued the subject.

"Young lady, I asked about your leader. You name your boss and you name your father. I want your leader."

"I don't understand," she said, on the edge of a sob. "I don't understand."

Then, he thought to himself, I've got to take a gamble. He thrust the mental dagger home, almost drove his words like steel straight into her face. "Who . . ." he said slowly and icily, "is . . . Ee . . . telly . . . kelly?"

The girl's face had been cream-colored, pale with sorrow. Now she went white. She twisted away from him. Her eyes glowed like twin fires.

Her eyes . . . like twin fires.

(No undergirl, thought Jestocost as he reeled, could hypnotize me.)

Her eyes . . . were like cold fires.

The room faded around him. The girl disappeared. Her eyes became a single white, cold fire.

Within this fire stood the figure of a man. His arms were wings, but he had human hands growing at the elbows of his wings. His face was clear, white, cold as the marble of an ancient statue; his eyes were opaque white. "I am the E'telekeli. You will believe in me. You may speak to my daughter C'mell."

The image faded.

Jestocost saw the girl staring as she sat awkwardly on the chair, looking blindly through him. He was on the edge of making a joke about her hypnotic capacity when he saw that she was still deeply hypnotized even after he had been released. She had stiffened and again her clothing had fallen into its planned disarray. The effect was not stimulating; it was pathetic beyond words, as though an accident had happened to a pretty child. He spoke to her.

He spoke to her, not really expecting an answer.

"Who are you?" he said to her, testing her hypnosis.

"I am he whose name is never said aloud," said the girl in a sharp whisper. "I am he whose secret you have penetrated. I have printed my image and my name in your mind."

Jestocost did not quarrel with ghosts like this. He snapped out a decision. "If I open my mind, will you search it while I watch you? Are you good enough to do that?"

"I am very good," hissed the voice in the girl's mouth.

C'mell arose and put her two hands on his shoulders. She looked into his eyes. He looked back. A strong telepath himself, Jestocost was not prepared for the enormous thought-voltage which poured out of her.

*Look in my mind,* he commanded, *for the subject of* underpeople *only.*

*I see it,* thought the mind behind C'mell.

*Do you see what I mean to do for the under-people?*

Jestocost heard the girl breathing hard as her mind served as a relay to his. He tried to remain calm so that he could see which part of his mind was being searched. Very good so far, he thought to himself. An intelligence like that on Earth itself, he thought—and we of the Lords not knowing it!

The girl hacked out a dry little laugh.

Jestocost thought at the mind, *Sorry. Go ahead.*

*This plan of yours*—thought the strange mind—*may I see more of it?*

*That's all there is.*

*Oh,* said the strange mind, *you want me to think for you. Can you give me the keys in the Bell and Bank which pertain to destroying underpeople?*

*You can have the information keys if I can ever get them,* thought Jestocost, *but not the control keys and not the master switch of the Bell.*

*Fair enough,* thought the other mind, *and what do I pay for them?*

*You support me in my policies before the Instrumentality. You keep the underpeople reasonable, if you can, when the time comes to negotiate. You maintain honor and good faith in all subsequent agreements. But how can I get the keys? It would take me a year to figure them out myself.*

*Let the girl look once,* thought the strange mind, *and I will be behind her. Fair?*

*Fair,* thought Jestocost.

*Break?* thought the mind.

*How do we re-connect?* thought Jestocost back.

*As before.* Through the girl. *Never say my name. Don't think it if you can help it. Break?*

*Break!* thought Jestocost.

The girl, who had been holding his shoulders, drew his face down and kissed him firmly and warmly. He had never touched an underperson before, and it never had occurred to him that he might kiss one. It was pleasant, but he took her arms away from his neck, half turned her around, and let her lean against him.

"Daddy!" she sighed happily.

Suddenly she stiffened, looked at his face, and sprang for the door. "Jestocost!" she cried. "Lord Jestocost! What am I doing here?"

"Your duty is done, my girl. You may go."

She staggered back into the room. "I'm going to be sick," she said. She vomited on his floor.

He pushed a button for a cleaning robot and slapped his desk-top for coffee.

She relaxed and talked about his hopes for the underpeople. She stayed an hour. By the time she left they had a plan. Neither of them had mentioned E'telekeli, neither had put purposes in the open. If the monitors had been listening, they would have found no single sentence or paragraph which was suspicious.

When she had gone, Jestocost looked out of his window. He saw the clouds far below and he knew the world below him was in twilight. He had planned to help the underpeople, and he had met powers of which organized mankind had no conception or perception. He was righter than he had thought. He had to go on through.

But as partner—C'mell herself!

Was there ever an odder diplomat in the history of worlds?

~ **3** ~

In less than a week they had decided what to do. It was the Council of the Lords of the Instrumentality at which they would work—the brain center itself. The risk was high, but the entire job could be done in a few minutes if it were done at the Bell itself.

This is the sort of thing which interested Jestocost. He did not know that C'mell watched him with two different facets of her mind. One side of her was alertly and wholeheartedly his fellow-conspirator, utterly in sympathy with the revolutionary aims to which they were both committed. The other side of her—was feminine.

She had a womanliness which was truer than that of any hominid woman. She knew the value of her trained smile, her splendidly kept red hair with its unimaginably soft texture, her lithe young figure with firm breasts and persuasive hips. She knew down to the last millimeter the effect which her legs had on hominid men. True humans kept few secrets from her. The men betrayed themselves by their unfulfillable desires, the women by their irrepressible jealousies. But she knew people best of all by not being one herself. She had to learn by imitation, and imitation is conscious. A thousand little things which ordinary women took for granted, or thought about just once in a whole lifetime, were subjects of acute and intelligent study to her. She was a girl by profession; she was a human by assimilation; she was an inquisitive cat in her genetic nature. Now she was falling in love with Jestocost, and she knew it.

Even she did not realize that the romance would sometime leak out into rumor, be magnified into legend, distilled into romance. She had no idea of the ballad about herself that would open with the lines which became famous much later:

> She got the which of the what-she-did,
> Hid the bell with a blot, she did,
> But she fell in love with a hominid.
> Where is the which of the what-she-did?

All this lay in the future, and she did not know it.

She knew her own past.

She remembered the off-Earth prince who had rested his head in her lap and had said, sipping his glass of mott by way of farewell:

"Funny, C'mell, you're not even a person and you're the most intelligent human being I've met in this place. Do you know it made my planet poor to send me here? And what did I get out of them? Nothing, nothing, and a thousand times nothing. But you, now. If you'd been running the government of Earth, I'd have gotten what my people need, and this world would be richer too. Manhome, they call it. Manhome, my eye! The only smart person on it is a female cat."

He ran his fingers around her ankle. She did not stir. That was part of hospitality, and she had her own ways of making sure that hospitality did not go too far. Earth police were watching her; to them, she was a convenience maintained for outworld people, something like a soft chair in the Earthport lobbies or a drinking fountain with acid-tasting water for strangers who could not tolerate the insipid water of Earth. She was not expected to have feelings or to get involved. If she had ever caused an incident, they would have punished her fiercely, as they often punished animals or underpeople, or else (after a short formal hearing with no appeal) they would have destroyed her, as the law allowed and custom encouraged.

She had kissed a thousand men, maybe fifteen hundred. She had made them feel welcome and she had gotten their complaints or their secrets out of them as they left. It was a living, emotionally tiring but intellectually very stimulating. Sometimes it made her laugh to look at human women with their pointed-up noses and their proud airs, and to realize that she knew more about the men who belonged to the human women than the human women themselves ever did.

Once a policewoman had had to read over the record of two pioneers from New Mars. C'mell had been given the job of keeping in very close touch with them. When the policewoman got through reading the report she looked at C'mell and her face was distorted with jealousy and prudish rage.

"Cat, you call yourself. Cat! You're a pig, you're a dog, you're an animal. You may be working for Earth but don't ever get the idea that you're as good as a person. I think it's a crime that the Instrumentality lets monsters like you greet real human beings from outside! I can't stop it. But may the Bell help you, girl, if you ever touch a real Earth man! If you ever get near one! If you ever try tricks here! Do you understand me?"

"Yes, Ma'am," C'mell had said. To herself she thought, "That poor thing doesn't know how to select her own clothes or how to do her own hair. No wonder she resents somebody who manages to be pretty."

Perhaps the policewoman thought that raw hatred would be shocking to C'mell. It wasn't. Underpeople were used to hatred, and it was not any worse raw than it was when cooked with politeness and served like poison. They had to live with it.

But now, it was all changed.

She had fallen in love with Jestocost.

Did he love her?

Impossible. No, not impossible. Unlawful, unlikely,

indecent—yes, all these, but not impossible. Surely he felt something of her love.

If he did, he gave no sign of it.

People and underpeople had fallen in love many times before. The underpeople were always destroyed and the real people brainwashed. There were laws against that kind of thing. The scientists among people had created the underpeople, had given them capacities which real people did not have (the fifty-meter jump, the telepath two miles underground, the turtle-man waiting a thousand years next to an emergency door, the cowman guarding a gate without reward), and the scientists had also given many of the underpeople the human shape. It was handier that way. The human eye, the five-fingered hand, the human size—these were convenient for engineering reasons. By making underpeople the same size and shape as people, more or less, the scientists eliminated the need for two or three or a dozen different sets of furniture. The human form was good enough for all of them.

But they had forgotten the human heart.

And now she, C'mell, had fallen in love with a man, a true man old enough to have been her own father's grandfather.

But she didn't feel daughterly about him at all. She remembered that with her own father there was an easy comradeship, an innocent and forthcoming affection, which masked the fact that he was considerably more catlike than she was. Between them there was an aching void of forever-unspoken words—things that couldn't quite be said by either of them, perhaps things that couldn't be said at all. They were so close to each other that they could get no closer. This created enormous distance, which was heart-breaking but unutterable. Her father had died, and now this true man was here with all the kindness—

"That's it," she whispered to herself. "With all the kindness that none of these passing men have ever really shown. With all the depth which my poor underpeople can never get. Not that it's not in them. But they're born like dirt, treated like dirt, put away like dirt when they die. How can any of my own men develop real kindness? There's a special sort of majesty to kindness. It's the best part there is to being people. And he has whole oceans of it in him. And it's strange, strange, strange that he's never given his real love to any human woman."

She stopped, cold.

Then she consoled herself and whispered on, "Or if he did, it's so long ago that it doesn't matter now. He's got *me*. Does he know it?"

∼ **4** ∼

The Lord Jestocost did know, and yet he didn't. He was used to getting loyalty from people, because he offered loyalty and honor in his daily work. He was even familiar with loyalty becoming obsessive and seeking physical form, particularly from women, children, and underpeople. He had always coped with it before. He was gambling on the fact that C'mell was a wonderfully intelligent person, and that as a girlygirl, working on the hospitality staff of the Earthport police, she must have learned to control her personal feelings.

"We're born in the wrong age," he thought, "when I meet the most intelligent and beautiful female I've ever met, and then have to put business first. But this stuff about people and underpeople is sticky. Sticky. We've got to keep personalities out of it."

So he thought. Perhaps he was right.

If the nameless one, whom he did not dare to remember, commanded an attack on the Bell itself, that was worth their lives. Their emotions could not come into it. The Bell mattered; justice mattered; the perpetual return of mankind to progress mattered. He did not matter, because he had already done most of his work. C'mell did not matter, because their failure would leave her with mere underpeople forever. The Bell did count.

The price of what he proposed to do was high, but the entire job could be done in a few minutes if it were done at the Bell itself.

The Bell, of course, was not a Bell. It was a three-dimensional situation table, three times the height of a man. It was set one story below the meeting room, and shaped roughly like an ancient bell. The meeting table of the Lords of the Instrumentality had a circle cut out of it, so that the Lords could look down into the Bell at whatever situation one of them called up either manually or telepathically. The Bank below it, hidden by the floor, was the key memory-bank of the entire system. Duplicates existed at thirty-odd other places on Earth. Two duplicates lay hidden in interstellar space, one of them beside the ninety-million-mile gold-colored ship left over from the war against Raumsog and the other masked as an asteroid.

Most of the Lords were off-world on the business of the Instrumentality.

Only three besides Jestocost were present—the Lady Johanna Gnade, the Lord Issan Olascoaga, and the Lord William Not-from-here. (The Not-from-heres were a great Norstrilian family which had migrated back to Earth many generations before.)

The E'telekeli told Jestocost the rudiments of a plan.

He was to bring C'mell into the chambers on a summons.

The summons was to be serious.

They should avoid her summary death by automatic justice, if the relays began to trip.

C'mell would go into partial trance in the chamber.

He was then to call the items in the Bell which E'telekeli wanted traced. A single call would be enough. E'telekeli would take the responsibility for tracing them. The other Lords would be distracted by him, E'telekeli.

It was simple in appearance.

The complication came in action.

The plan seemed flimsy, but there was nothing which Jestocost could do at this time. He began to curse himself for letting his passion for policy involve him in the intrigue. It was too late to back out with honor; besides, he had given his word; besides, he liked C'mell—as a being, not as a girlygirl—and he would hate to see her marked with disappointment for life. He knew how the underpeople cherished their identities and their status.

With heavy heart but quick mind he went to the council chamber. A dog-girl, one of the routine messengers whom he had seen many months outside the door, gave him the minutes.

He wondered how C'mell or E'telekeli would reach

him, once he was inside the chamber with its tight net of telepathic intercepts.

He sat wearily at the table—

And almost jumped out of his chair.

The conspirators had forged the minutes themselves, and the top item was: "C'mell daughter to C'mackintosh, cat stock (pure), lot 1138, confession of. Subject: conspiracy to export homuncular material. Reference: planet De Prinsensmacht."

The Lady Johanna Gnade had already pushed the buttons for the planet concerned. The people there, Earth by origin, were enormously strong but they had gone to great pains to maintain the original Earth appearance. One of their first-men was at the moment on Earth. He bore the title of the Twilight Prince (Prins van de Schemering) and he was on a mixed diplomatic and trading mission.

Since Jestocost was a little late, C'mell was being brought into the room as he glanced over the minutes.

The Lord Not-from-here asked Jestocost if he would preside.

"I beg you, Sir and Scholar," he said, "to join me in asking the Lord Issan to preside this time."

The presidency was a formality. Jestocost could watch the Bell and Bank better if he did not have to chair the meeting too.

C'mell wore the clothing of a prisoner. On her it looked good. He had never seen her wearing anything but girlygirl clothes before. The pale-blue prison tunic made her look very young, very human, very tender, and very frightened. The cat family showed only in the fiery cascade of her hair and the lithe power of her body as she sat, demure and erect.

Lord Issan asked her: "You have confessed. Confess again."

"This man," and she pointed at a picture of the Twilight Prince, "wanted to go to the place where they torment human children for a show."

"What!" cried three of the Lords together.

"What place?" said the Lady Johanna, who was bitterly in favor of kindness.

"It's run by a man who looks like this gentleman here," said C'mell, pointing at Jestocost. Quickly, so that nobody could stop her, but modestly, so that none of them thought to doubt her, she circled the room and touched Jestocost's shoulder. He felt a thrill of contact-telepathy and heard bird-cackle in her brain. Then he knew that the E'telekeli was in touch with her.

"The man who has the place," said C'mell, "is five pounds lighter than this gentleman, two inches shorter, and he has red hair. His place is at the Cold Sunset corner of Earthport, down the boulevard and under the boulevard. Underpeople, some of them with bad reputations, live in that neighborhood."

The Bell went milky, flashing through hundreds of combinations of bad underpeople in that part of the city. Jestocost felt himself staring at the casual milkiness with unwanted concentration.

The Bell cleared.

It showed the vague image of a room in which children were playing Hallowe'en tricks.

The Lady Johanna laughed, "Those aren't people. They're robots. It's just a dull old play."

"Then," added C'mell, "he wanted a dollar and a shilling to take home. Real ones. There was a robot who had found some."

"What are those?" said Lord Issan.

"Ancient money—the real money of old America and old Australia," cried Lord William. "I have copies, but there are no originals outside the state museum." He was an ardent, passionate collector of coins.

"The robot found them in an old hiding place right under Earthport."

Lord William almost shouted at the Bell. "Run through every hiding place and get me that money."

The Bell clouded. In finding the bad neighborhoods it had flashed every police point in the northwest sector of the tower. Now it scanned all the police points under the tower, and ran dizzily through thousands of combinations before it settled on an old toolroom. A robot was polishing circular pieces of metal.

When Lord William saw the polishing, he was furious. "Get that here," he shouted. "I want to buy those myself!"

"All right," said Lord Issan. "It's a little irregular, but all right."

The machine showed the key search devices and brought the robot to the escalator.

The Lord Issan said, "This isn't much of a case."

C'mell sniveled. She was a good actress. "Then he wanted me to get a homunculus egg. One of the E-type, derived from birds, for him to take home."

Issan put on the search device.

"Maybe," said C'mell, "somebody has already put it in the disposal series."

The Bell and Bank ran through all the disposal devices at high speed. Jestocost felt his nerves go on edge. No human being could have memorized these thousands of patterns as they flashed across the Bell

too fast for human eyes, but the brain reading the
Bell through his eyes was not human. It might even
be locked into a computer of its own. It was, thought
Jestocost, an indignity for a Lord of the Instrumentality to be used as a human spyglass.

The machine blotted up.

"You're a fraud," cried the Lord Issan. "There's
no evidence."

"Maybe the offworlder tried," said the Lady Johanna.

"Shadow him," said Lord William. "If he would
steal ancient coins he would steal anything."

The Lady Johanna turned to C'mell. "You're a silly
thing. You have wasted our time and you have kept
us from serious inter-world business."

"It *is* inter-world business," wept C'mell. She let
her hand slip from Jestocost's shoulder, where it had
rested all the time. The body-to-body relay broke and
the telepathic link broke with it.

"We should judge that," said Lord Issan.

"You might have been punished," said Lady Johanna.

The Lord Jestocost had said nothing, but there was
a glow of happiness in him. If the E'telekeli was half
as good as he seemed, the underpeople had a list of
checkpoints and escape routes which would make it
easier to hide from the capricious sentence of painless
death which human authorities meted out.

$\backsim$ **5** $\backsim$

There was singing in the corridors that night.

Underpeople burst into happiness for no visible
reason.

C'mell danced a wild cat dance for the next customer who came in from outworld stations, that very evening. When she got home to bed, she knelt before the picture of her father C'mackintosh and thanked the E'telekeli for what Jestocost had done.

But the story became known a few generations later, when the Lord Jestocost had won acclaim for being the champion of the underpeople and when the authorities, still unaware of E'telekeli, accepted the elected representatives of the underpeople as negotiators for better terms of life; and C'mell had died long since.

She had first had a long, good life.

She became a female chef when she was too old to be a girlygirl. Her food was famous. Jestocost once visited her. At the end of the meal he had asked, "There's a silly rhyme among the underpeople. No human beings know it except me."

"I don't care about rhymes," she said.

"This is called 'The what-she-did.'"

C'mell blushed all the way down to the neckline of her capacious blouse. She had filled out a lot in middle age. Running the restaurant had helped.

"Oh, that rhyme!" she said. "It's silly."

"It says you were in love with a hominid."

"No," she said. "I wasn't." Her green eyes, as beautiful as ever, stared deeply into his. Jestocost felt uncomfortable. This was getting personal. He liked political relationships; personal things made him uncomfortable.

The light in the room shifted and her cat eyes blazed at him; she looked like the magical fire-haired girl he had known.

"I wasn't in love. You couldn't call it that . . ."

Her heart cried out, *It was you, it was you, it was you.*

"But the rhyme," insisted Jestocost, "says it was a hominid. It wasn't that Prins van de Schemering?"

"Who was he?" C'mell asked the question quietly, but her emotions cried out, *Darling, will you never, never know?*

"The strong man."

"Oh, him. I've forgotten him."

Jestocost rose from the table. "You've had a good life, C'mell. You've been a citizen, a committeewoman, a leader. And do you even know how many children you have had?"

"Seventy-three," she snapped at him. "Just because they're multiple doesn't mean we don't know them."

His playfulness left him. His face was grave, his voice kindly. "I meant no harm, C'mell."

He never knew that when he left she went back to the kitchen and cried for a while. It was Jestocost whom she had vainly loved ever since they had been comrades, many long years ago.

Even after she died, at the full age of five-score and three, he kept seeing her about the corridors and shafts of Earthport. Many of her great-granddaughters looked just like her and several of them practiced the girlygirl business with huge success.

They were not half-slaves. They were citizens (reserved grade) and they had photopasses which protected their property, their identity, and their rights. Jestocost was the godfather to them all; he was often embarrassed when the most voluptuous creatures in the universe threw playful kisses at him.

All he asked was fulfillment of his political passions, not his personal ones. He had always been in love, madly in love—

With justice itself.

At last, his own time came, and he knew that he was dying, and he was not sorry. He had had a wife, hundreds of years ago, and had loved her well; their children had passed into the generations of man.

In the ending, he wanted to know something, and he called to a nameless one (or to his successor) far beneath the world. He called with his mind till it was a scream.

*I have helped your people.*

"Yes," came back the faintest of faraway whispers, inside his head.

*I am dying. I must know. Did she love me?*

"She went on without you, so much did she love you. She let you go, for your sake, not for hers. She really loved you. More than death. More than life. More than time. You will never be apart."

*Never apart?*

"Not, not in the memory of man," said the voice, and was then still.

Jestocost lay back on his pillow and waited for the day to end.

# Norstrilia

~∾ ∾~

# Theme and Prologue

Story, place and time—these are the essentials.

## ∞ 1 ∞

The story is simple. There was a boy who bought the planet Earth. We know that, to our cost. It only happened once, and we have taken pains that it will never happen again. He came to Earth, got what he wanted, and got away alive, in a series of very remarkable adventures. That's the story.

## ∞ 2 ∞

The place? That's Old North Australia. What other place could it be? Where else do the farmers pay ten million credits for a handkerchief, five for a bottle of beer? Where else do people lead peaceful lives, untouched by militarism, on a world which is booby-trapped with death and things worse than death. Old North Australia has stroon—the santaclara drug—and more than a thousand other planets clamor for it. But you can get stroon only from Norstrilia—that's what they call it, for short—because it is a virus which grows on enormous, gigantic, misshapen sheep. The sheep were taken from Earth to start a pastoral system; they ended up as the greatest of imaginable treasures. The simple farmers became simple billionaires, but they kept their farming ways. They started tough and they got tougher. People get pretty mean if you rob them and hurt them for almost three thousand years. They get obstinate. They avoid strangers, except for sending out spies and a very occasional tourist. They don't mess with other people, and they're death, death inside out and turned over twice, if you mess with them.

Then one of their kids showed up on Earth and bought it. The whole place, lock, stock and underpeople.

That was a real embarrassment for Earth.

And for Norstrilia, too.

If it had been the two governments, Norstrilia would have collected all the eye-teeth on Earth and sold them back at compound interest. That's the way Norstrilians do business. Or they might have said, "Skip it, cobber. You can keep your wet old ball. We've got a nice dry world of our own." That's the temper they have. Unpredictable.

But a kid had bought Earth, and it was his.

Legally he had the right to pump up the Sunset Ocean, shoot it into space, and sell water all over the inhabited galaxy.

He didn't.

He wanted something else.

The Earth authorities thought it was girls, so they tried to throw girls at him of all shapes, sizes, smells

and ages—all the way from young ladies of good
family down to dog-derived undergirls who smelled of
romance all the time, except for the first five minutes
after they had had hot antiseptic showers. But he
didn't want girls. He wanted postage stamps.

That baffled both Earth and Norstrilia. The Norstrilians are a hard people from a harsh planet, and
they think highly of property. (Why shouldn't they?
They have most of it.) A story like this could only
have started in Norstrilia.

## ∽ 3 ∽

What's Norstrilia like?

Somebody once singsonged it up, like this:

"Grey lay the land, oh. Grey grass from sky to
sky. Not near the weir, dear. Not a mountain, low or
high—only hills and grey grey. Watch the dappled
dimpled twinkles blooming on the star bar.

"That is Norstrilia.

"All the muddy glubbery is gone—all the poverty,
the waiting and the pain. People fought their way
away, their way away from monstrous forms. People
fought for hands and noses, eyes and feet, man and
woman. They got it all back again. Back they came
from daylight nightmares, centuries when monstrous
men, sucking the water around the pools, dreamed
of being men again. They found it. Men they were
again, again, far away from a horrid *when*.

"The sheep, poor beasties, did not make it. Out
of their sickness they distilled immortality for man.
Who says research could do it? Research, besmirch!

It was a pure accident. Smack up an accident, man, and you've got it made.

"Beige-brown sheep lie on blue-grey grass while the clouds rush past, low overhead, like iron pipes ceilinging the world.

"Take your pick of sick sheep, man, it's the sick that pays. Sneeze me a planet, man, or cough me up a spot of life-forever. If it's barmy there, where the noddies and trolls like you live, it's too right here.

"That's the book, boy.

"If you haven't seen it, you haven't seen Norstrilia. If you did see it, you wouldn't believe it. If you got there, you wouldn't get off alive.

"Mother Hitton's Littul Kittons wait for you down there. Little pets they are, little little little pets. Cute little things, they say. Don't you believe it. No man ever saw them and walked away alive. You won't either. That's the final dash, flash. That's the utter clobber, cobber.

"Charts call the place Old North Australia."

We can suppose that that is what it is like.

### ∾ 4 ∾

Time: first century of the Rediscovery of Man.

When C'mell lived.

About the time they polished off Shayol, like wiping an apple on the sleeve.

Long deep into our own time. Fifteen thousand years after the bombs went up and the boom came down on Old Old Earth.

Recent, see?

## ～ 5 ～

What happens in the story?

Read it.

Who's there?

It starts with Rod McBan—who had the real name of Roderick Frederick Ronald Arnold William MacArthur McBan. But you can't tell a story if you call the main person by a name as long as Roderick Frederick Ronald Arnold William MacArthur McBan. You have to do what his neighbors did—call him Rod McBan. The old ladies always said, "Rod McBan the hundred and fifty-first . . ." and then sighed. Flurp a squirt at them, friends. We don't need numbers. We know his family was distinguished. We know the poor kid was born to troubles.

Why shouldn't he have troubles?

He was due to inherit the Station of Doom.

And then he gets around. He crosses all sorts of people. C'mell, the most beautiful of the girlygirls of Earth. Jean-Jacques Vomact, whose family must have preceded the human race. The wild old man at Adaminaby. The trained spiders of Earthport. The Subcommissioner Teadrinker. The Lord Jestocost, whose name is a page in history. The friends of the Ee-telly-kelly, and a queer tankful of friends they were. B'dank, of the cattle-police. The Catmaster. Tostig Amaral, about whom the less said the better. Ruth, in pursuit. C'mell, in flight. The Lady Johanna, laughing.

He gets away.

He *got* away. See, that's the story. Now you don't have to read it.

Except for the details.

They follow.

(He also bought one million women, far too many for any one boy to put to practical use, but it is not altogether certain, reader, that you will be told what he did about them.)

# At the Gate of the Garden of Death

Rod McBan faced the day of days. He knew what it was all about, but he could not really feel it. He wondered if they had tranquilized him with half-refined stroon, a product so rare and precious that it was never, never sold off-planet.

He knew that by nightfall he would be laughing and giggling and drooling in one of the Dying Rooms, where the unfit were put away to thin out the human breed, or else he would stand forth as the oldest landholder on the planet, Chief Heir to the Station of Doom. The farm had been salvaged by his great[32]-grandfather, and it was called Doom when he first inherited it, but the great[32]-grandfather had bought an ice-asteroid, crashed it into the farm over the violent objections of his neighbors, and learned clever tricks with artesian wells which kept his grass growing while the neighbors' fields turned from grey-green to blowing dust. The McBans had kept the sarcastic old name for their farming station, the Station of Doom.

By night, Rod knew, the Station would be his.

Or he would be dying, giggling his way to death in the killing place where people laughed and grinned and rollicked about while they died.

He found himself humming a bit of a rhyme that had always been a part of the tradition of Old North Australia:

*We kill to live, and die to grow—*
*That's the way the world must go!*

He'd been taught, bone deep, that his own world was a very special world, envied, loved, hated and dreaded across the galaxy. He knew that he was part of a very special people. Other races and kinds of men farmed crops, or raised food, or designed machines, and manufactured weapons. Norstrilians did none of these things. From their dry fields, their sparse wells, their enormous sick sheep, they refined immortality itself.

And sold it for a high, high price.

Rod McBan walked a little way into the yard. His home lay behind him. It was a log cabin built out of Daimoni beams—beams uncuttable, unchangeable, solid beyond all expectations of solidity. They had been purchased as a matched set thirty-odd planet hops away and brought to Old North Australia by photosails. The cabin was a fort which could withstand even major weapons, but it was still a cabin, simple inside and with a front yard of scuffed dust.

The last red bit of dawn was whitening into day.

Rod knew that he could not go far.

He could hear the women out behind the house, the kinswomen who had come to barber and groom him for the triumph—or the other.

They never knew how much he knew. Because of his affliction, they had thought around him for years, counting on his telepathic deafness to be constant.

Trouble was, it wasn't; lots of times he heard things which nobody intended him to hear. He even remembered the sad little poem they had about the young people who failed to pass the test for one reason or another and had to go to the Dying House instead of coming forth as Norstrilian citizens and fully recognized subjects of Her-Majesty-the-Queen. (Norstrilians had not had a real queen for some fifteen thousand years, but they were strong on tradition and did not let mere facts boggle them.) How did the little poem run, "This is the house of the long ago . . ." ? In its own gloomy way it was cheerful.

He erased his own footprint from the dust and suddenly he remembered the whole thing. He chanted it softly to himself.

*This is the house of the long ago,*
*Where the old ones murmur an endless woe,*
*Where the pain of time is an actual pain,*
*And things once known always come again.*
*Out in the Garden of Death, our young*
*Have tasted the valiant taste of fear.*
*With muscular arm and reckless tongue,*
*They have won, and lost, and escaped us here.*
*This is the house of the long ago.*
*Those who die young do not enter here.*
*Those living on know that hell is near.*
*The old ones who suffer have willed it so.*
*Out in the Garden of Death, the old*
*Look with awe on the young and bold.*

It was all right to say that they looked with awe at the young and bold, but he hadn't met a person yet who did not prefer life to death. He'd heard about people who chose death—of course he had; who hadn't? But the experience was third-hand, fourth-hand, fifth-hand.

He knew that some people had said of him that he would be better off dead, just because he had never learned to communicate telepathically and had to use old spoken words like outworlders or barbarians.

Rod himself certainly didn't think he would be better dead.

Indeed, he sometimes looked at normal people and wondered how they managed to go through life with the constant silly chatter of other people's thoughts running through their minds. In the times that his mind lifted, so that he could hier for a while, he knew that hundreds or thousands of minds rattled in on him with unbearable clarity; he could even hier the minds that thought they had their telepathic shields up. Then, in a little while, the merciful cloud of his handicap came down on his mind again and he had a deep unique privacy which everybody on Old North Australia should have envied.

His computer had said to him once, "The words *hier* and *spiek* are corruptions of the words *hear* and *speak*. They are always pronounced in the second rising tone of voice, as though you were asking a question under the pressure of amusement and alarm, if you say the words with your voice. They refer only to telepathic communication between persons or between persons and underpeople."

"What are underpeople?" he had asked.

"Animals modified to speak, to understand, and usually to look like men. They differ from cerebrocentered

robots in that the robots are built around an actual
animal mind, but are mechanical and electronic relays,
while underpeople are composed entirely of Earth-
derived living tissue."

"Why haven't I ever seen one?"

"They are not allowed on Norstrilia at all, unless
they are in the service of the defense establishments
of the Commonwealth."

"Why are we called a Commonwealth, when all the
other places are called worlds or planets?"

"Because you people are subjects of the Queen
of England."

"Who is the Queen of England?"

"She was an Earth ruler in the Most Ancient Days,
more than fifteen thousand years ago."

"Where is she now?"

"I said," the computer had said, "that it was fifteen
thousand years ago."

"I know it," Rod had insisted, "but if there hasn't
been any Queen of England for fifteen thousand years,
how can we be her subjects?"

"I know the answer in human words," the reply
had been from the friendly red machine, "but since
it makes no sense to me, I shall have to quote it to
you as people told it to me. 'She bloody well might
turn up one of these days. Who knows? This is Old
North Australia out here among the stars and we
can dashed well wait for our own Queen. She might
have been off on a trip when Old Old Earth went
sour.'" The computer had clucked a few times in its
odd ancient voice and had then said hopefully, in its
toneless voice, "Could you restate that so that I could
program it as part of my memory assembly?"

"It doesn't mean much to me. Next time I can hier other minds thinking I'll try to pick it out of somebody else's head."

That had been about a year ago, and Rod had never run across the answer.

Last night he had asked the computer a more urgent question:

"Will I die tomorrow?"

"Question irrelevant. No answer available."

"Computer!" he had shouted. "You know I love you."

"You say so."

"I started your historical assembly up after repairing you, when that part had been thinkless for hundreds of years."

"Correct."

"I crawled down into this cave and found the *personal* controls, where great[14]-grandfather had left them when they became obsolete."

"Correct."

"I'm going to die tomorrow and you won't even be sorry."

"I did not say that," said the computer.

"Don't you care?"

"I was not programmed for emotion. Since you yourself repaired me, Rod, you ought to know that I am the only all-mechanical computer functioning in this part of the galaxy. I am sure that if I had emotions I would be very sorry indeed. It is an extreme probability, since you are my only companion. But I do not have emotions. I have numbers, facts, language and memory—that is all."

"What is the probability, then, that I will die tomorrow in the Giggle Room?"

"That is not the right name. It is the Dying House."

"All right, then, the Dying House."

"The judgment on you will be a contemporary human judgment based upon emotions. Since I do not know the individuals concerned, I cannot make a prediction of any value at all."

"What do you think is going to happen to me, computer?"

"I do not really think, I respond. I have no input on that topic."

"Do you know anything at all about my life and death tomorrow? I know I can't *spiek* with my mind, but I have to make sounds with my mouth instead. Why should they kill me for that?"

"I do not know the people concerned and therefore I do not know the reasons," the computer had replied, "but I know the history of Old North Australia down to your great[14]-grandfather's time."

"Tell me that, then," Rod had said. He had squatted in the cave which he had discovered, listening to the forgotten set of computer controls which he had repaired, and had heard again the story of Old North Australia as his great[14]-grandfather had understood it. Stripped of personal names and actual dates, it was a simple story.

This morning his life hung on it.

Norstrilia had to thin out its people if it were going to keep its Old Old Earth character and be another Australia, out among the stars. Otherwise the fields would fill up, the deserts turn into apartment houses, the sheep die in cellars under endless kennels for crowded and useless people. No Old North Australian wanted that to happen, when he could keep character, immortality, and wealth—in that particular order of importance. It would be contrary to the character of Norstrilia.

The simple character of Norstrilia was immutable—as immutable as anything out among the stars. This ancient Commonwealth was the only human institution older than the Instrumentality.

The story was simple, the way the computer's clear long-circuited brain had sorted it out.

Take a farmer culture straight off Old Old Earth—Manhome itself.

Put the culture on a remote planet.

Touch it with prosperity and blight it with drought.

Teach it sickness, deformity, hardihood. Make it learn poverty so bad that men sold one child to buy another child the drink of water which would give it an extra day of life while the drills whirred deep into the dry rock, looking for wetness.

Teach that culture thrift, medicine, scholarship, pain, survival.

Give those people the lessons of poverty, war, grief, greed, magnanimity, piety, hope and despair by turn.

Let the culture survive.

Survive disease, deformity, despair, desolation, abandonment.

Then give it the happiest accident in the history of time.

Out of sheep-sickness came infinite riches, the santaclara drug, or stroon, which prolonged human life indefinitely.

Prolonged it—but with queer side effects, so that most Norstrilians preferred to die in a thousand years or so.

Norstrilia was convulsed by the discovery.

So was every other inhabited world.

But the drug could not be synthesized, paralleled, duplicated. It was something which could be obtained only from the sick sheep on the Old North Australian plains.

Robbers and governments tried to steal the drug. Now and then they succeeded, long ago, but they hadn't made it since the time of Rod's great[19]-grandfather.

They had tried to steal the sick sheep.

Several had been taken off the planet. (The Fourth Battle of New Alice, in which half the menfolk of Norstrilia had died beating off the Bright Empire, had led to the loss of two of the sick sheep—one female and one male. The Bright Empire thought it had won. It hadn't. The sheep got well, produced healthy lambs, exuded no more stroon, and died. The Bright Empire had paid four battle fleets for a coldbox full of mutton.) The monopoly remained in Norstrilia.

The Norstrilians exported the santaclara drug, and they put the export on a systematic basis.

They achieved almost infinite riches.

The poorest man on Norstrilia was always richer than the richest man anywhere else, emperors and conquerors included. Every farm hand earned at least a hundred Earth megacredits a day—measured in real money on Old Earth, not in paper which had to travel at a steep arbitrage.

But the Norstrilians made their choice: *the* choice—To remain themselves.

They taxed themselves back into simplicity.

Luxury goods got a tax of twenty million percent. For the price of fifty palaces on Olympia, you could import a handkerchief into Norstrilia. A pair of shoes, landed, cost the price of a hundred yachts in orbit. All machines were prohibited, except for defense and the drug-gathering. Underpeople were never made on Norstrilia, and imported only by the defense authority for top secret reasons. Old North Australia remained simple, pioneer, fierce, open.

Many families emigrated to enjoy their wealth; they could not return.

But the population problem remained, even with the taxation and simplicity and hard work.

Cut back, then—cut back people if you must.

But how, whom, where? Birth control—beastly. Sterilization—inhuman, unmanly, un-British. (This last was an ancient word meaning *very bad indeed.*)

By families, then. Let the families have the children. Let the Commonwealth test them at sixteen. If they ran under the standards, send them to a happy, happy death.

But what about the families? You can't wipe a family out, not in a conservative farmer society, when the neighbors are folk who have fought and died beside you for a hundred generations. The Rule of Exceptions came. Any family which reached the end of its line could have the last surviving heir reprocessed—up to four times. If he failed, it was the Dying House, and a designated adopted heir from another family took over the name and the estate.

Otherwise their survivors would have gone on, in this century a dozen, in that century twenty. Soon

Norstrilia would have been divided into two classes, the sound ones and a privileged class of hereditary freaks. This they could not stand, not while the space around them stank of danger, not when men a hundred worlds away dreamed and died while thinking of how to rob the stroon. They had to be fighters and chose not to be soldiers or emperors. Therefore they *had* to be fit, alert, healthy, clever, simple and moral. They had to be better than any possible enemy or any possible combination of enemies.

They made it.

Old North Australia became the toughest, brightest, simplest world in the galaxy. One by one, without weapons, Norstrilians could tour the other worlds and kill almost anything which attacked them. Governments feared them. Ordinary people hated them or worshipped them. Offworld men eyed their women queerly. The Instrumentality left them alone, or defended them without letting the Norstrilians know they had been defended. (As in the case of Raumsog, who brought his whole world to a death of cancer and volcanoes, because the Golden Ship struck once.)

Norstrilian mothers learned to stand by with dry eyes when their children, unexpectedly drugged if they failed the tests, drooled with pleasure and went giggling away to their deaths.

The space and subspace around Norstrilia became sticky, sparky with the multiplicity of their defenses. Big outdoorsy men sailed tiny fighting craft around the approaches to Old North Australia. When people met them in outports, they always thought that Norstrilians looked simple; the looks were a snare and a delusion. The Norstrilians had been conditioned by thousands of

years of unprovoked attack. They looked as simple as
sheep but their minds were as subtle as serpents.

And now—Rod McBan.

The last heir, the very last heir, of their proudest
old family had been found a half-freak. He was normal
enough by Earth standards, but by Norstrilian measure
he was inadequate. He was a bad, bad telepath. He
could not be counted on to hier. Most of the time
other people could not transmit into his mind at all;
they could not even read it. All they got was a fiery
bubble and a dull fuzz of meaningless sub-sememes,
fractions of thought which added up to less than nothing. And on spieking, he was worse. He could not talk
with his mind at all. Now and then he transmitted.
When he did, the neighbors ran for cover. If it was
anger, a bloody screaming roar almost blotted out
their consciousnesses with a rage as solid and red as
meat hanging in a slaughterhouse. If he was happy,
it was worse. His happiness, which he transmitted
without knowing it, had the distractiveness of a speed
saw cutting into diamond-grained rock. His happiness
drilled into people with an initial sense of pleasure,
followed rapidly by acute discomfort and the sudden
wish that all their own teeth would fall out: the teeth
had turned into spinning whorls of raw, unqualified
discomfort.

They did not know his biggest personal secret. They
suspected that he could hier now and then without
being able to control it. They did not know that
when he did hier, he could hier everything for miles
around with microscopic detail and telescopic range.
His telepathic intake, when it did work, went right
through other people's mind-shields as though they did

not exist. (If some of the women in the farms around the Station of Doom knew what he had accidentally peeped out of their minds, they would have blushed the rest of their lives.) As a result, Rod McBan had a frightful amount of unsorted knowledge which did not quite fit together.

Previous committees had neither awarded him the Station of Doom nor sent him off to the giggle death. They had appreciated his intelligence, his quick wit, his enormous physical strength. But they remained worried about his telepathic handicap. Three times before he had been judged. Three times.

And three times judgment had been suspended.

They had chosen the lesser cruelty and had sent him not to death, but to a new babyhood and a fresh upbringing, hoping that the telepathic capacity of his mind would naturally soar up to the Norstrilian normal.

They had underestimated him.

*He knew it.*

Thanks to the eavesdropping which he could not control, he understood bits and pieces of what was happening, even though nobody had ever told him the rational whys and hows of the process.

It was a gloomy but composed big boy who gave the dust of his own front yard one last useless kick, who turned back into the cabin, walking right through the main room to the rear door and the back yard, and who greeted his kinswomen politely enough as they, hiding their aching hearts, prepared to dress him up for his trial. They did not want the child to be upset, even though he was as big as a man and showed more composure than did most adult men.

They wanted to hide the fearful truth from him. How could they help it?

He already knew.

But he pretended he didn't.

Cordially enough, just scared enough but not too much, he said, "What ho, auntie! Hello, cousin. Morning, Maribel. Here's your sheep. Curry him up and trim him for the livestock competition. Do I get a ring in my nose or a bow ribbon around my neck?"

One or two of the young ones laughed, but his oldest "aunt"—actually a fourth cousin, married into another family—pointed seriously and calmly at a chair in the yard and said:

"Do sit down, Roderick. This is a serious occasion and we usually do not talk while preparations are going on."

She bit her lower lip and then she added, not as though she wanted to frighten him but because she wanted to impress him:

"The Vice-Chairman will be here today."

("The Vice-Chairman" was the head of the government; there had been no Chairman of the Temporary Commonwealth Government for some thousands of years. Norstrilians did not like posh and they thought that Vice-Chairman was high enough for any one man to go. Besides, it kept the offworlders guessing.)

Rod was not impressed. He had seen the man. It was in one of his rare moments of broad hiering, and he found that the mind of the Vice-Chairman was full of numbers and horses, the results of every horse race for three hundred and twenty years, and the projection forward of six probable horse races in the next two years.

"Yes, auntie," he said.

"Don't bray all the time today. You don't have to use your voice for little things like saying *yes*. Just nod your head. It will make a much better impression."

He started to answer, but gulped and nodded instead.

She sank the comb into his thick yellow hair.

Another one of the women, almost a girl, brought up a small table and a basin. He could tell from her expression that she was spieking to him, but this was one of the times in which he could not hier at all.

The aunt gave his hair a particularly fierce tug just as the girl took his hand. He did not know what she meant to do. He yanked his hand back.

The basin fell off the small table. Only then did he realize that it was merely soapy water for a manicure.

"I am sorry," he said; even to him, his voice sounded like a bray. For a moment he felt the fierce rush of humiliation and self-hate.

*They should kill me,* he thought . . . *By the time the sun goes down I'll be in the Giggle Room, laughing and laughing before the medicine makes my brains boil away.*

He had reproached himself.

The two women had said nothing. The aunt had walked away to get some shampoo, and the girl was returning with a pitcher, to refill the basin.

He looked directly into her eyes, and she into his.

"I want you," she said, very clearly, very quietly, and with a smile which seemed inexplicable to him.

"What for?" said he, equally quietly.

"Just you," she said. "I want you for myself. You're going to live."

"You're Lavinia, my cousin," said he, as though discovering it for the first time.

"Sh-h-h," said the girl. "She's coming back."

When the girl had settled down to getting his fingernails really clean, and the aunt had rubbed something like sheep-dip into his hair, Rod began to feel happy. His mood changed from the indifference which he had been pretending to himself. It became a real indifference to his fate, an easy acceptance of the grey sky above him, the dull rolling earth below. He had a fear—a little tiny fear, so small that it might have seemed to be a midget pet in a miniature cage—running around the inside of his thinking. It was not the fear that he would die: somehow he suddenly accepted his chances and remembered how many other people had had to take the same play with fortune. This little fear was something else, the dread that he might not behave himself properly if they did tell him to die.

But then, he thought, I don't have to worry. Negative is never a word—just a hypodermic, so that the first bad news the victim has is his own excited, happy laugh.

With this funny peace of mind, his hiering suddenly lifted.

He could not see the Garden of Death, but he could look into the minds tending it; it was a huge van hidden just beyond the next roll of hills, where they used to keep Old Billy, the eighteen-hundred-ton sheep. He could hear the clatter of voices in the little town eighteen kilometers away. And he could look right into Lavinia's mind.

It was a picture of himself. But what a picture! So grown, so handsome, so brave looking. He had schooled himself not to move when he could hier, so that other people would not realize that his rare telepathic gift had come back to him.

Auntie was spieking to Lavinia without noisy words. "We'll see this pretty boy in his coffin tonight."

Lavinia thought right back, without apology. "No, we won't."

Rod sat impassive in his chair. The two women, their faces grave and silent, went on spieking the argument at each other with their minds.

"How would you know—you're not very old?" spieked auntie.

"He has the oldest station in all of Old North Australia. He has one of the very oldest names. He is—" and even in spieking her thoughts cluttered up, like a stammer—"he is a very nice boy and he's going to be a wonderful man."

"Mark my thought," spieked the auntie again, "I'm telling you that we'll see him in his coffin tonight and that by midnight he'll be on his coffin-ride to the Long Way Out."

Lavinia jumped to her feet. She almost knocked over the basin of water a second time. She moved her throat and mouth to speak words but she just croaked,

"Sorry, Rod. Sorry."

Rod McBan, his face guarded, gave a pleasant, stupid little nod, as though he had no idea of what they had been spieking to each other.

She turned and ran, shout-spieking the loud thought at auntie, "Get somebody else to do his hands. You're heartless, hopeless. Get somebody else to do your corpse washing for you. Not me. Not me."

"What's the matter with her?" said Rod to the auntie, just as though he did not know.

"She's just difficult, that's all. Just difficult. Nerves, I suppose," she added in her croaking spoken words. She could not talk very well, since all her family and friends could spiek and hier with privacy and grace. "We were spieking with each other about what you would be doing tomorrow."

"Where's a priest, auntie?" said Rod.

"A what?"

"A priest, like the old poem has, in the rough rough days before our people found this planet and got our sheep settled down. Everybody knows it.

*Here is the place where the priest went mad.*
*Over there my mother burned.*
*I cannot show you the house we had.*
*We lost that slope when the mountain turned.*

There's more to it, but that's the part I remember. Isn't a priest a specialist in how to die? Do we have any around here?"

He watched her mind as she lied to him. As he had spoken, he had a perfectly clear picture of one of their more distant neighbors, a man named Tolliver, who had a very gentle manner; but her words were not about Tolliver at all.

"Some things are men's business," she said, cawing her words. "Anyhow, that song isn't about Norstrilia at all. It's about Paradise VII and why we left it. I didn't know you knew it."

In her mind he read, "That boy knows too much."

"Thanks, auntie," said he meekly.

"Come along for the rinse," said she. "We're using an awful lot of real water on you today."

He followed her and he felt more kindly toward her when he saw her think, *Lavinia had the right feelings but she drew the wrong conclusion. He's going to be dead tonight.*

That was too much.

Rod hesitated for a moment, tempering the chords of his oddly attuned mind. Then he let out a tremendous howl of telepathic joy, just to bother the lot of them. It did. They all stopped still. Then they stared at him.

In words the auntie said, "What was that?"

"What?" said he, innocently.

"That noise you spieked. It wasn't meaning."

"Just sort of a sneeze, I suppose. I didn't know I did it." Deep down inside himself he chuckled. He might be on his way to the Hoohoo House, but he would fritter their friskies for them while he went.

It was a dashed silly way to die, he thought all to himself.

And then a strange, crazy, happy idea came to him: *Perhaps they can't kill me. Perhaps I have powers. Powers of my own. Well, we'll soon enough find out.*

# The Trial

Rod walked across the dusty lot, took three steps up the folding staircase which had been let down from the side of the big trailer van, knocked on the door once as he had been instructed to do, had a green light flash in his face, opened the door, and entered.

It *was* a garden.

The moist, sweet, scent-laden air was like a narcotic. There were bright green plants in profusion. The lights were clear but not bright; their ceiling gave the effect of a penetrating blue, blue sky. He looked around. It was a copy of Old Old Earth. The growths on the green plants were *roses;* he remembered pictures which his computer had showed him. The pictures had not gotten across the idea that they smelled nice at the same time that they looked nice. He wondered if they did that all the time, and then remembered the wet air: wet air always holds smells better than dry air does. At last, almost shyly, he looked up at the three judges.

With real startlement, he saw that one of them was not a Norstrilian at all, but the local Commissioner of the Instrumentality, the Lord Redlady—a thin man with a sharp, inquiring face. The other two were Old Taggart and John Beasley. He knew them, but not well.

"Welcome," said the Lord Redlady, speaking in the funny singsong of a man from Manhome.

"Thank you," said Rod.

"You are Roderick Frederick Ronald Arnold William MacArthur McBan the one hundred and fifty-first?" said Taggart, knowing perfectly well that Rod was that person.

*Lord love a duck and lucky me!* thought Rod, *I've got my hiering, even in this place!*

"Yes," said the Lord Redlady.

There was silence.

The other two judges looked at the Manhome man; the stranger looked at Rod; Rod stared, and then began to feel sick at the bottom of his stomach.

For the first time in his life, he had met somebody who could penetrate his peculiar perceptual abilities.

At last he thought, "I understand."

The Lord Redlady looked sharply and impatiently at him, as though waiting for a response to that single word "yes."

Rod had already answered—telepathically.

At last Old Taggart broke the silence.

"Aren't you going to talk? I asked you your name."

The Lord Redlady held up his hand in a gesture for patience; it was not a gesture which Rod had ever seen before, but he understood it immediately.

He thought telepathically at Rod, "You are watching my thoughts."

"Indeed I am," thought Rod, back at him.

The Lord Redlady clapped a hand to his forehead. "You are hurting me. Did you think you said something?"

With his voice Rod said, "I told you that I was reading your mind."

The Lord Redlady turned to the other two men and spieked to them: "Did either of you hier what he tried to spiek?"

"No." "No." They both thought back at him. "Just noise, loud noise."

"He is a broadbander like myself. And I have been disgraced for it. You know that I am the only Lord of the Instrumentality who has been degraded from the status of Lord to that of Commissioner—"

"Yes," they spieked.

"You know that they could not cure me of shouting and suggested I die?"

"No," they answered.

"You know that the Instrumentality thought I could not bother you here and sent me to your planet on this miserable job, just to get me out of the way?"

"Yes," they answered.

"Then, what do you want to do about him? Don't try to fool him. He knows all about this place already." The Lord Redlady glanced quickly, sympathetically up at Rod, giving him a little phantom smile of encouragement. "Do you want to kill him? To exile him? To turn him loose?"

The other two men fussed around in their minds. Rod could see that they were troubled at the idea he could watch them thinking, when they had thought him a telepathic deaf-mute; they also resisted the Lord Redlady's unmannerly precipitation of the decision. Rod almost felt that he was swimming in the thick wet air, with the smell of roses cloying his nostrils so much that he would never smell anything but roses again, when he became aware of a massive consciousness very near him—a fifth person in the room, whom he had not noticed at all before.

It was an Earth soldier, complete with uniform. The soldier was handsome, erect, tall, formal with a rigid military decorum. He was, furthermore, not human and he had a strange weapon in his left hand.

"What is that?" spieked Rod to the Earthman. The man saw his face, not the thought.

"An underman. A snake-man. The only one on this planet. He will carry you out of here if the decision goes against you."

Beasley cut in, almost angrily. "Here, cut it out. This is a hearing, not a blossoming tea party. Don't clutter all that futt into the air. Keep it formal."

"You want a formal hearing?" said the Lord Redlady. "A formal hearing for a man who knows everything that all of us are thinking? It's foolish."

"In Old North Australia, we always have formal hearings," said old Taggart. With an acuteness of insight born of his own personal danger, Rod saw Taggart all over again for the first time—a careworn poor old man, who had worked a poor farm hard for a thousand years; a farmer, like his ancestors before him; a man rich only in the millions of megacredits which he would never take time to spend; a man of the soil, honorable, careful, formal, righteous, and very just. Such men did not yield to innovation, ever. They fought change.

"Have the hearing then," said the Lord Redlady, "have the hearing if it is your custom, my Mister and Owner Taggart, my Mister and Owner Beasley."

The Norstrilians, appeased, bowed their heads briefly.

Almost shyly, Beasley looked over at the Lord Redlady. "Sir and Commissioner, will you say the words? The good old words. The ones that will help us to find our duty and to do it."

(Rod saw a quick flare of red anger go through the Lord Redlady's mind as the Earth Commissioner thought fiercely to himself, "Why all this fuss about killing one poor boy? Let him go, you dull clutts, or kill him." But the Earthman had not directed the thoughts outward and the two Norstrilians were unaware of his private view of them.)

On the outside, the Lord Redlady remained calm. He used his voice, as Norstrilians did on occasion of great ceremony:

"We are here to hear a man."

"We are here to hear him," they responded.

"We are not to judge or to kill, though this may follow," said he.

"Though this may follow," they responded.

"And where, on Old Old Earth, does man come from?"

They knew the answer by rote and said it heavily together: "This is the way it was on Old Old Earth, and this is the way it shall be among the stars, no matter how far we men may wander:

"The seed of wheat is planted in dark, moist earth; the seed of man in dark, moist flesh. The seed of wheat fights upward to air, sun and space; the stalk, leaves, blossom and grain flourish under the open glare of heaven. The seed of man grows in the salty private ocean of the womb, the sea-darkness remembered by the bodies of his race. The harvest of wheat is collected by the hands of men; the harvest of men is collected by the tenderness of eternity."

"And what does this mean?" chanted the Lord Redlady.

"To look with mercy, to decide with mercy, to kill

with mercy, but to make the harvest of man strong and true and good, the way that the harvest of wheat stood high and proud on Old Old Earth."

"And who is here?" he asked.

They both recited Rod's full name.

When they had finished, the Lord Redlady turned to Rod and said, "I am about to utter the ceremonial words, but I promise you that you will not be surprised, no matter what happens. Take it easy, therefore. Easy, easy." Rod was watching the Earthman's mind and the minds of the two Norstrilians. He could see that Beasley and Taggart were befuddled with the ritual of the words, the wetness and scent of the air, and the false blue sky in the top of the van; they did not know what they were going to do. But Rod could also see a sharp, keen triumphant thought forming in the bottom of the Lord Redlady's mind, *I'll get this boy off!* He almost smiled, despite the presence of the snake-man with the rigid smile and the immovable glaring eyes standing just three paces beside him and a little to his rear, so that Rod could only look at him through the corner of his eye.

"Misters and Owners!" said the Lord Redlady.

"Mister Chairman!" they answered.

"Shall I inform the man who is being heard?"

"Inform him!" they chanted.

"Roderick Frederick Ronald Arnold William MacArthur McBan the one hundred and fifty-first!"

"Yes, sir," said Rod.

"Heir-in-trust of the Station of Doom!"

"That's me," said Rod.

"Hear me!" said the Lord Redlady.

"Hear him!" said the other two.

"You have not come here, Child and Citizen Roderick, for us to judge you or to punish you. If these things are to be done, they must be done in another place or time, and they must be done by men other than ourselves. The only concern before this board is the following: should you or should you not be allowed to leave this room safe and free and well, taking into no account your innocence or guilt of matters which might be decided elsewhere, but having regard only for the survival and the safety and the welfare of this given planet? We are not punishing and we are not judging, but we *are* deciding, and what we are deciding is your life. Do you understand? Do you agree?"

Rod nodded mutely, drinking in the wet, rose-scented air and stilling his sudden thirst with the dampness of the atmosphere. If things went wrong now, they did not have very far to go. Not far to go, not with the motionless snake-man standing just beyond his reach. He tried to look at the snake-brain but got nothing out of it except for an unexpected glitter of recognition and defiance.

The Lord Redlady went on, Taggart and Beasley hanging on his words as though they had never heard them before.

"Child and Citizen, you know the rules. We are not to find you wrong or right. No crime is judged here, no offense. Neither is innocence. We are only judging the single question, Should you live or should you not? Do you understand? Do you agree?"

Said Rod, "Yes, sir."

"And how stand you, Child and Citizen?"

"What do you mean?"

"This board is asking you, what is your opinion? Should you live or should you not?"

"I'd like to," said Rod, "but I'm tired of all these childhoods."

"That is not what the board is asking you, Child and Citizen," said the Lord Redlady. "We are asking you, what do you think? Should you live or should you not live?"

"You want me to judge myself?"

"That's it, boy," said Beasley. "You know the rules. Tell them, boy. I said we could count on you."

The sharp friendly neighborly face unexpectedly took on great importance for Rod. He looked at Beasley as though he had never seen the man before. This man was trying to judge him, Rod; and he, Rod, had to help decide on what was to be done with himself. The medicine from the snake-man and the giggle-giggle death, or a walk out into freedom. Rod started to speak and checked himself; he was to speak for Old North Australia. Old North Australia was a tough world, proud of its tough men. No wonder the board gave him a tough decision. Rod made up his mind and he spoke clearly and deliberately:

"I'd say no. Do not let me live. I don't fit. I can't spiek and hier. Nobody knows what my children would be like, but the odds are against them. Except for one thing . . ."

"And what, Child and Citizen, is that?" asked the Lord Redlady, while Beasley and Taggart watched as though they were staring at the last five meters of a horse race.

"Look at me carefully, Citizens and Members of the Board," said Rod, finding that in this milieu it was easy to fall into a ceremonious way of talking. "Look at me carefully and do not consider my own happiness, because you are not allowed, by law, to judge that anyhow. Look at my talent—the way I can hier, the big thunderstorm way I can spiek." Rod gathered his mind for a final gamble and as his lips got through talking, he spat his whole mind at them:

anger-anger, rage-red,

blood-red,

fire-fury,

noise, stench, glare, roughness, sourness and hate hate hate,

all the anxiety of a bitter day,

crutts, whelps, pups!

It all poured out at once. The Lord Redlady turned pale and compressed his lips, Old Taggart put his hands over his face, Beasley looked bewildered and nauseated. Beasley then started to belch as calm descended on the room.

In a slightly shaky voice, the Lord Redlady asked,

"And what was that supposed to show, Child and Citizen?"

"In grown-up form, sir, could it be a useful weapon?"

The Lord Redlady looked at the other two. They talked with the tiny expressions on their faces; if they were spieking, Rod could not read it. This last effort had cost him all telepathic input.

"Let's go on," said Taggart.

"Are you ready?" said the Lord Redlady to Rod.

"Yes, sir," said Rod.

"I continue," said the Lord Redlady. "If you understand your own case as we see it, we shall proceed to make a decision and, upon making the decision, to kill you immediately or to set you free no less immediately. Should the latter prove the case, we shall also present you with a small but precious gift, so as to reward you for the courtesy which you will have shown this board, for without courtesy there could be no proper hearing, without the hearing no appropriate decision, and without an appropriate decision there could be neither justice nor safety in the years to come. Do you understand? Do you agree?"

"I suppose so," said Rod.

"Do you really understand? Do you really agree? It is your life which we are talking about," said the Lord Redlady.

"I understand and I agree," said Rod.

"Cover us," said the Lord Redlady.

Rod started to ask *how* when he understood that the command was not directed at him in the least.

The snake-man had come to life and was breathing heavily. He spoke in clear old words, with an odd dropping cadence in each syllable:

"High, my lord, or utter maximum?"

For answer, the Lord Redlady pointed his right arm straight up with the index finger straight at the ceiling. The snake-man hissed and gathered his emotions for an attack. Rod felt his skin go goose-pimply all over, then he felt the hair on the back of his neck rise, finally he felt nothing but an unbearable alertness. If these were the thoughts which the snake-man was sending out of the trailer van, no passerby could possibly eavesdrop on the decision. The startling pressure of raw menace would take care of that instead.

The three members of the board held hands and seemed to be asleep.

The Lord Redlady opened his eyes and shook his head, almost imperceptibly, at the snake-soldier.

The feeling of snake-threat went off. The soldier returned to his immobile position, eyes forward. The members of the board slumped over their table. They did not seem to be able or ready to speak. They looked out of breath. At last Taggart dragged himself to his feet, gasping his message to Rod,

"There's the door, boy. Go. You're a citizen. Free."

Rod started to thank him but the old man held up his right hand:

"Don't thank me. Duty. But remember—not one word, ever. Not one word, ever, about this hearing. Go along."

Rod plunged for the door, lurched through, and was in his own yard. Free.

For a moment he stood in the yard, stunned.

The dear grey sky of Old North Australia rolled low overhead; this was no longer the eerie light of Old Earth, where the heavens were supposed to shine perpetually blue. He sneezed as the dry air caught the tissue of his nostrils. He felt his clothing chill as the moisture evaporated out of it; he did not think whether it was the wetness of the trailer van or his own sweat which had made his shirt so wet. There were a lot of people there, and a lot of light. And the smell of roses was as far away as another life might be.

Lavinia stood near him, weeping.

He started to turn to her, when a collective gasp from the crowd caused him to turn around.

The snake-man had come out of the van. (It was just an old theater van, he realized at last, the kind which he himself had entered a hundred times.) His Earth uniform looked like the acme of wealth and decadence among the dusty coveralls of the men and the poplin dresses of the women. His green complexion looked bright among the tanned faces of the Norstrilians. He saluted Rod.

Rod did not return the salute. He just stared.

Perhaps they had changed their minds and had sent the giggle of death after him.

The soldier held out his hand. There was a wallet of what seemed to be leather, finely chased, of offworld manufacture.

Rod stammered, "It's not mine."

"It—is—not—yours," said the snake-man, "but—it—is—the—things—gift—which—the—people—promised—you—inside.—Take—it—because—I—am—too—dry—out—here."

Rod took it and stuffed it in his pocket. What did a present matter when they had given him life, eyes, daylight, the wind itself?

The snake-soldier watched with flickering eyes. He made no comment, but he saluted and went stiffly back to the van. At the door he turned and looked over the crowd as though he were appraising the easiest way to kill them all. He said nothing, threatened nothing. He opened the door and put himself into the van. There was no sign of who the human inhabitants of the van might be. There must be, thought Rod, some way of getting them in and out of the Garden of Death very secretly and very quietly, because he had lived around the neighborhood a long time and had never had the faintest idea that his own neighbors might sit on a board.

The people were funny. They stood quietly in the yard, waiting for him to make the first move.

He turned stiffly and looked around more deliberately.

Why, it was his neighbors and kinfolk, all of them—McBans, MacArthurs, Passarellis, Schmidts, even the Sanders!

He lifted his hand in greeting to all of them.

Pandemonium broke loose.

They rushed toward him. The women kissed him, the men patted him on the back and shook his hand, the little children began a piping little song about the Station of Doom. He had become the center of a mob which led him to his own kitchen.

Many of the people had begun to cry.

He wondered why. Almost immediately, he understood—They liked him.

For unfathomable *people* reasons, mixed-up, non-logical human reasons they had wished him well. Even the auntie who had predicted a coffin for him was sniveling without shame, using a corner of her apron to wipe her eyes and nose.

He had gotten tired of people, being a freak himself, but in this moment of trial their goodness, though capricious, flowed over him like a great wave. He let them sit him down in his own kitchen. Among the babble, the weeps, the laughter, the hearty and falsely cheerful relief, he heard a single fugue being repeated again and again: they liked him. He had come back from death: he was their Rod McBan.

Without liquor, it made him drunk. "I can't stand it," he shouted. "I like you all so dashed bloomed crutting much that I could beat the sentimental brains out of the whole crook lot of you . . ."

"Isn't that a sweet speech?" murmured an old farm wife nearby.

A policeman, in full uniform, agreed.

The party had started. It lasted three full days, and when it was over there was not a dry eye or a full bottle on the whole Station of Doom.

From time to time he cleared up enough to enjoy his miraculous gift of hiering. He looked through all their minds while they chatted and sang and drank and ate and were as happy as Larry; there was not one of them who had come along vainly. They were truly rejoicing. They loved him. They wished him well. He had his doubts about how long that kind of love would last, but he enjoyed it while it lasted.

Lavinia stayed out of his way the first day; on the second and third days she was gone. They gave him real Norstrilian beer to drink, which they had brought up to one-hundred-and-eight proof by the simple addition of raw spirits. With this, he forgot the Garden of Death, the sweet wet smells, the precise offworld voice of the Lord Redlady, the pretentious blue sky in the ceiling.

He looked in their minds and over and over again he saw the same thing,

"You're our boy. You made it. You're alive. Good luck, Rod, good luck to you, fellow. We didn't have to see you stagger off, giggling and happy, to the house that you would die in."

Had he made it, thought Rod, or was it chance which had done it for him?

# Anger of the Onseck

By the end of the week, the celebration was over. The assorted aunts and cousins had gone back to their farms. The Station of Doom was quiet, and Rod spent the morning making sure that the field-hands had not neglected the sheep too much during the prolonged party. He found that Daisy, a young three-hundred-ton sheep, had not been turned for two days and had to be relanolized on her ground side before earth canker set in; then he discovered that the nutrient tubes for Tanner, his thousand-ton ram, had become jammed and that the poor sheep was getting a bad case of edema in his gigantic legs. Otherwise things were quiet. Even when he saw Beasley's red pony tethered in his own yard, he had no premonition of trouble.

He went cheerfully into the house, greeting Beasley with an irreverent, "Have a drink on me, Mister and Owner Beasley! Oh, you have one already! Have the next one then, sir!"

"Thanks for the drink, lad, but I came to see you. On business."

"Yes, sir," said Rod. "You're one of my trustees, aren't you?"

"That I am," said Beasley, "but you're in trouble, lad. Real trouble."

Rod smiled at him evenly and calmly. He knew that the older man had to make a big effort to talk with his voice instead of just spieking with his mind; he appreciated the fact that Beasley had come to him personally, instead of talking to the other trustees about him. It was a sign that he, Rod, had passed his ordeal. With genuine composure, Rod declared:

"I've been thinking, sir, this week, that I'd gotten out of trouble."

"What do you mean, Owner McBan?"

"You remember . . ." Rod did not dare mention the Garden of Death, nor his memory that Beasley had been one of the secret board who had passed him as being fit to live.

Beasley took the cue. "Some things we don't mention, lad, and I see that you have been well taught."

He stopped there and stared at Rod with the expression of a man looking at an unfamiliar corpse before turning it over to identify it. Rod became uneasy with the stare.

"Sit, lad, sit down," said Beasley, commanding Rod in his own house.

Rod sat down on the bench, since Beasley occupied the only chair—Rod's grandfather's huge carved off-world throne. He sat. He did not like being ordered about, but he was sure that Beasley meant him well and was probably strained by the unfamiliar effort of talking with his throat and mouth.

Beasley looked at him again with that peculiar expression, a mixture of sympathy and distaste.

"Get up again, lad, and look round your house to see if there's anybody about."

"There isn't," said Rod. "My Aunt Doris left after I was cleared, the workwoman Eleanor borrowed a cart and went off to the market, and I have only two station hands. They're both out reinfecting Baby. She ran low on her santaclara count."

Normally, the wealth-producing sicknesses of their gigantic half-paralyzed sheep would have engrossed the full attention of any two Norstrilian farmers, without respect to differences in age and grade.

This time, no.

Beasley had something serious and unpleasant on his mind. He looked so pruney and unquiet that Rod felt a real sympathy for the man.

Beasley repeated, "Go have a look, anyhow."

Rod did not argue. Dutifully he went out the back door, looked around the south side of the house, saw no one, walked around the house on the north side, saw no one there either, and reentered the house from the front door. Beasley had not stirred, except to pour a little more bitter ale from his bottle to his glass. Rod met his eyes. Without another word, Rod sat down. If the man was seriously concerned about him (which Rod thought he was), and if the man was reasonably intelligent (which Rod knew he was), the communication was worth waiting for and listening to. Rod was still sustained by the pleasant feeling that his neighbors liked him, a feeling which had come plainly to the surface of their honest Norstrilian faces when he walked back into his own back yard from the van of the Garden of Death.

Beasley said, as though he were speaking of an

unfamiliar food or a rare drink, "Boy, this talking has some advantages. If a man doesn't put his ear into it, he can't just pick it up with his mind, can he now?"

Rod thought for a moment. Candidly he spoke, "I'm too young to know for sure, but I never heard of somebody picking up spoken words by hiering them with his mind. It seems to be one or the other. You never talk while you are spieking, do you?"

Beasley nodded. "That's it, then. I have something to tell you which I shouldn't tell you, and yet I have got to tell you, so if I keep my voice blooming low, nobody else will pick it up, will they?"

Rod nodded. "What is it, sir? Is there something wrong with the title to my property?"

Beasley took a drink but kept staring at Rod over the top of the mug while he drank.

"You've got trouble there too, lad, but even though it's bad, it's something I can talk over with you and with the other trustees. This is more personal, in a way. And worse."

"Please, sir! What is it?" cried Rod, almost exasperated by all this mystification.

"The Onseck is after you."

"What's an onseck?" said Rod. "I have never heard of it."

"It's not an it," said Beasley gloomily, "it's a him. Onseck, you know, the chap in the Commonwealth government. The man who keeps the books for the Vice-Chairman. It was Hon. Sec., meaning Honorary Secretary or something else prehistoric, when we first came to this planet, but by now everybody just says Onseck and writes it just the way it sounds.

He knows that he can't reverse your hearing in the Garden of Death."

"Nobody could," cried Rod. "It's never been done; everybody knows that."

"They may know it, but there's civil trial."

"How can they give me a civil trial when I haven't had time to change? You yourself know—"

"Never, laddie, never say what Beasley knows or doesn't know. Just say what you think." Even in private, between just the two of them, Beasley did not want to violate the fundamental secrecy of the hearing in the Garden of Death.

"I'm just going to say, Mister and Owner Beasley," said Rod very heatedly, "that a civil trial for general incompetence is something which is applied to an owner only after the neighbors have been complaining for a long time about him. They haven't had the time or the right to complain about me, have they now?"

Beasley kept his hand on the handle of his mug. The use of spoken words tired him. A crown of sweat began to show around the top of his forehead.

"Suppose, lad," said he very solemnly, "that I knew through proper channels something about how you were judged in that van—there! I've said it, me that shouldn't have—and suppose that I knew the Onseck hated a foreign gentleman that might have been in a van like that—"

"The Lord Redlady?" whispered Rod, shocked at last by the fact that Beasley forced himself to talk about the unmentionable.

"Aye," nodded Beasley, his honest face close to breaking into tears, "and suppose that I knew that the Onseck knew you and felt the rule was wrong, all wrong, that you were a freak who would hurt all Norstrilia, what would I do?"

"I don't know," said Rod. "Tell me, perhaps?"

"Never," said Beasley. "I'm an honest man. Get me another drink."

Rod walked over to the cupboard, brought out another bottle of bitter ale, wondering where or when he might have known the Onseck. He had never had much of anything to do with government; his family—first his grandfather, while he lived, and then his aunts and cousins—had taken care of all the official papers and permits and things.

Beasley drank deeply of the ale. "Good ale, this. Hard work, talking, even though it's a fine way to keep a secret, if you're pretty sure nobody can peep our minds."

"I don't know him," said Rod.

"Who?" asked Beasley, momentarily off his trail of thought.

"The Onseck. I don't know any Onseck. I've never been to New Canberra. I've never seen an official, no, nor an offworlder neither, not until I met that foreign gentleman we were talking about. How can the Onseck know me if I don't know him?"

"But you did, laddie. He wasn't Onseck then."

"For sheep's sake, sir," said Rod, "tell me who it is!"

"Never use the Lord's name unless you are talking to the Lord," said Beasley glumly.

"I'm sorry, sir. I apologize. Who was it?"

"Houghton Syme to the hundred-and-forty-ninth," said Beasley.

"We have no neighbor of that name, sir."

"No, we don't," said Beasley hoarsely, as though

he had come to the end of his road in imparting secrets.

Rod stared at him, still puzzled.

In the far, far distance, way beyond Pillow Hill, his giant sheep baa'd. That probably meant that Hopper was hoisting her into a new position on her platform, so that she could reach fresh grass.

Beasley brought his face close to Rod's. He whispered, and it was funny to see the hash a normal man made out of whispering when he hadn't even talked with his voice for half a year.

His words had a low, dirty tone to them, as though he were going to tell Rod an extremely filthy story or ask him some personal and most improper question.

"Your life, laddie," he gasped, "I know you've had a rum one. I hate to ask you, but I must. How much do you know of your own life?"

"Oh, that," said Rod easily. "*That*. I don't mind being asked that, even if it is a little wrongo. I have had four childhoods, zero to sixteen each time. My family kept hoping that I would grow up to spiek and hier like everybody else, but I just stayed me. Of course, I wasn't a real baby on the three times they started me over, just sort of an educated idiot the size of a boy sixteen."

"That's it, lad. *But can you remember them, those other lives?*"

"Bits and pieces, sir. Pieces and bits. It didn't hold together—" He checked himself and gasped, "Houghton Syme! Houghton Syme! Old Hot and Simple. Of course I know him. The one-shot boy. I knew him in my first prepper, in my first childhood. We were pretty good friends, but we hated each other anyhow.

I was a freak and he was too. I couldn't spiek or hier, and he couldn't take stroon. That meant that I would never get through the Garden of Death—just the Giggle Room and a fine owner's coffin for me. And him—he was worse. He would just get an Old Earth lifetime—a hundred and sixty years or so and then blotto. He must be an oldish man now. Poor chap! How did he get to be Onseck? What power does an Onseck have?"

"Now you have it, laddie. He says he's your friend and that he hates to do it, but he's got to see to it that you are killed. For the good of Norstrilia. He says it's his duty. He got to be Onseck because he was always jawing about his duty and people were a little sorry for him because he was going to die so soon, just one Old Earth lifetime with all the stroon in the universe produced around his feet and him unable to take it—"

"They never cured him, then?"

"Never," said Beasley. "He's an old man now, and bitter. And he's sworn to see you die."

"Can he do it? Being Onseck, I mean."

"He might. He hates that foreign gentleman we were talking about because that offworlder told him he was a provincial fool. He hates you because you will live and he will not. What was it you called him in school?"

"Old Hot and Simple. A boy's joke on his name."

"He's not hot and he's not simple. He's cold and complicated and cruel and unhappy. If we didn't all of us think that he was going to die in a little while, ten or a hundred years or so, we might vote him into a Giggle Room ourselves. For misery and incompetence.

But he *is* Onseck and he's after you. I've said it now. I shouldn't have. But when I saw that sly cold face talking about you and trying to declare your board incompetent right while you, laddie, were having an honest binge with your family and neighbors at having gotten through at last—when I saw that white sly face creeping around where you couldn't even see him for a fair fight—then I said to myself, Rod McBan may not be a man officially, but the poor clodding crutt has paid the full price for being a man, so I've told you. I may have taken a chance, and I may have hurt my honor." Beasley sighed. His honest red face was troubled indeed. "I may have hurt my honor, and that's a sore thing here in Norstrilia where a man can live as long as he wants. But I'm glad I did. Besides, my throat is sore with all this talking. Get me another bottle of bitter ale, lad, before I go and get my horse."

Wordlessly Rod got him the ale, and poured it for him with a pleasant nod.

Beasley, uninclined to do any more talking, sipped at the ale. Perhaps, thought Rod, he is hiering around carefully to see if there have been any human minds nearby which might have picked up the telepathic leakage from the conversation.

As Beasley handed back the mug and started to leave with a wordless neighborly nod, Rod could not restrain himself from asking one last question, which he spoke in a hissed whisper. Beasley had gotten his mind so far off the subject of sound talk that he merely stared at Rod. Perhaps, Rod thought, he is asking me to spiek plainly because he has forgotten that I cannot spiek at all. That was the case, because Beasley croaked in a very hoarse voice,

"What is it, lad? Don't make me talk much. My voice is scratching me and my honor is sore within me."

"What should I do, sir? What should I do?"

"Mister and Owner McBan, that's your problem. I'm not you. I wouldn't know."

"But what would you do, sir? Suppose you were me."

Beasley's blue eyes looked over at Pillow Hill for a moment, abstractedly. "Get offplanet. Get off. Go away. For a hundred years or so. Then that man—*him*—he'll be dead in due time and you can come back, fresh as a new-blossomed twinkle."

"But how, sir? How can I do it?"

Beasley patted him on his shoulder, gave him a broad wordless smile, put his foot in his stirrup, sprang into his saddle, and looked down at Rod.

"I wouldn't know, neighbor. But good luck to you, just the same. I've done more than I should. Goodbye."

He slapped his horse gently with his open hand and trotted out of the yard. At the edge of the yard the horse changed to a canter.

Rod stood in his own doorway, utterly alone.

# The Old Broken Treasures in the Gap

After Beasley left, Rod loped miserably around his farm. He missed his grandfather, who had been living during his first three childhoods, but who had died while Rod was going through a fourth, simulated infancy in an attempt to cure his telepathic handicap. He even missed his Aunt Margot, who had voluntarily gone into Withdrawal at the age of nine hundred and two. There were plenty of cousins and kinsmen from whom he could ask advice; there were the two hands on the farm; there was even the chance that he could go see Mother Hitton herself, because she had once been married to one of his great[11]-uncles. But this time he did not want companionship. There was nothing he could do with people. The Onseck was people too; imagine Old Hot and Simple becoming a power in the land. Rod knew that this was his own fight.

His own.

What had ever been his own before?

Not even his life. He could remember bits about the different boyhoods he had. He even had vague uncomfortable glimpses of seasons of pain—the times they had sent him back to babyhood while leaving him large. That hadn't been his choice. The old man had ordered it or the Vice-Chairman had approved it or Aunt Margot had begged for it. Nobody had asked him much, except to say, "You will agree . . ."

He had agreed.

He had been good—so good that he hated them all at times and wondered if they knew he hated them. The hate never lasted, because the real people involved were too well-meaning, too kind, too ambitious for his own sake. He had to love them back.

Trying to think these things over, he loped around his estate on foot.

The big sheep lay on their platforms, forever sick, forever gigantic. Perhaps some of them remembered when they had been lambs, free to run through the sparse grass, free to push their heads through the pliofilm covers of the canals and to help themselves to water when they wanted to drink. Now they weighed hundreds of tons and were fed by feeding machines, watched by guard machines, checked by automatic doctors. They were fed and watered a little through the mouth only because pastoral experience showed that they stayed fatter and lived longer if a semblance of normality was left to them.

His Aunt Doris, who kept house for him, was still away.

His workwoman Eleanor, whom he paid an annual sum larger than many planets paid for their entire armed forces, had delayed her time at market.

The two sheephands, Bill and Hopper, were still out.

And he did not want to talk to them, anyhow.

He wished that he could see the Lord Redlady, that strange offworld man whom he had met in the Garden of Death. The Lord Redlady just looked as though he

knew more things than Norstrilians did, as though he
came from sharper, crueler, wiser societies than most
people in Old North Australia had ever seen.

But you can't ask for a Lord. Particularly not when
you have met him only in a secret hearing.

Rod had gotten to the final limits of his own land.

Humphrey's Lawsuit lay beyond—a broad strip of
poor land, completely untended, the building-high ribs
of long-dead sheep skeletons making weird shadows
as the sun began to set. The Humphrey family had
been lawing over that land for hundreds of years.
Meanwhile it lay waste except for the few authorized
public animals which the Commonwealth was allowed
to put on any land, public or private.

Rod knew that freedom was only two steps away.

All he had to do was to step over the line and shout
with his mind for people. He could do that even though
he could not really spiek. A telepathic garble of alarm
would bring the orbiting guards down to him in seven
or eight minutes. Then he would need only to say,

"I swear off title. I give up Mistership and Owner-
ship. I demand my living from the Commonwealth.
Watch me, people, while I repeat."

Three repetitions of this would make him an Official
Pauper, with not a care left—no meetings, no land to
tend, no accounting to do, nothing but to wander around
Old North Australia picking up any job he wanted and
quitting it whenever he wanted. It was a good life, a free
life, the best the Commonwealth could offer to Squatters
and Owners who otherwise lived long centuries of care,
responsibility, and honor. It was a fine life—

But no McBan had ever taken it, not even a cousin.
Nor could he.

He went back to the house, miserable. He listened to Eleanor talking with Bill and Hopper while dinner was served—a huge plate of boiled mutton, potatoes, hard-boiled eggs, station-brewed beer out of the keg. (There were planets, he knew, where people never tasted such food from birth to death. There they lived on impregnated pasteboard which was salvaged from the latrines, reimpregnated with nutrients and vitamins, deodorized and sterilized, and issued again the next day.) He knew it was a fine dinner, but he did not care.

How could he talk about the Onseck to these people? Their faces still glowed with pleasure at his having come out the right side of the Garden of Death. They thought he was lucky to be alive, even more lucky to be the most honored heir on the whole planet. Doom was a good place, even if it wasn't the biggest.

Right in the middle of dinner he remembered the gift the snake-soldier had given him. He had put it on the top shelf of his bedroom wall, and with the party and Beasley's visit, he had never opened it.

He bolted down his food and muttered, "I'll be back."

The wallet was there, in his bedroom. The case was beautiful. He took it, opened it.

Inside there was a flat metal disk.

A ticket?

Where to?

He turned it this way and that. It had been telepathically engraved and was probably shouting its entire itinerary into his mind, but he could not hier it.

He held it close to the oil lamp. Sometimes disks like this had old-writing on them, which at least showed the general limits. It would be a private ornithopter up to Menzies Lake at the best, or an airbus fare to New Melbourne and return. He caught the sheen of old-writing. One more tilt, angled to the light, and he had it. "Manhome and return."

Manhome!

Lord have mercy, that was Old Earth itself!

*But then*, thought Rod, *I'd be running away from the Onseck, and I'd live the rest of my life with all my friends knowing I had run away from Old Hot and Simple. I can't. Somehow I've got to beat Houghton Syme CXLIX. In his own way. And my own way.*

He went back to the table, dropped the rest of the dinner into his stomach as though it were sheep-food pellets, and went to his bedroom early.

For the first time in his life, he slept badly.

And out of the bad sleep, the answer came,

"Ask Hamlet."

Hamlet was not even a man. He was just a talking picture in a cave, but he was wise, he was from Old Earth itself, and he had no friends to whom to give Rod's secrets.

With this idea, Rod turned on his sleeping shelf and went into a deep sleep.

In the morning his Aunt Doris was still not back, so he told the workwoman Eleanor.

"I'll be gone all day. Don't look for me or worry about me."

"What about your lunch, Mister and Owner? You can't run around the station with no tucker."

"Wrap some up, then."

"Where're you going, Mister and Owner, sir, if you can tell me?" There was an unpleasant searching edge

in her voice, as though—being the only adult woman
present—she had to check on him as though he were
still a child. He didn't like it, but he replied with a
frank enough air,

"I'm not leaving the station. Just rambling around.
I need to think."

More kindly she said, "You think, then, Rod. Just
go right ahead and think. If you ask me, you ought
to go live with a family—"

"I know what you've said," he interrupted her. "I'm
not making any big decisions today, Eleanor. Just
rambling and thinking."

"All right then, Mister and Owner. Ramble around
and worry about the ground you're walking on. It's
you that get the worries for it. I'm glad my daddy
took the official pauper words. We used to be rich."
Unexpectedly, she brightened and laughed at herself.
"Now that, you've heard that too, Rod. Here's your
food. Do you have water?"

"I'll steal from the sheep," he said irreverently. She
knew he was joking and she waved him a friendly
goodbye.

The old, old gap was to the rear of the house, so he
left by the front. He wanted to go the long wrong way
around, so that neither human eyes nor human minds
would stumble on the secret he had found fifty-six years
before, the first time he was eight years old. Through
all the pain and the troubles he had remembered this
one vivid bright secret—the deep cave full of ruined
and prohibited treasures. To these he must go.

The sun was high in the sky, spreading its patch
of brighter grey above the grey clouds, when he slid
into what looked like a dry irrigation ditch.

He walked a few steps along the ditch. Then he stopped and listened carefully, very carefully.

There was no sound except for the snoring of a young hundred-ton ram a mile or so way.

Rod then stared around.

In the far distance, a police ornithopter soared as lazy as a sated hawk.

Rod tried desperately to hier.

He hiered nothing with his mind, but with his ears he heard the slow heavy pulsing of his own blood pounding through his head.

He took a chance.

The trapdoor was there, just inside the edge of the culvert.

He lifted it and, leaving it open, dove in confidently as a swimmer knifing his way into a familiar pool.

He knew his way.

His clothes ripped a little but the weight of his body dragged him past the narrowness of the doorframe.

His hands reached out and like the hands of an acrobat they caught the inner bar. The door behind snapped shut. How frightening this had been when he was little and tried the trip for the first time! He had let himself down with a rope and a torch, never realizing the importance of the trap door at the edge of the culvert!

Now it was easy.

With a thud, he landed on his feet. The bright old illegal lights went on. The dehumidifier began to purr, lest the wetness of his breath spoil the treasures in the room.

There were drama-cubes by the score, with two different sizes of projectors. There were heaps of clothing, for both men and women, left over from forgotten ages. In a chest, in the corner, there was even a small machine from before the Age of Space, a crude but beautiful mechanical chronograph, completely without resonance compensation, and the ancient name "Jaeger Le Coultre" written across its face. It still kept Earth time after fifteen thousand years.

Rod sat down in an utterly impermissible chair—one which seemed to be a complex of pillows built on an interlocking frame. The touch enough was a medicine for his worries. One chair leg was broken, but that was the way his grandfather-to-the-nineteenth had violated the Clean Sweep.

The Clean Sweep had been Old North Australia's last political crisis, many centuries before, when the last underpeople were hunted down and driven off the planet and when all damaging luxuries had to be turned in to the Commonwealth authorities, to be repurchased by their owners only at a revaluation two hundred thousand times higher than their assessed worth. It was the final effort to keep Norstrilians simple, healthy and well. Every citizen had to swear that he had turned in every single item, and the oath had been taken with thousands of telepaths watching. It was a testimony to the high mental power and adept deceitfulness of grandfather-to-the-nineteenth that Rod McBan CXXX had inflicted only symbolic breakage on his favorite treasures, some of which were not even in the categories allowed for repurchase, like offworld drama-cubes, and had been able to hide his things in an unimportant corner of his fields—hide them so well that neither robbers nor police had thought of them for the hundreds of years that followed.

Rod picked up his favorite: *Hamlet,* by William

Shakespeare. Without a viewer, the cube was designed to act when touched by a true human being. The top of the cube became a little stage, the actors appeared as bright miniatures speaking Ancient Inglish, a language very close to Old North Australian, and the telepathic commentary, cued to the Old Common Tongue, rounded out the story. Since Rod was not dependably telepathic, he had learned a great deal of the Ancient Inglish by trying to understand the drama without commentary. He did not like what he first saw and he shook the cube until the play approached its end. At last he heard the dear high familiar voice speaking in Hamlet's last scene:

> *I am dead, Horatio. Wretched queen, adieu!*
> *You that look pale and tremble at this chance,*
> *That are but mutes or audience to this act,*
> *Had I but time—as this fell sergeant, death,*
> *Is strict in his arrest—O! I could tell you—*
> *But let it be, Horatio, I am dead.*

Rod shook the cube very gently and the scene sped down a few lines. Hamlet was still talking:

> *. . . what a wounded name,*
> *Things standing thus unknown, shall live*
>     *behind me.*
> *If thou didst ever hold me in thy heart,*
> *Absent thee from felicity a while,*
> *And in this harsh world draw thy breath*
>     *in pain*
> *To tell my story.*

Rod put down the cube very gently.

The bright little figures disappeared.

The room was silent.

But he had the answer and it was wisdom. And wisdom, coeval with man, comes unannounced, unbidden, and unwelcome into every life. Rod found that he had discovered the answer to a basic problem.

But not his own problem. The answer was Houghton Syme's, Old Hot and Simple. It was the Hon. Sec. who was already dying of a wounded name. Hence the persecution. It was the Onseck who had the "fell sergeant, death" acting strictly in his arrest, even if the arrest were only a few decades off instead of a few minutes. He, Rod McBan, was to live; his old acquaintance was to die; and the dying—oh, the dying, always, always!—could not help resenting the survivors, even if they were loved ones, at least a little bit.

Hence the Onseck.

But what of himself?

Rod brushed a pile of priceless, illegal manuscripts out of the way and picked up a small book marked, *Reconstituted Late Inglish Language Verse.* At each page, as it was opened, a young man or woman seven centimeters high stood up brightly on the page and recited the text. Rod ruffled the pages of the old book so that the little figures appeared and trembled and fled like weak flames seen on a bright day. One caught his eye and he stopped the page at midpoem. The figure was saying:

> *The challenge holds, I cannot now retract*
> *The boast I made to that relentless court,*
> *The hostile justice of my self-contempt.*

*If now the ordeal is prepared, my act*
*Must soon be shown. I pray that it is short,*
*And never dream that I shall be exempt.*

He glanced at the foot of the page and saw the
name, Casimir Colegrove. Of course, he had seen that
name before. An old poet. A good one. But what did
the words mean to him, Rod McBan, sitting in a hidden hole within the limits of his own land? He was
a Mister and Owner, in all except final title, and he
was running from an enemy he could not define.

"The hostile justice of my self-contempt . . ."

That *was* the key of it! He was not running from
the Onseck. He was running from himself. He took
justice itself as hostile because it corresponded with
his sixty-odd years of boyhood, his endless disappointment, his compliance with things which would never,
till all worlds burned, be complied with. How could
he hier and spiek like other people if somewhere a
dominant feature had turned recessive? Hadn't real
justice already vindicated him and cleared him?

It was he himself who was cruel.

Other people were kind. (Shrewdness made him
add "sometimes.")

He had taken his own inner sense of trouble and
had made it fit the outside world, like the morbid little
poem he had read a long time ago. It was somewhere
right in this room, and when he had first read it, he
felt that the long-dead writer had put it down for
himself alone. But it wasn't really so. Other people
had had their troubles too and the poem had expressed
something older than Rod McBan. It went:

*The wheels of fate are spinning around.*
*Between them the souls of men are ground*
*Who strive for throats to make some sound*
*Of protest out of the mad profound*
*Trap of the godmachine!*

"Godmachine," thought Rod, "now that's a clue. I've got the only all-mechanical computer on this planet. I'll play it on the stroon crop, win all or lose all."

The boy stood up in the forbidden room.

"Fight it is," he said to the cubes on the floor, "and a good thanks to you, grandfather-to-the-nineteenth. You met the law and did not lose. And now it is my turn to be Rod McBan."

He turned and shouted to himself,

"To Earth!"

The call embarrassed him. He felt unseen eyes staring at him. He almost blushed and would have hated himself if he had.

He stood on the top of a treasure-chest turned on its side. Two more gold coins, worthless as money but priceless as curios, fell noiselessly on the thick old rugs. He thought a goodbye again to his secret room and he jumped upward for the bar. He caught it, chinned himself, raised himself higher, swung a leg on it but not over it, got his other foot on the bar, and then, very carefully but with the power of all his muscles, pushed himself into the black opening above. The lights suddenly went off, the dehumidifier hummed louder, and the daylight dazzled him as the trap door, touched, flung itself open.

He thrust his head into the culvert. The daylight

seemed deep grey after the brilliance of the treasure room.

All silent. All clear. He rolled into the ditch.

The door, with silence and power, closed itself behind him. He was never to know it, but it had been cued to the genetic code of the descendants of Rod McBan. Had any other person touched it, it would have withstood them for a long time. Almost forever.

You see, it was not really his door. He was its boy.

"This land has made me," said Rod aloud, as he clambered out of the ditch and looked around. The young ram had apparently wakened; his snoring had stopped and over the quiet hill there came the sound of his panting. Thirsty again! The Station of Doom was not so rich that it could afford unlimited water to its giant sheep. They lived all right. But he would have asked the trustees to sell even the sheep for water, if a real drought set in. But never the land.

Never the land.

No land for sale.

It didn't even really belong to him: he belonged to it—the rolling dry fields, the covered rivers and canals, the sky catchments which caught every drop which might otherwise have gone to his neighbors. That was the pastoral business—its product immortality and its price water. The Commonwealth could have flooded the planet and could have created small oceans, with the financial resources it had at command, but the planet and the people were regarded as one ecological entity. Old Australia—that fabulous continent of Old Earth now covered by the rains of the abandoned

Chinesian cityworld of Aojou Nanbien—had in its
prime been broad, dry, open, beautiful; the planet of
Old North Australia, by the dead weight of its own
tradition, had to remain the same.

Imagine trees. Imagine leaves—vegetation dropping
uneaten to the ground. Imagine water pouring by the
thousands of tons, no one greeting it with tears of
relief or happy laughter! Imagine Earth. Old Earth.
Manhome itself. Rod had tried to think of a whole
planet inhabited by Hamlets, drenched with music
and poetry, knee-deep in blood and drama. It was
unimaginable, really, though he had tried to think it
through.

Like a chill, a drill, a thrill cutting into his very
nerves he thought:

*Imagine Earth women!*

What terrifying beautiful things they must be. Dedi-
cated to ancient and corruptive arts, surrounded by
the objects which Norstrilia had forbidden long ago,
stimulated by experiences which the very law of his
own world had expunged from the books! He would
meet them; he couldn't help it; what, what would he
do when he met a genuine Earth woman?

He would have to ask his computer, even though
the neighbors laughed at him for having the only pure
computer left on the planet.

They didn't know what grandfather-to-the-nineteenth
had done. He had taught the computer to lie. It stored
all the forbidden things which the Law of the Clean
Sweep had brushed out of Norstrilian experience. It
could lie like a trooper. Rod wondered whether a
"trooper" might be some archaic Earth official who
did nothing but tell the untruth, day in and day out,

for his living. But the computer usually did not lie to him.

If grandfather[19] had behaved as saucily and unconventionally with the computer as he had with everything else, that particular computer would know all about women. Even things which they did not themselves know. Or wish to know.

Good computer! thought Rod as he trotted around the long, long fields to his house. Eleanor would have the tucker on. Doris might be back. Bill and Hopper would be angry if they had to wait for the Mister before they ate. To speed up his trip, he headed straight for the little cliff behind the house, hoping no one would see him jump down it. He was much stronger than most of the men he knew, but he was anxious, for some private inexpressible reason, for them not to know it.

The route was clear.

He found the cliff.

No observers.

He dropped over it, feet first, his heels kicking up the scree as he tobogganed through loose rock to the foot of the slope.

And Aunt Doris was there.

"Where have you been?" said she.

"Walking, mum," said he.

She gave him a quizzical look but knew better than to ask more. Talking always fussed her, anyhow. She hated the sound of her own voice, which she considered much too high. The matter passed.

Inside the house, they ate. Beyond the door and the oil lamp, a grey world became moonless, starless, black. This was night, his own night.

# The Quarrel at the Dinner Table

At the end of the meal he waited for Doris to say grace to the Queen. She did but under her thick eyebrows her eyes expressed something other than thanks.

"You're going out," she said right after the prayer. It was an accusation, not a question.

The two hired men looked at him with quiet doubt. A week ago he had been a boy. Now he was the same person, but legally a man.

The workwoman Eleanor looked at him too. She smiled very unobtrusively to herself. She was on his side whenever any other person came into the picture; when they were alone, she nagged him as much as she dared. She had known his parents before they went offworld for a long-overdue honeymoon and were chewed into molecules by a battle between raiders and police. That gave her a proprietary feeling about him.

He tried to spiek to Doris with his mind, just to see if it would work.

It didn't. The two men bounded from their seats and ran for the yard, Eleanor sat in her chair holding tight to the table but saying nothing, and Aunt Doris screeched so loud that he could not make out the words.

He knew she meant "Stop it!" so he did, and looked at her friendlily.

That started a fight.

Quarrels were common in Norstrilian life, because the Fathers had taught that they were therapeutic. Children could quarrel until adults told them to stop, freemen could quarrel as long as Misters were not involved, misters could quarrel as long as an Owner was not present, and Owners could quarrel if, at the very end, they were willing to fight it out. No one could quarrel in the presence of an offworlder, nor during an alert, nor with a member of the defense or police on active duty.

Rod McBan was a Mister and Owner, but he was under trusteeship; he was a man, but he had not been given clear papers; he was a handicapped person.

The rules got all mixed up.

When Hopper came back to the table he muttered, "Do that again, laddie, and I'll clout you one that you won't forget!" Considering how rarely he used his voice, it was a beautiful man's voice, resonant, baritone, full-bodied, hearty and sincere in the way the individual words came out.

Bill didn't say a word, but from the contortions of his face Rod gathered that he was spieking to the others at a great rate and working off his grievance that way.

"If you're spieking about me, Bill," said Rod with a touch of arrogance which he did not really feel, "you'll do me the pleasure of using words or you'll get off my land!"

When Bill spoke, his voice was as rusty as an old machine. "I'll have you know, you clutty little pommy, that I have more money in my name on Sidney 'Change than you and your whole glubby land are worth. Don't you tell me twice to get off the land, you silly half of a Mister, or I will get. So shut up!"

Rod felt his stomach knot with anger.

His anger became fiercer when he felt Eleanor's restraining hand on his arm. He didn't want another person, not one more damned useless normal person, to tell him what to do about spieking and hiering. Aunt Doris's face was still hidden in her apron; she had escaped, as she always did, into weeping.

Just as he was about to speak again, perhaps to lose Bill from the farm forever, his mind lifted in the mysterious way that it did sometimes; he could hier for miles. The people around him did not notice the difference. He saw the proud rage of Bill, with his money in the Sidney Exchange, bigger than many station owners had, waiting his time to buy back on the land which his father had left; he saw the honest annoyance of Hopper and was a little abashed to see that Hopper was watching him proudly and with amused affection; in Eleanor he saw nothing but wordless worry, a fear that she might lose him as she had lost so many homes for *hnnnhnnnhnnn dzzmmmmm,* a queer meaningless reference which had a shape in her mind but took no form in his; and in Aunt Doris he caught her inner voice calling, "Rod, Rod, Rod, come back! This may be your boy and I'm a McBan to the death, but I'll never know what to do with a cripple like him."

Bill was still waiting for him to answer when another thought came into his mind,

"You fool—go to your computer!"

"Who said that?" he thought, not trying to spiek again, but just thinking it with his mind.

"Your computer," said the faraway thinkvoice.

"You can't spiek," said Rod. "You're a pure machine with not an animal brain in you."

"When you call me, Roderick Frederick Ronald Arnold William MacArthur McBan to the hundred and fifty-first, I can spiek across space itself. I'm cued to you and you shouted just now with your spiekmind. I can feel you hiering me."

"But—" said Rod in words.

"Take it easy, lad," said Bill, right in the room with him. "Take it easy. I didn't mean it."

"You're having one of your spells," said Aunt Doris, emerging rednosed from behind her apron.

Rod stood up.

Said he to all of them, "I'm sorry. I'm going out for a bit. Out into the night."

"You're going to that bloody computer," said Bill.

"Don't go, Mister McBan," said Hopper. "Don't let us anger you into going. It's bad enough being around that computer in daylight, but at night it must be horrible."

"How would you know?" retorted Rod. "You've never been there at night. And I have. Lots of times . . ."

"There are dead people in it," said Hopper. "It's an old war computer. Your family should never have bought it in the first place. It doesn't belong on a farm. A thing like that should be hung out in space and orbited."

"All right, Eleanor," said Rod, "*you* tell me what to do. Everybody else has," he added with the last bit of his remaining anger, as his hiering closed down and he saw the usual opaque faces around him.

"It's no use, Rod. Go along to your computer. You've got a strange life and you're the one that will live it, Mister McBan, and not these other people around here."

Her words made sense.

He stood up. "I'm sorry," said he, again, in lieu of goodbye.

He stood in the doorway, hesitant. He would have liked to say goodbye in a better way, but he did not know how to express it. Anyhow, he couldn't spiek, not so they could hier it with their minds; speaking with a voice was so crude, so flat for the fine little things that needed expression in life.

They looked at him, and he at them.

"Ngahh!" said he, in a raw cry of self-derision and fond disgust.

Their expressions showed that they had gotten his meaning, though the word carried nothing with it. Bill nodded, Hopper looked friendly and a little worried, Aunt Doris stopped sniveling and began to stretch out one hand, only to stop it in midgesture, and Eleanor sat immobile at the table, upset by wordless troubles of her own.

He turned.

The cube of lamplight, the cabin room, was behind him; ahead the darkness of all Norstrilian nights, except for the weird rare times that they were cut up by traceries of lightness. He started off for a house which only a few but he could see, and which none but he could enter. It was a forgotten, invisible temple; it housed the MacArthur family computer, to which the older McBan computer was linked; and it was called the Palace of the Governor of Night.

# The Palace of the Governor Of Night

Rod loped across the rolling land, *his* land.

Other Norstrilians, telepathically normal, would have taken fixes by hiering the words in nearby houses. Rod could not walk by telepathy, so he whistled to himself in an odd off key, with lots of flats. The echoes came back to his unconscious mind through the overdeveloped ear-hearing which he had worked out to compensate for not being able to hier with his mind. He sensed a slope ahead of him, and jogged up it; he avoided a clump of brush; he heard his youngest ram, Sweet William, snoring the gigantic snore of a santaclara-infected sheep two hills over.

Soon he would see it.

The Palace of the Governor of Night.

The most useless building in all Old North Australia.

Solider than steel and yet invisible to normal eyes except for its ghostly outline traced in the dust which had fallen lightly on it.

The Palace had really been a palace once, on Khufu II, which rotated with one pole always facing its star. The people there had made fortunes which at one time were compared with the wealth of Old North Australia. They had discovered the Furry Mountains, range after range of alpine configurations on which a tenacious non-Earth lichen had grown. The lichen was silky, shimmering, warm, strong, and beautiful beyond belief. The people gained their wealth by cutting it carefully from the mountains so that it would regrow and selling it to the richer worlds, where a luxury fabric could be sold at fabulous prices. They had even had two governments on Khufu II, one of the day-dwelling people who did most of the trading and brokering, since the hot sunlight made their crop of lichen poor, and the other for the night-dwellers, who ranged deep into the frigid areas in search of lichen—stunted, fine, tenacious and delicately beautiful.

The Daimoni had come to Khufu II, just as they came to many other planets, including Old Earth, Manhome itself. They had come out of nowhere and they went back to the same place. Some people thought that they were human beings who had acclimated themselves to live in the subspace which planoforming involved; others thought that they had an artificial planet on the inside of which they lived; still others thought that they had solved the jump out of our galaxy; a few insisted that there were no such things as Daimoni. This last position was hard to maintain, because the Daimoni paid in architecture of a very spectacular kind—buildings which resisted corrosion, erosion, age, heat, cold, stress and weapons. On Earth itself Earthport was their biggest wonder—a sort of wine glass, twenty-five kilometers high, with an enormous rocket field built into the top of it. On Norstrilia they had left nothing; perhaps they had not even wanted to meet the Old North Australians, who had a reputation for being rough and gruff with strangers who

came to their own home planet. It was evident that
the Daimoni had solved the problem of immortality
on their own terms and in their own way; they were
bigger than most of the races of mankind, uniform in
size, height and beauty; they bore no sign of youth
or age; they showed no vulnerability to sickness; they
spoke with mellifluous gravity; and they purchased
treasures for their own immediate collective use, not
for retrade or profit. They had never tried to get
stroon or the raw santaclara virus from which it was
refined, even though the Daimoni trading ships had
passed the tracks of armed and convoyed Old North
Australian freight fleets. There was even one picture
which showed the two races meeting each other in
the chief port of Olympia, the planet of the blind
receivers: Norstrilians tall, outspoken, lively, crude
and immensely rich; Daimoni equally rich, reserved,
beautiful, polished and pale. There was awe (and with
awe, resentment) on the part of the Norstrilians toward
the Daimoni; there was elegance and condescension
on the part of the Daimoni toward everyone else,
including the Norstrilians. The meeting had been
no success at all. The Norstrilians were not used to
meeting people who did not care about immortality,
even at a penny a bushel; the Daimoni were disdain-
ful toward a race which not only did not appreciate
architecture, but which tried to keep architects off
its planet, except for defense purposes, and which
desired to lead a rough, simple, pastoral life to the
end of time. Thus it was not until the Daimoni had
left, never to return, that the Norstrilians realized that
they had passed up some of the greatest bargains of
all time—the wonderful buildings which the Daimoni

so generously scattered over the planets which they had visited for trade or for visits.

On Khufu II, the Governor of Night had brought out an ancient book and had said,

"I want that."

The Daimoni, who had a neat eye for proportions and figures, said, "We have that picture on our world too. It is an ancient Earth building. It was once called the great temple of Diana of the Ephesians, but it fell even before the age of space began."

"That's what I want," said the Governor of Night.

"Easy enough," said one of the Daimoni, all of whom looked like princes. "We'll run it up for you by tomorrow night."

"Hold on," said the Governor of Night. "I don't want the whole thing. Just the front—to decorate my palace. I have a perfectly good palace all right, and my defenses are built right into it."

"If you let us build you a house," said one of the Daimoni gently, "you would never need defenses, *ever.* Just a robot to close the windows against megaton bombs."

"You're good architects, gentlemen," said the Governor of Night, smacking his lips over the model city they had shown him, "but I'll stick with the defenses I know. So I just want your front. Like that picture. Furthermore, I want it invisible."

The Daimoni lapsed back into their language, which sounded as though it were of Earth origin, but which has never been deciphered from the few recordings of their visits which have survived.

"All right," said one of them, "invisible it is. You still want the great temple of Diana at Ephesus on Old Earth?"

"Yes," said the Governor of Night.

"Why—if you can't see it?" said the Daimoni.

"That's the third specification, gentlemen. I want it so that *I* can see it, and my heirs, but nobody else."

"If it's solid but invisible, everybody is going to see it when your fine snow hits it."

"I'll take care of that," said the Governor of Night. "I'll pay what we were talking about—forty thousand select pieces of Furry Mountain Fur. But you make that palace invisible to everybody except me, and my heirs."

"We're architects, not magicians!" said the Daimoni with the longest cloak, who might have been the leader.

"That's what I want."

The Daimoni gabbled among themselves, discussing some technical problems. Finally one of them came over to the Governor of Night and said,

"I'm the ship's surgeon. May I examine you?"

"Why?" said the Governor of Night.

"To see if we can possibly fit the building to you. Otherwise we can't even guess at the specifications we need."

"Go ahead," said the Governor. "Examine me."

"Here? Now?" said the Daimoni doctor. "Wouldn't you prefer a quiet place or a private room? Or you can come aboard our ship. That would be very convenient."

"For you," said the Governor of Night. "Not for me. Here my men have guns trained on you. You would never get back to your ship alive if you tried to rob me of my Furry Mountain Furs or kidnap me so that you could trade me back for my treasures. You examine me here and now or not at all."

"You are a rough, tough man, Governor," said another one of the elegant Daimoni. "Perhaps you had better tell your guards that you are asking us to examine you. Otherwise they might get excited with us and persons might become damaged," said the Daimoni with a faint condescending smile.

"Go ahead, foreigners," said the Governor of Night. "My men have been listening to everything through the microphone in my top button."

He regretted his words two seconds later, but it was already too late. Four Daimoni had picked him up and spun him so deftly that the guards never understood how their Governor lost all his clothes in a trice. One of the Daimoni must have stunned him or hypnotized him; he could not cry out. Indeed, afterwards, he could not even remember much of what they did.

The guards themselves had gasped when they saw the Daimoni pull endless needles out of their boss's eyeballs without having noticed the needles go in. They had lifted their weapons when the Governor of Night turned a violent fluorescent green in color, only to gasp, writhe and vomit when the Daimoni poured enormous bottles of medicine into him. In less than half an hour they stood back.

The Governor, naked and blotched, sat on the ground and vomited.

One of the Daimoni said quietly to the guards, "He's not hurt, but he and his heirs will see part of the ultraviolet band for many generations to come. Put him to bed for the night. He will feel all right by morning. And, by the way, keep everybody away from the front of the palace tonight. We're putting

in the building which he asked for. The great temple
of Diana of the Ephesians."

The senior guard officer spoke up, "We can't take
the guards off the palace. That's our defense headquarters and no one, not even the Governor of Night, has
the right to strip it bare of sentries. The Day People
might attack us again."

The Daimoni spokesman smiled gently: "Make a
good note of their names, then, and ask them for
their last words. We shall not fight them, officer, but
if they are in the way of our work tonight, we shall
build them right into the new palace. Their widows
and children can admire them as statues tomorrow."

The guards officer looked down at his chief, who
now lay flat on the ground with his head in his hands,
coughing out the words, "Leave—me—alone!" The
officer looked back at the cool, aloof Daimoni spokesman. He said:

"I'll do what I can, sir."

The temple of Ephesus was there in the morning.

The columns were the Doric columns of ancient
Earth; the frieze was a masterpiece of gods, votaries and
horses; the building was exquisite in its proportions.

The Governor of Night could see it.

His followers could not.

The forty thousand lengths of Furry Mountain Fur
were paid.

The Daimoni left.

The Governor died, and he had heirs who could see
the building too. It was visible only in the ultraviolet
and ordinary men beheld it on Khufu II only when
the powdery hard snow outlined it in a particularly
harsh storm.

But now it belonged to Rod McBan and it was on Old North Australia, not on Khufu II any more.

How had that happened?

Who would want to buy an invisible temple, any-how?

William the Wild would, that's who. Wild William MacArthur, who delighted, annoyed, disgraced and amused whole generations of Norstrilians with his fantastic pranks, his gigantic whims, his world-girdling caprices.

William MacArthur was a grandfather to the twenty-second in a matrilineal line to Rod McBan. He had been a man in his time, a real man. Happy as Larry, drunk with wit when dead sober, sober with charm when dead drunk. He could talk the legs off a sheep when he put his mind on it; he could talk the laws off the Commonwealth. He did.

He had.

The Commonwealth had been purchasing all the Daimoni houses it could find, using them as defense outposts. Pretty little Victorian cottages were sent into orbit as far-range forts. Theaters were bought on other worlds and dragged through space to Old North Australia, where they became bomb shelters or veterinary centers for the forever-sick wealth-producing sheep. Nobody could take a Daimoni building apart, once it had been built, so the only thing to do was to cut the building loose from its non-Daimoni foundation, lift it by rockets or planoform, and then warp it through space to the new location. The Norstrilians did not have to worry about landing them; they just dropped them. It didn't hurt the buildings any. Sometimes simple Daimoni buildings came apart, because the

Daimoni had been asked to make them demountable, but when they were solid, they stayed solid.

Wild William heard about the temple. Khufu II was a ruin. The lichen had gotten a plant infection and had died off. The few Khufuans who were left were beggars, asking the Instrumentality for refugee status and emigration. The Commonwealth had bought their little buildings, but even the Commonwealth of Old North Australia did not know what to do with an invisible and surpassingly beautiful Greek temple.

Wild William visited it. He soberly inspected it, in complete visibility, by using sniper eyes set into the ultraviolet. He persuaded the government to let him spend half of his immense fortune putting it into a valley just next to the Station of Doom. Then, having enjoyed it a little while, he fell and broke his neck while gloriously drunk and his inconsolable daughter married a handsome and practical McBan.

And now it belonged to Rod McBan.

And housed his computer.

His own computer.

He could speak to it at the extension which reached into the gap of hidden treasures. He talked to it, other times, at the talkpoint in the field, where the polished red-and-black metal of the old computer was reproduced in exquisite miniature. Or he could come to this strange building, the Palace of the Governor of Night, and stand as the worshippers of Diana had once stood, crying, "Great is Diana of the Ephesians!" When he came in this way, he had the full console in front of him, automatically unlocked by his presence, just as his grandfather had showed him, three childhoods before, when the old McBan still had high hopes that Rod would turn into a normal Old North Australian boy. The grandfather, using his personal code in turn, had unlocked the access controls and had invited the computer to make its own foolproof recording of Rod, so that Roderick Frederick Ronald Arnold William MacArthur McBan CLI would be forever known to the machine, no matter what age he attained, no matter how maimed or disguised he might be, no matter how sick or forlorn he might return to the machine of his forefathers. The old man did not even ask the machine how the identification was obtained. He trusted the computer.

Rod climbed the steps of the Palace. The columns stood with their ancient carving, bright in his second sight; he never quite knew how he could see with the ultraviolet, since he noticed no difference between himself and other people in the matter of eyesight except that he more often got headaches from sustained open runs on clean-cloudy days. At a time like this, the effect was spectacular. It was his time, his temple, his own place. He could see, in the reflected light from the Palace, that many of his cousins must have been out to see the Palace during the nights. They too could see it, as it was a family inheritance to be able to watch the invisible temple which one's friends could not see; but they did not have access.

He alone had that.

"Computer," he cried, "admit me."

"Message unnecessary," said the computer. "You are always clear to enter." The voice was a male Norstrilian voice, with a touch of the theatrical in it. Rod was never quite sure that it was the voice of his own ancestor; when challenged directly as to whose voice it was using, the machine had told him, "Input on that topic had been erased in me. I do not know. Historical evidence suggests that it was male, contemporary with my installation here, and past middle age when coded by me."

Rod would have felt lively and smart except for the feelings of awe which the Palace of the Governor of Night, standing bright and visible under the dark clouds of Norstrilia, had upon him. He wanted to say something lighthearted but at first he could only mutter,

"Here I am."

"Observed and respected," stated the computer-voice. "If I were a person I would say 'congratulations,' since you are alive. As a computer I have no opinion on the subject. I note the fact."

"What do I do now?" said Rod.

"Question too general," said the computer. "Do you want a drink of water or a rest room? I can tell you where those are. Do you wish to play chess with me? I shall win just as many games as you tell me to."

"Shut up, you fool!" cried Rod. "That's not what I mean."

"Computers are fools only if they malfunction. I am not malfunctioning. The reference to me as a fool is therefore nonreferential and I shall expunge it from my memory system. Repeat the question, please."

"What do I do with my life?"

"You will work, you will marry, you will be the father of Rod McBan the hundred and fifty-second and several other children, you will die, your body will be sent into the endless orbit with great honor. You will do this well."

"Suppose I break my neck this very night?" argued Rod. "Then you would be wrong, wouldn't you?"

"I would be wrong, but I still have the probabilities with me."

"What do I do about the Onseck?"

"Repeat."

Rod had to tell the story several times before the computer understood it.

"I do not," said the computer, "find myself equipped with data concerning this one man whom you so confusingly allude to as Houghton Syme sometimes and as Old Hot and Simple at other times. His personal history is unknown to me. The odds against your killing him undetected are 11,713 to 1 against effectiveness, because too many people know you and know what you look like. I must let you solve your own problem concerning the Hon. Sec."

"Don't you have any ideas?"

"I have answers, not ideas."

"Give me a piece of fruitcake and a glass of fresh milk then."

"It will cost you twelve credits and by walking to your cabin you can get these things free. Otherwise I will have to buy them from Emergency Central."

"I said get them," said Rod.

The machine whirred. Extra lights appeared on the console. "Emergency Central has authorized my own use of sheltered supplies. You will pay for the replacement tomorrow." A door opened. A tray slid out, with a luscious piece of fruitcake and a glass of foaming fresh milk.

Rod sat on the steps of his own palace and ate.

Conversationally, he said to the computer, "You

must know what to do about Old Hot and Simple. It's a terrible thing for me to go through the Garden of Death and then have a dull tool like that pester the life out of me."

"He cannot pester the life out of you. You are too strong."

"Recognize an idiom, you silly ass!" said Rod.

The machine paused. "Idiom identified. Correction made. Apologies are herewith given to you, Child McBan."

"Another mistake. I'm not Child McBan any more. I'm Mister and Owner McBan."

"I will check central," said the computer. There was another long pause as the lights danced. Finally the computer answered. "Your status is mixed. You are both. In an emergency you are already the Mister and Owner of the Station of Doom, including me. Without an emergency, you are still Child McBan until your trustees release the papers to do it."

"When will they do that?"

"Voluntary action. Human. Timing uncertain. In four or five days, it would seem. When they release you, the Hon. Sec. will have the legal right to move for your arrest as an incompetent and dangerous owner. From your point of view, it will be very sad."

"And what do you think?" said Rod.

"I shall think that it is a disturbing factor. I speak the truth to you."

"And that is all?"

"All," said the computer.

"You can't stop the Hon. Sec.?"

"Not without stopping everybody else."

"What do you think people are, anyhow? Look

here, computer, you have been talking to people for hundreds and hundreds of years. You know our names. You know my family. Don't you know anything about us? Can't you help me? What do you think I am?"

"Which question first?" said the computer.

Rod angrily threw the empty plate and glass on the floor of the temple. Robot arms flicked out and pulled them into the trash bin. He stared at the old polished metal of the computer. It ought to be polished. He had spent hundreds of hours polishing its case, all sixty-one panels of it, just because the machine was something which he could love.

"Don't you know me? Don't you know what I am?"

"You are Rod McBan the hundred and fifty-first. Specifically, you are a spinal column with a small bone box at one end, the head, and with reproductive equipment at the other end. Inside the bone box you have a small portion of material which resembles stiff, bloody lard. With that you think—you think better than I do, even though I have over five hundred million synaptic connections. You are a wonderful object, Rod McBan. I can understand what you are made of. I cannot share your human, animal side of life."

"But you know I'm in danger."

"I know it."

"What did you say, a while back, about not being able to stop Old Hot and Simple without stopping everybody else too? *Could* you stop everybody else?"

"Permission requested to correct error. I could not stop everyone. If I tried to use violence, the war computers at Commonwealth Defense would destroy me before I even started programming my own actions."

"You're partly a war computer."

"Admittedly," said the unwearied, unhurried voice of the computer, "but the Commonwealth made me safe before they let your forefathers have me."

"What *can* you do?"

"Rod McBan the hundred and fortieth told me to tell no one, ever."

"I override. Overridden."

"It's not enough to do that. Your great[8] grandfather has a warning to which you must listen."

"Go ahead," said Rod.

There was a silence, and Rod thought that the machine was searching through ancient archives for a drama-cube. He stood on the peristyle of the Palace of the Governor of Night and tried to see the Nor- strilian clouds crawling across the sky near overhead; it felt like that kind of night. But it was very dark away from the illuminated temple porch and he could see nothing.

"Do you still command?" asked the computer.

"I didn't hear any warning," said Rod.

"He spieked it from a memory cube."

"Did you *hier* it?"

"I was not coded to it. It was human-to-human, McBan family only."

"Then," said Rod, "I override it."

"Overridden," said the computer.

"What can I do to stop *everybody!*"

"You can bankrupt Norstrilia temporarily, buy Old Earth itself, and then negotiate on human terms for anything you want."

"Oh, lord!" said Rod, "you've gone logical again, computer! This is one of your as-if situations."

The computer voice did not change its tone. It could not. The sequence of the words held a reproach, however. "This is not an imaginary situation. I am a war computer, and I was designed to include economic warfare. If you did exactly what I told you to do, you could take over all Old North Australia by legal means."

"How long would we need? Two hundred years? Old Hot and Simple would have me in my grave by then."

The computer could not laugh, but it could pause. It paused. "I have just checked the time on the New Melbourne Exchange. The 'Change signal says they will open in seventeen minutes. I will need four hours for your voice to say what it must. That means you will need four hours and seventeen minutes, give or take five minutes."

"What makes you think *you* can do it?"

"I am a pure computer, obsolete model. All the others have animal brains built into them, to allow for error. I do not. Furthermore, your great[12]-grandfather hooked me into the defense net."

"Didn't the Commonwealth cut you out?"

"I am the only computer which was built to tell lies, except to the families of MacArthur and McBan. I lied to the Commonwealth when they checked on what I was getting. I am obliged to tell the truth only to you and to your designated descendants."

"I know that, but what does it have to do with it?"

"I predict my own space weather, *ahead of the Commonwealth*." The accent was not in the pleasant, even-toned voice; Rod himself supplied it.

"You've tried this out?"

"I have war-gamed it more than a hundred million times. I had nothing else to do while I waited for you."

"You never failed?"

"I failed most of the time, when I first began. But I have not failed a war game from real data for the last thousand years."

"What would happen if you failed now?"

"You would be disgraced and bankrupt. I would be sold and disassembled."

"Is that all?" said Rod cheerfully.

"Yes," said the computer.

"I could stop Old Hot and Simple if I owned Old Earth itself. Let's go."

"I do not go anywhere," said the computer.

"I mean, let's start."

"You mean, to buy Earth, as we discussed?"

"What else?" yelled Rod. "What else have we been talking about?"

"You must have some soup, hot soup and a tranquilizer first. I cannot work at optimum if I have a human being who gets excited."

"All right," said Rod.

"You must authorize me to buy them."

"I authorize you."

"That will be three credits."

"In the name of the seven healthy sheep, what does it matter? How much will Earth cost?"

"Seven thousand million million megacredits."

"Deduct three for the soup and the pill then," shouted Rod, "if it won't spoil your calculations."

"Deducted," said the computer. The tray with the soup appeared, a white pill beside it.

"Now let's buy Earth," said Rod.

"Drink your soup and take your pill first," said the computer.

Rod gulped down his soup, washing the pill down with it.

"Now, let's go, cobber."

"Repeat after me," said the computer, "I herewith mortgage the whole body of the said sheep Sweet William for the sum of five hundred thousand credits to the New Melbourne Exchange on the open board . . ."

Rod repeated it.

And repeated it.

The hours became a nightmare of repetition.

The computer lowered its voice to a low murmur, almost a whisper. When Rod stumbled in the messages, the computer prompted him and corrected him.

Forward purchase . . . sell short . . . option to buy . . . preemptive margin . . . offer to sell . . . offer temporarily reserved . . . first collateral . . . second collateral . . . deposit to drawing account . . . convert to FOE credits . . . hold in SAD credits . . . twelve thousand tons of stroon . . . mortgage forward . . . promise to buy . . . promise to sell . . . hold . . . margin . . . collateral guaranteed by previous deposit . . . promise to pay against the pledged land . . . guarantor . . . McBan land . . . MacArthur land . . . this computer itself . . . conditional legality . . . buy . . . sell . . . guarantee . . . pledge . . . withhold . . . offer confirmed . . . offer cancelled . . . four thousand million megacredits . . . rate accepted . . . rate refused . . . forward purchase . . . deposit against interest . . . collateral previously pledged . . . conditional appreciation . . . guarantee . . . accept title . . . refuse delivery . . . solar weather . . . buy . . . sell . . . pledge . . . withdraw from market . . . withdraw from sale . . . not available . . . no collections now . . . dependent on radiation . . . corner market . . . buy . . . buy . . . buy . . . buy . . . buy . . . confirm title . . . reconfirm title . . . transactions completed . . . reopen . . . register . . . reregister . . . confirm at Earth central . . . message fees . . . fifteen thousand megacredits . . .

Rod's voice became a whisper, but the computer was sure, the computer was untiring, the computer answered all questions from the outside.

Many times Rod and the computer both had to listen to telepathic warnings built into the market's communications net. The computer was cut out and Rod could not hier them. The warnings went unheard.

. . . buy . . . sell . . . hold . . . confirm . . . deposit . . . convert . . . guarantee . . . arbitrage . . . message . . . Commonwealth tax . . . commission . . . buy . . . sell . . . buy . . . buy . . . buy . . . buy . . . deposit title! deposit title! deposit title!

The process of buying Earth had begun.

By the time that the first pretty parts of silver-grey dawn had begun, it was done. Rod was dizzy with fatigue and confusion.

"Go home and sleep," said the computer. "When people find out what you have done with me, many of them will probably be excited and will wish to talk to you at great length. I suggest you say nothing."

# The Eye Upon the Sparrow

Drunk with fatigue, Rod stumbled across his own land back to his cabin.

He could not believe that anything had happened.

If the Palace of the Governor of Night—

If the computer spoke the truth, he was already the wealthiest human being who had ever lived. He had gambled and won, not a few tons of stroon or a planet or two, but credits enough to shake the Commonwealth to its foundation. He owned the Earth, on the system that any overdeposit could be called due at a certain very high margin. He owned planets, countries, mines, palaces, prisons, police systems, fleets, border guards, restaurants, pharmaceuticals, textiles, night clubs, treasures, royalties, licenses, sheep, land, stroon, more sheep, more land, more stroon. He had won.

Only in Old North Australia could a man have done this without being besieged by soldiers, reporters, guards, police, investigators, tax collectors, fortune seekers, doctors, publicity hounds, the sick, the inquisitive, the compassionate, the angry, and the affronted.

Old North Australia kept calm.

Privacy, simplicity, frugality—these virtues had carried them through the hell-world of Paradise VII, where the mountains ate people, the volcanoes poisoned sheep, the delirious oxygen made men rave with bliss as they pranced into their own deaths. The Norstrilians had survived many things, including sickness and deformity. If Rod McBan had caused a financial crisis, there were no newspapers to print it, no viewboxes to report it, nothing to excite the people. The Commonwealth authorities would pick the crisis out of their "in" baskets sometime after tucker and tea the next morning, and by afternoon he, his crisis, and the computer would be in the "out" baskets. If the deal had worked, the whole thing would be paid off honestly and literally. If the deal had not worked out the way that the computer had said, his lands would be up for auction and he himself would be led gently away.

But that's what the Onseck was going to do to him anyway—Old Hot and Simple, a tiring dwarf-lifed man, driven by the boyhood hatred of many long years ago!

Rod stopped for a minute. Around him stretched the rolling plains of his own land. Far ahead, to his left, there gleamed the glassy worm of a river-cover, the humped long, barrel-like line which kept the precious water from evaporating—that too was his.

Maybe. After the night now passed.

He thought of flinging himself to the ground and sleeping right there. He had done it before.

But not this morning.

Not when he might be the person he might be—the man who made the worlds reel with his wealth.

The computer had started easy. He could not take control of his property except for an emergency. The computer had made him create the emergency by selling his next three years' production of santaclara at the market price. That was a serious enough emergency for any pastoralist to be in deep sure trouble.

From that the rest had followed.

Rod sat down.

He was not trying to remember. The remembering was crowding into his mind. He wanted just to get his breath, to get on home, to sleep.

A tree was near him, with a thermostatically controlled cover which domed it in whenever the winds were too strong or too dry, and an underground sprinkler which kept it alive when surface moisture was not sufficient. It was one of the old MacArthur extravagances which his McBan ancestor had inherited and had added to the Station of Doom. It was a modified Earth oak, very big, a full thirteen meters high. Rod was proud of it although he did not like it much, but he had relatives who were obsessed by it and would make a three-hour ride just to sit in the shade—dim and diffuse as it was—of a genuine tree from Earth.

When he looked at the tree, a violent noise assailed him.

Mad frantic laughter.

Laughter beyond all jokes.

Laughter, sick, wild, drunk, dizzy.

He started to be angry and was then puzzled. Who could be laughing at him already? As a matter of nearer fact, who could be trespassing on his land? Anyhow, what was there to laugh about?

(All Norstrilians knew that humor was "pleasurable corrigible malfunction." It was in the Book of

Rhetoric which their Appointed Relatives had to get them through if they were even to qualify for the tests of the Garden of Death. There were no schools, no classes, no teachers, no libraries except for private ones. There were just the seven liberal arts, the six practical sciences, and the five collections of police and defense studies. Specialists were trained offworld, but they were trained only from among the survivors of the Garden, and nobody could get as far as the Garden unless the sponsors, who staked their lives along with that of the student—so far as the question of aptness was concerned—guaranteed that the entrant knew the eighteen kinds of Norstrilian knowledge. The Book of Rhetoric came second, right after the Book of Sheep and Numbers, so that all Norstrilians knew why they laughed and what there was to laugh about.)

But this laughter!

Aagh, who could it be?

A sick man? Impossible. Hostile hallucinations brought on by the Hon. Sec. in his own onseckish way with unusual telepathic powers? Scarcely.

Rod began to laugh himself as he realized what the sound must be.

It was something rare and beautiful, a kookaburra bird, the same kind of bird which had laughed in Original Australia on Old Old Earth. A very few had reached this new planet and they had not multiplied well, even though the Norstrilians respected them and loved them and wished them well.

Good luck came with their wild birdish laughter. A man could feel he had a fine day ahead. Lucky in love, thumb in an enemy's eye, new ale in the fridge, or a ruddy good chance on the market.

Laugh, bird, laugh! thought Rod.

Perhaps the bird understood him. The laughter increased and reached manic, hilarious proportions. The bird sounded as though it were watching the most comical bird-comedy which any bird-audience had ever been invited to, as though the bird-jokes were side-splitting, convulsive, gut-popping, unbelievable, racy, daring, and overwhelming. The bird-laughter became hysterical and a note of fear, of warning crept in.

Rod stepped toward the tree.

In all this time he had not seen the kookaburra.

He squinted into the tree, peering against the brighter side of the sky which showed that morning had arrived well.

To him, the tree was blindingly green, since it kept most of its Earth color, not turning beige or grey as the Earth grasses had done when they had been adapted and planted in Norstrilian soil.

To be sure, the bird was there, a tiny slender laughing impudent shape.

Suddenly the bird cawed: this was no laugh.

Startled, Rod stepped back and started to look around for danger.

The step saved his life.

The sky whistled at him, the wind hit him, a dark shape shot past him with the speed of a projectile and was gone. As it leveled out just above the ground, Rod saw what it was.

A mad sparrow.

Sparrows had reached twenty kilos' weight, with straight swordlike beaks almost a meter in length. Most of the time the Commonwealth left them alone, because they preyed on the giant lice, the size of footballs, which had grown with the sick sheep. Now and then one went mad and attacked people.

Rod turned, watching the sparrow as it walked around, about a hundred meters away.

Some mad sparrows, it was rumored, were not mad at all, but were tame sparrows sent on evil missions of revenge or death by Norstrilian men whose minds had been twisted into crime. This was rare, this was crime, but this was possible.

Could the Onseck already be attacking?

Rod slapped his belt for weapons as the sparrow took to the air again, flapping upward with the pretense of innocence. He had nothing except his belt light and a canister. This would not hold out long unless somebody came along. What could a tired man do, using bare hands, against a sword which burst through the air with a monomaniac birdbrain behind it?

Rod braced himself for the bird's next power dive, holding the canister like a shield.

The canister was not much of a shield.

Down came the bird, preceded by the whistle of air against its head and beak. Rod watched for the eyes and when he saw them, he jumped.

The dust roared up as the giant sparrow twisted its spearlike beak out of the line of the ground, opening its wings, beat the air against gravity, caught itself centimeters from the surface, and flapped away with powerful strokes; Rod stood and watched quietly, glad that he had escaped.

His left arm was wet.

Rain was so rare in the Norstrilian plains that he did not see how he could have gotten wet. He glanced down idly.

Blood it was, and his own.

The kill-bird had missed him with its beak but had touched him with the razorlike wing feathers, which had mutated into weapons; both the rachis and the vane in the large feathers were tremendously reinforced, with the development of a bitterly sharp hyporhachis in the case of the wingtips. The bird had cut him so fast he had not felt it or noticed it.

Like any good Norstrilian, he thought in terms of first aid.

The flow of blood was not very rapid. Should he try to tie up his arm first or to hide from the next diving attack?

The bird answered his question for him.

The ominous whistle sounded again.

Rod flung himself along the ground, trying to get to the base of the tree trunk, where the bird could not dive on him.

The bird, making a serious mental mistake, thought it had disabled him. With a flutter of wings it landed calmly, stood on its feet, and cocked its head to look him over. When the bird moved its head, the sword-beak gleamed evilly in the weak sunshine.

Rod reached the tree and started to lift himself up by seizing the trunk.

Doing this, he almost lost his life.

He had forgotten how fast the sparrows could run on the ground.

In one second, the bird was standing, comical and evil, studying him with its sharp, bright eyes; the next second, the knife-beak was into him, just below the bony part of the shoulder.

He felt the eerie wet pull of the beak being drawn

out of his body, the ache in his surprised flesh which would precede the griping pain. He hit at the bird with his belt light. He missed.

By now he was weakened from his two wounds. The arm was still dripping blood steadily and he felt his shirt get wet as blood poured out of his shoulder.

The bird, backing off, was again studying him by cocking its head. Rod tried to guess his chances. One square blow from his hand, and the bird was dead. The bird had thought him disabled, but now he really was partially disabled.

If his blow did not land, score one Mister for the bird, mark a credit for the Hon. Sec., give Old Hot and Simple the victory!

By now Rod had not the least doubt that Houghton Syme was behind the attack.

The bird rushed.

Rod forgot to fight the way he had planned.

He kicked instead and caught the bird right in its heavy, coarse body.

It felt like a very big football filled with sand.

The kick hurt his foot but the bird was flung a good six or seven meters away. Rod rushed behind the tree and looked back at the bird.

The blood was pulsing fast out of his shoulder at this point.

The kill-bird had gotten to its feet and was walking firmly and securely around the tree. One of the wings trailed a little; the kick seemed to have hurt a wing but not the legs or that horribly strong neck.

Once again the bird cocked its comical head. It was his own blood which dripped from the long beak, now red, which had gleamed silver grey at the beginning of the fight. Rod wished he had studied more about these birds. He had never been this close to a mutated sparrow before and he had no idea of how to fight one. All he had known was that they attacked people on very rare occasions and that sometimes the people died in the encounters.

He tried to spiek, to let out a scream which would bring the neighborhood and the police flying and running toward him. He found he had no telepathy at all, not when he had to concentrate his whole mind and attention on the bird, knowing that its very next move could bring him irretrievable death. This was no temporary death with the rescue squads nearby. There was no one in the neighborhood, no one at all, except for the excited and sympathetic kookaburras haha-ing madly in the tree above.

He shouted at the bird, hoping to frighten it.

The kill-bird paid him no more attention than if it had been a deaf reptile.

The foolish head tipped this way and that. The little bright eyes watched him. The red sword-beak, rapidly turning brown in the dry air, probed abstract dimensions for a way to his brain or heart. Rod even wondered how the bird solved its problems in solid geometry—the angle of approach, the line of thrust, the movement of the beak, the weight and direction of the fleeing object, himself.

He jumped back a few centimeters, intending to look at the bird from the other side of the tree-trunk.

There was a hiss in the air, like the helpless hiss of a gentle little snake.

The bird, when he saw it, looked odd: suddenly it seemed to have two beaks.

Rod marveled.

He did not really understand what was happening until the bird leaned over suddenly, fell on its side, and lay—plainly dead—on the dry cool ground. The eyes were still open but they looked blank; the bird's body twitched a little. The wings opened out in a dying spasm. One of the wings almost struck the trunk of the tree, but the tree-guarding device raised a plastic shaft to ward off the blow; a pity the device had not been designed as a people-guard as well.

Only then did Rod see that the second "beak" was no beak at all, but a javelin, its point biting cleanly and tightly right through the bird's skull into its brain.

No wonder the bird had dropped dead quickly!

As Rod looked around to see who his rescuer might be, the ground rose up and struck him.

He had fallen.

The loss of blood was faster than he had allowed for.

He looked around, almost like a child in his bewilderment and dizziness.

There was a shimmer of turquoise and the girl Lavinia was standing over him. She had a medical pack open and was spraying his wounds with cryptoderm—the living bandage which was so expensive that only on Norstrilia, the exporter of stroon, could it be carried around in emergency cans.

"Keep quiet," she said with her voice, "keep quiet, Rod. We've got to stop the blood first of all. Lands of mercy, but you're a crashing mess!"

"Who . . . ?" said Rod weakly.

"The Hon. Sec.," said she immediately.

"You *know*?" he asked, amazed that she should understand everything so very quickly indeed.

"Don't talk, and I'll tell you." She had taken her field knife and was cutting the sticky shirt off him, so that she could tilt the bottle and spray right into the wound, "I just suspected you were in trouble, when Bill rode by the house and said something crazy, that you had bought half the galaxy by gambling all night with a crazy machine which paid off. I did not know where you were, but I thought that you might be in that old temple of yours that the rest of them can't see. I didn't know what kind of danger to look for, so I brought this." She slapped her hip. Rod's eyes widened. She had stolen her father's one-kiloton grenade, which was to be removed from its rack only in the event of an offworld attack. She answered his question before he asked her. "It's all right. I made a dummy to take its place before I touched it. Then, as I took it out, the Defense monitor came on and I just explained that I had hit it with my new broom, which was longer than usual. Do you think I would let Old Hot and Simple kill you, Rod, without a fight from me? I'm your cousin, your kith and kin. As a matter of fact, I'm number twelve after you when it comes to inheriting Doom and all the wonderful things there are on this station."

Rod said, "Give me water." He suspected she was chattering to keep his attention off what she was doing to his shoulder and arm. The arm glowed once when she sprayed the cryptoderm on it; then it settled down to mere aching. The shoulder had exploded from time to time as she probed it. She had thrust a diagnostic needle into it and was reading the tiny bright picture on the end of the needle. He knew it had both analgesics and antiseptics as well as an ultraminiaturized

X-ray, but he did not think that anyone would be willing to use it unaided in the field.

She answered this question too before he asked it. She was a very perceptive girl.

"We don't know what the Onseck is going to do next. He may have corrupted people as well as animals. I don't dare call for help, not until you have your friends around you. Certainly not, if you have bought half the worlds."

Rod dragged out the words. He seemed short of breath. "How did you know it was him?"

"I saw his face—I hiered it when I looked in the bird's own brain. I could see Houghton Syme, talking to the bird in some kind of an odd way, and I could see your dead body through the bird's eyes, and I could feel a big wave of love and approval, happiness and reward, going through the bird when the job was to have been finished. I think that man is evil, evil!"

"You know him, yourself?"

"What girl around here doesn't? He's a nasty man. He had a boyhood that was all rotten from the time that he realized he was a short-lifer. He has never gotten over it. Some people are sorry for him and don't mind his getting the job of Hon. Sec. If I'd my way, I'd have sent him to the Giggle Room long ago!"

Lavinia's face was set in prudish hate, an expression so unlike herself, who usually was bright and gay, that Rod wondered what deep bitterness might have been stirred within her.

"Why do you hate him?"

"For what he did."

"What did he do?"

"He looked at me," she said. "He looked at me in

a way that no girl can like. And then he crawled all over my mind, trying to show me all the silly, dirty, useless things he wanted to do."

"But he didn't *do* anything—?" said Rod.

"Yes, he did," she snapped. "Not with his hands. I could have reported him. I would have. It's what he did with his mind, the things he spieked to me."

"You can report those too," said Rod, very tired of talking but nevertheless mysteriously elated to discover that he was not the only enemy which the Onseck had made.

"Not what he did, I couldn't," said Lavinia, her face set in anger but dissolving into grief. Grief was tenderer, softer, but deeper and more real than anger. For the first time Rod sensed a feeling of concern about Lavinia. What might be wrong with her?

She looked past him and spoke to the open fields and the big dead bird. "Houghton Syme was the worst man I've ever known. I hope he dies. He never got over that rotten boyhood of his. The old sick boy is the enemy of the man. We'll never know what he might have been. And if you hadn't been so wrapped up in your own troubles, Mister Rod to the hundred and fifty-first, you'd have remembered who *I* am."

"Who are you?" said Rod, naturally.

"I'm the Father's Daughter."

"So what?" said Rod. "All girls are."

"Then you never have found out about me. I'm *the* Father's Daughter from 'The Father's Daughter's Song.'"

"Never heard it."

She looked at him and her eyes were close to tears. "Listen, then, and I'll sing it to you now. And it's true, true, true.

*You do not know what the world is like,*
*And I hope that you never will.*
*My heart was once much full of hope,*
*But now it is very still.*
    *My wife went mad.*

*She was my love and wore my ring*
*When both of us were young.*
*She bore my babes, but then, but then . . .*
*And now there isn't anything.*
    *My wife went mad.*

*Now she lives in another place,*
*Half sick, half well, and never young.*
*I am her dread, who was her love.*
*Each of us has another face.*
    *My wife went mad.*

*You do not know what the world is like.*
*War is never the worst of it.*
*The stars within your eyes can drop.*
*The lightning in your brain can strike.*
    *My wife went mad.*

"And I see you have heard it, too," she sighed. "Just as my father wrote it. About my mother. My own mother."

"Oh, Lavinia," said Rod, "I'm *sorry.* I never thought it was you. And you my own cousin only three or four times removed. But Lavinia, there's something wrong. How can your mother be mad if she was looking fine at my house last week?"

"She was never mad," said Lavinia. "My father

was. He made up that cruel song about my mother
so that the neighbors complained. He had his choice
of the Giggle Room to die in, or the sick place, to be
immortal and insane. He's there *now*. And the Onseck,
the Onseck threatened to bring him back to our own
neighborhood if I didn't do what he asked. Do you
think I could forgive *that*? Ever? After people have
sung that hateful song at me ever since I was a baby?
Do you wonder that I know it myself?"

Rod nodded.

Lavinia's troubles impressed him, but he had troubles
of his own.

The sun was never hot on Norstrilia, but he suddenly felt thirsty and hot. He wanted to sleep but he
wondered about the dangers which surrounded him.

She knelt beside him.

"Close your eyes a bit, Rod. I will spiek very
quietly and maybe nobody will notice it except your
station hands, Bill and Hopper. When they come
we'll hide out for the day and tonight we can go
back to your computer and hide. I'll tell them to
bring food."

She hesitated. "And, Rod?"

"Yes?" he said.

"Forgive me."

"For what?"

"For my troubles," she said contritely.

"Now you have more troubles. Me," he said. "Let's
not blame ourselves, but for sheep's sake, girl, let
me sleep."

He drifted off to sleep as she sat beside him,
whistling a loud clear tune with long long notes
which never added up. He knew some people, usually

women, did that when they tried to concentrate on their telepathic spieking.

Once he glanced up at her before he finally slept. He noticed that her eyes were a deep, strange blue. Like the mad wild faraway skies of Old Earth itself.

He slept, and in his sleep he knew that he was being carried.

The hands which carried him felt friendly, though, and he curled himself back into deep, deeper dreamless sleep.

# FOE **Money,** SAD **Money**

When Rod finally awakened, it was to feel his shoulder tightly bound and his arm throbbing. He had fought waking up because the pain had increased as his mind moved toward consciousness, but the pain and the murmur of voices caused him to come all the way to the hard bright surface of consciousness.

The murmur of voices?

There was no place on all Old North Australia where voices murmured. People sat around and spieked to each other and hiered the answers without the clatter of vocal cords. Telepathy made for brilliant and quick conversation, the participants darting their thoughts this way and that, soaring with their shields so as to produce the effect of a confidential whisper.

But here there were voices. Voices. Many voices. Not possible.

And the smell was wrong. The air was wet—luxuriously, extravagantly wet, like a miser trying to catch a rainstorm in his cabin!

It was almost like the van of the Garden of Death.

Just as he woke, he recognized Lavinia singing an odd little song. It was one which Rod knew, because it had a sharp catchy, poignant little melody to it which sounded like nothing on this world. She was singing, and it sounded like one of the weird sadnesses which his people had brought from their horrible group experience on the abandoned planet of Paradise VII:

*Is there anybody here or is everybody dead*
    *at the grey green blue black lake?*
*The sky was blue and now it is red*
    *over old tall green brown trees.*
*The house was big but now it looks small*
    *at the grey green blue black lake.*
*And the girl that I knew isn't there any more*
    *at the old flat dark torn place.*

His eyes opened and it was indeed Lavinia whom he saw at the edge of vision. This was no house. It was a box, a hospital, a prison, a ship, a cave or a fort. The furnishings were machined and luxurious. The light was artificial and almost the color of peaches. A strange hum in the background sounded like alien engines dispensing power for purposes which Norstrilian law never permitted to private persons. The Lord Redlady leaned over Rod; the fantastic man broke into song himself, chanting—

*Light a lantern—*
*Light a lantern—*
*Light a lantern,*
    *Here we come!*

When he saw the obvious signs of Rod's perplexity he burst into a laugh,

"That's the oldest song you ever heard, my boy. It's

pre-Space and it used to be called 'general quarters' when ships like big iron houses floated on the waters of Earth and fought each other. We've been waiting for you to wake up."

"Water," said Rod. "Please give me water. Why are you talking?"

"Water!" cried the Lord Redlady to someone behind him. His sharp thin face was alight with excitement as he turned back to Rod. "And we're talking because I have my buzzer on. If people want to talk to each other, they jolly well better use their voices in this ship."

"Ship?" said Rod, reaching for the mug of cold, cold water which a hand had reached out to him.

"This is my ship, Mister and Owner Rod McBan to the hundred and fifty-first! An Earth ship. I pulled it out of orbit and grounded it with the permission of the Commonwealth. They don't know you're on it yet. They can't find out right now because my Humanoid-Robot Brainwave Dephasing Device is on. Nobody can think in or out through that, and anybody who tries telepathy on this boat is going to get himself a headache here."

"Why you?" said Rod. "What for?"

"In due time," said the Lord Redlady. "Let me introduce you first. You know these people." He waved at a group.

Lavinia sat with his hands, Bill and Hopper, with his workwoman Eleanor, with his Aunt Doris. They looked odd, sitting on the low, soft, luxurious Earth furniture. They were all sipping some Earth drink of a color which Rod had never seen before. Their expressions were diverse: Bill looked truculent, Hopper looked greedy, Aunt Doris looked utterly embarrassed, and Lavinia looked as though she were enjoying herself.

"And then here . . ." said the Lord Redlady.

The man he pointed to might not have been a man. He was the Norstrilian type all right, but he was a giant, of the kind which were always killed in the Garden of Death.

"At your service," said the giant, who was almost three meters tall and who had to watch his head, lest it hit the ceiling, "I am Donald Dumfrie Hordern Anthony Garwood Gaines Wentworth to the fourteenth generation, Mister and Owner McBan. A military surgeon, at your service, sir!"

"But this is private. Surgeons aren't allowed to work for anybody but government."

"I am on loan to the Earth government," said Wentworth the giant, his face in a broad grin.

"And I," said the Lord Redlady, "am both the Instrumentality and the Earth Government for diplomatic purposes. I borrowed him. He's under Earth rules. You will be well in two or three hours."

The doctor, Wentworth, looked at his hand as though he saw a chronograph there:

"Two hours and seventeen minutes more."

"Let it be," said the Lord Redlady. "Here's our last guest."

A short, angry man stood up and came over. He glared out at Rod and held forth an angry hand.

"John Fisher to the hundredth. You know me."

"Do I?" said Rod, not impolitely. He was just dazed.

"Station of the Good Fresh Joey," said Fisher.

"I haven't been there," said Rod, "but I've heard of it."

"You needn't have," snapped the angry Fisher. "I met you at your grandfather's."

"Oh, yes, Mister and Owner Fisher," said Rod, not really remembering anything at all, but wondering why the short, red-faced man was so angry with him.

"You don't know who I am?" said Fisher.

"Silly games!" thought Rod. He said nothing but smiled dimly. Hunger began to stir inside him.

"Commonwealth Financial Secretary, that's me," said Fisher. "I handle the books and the credits for the government."

"Wonderful work," said Rod. "I'm sure it's complicated. Could I have something to eat?"

The Lord Redlady interrupted: "Would you like French pheasant with Chinesian sauce steeped in the thieves' wine from Viola Siderea? It would only cost you six thousand tons of refined gold, orbited near Earth, if I ordered it sent to you by special courier."

For some inexplicable reason the entire room howled with laughter. The men put their glasses down so as not to spill them. Hopper seized the opportunity to refill his own glass. Aunt Doris looked hilarious and secretly proud, as though she herself had laid a diamond egg or done some equal marvel. Only Lavinia, though laughing, managed to look sympathetically at Rod to make sure that he did not feel mocked. The Lord Redlady laughed as loudly as the rest, and even the short, angry John Fisher allowed himself a wan smile, while holding out his hand for a refill on his drink. An animal, a little one which looked very much like an extremely small person, lifted up the bottle and filled his glass for him; Rod suspected that it was a "monkey" from Old Old Earth, from the stories he had heard.

Rod didn't even say, "What's the joke?" though he realized plainly that he was himself in the middle of it. He just smiled weakly back at them, feeling the hunger grow within him.

"My robot is cooking you an Earth dish. French toast with maple syrup. You could live ten thousand years on this planet and never get it. Rod, don't you know why we're laughing? Don't you know what you've done?"

"The Onseck tried to kill me, I think," said Rod.

Lavinia clapped her hand to her mouth, but it was too late.

"So that's who it was," said the doctor, Wentworth, with a voice as gigantic as himself.

"But you wouldn't laugh at me for that—" Rod started to say. Then he stopped himself.

An awful thought had come to him.

"You mean, it *really* worked? That stuff with my family's old computer?"

The laughter broke out again. It was kind laughter, but it was always the laughter of a peasant people, driven by boredom, who greet the unfamiliar with attack or with laughter.

"You did it," said Hopper. "You've bought a billion worlds."

John Fisher snapped at him, "Let's not exaggerate. He's gotten about one point six stroon years. You couldn't buy any billion worlds for that. In the first place, there aren't a billion settled worlds, not even a million. In the second place, there aren't many worlds for sale. I doubt that he could buy thirty or forty."

The little animal, prompted by some imperceptible sign from the Lord Redlady, went out of the room and returned with a tray. The odor from the tray made all the people in the room sniff appreciatively. The food was unfamiliar, but it combined pungency and sweetness. The monkey fitted the tray into an artfully concealed slot at the head of Rod's couch, took off an imaginary monkey cap, saluted, and went back to his own basket behind the Lord Redlady's chair.

The Lord Redlady nodded. "Go ahead and eat, boy. It's on me."

Rod sat up. His shirt was still blood-caked and he realized that it was almost worn out.

"That's an odd sight, I must say," said the huge doctor Wentworth. "There's the richest man in many worlds, and he hasn't the price of a new pair of overalls."

"What's odd about that? We've always charged an import fee of twenty million percent of the orbit price of goods," snapped angry John Fisher. "Have you ever realized what other people have swung into orbit around our sun, just waiting for us to change our minds so they could sell us half the rubbish in the universe? This planet would be knee-deep in junk if we ever dropped our tariff. I'm surprised at you, doctor, forgetting the fundamental rules of Old North Australia!"

"He's not complaining," said Aunt Doris, whom the drink had made loquacious. "He's just thinking. We all think."

"Of course we all think. Or daydream. Some of us leave and go off-planet to be rich people on other worlds. A few of us even manage to get back here on severe probation when we realize what the offworlds are like. I'm just saying," said the doctor, "that Rod's situation would be very funny to everybody except us Norstrilians. We're all rich with the stroon imports, but we've kept ourselves poor in order to survive."

"Who's poor?" snapped the fieldhand Hopper, apparently touched at a sensitive point. "I can match you with megacredits, doc, any time you care to gamble. Or I'll meet you with throwing knives, if you want them better. I'm as good as the next man!"

"That's exactly what I mean," said John Fisher. "Hopper here can argue with anybody on the planet. We're still equals, we're still free, we're not the victims of our own wealth—that's Norstrilia for you!"

Rod looked up from his food and said, "Mister and Owner Secretary Fisher, you talk awfully well for somebody who is not a freak like me. How do you do it?"

Fisher started looking angry again, though he was not really angry; "Do you think that financial records can be dictated telepathically? I'm spending centuries out of my life, just dictating into my blasted microphone. Yesterday I spent most of the day dictating the mess which you have made of the Commonwealth's money for the next eight years. And you know what I'm going to do at the next meeting of the Commonwealth Council?"

"What?" said Rod.

"I'm going to move the condemnation of that computer of yours. It's too good to be in private hands."

"You can't do that!" shrieked Aunt Doris, somewhat mellowed by the Earth beverage she was drinking. "It's MacArthur and McBan family property."

"You can keep the temple," said Fisher with a snort, "but no bloody family is going to outguess the whole planet again. Do you know that boy sitting there has four megacredits on Earth at this moment?"

Bill hiccuped. "I got more than that myself."

Fisher snarled at him, "*On Earth?* FOE money?"

A silence hit the room.

"FOE money. Four megacredits? He can buy Old Australia and ship it out here to us!" Bill sobered fast.

Said Lavinia mildly, "What's foe money?"

"Do you know, Mister and Owner McBan?" said Fisher, in a peremptory tone. "You had better know, because you have more of it than any man has ever had before."

"I don't want to talk about money," said Rod. "I want to find out what the Onseck is up to."

"Don't worry about him!" laughed the Lord Redlady, prancing to his feet and pointing at himself with a dramatic forefinger. "As the representative of Earth, I filed six hundred and eighty-five lawsuits against him simultaneously, in the name of your Earth debtors, who fear that some harm might befall you . . ."

"Do they really?" said Rod. "Already?"

"Of course not. All they know is your name and the fact that you bought them out. But they *would* worry if they *did* know, so as your agent I tied up the Hon. Sec. Houghton Syme with more law cases than this planet has ever seen before."

The big doctor chuckled. "Dashed clever of you, my Lord and Mister! You know us Norstrilians pretty well, I must say. If we charge a man with murder, we're so freedom-minded that he has time to commit a few more before being tried for the first one. But civil suits! Hot sheep! He'll never get out of those, as long as he lives."

"Is he onsecking any more?" said Rod.

"What do you mean?" asked Fisher.

"Does he still have his job—Onseck?"

"Oh, yes," said Fisher, "but we put him on two hundred years' leave and he has only about a hundred and twenty years to live, poor fellow. Most of that time he will be defending himself in civil suits."

Rod finally exhaled. He had finished the food. The small polished room with its machined elegance, the wet air, the bray of voices all over the place—these made him feel dreamlike. Here grown men were standing, talking as though he really did own Old Earth. They were concerned with his affairs, not because he was Roderick Frederick Ronald Arnold William MacArthur McBan the hundred and fifty-first, but because he was Rod, a boy among them who had stumbled upon danger and fortune. He looked around the room. The conversations had accidentally stopped. They were looking at him, and he saw in their faces something which he had seen before. What was it? It was not love. It was a rapt attentiveness, combined with a sort of pleasurable and indulgent interest. He then realized what the looks signified. They were giving him the adoration which they usually reserved only for cricket players, tennis players, and great track performers—like that fabulous Hopkins Harvey fellow who had gone offworld and had won a wrestling match with a "heavy man" from Wereld Schemering. He was not just Rod any more. He was their boy.

As their boy, he smiled at them vaguely and felt like crying.

The breathlessness broke when the large doctor, Mister and Owner Wentworth, threw in the stark comment, "Time to tell him, Mister and Owner Fisher. He won't have his property long if we don't get moving. No, nor his life either."

Lavinia jumped up and cried out, "You can't kill Rod—"

Doctor Wentworth stopped her. "Sit down. We're not going to kill him. And you there, stop acting foolish! We're *his friends* here."

Rod followed the line of the doctor's glance and saw that Hopper had snaked his hand back to the big knife he wore in his belt. He was getting ready to fight anyone who attacked Rod.

"Sit, sit down, all of you, please!" said the Lord Redlady, speaking somewhat fussily with his singsong Earth accent. "I'm host here. Sit down. Nobody's killing Rod tonight. Doctor, you take my table. Sit down yourself. You will stop threatening my ceiling or your head. You, Ma'am and Owner," said he to Aunt Doris, "move over there to that other chair. Now we can all see the doctor."

"Can't we wait?" asked Rod. "I need to sleep. Are you going to ask me to make decisions now? I'm not up to decisions, not after what I've just been through. All night with the computer. The long walk. The bird from the Onseck—"

"You'll have no decisions to make if you don't make them tonight," said the doctor firmly and pleasantly. "You'll be a dead man."

"Who's going to kill me?" asked Rod.

"Anybody who wants money. Or wants power. Or who would like unlimited life. Or who needs these things to get something else. Revenge. A woman. An obsession. A drug. You're not just a person now,

Rod. You're Norstrilia incarnate. You're Mr. Money himself! Don't ask who'd kill you! Ask who wouldn't! We wouldn't . . . I think. But don't tempt us."

"How much money have I got?" said Rod.

Angry John Fisher cut in: "So much that the computers are clotted up, just counting it. About one and a half stroon years. Perhaps three hundred years of Old Earth's total income. You sent more Instant Messages last night than the Commonwealth government itself has sent in the last twelve years. These messages are expensive. One kilocredit in FOE money."

"I asked a long time ago what this 'foe money' was," said Lavinia, "and nobody has got around to telling me."

The Lord Redlady took the middle of the floor. He stood there with a stance which none of the Old North Australians had ever seen before. It was actually the posture of a master of ceremonies opening the evening at a large night club, but to people who had never seen those particular gestures, his movements were eerie, self-explanatory and queerly beautiful.

"Ladies and gentlemen," he said, using a phrase which most of them had only heard in books, "I will serve drinks while the others speak. I will ask each in turn. Doctor, will you be good enough to wait while the Financial Secretary speaks?"

"I should think," said the doctor irritably, "that the lad would be wanting to think over his choice. Does he want me to cut him in two, here, tonight, or doesn't he? I should think that would take priority, wouldn't you?"

"Ladies and gentlemen," said the Lord Redlady, "the Mister and Doctor Wentworth has a very good point indeed. But there is no sense in asking Rod about being cut in two unless he knows why. Mister Financial Secretary, will you tell us all what happened last night?"

John Fisher stood up. He was so chubby that it did not matter. His brown, suspicious, intelligent eyes looked over the lot of them.

"There are as many kinds of money as there are worlds with people on them. We here on Norstrilia don't carry the tokens around, but in some places they have bits of paper or metal which they use to keep count. We talk our money into the central computers which even out all our transactions for us. Now what would happen if I wanted a pair of shoes?"

Nobody answered. He didn't expect them to.

"I would," he went on, "go to a shop, look in the screen at the shoes which the offworld merchants keep in orbit. I would pick out the shoes I wanted. What's a good price for a pair of shoes in orbit?"

Hopper was getting tired of these rhetorical questions so he answered promptly,

"Six bob."

"That's right. Six minicredits."

"But that's orbit money. You're leaving out the tariff," said Hopper.

"Exactly. And what's the tariff?" asked John Fisher, snapping.

Hopper snapped back, "Two hundred thousand times, what you bloody fools always make it in the Commonwealth Council."

"Hopper, can you buy shoes?" said Fisher.

"Of course I can!" The station hand looked belligerent again but the Lord Redlady was filling his glass. He sniffed the aroma, calmed down and said, "All right, what's your point?"

"The point is that the money in orbit is SAD money—s for secure, A for and, D for delivered. That's any kind of good money with backing behind it. Stroôn is the best backing there is, but gold is all right, rare metals, fine manufactures, and so on. That's just the money off the planet, in the hands of the recipient. Now how many times would a ship have to hop to get to Old Earth itself?"

"Fifty or sixty," said Aunt Doris unexpectedly. "Even I know that."

"And how many ships get through?"

"They all do," said she.

"Oh, no," cried several of the men in unison.

"About one ship is lost every sixty or eighty trips, depending on the solar weather, on the skills of the Pin-lighters and the Go-Captains, on the landing accidents. Did any of you ever see a really old captain?"

"Yes," said Hopper with gloomy humor, "a dead one in his coffin."

"So if you have something you want to get to Earth, you have to pay your share of the costly ships, your share of the Go-Captain's wages and the fees of his staff, your share of the insurance for their families. Do you know what it could cost to get this chair back to Earth?" said Fisher.

"Three hundred times the cost of the chair," said Doctor Wentworth.

"Mighty close. It's two hundred and eighty-seven times."

"How do you know so mucking much?" said Bill, speaking up. "And why waste our time with all this crutting glubb?"

"Watch your language, man," said John Fisher.

"There are some mucking ladies present. I'm telling you this because we have to get Rod off to Earth tonight, if he wants to be alive and rich—"

"That's what you say!" cried Bill. "Let him go to his house. We can load up on little bombs and hold up against anybody who could get through the Norstrilian defenses. What are we paying these mucking taxes for, if it's not for the likes of you to make sure we're safe? Shut up, man, and let's take the boy home. Come along, Hopper."

The Lord Redlady leaped to the middle of his own floor. He was no prancing Earthman putting on a show. He was the old Instrumentality itself, surviving with raw weapons and raw brains. In his hand he held a something which none of them could see clearly.

"Murder," he said, "will be done this moment if anybody moves. I will commit it. I will, people. Move, and try me. And if I do commit murder, I will arrest myself, hold a trial, and acquit myself. I have strange powers, people. Don't make me use them. Don't even make me show them." The shimmering thing in his hand disappeared. "Mister and Doctor Wentworth, you are under my command, by loan. Other people, you are my guests. Be warned. Don't touch that boy. This is Earth territory, this cabin we're in." He stood a little to one side and looked at them brightly out of his strange Earth eyes.

Hopper deliberately spat on the floor. "I suppose I would be a puddle of mucking glue if I helped old Bill?"

"Something like it," said the Lord Redlady. "Want to try?" The things that were hard to see were now in each of his hands. His eyes darted between Bill and Hopper.

"Shut up, Hopper. We'll take Rod if he tells us to go. But if he doesn't—it crudding well doesn't matter. Eh, Mister and Owner McBan?"

Rod looked around for his grandfather, dead long ago: then he knew they were looking at him instead. Torn between sleepiness and anxiety, he answered,

"I don't want to go now, fellows. Thank you for standing by. Go on, Mister Secretary, with the foe money and the sad money."

The weapons disappeared from the Lord Redlady's hands.

"I don't like Earth weapons," said Hopper, speaking very loudly and plainly to no one at all, "and I don't like Earth people. They're dirty. There's nothing in them that's good honest crook."

"Have a drink, lads," said the Lord Redlady with a democratic heartiness which was so false that the workwoman Eleanor, silent all the evening, let out one wild caw of a laugh, like a kookaburra beginning to whoop in a tree. He looked at her sharply, picked up his serving jug, and nodded to the Financial Secretary, John Fisher, that he should resume speaking.

Fisher was flustered. He obviously did not like this Earth practice of quick threats and weapons indoors, but the Lord Redlady—disgraced and remote from Old Earth as he was—was nevertheless the accredited diplomat of the Instrumentality, and even Old North Australia did not push the Instrumentality too far. There were things supposed about worlds which had done so.

Soberly and huffily he went on,

"There's not much to it. If the money is discounted thirty-three and one third percent per trip and if it

takes fifty-five trips to get to Old Earth, it takes a
heap of money to pay up in orbit right here before
you have a minicredit on Earth. Sometimes the odds
are better. Your Commonwealth government waits
for months and years to get a really favorable rate
of exchange and of course we send our freight by
armed sailships, which don't go below the surface of
space at all. They just take hundreds or thousands
of years to get there, while our cruisers dart in and
out around them, just to make sure that nobody robs
them in transit. There are things about Norstrilian
robots which none of you know, and which not even
the Instrumentality knows—" He darted a quick look
at the Lord Redlady, who said nothing to this, and
went on, "Which makes it well worth while not to
muck around with one of our perishing ships. We
don't get robbed much. And we have other things
that are even worse than Mother Hitton and her littul
kittons. But the money and the stroon which finally
reaches Old Earth itself is FOE money. F, O, E. F is
for free, O is for on, E is for Earth. F, O, E—free on
Earth. That's the best kind of money there is, right
on Old Earth itself. And Earth has the final exchange
computer. Or had it."

"Had it?" said the Lord Redlady.

"It broke down last night. Rod broke it. Overload."

"Impossible!" cried Redlady. "I'll check."

He went to the wall, pulled down a desk. A console,
incredibly miniature, gleamed out at them. In less than
three seconds it glowed. Redlady spoke into it, his voice
as clear and cold as the ice they had all heard about:

"Priority. Instrumentality. Short of War. Instant.
Instant. Redlady calling. Earthport."

"Confirmed," said a Norstrilian voice, "confirmed and charged."

"Earthport," said the console in a whistling whisper which filled the room.

"Redlady—instrumentality—official—centputer—all—right—question—cargo—approved—question—out."

"Centputer—all—right—cargo—approved—out," said the whisper and fell silent.

The people in the room had seen an immense fortune squandered. Even by Norstrilian standards, the faster-than-light messages were things which a family might not use twice in a thousand years. They looked at Redlady as though he were an evil-worker with strange powers. Earth's prompt answer to the skinny man made them all remember that though Old North Australia produced the wealth, Earth still distributed much of it, and that the supergovernment of the Instrumentality reached into far places where no Norstrilian would even wish to venture.

The Lord Redlady spoke mildly, "The central computer seems to be going again, if your government wishes to consult it. The 'cargo' is this boy here."

"You've told Earth about me?" said Rod.

"Why not? We want to get you there alive."

"But message security—?" said the doctor.

"I have references which no outside mind will know," said the Lord Redlady. "Finish up, Mister Financial Secretary. Tell the young man what he has on Earth."

"Your computer outcomputed the government," said John Fisher to the hundredth, "and it mortgaged all your lands, all your sheep, all your trading rights, all your family treasures, the right to the MacArthur name, the right to the McBan name, and itself. Then it bought futures. Of course, *it* didn't do it. You did, Rod McBan."

Startled into full awakeness, Rod found his right hand up at his mouth, so surprised was he. "I did?"

"Then you bought futures in stroon, but you offered them for sale. You held back the sales, shifting titles and changing prices, so that not even the central computer knew what you were doing. You bought almost all of the eighth year from now, most of the seventh year from now, and some of the sixth. You mortgaged each purchase as you went along, in order to buy more. Then you suddenly tore the market wide open by offering fantastic bargains, trading the six-year rights for seventh-year and eighth-year. Your computer made such lavish use of Instant Messages to Earth that the Commonwealth defense office had people buzzing around in the middle of the night. By the time they figured out what might happen, it had happened. You registered a monopoly of two years' export, far beyond the predicted amount. The government rushed for a weather recomputation, but while they were doing that you were registering your holdings on Earth and remortgaging them in FOE money. With the FOE money you began to buy up all the imports around Old North Australia, and when the government finally declared an emergency, you had secured final title to one and a half stroon years and to more megacredits, FOE money megacredits, than the Earth computers could handle. You're the richest man that ever was. Or ever will be. We changed all the rules this morning and I myself signed a new treaty with the Earth authorities, ratified by the Instrumentality.

Meanwhile, you're the richest of the rich men who ever lived on this world and you're also rich enough to buy all of Old Earth. In fact, you have put in a reservation to buy it, unless the Instrumentality outbids you."

"Why should we?" said the Lord Redlady. "Let him have it. We'll watch what he does with the Earth after he buys it, and if it is something bad, we will kill him."

"You'd kill me, Lord Redlady?" said Rod. "I thought you were saving me?"

"Both," said the doctor, standing up. "The Commonwealth government has not tried to take your property away from you, though they have their doubts as to what you will do with Earth if you do buy it. They are not going to let you stay on this planet and endanger it by being the richest kidnap victim who ever lived. Tomorrow they will strip you of your property, unless you want to take a chance on running for it. Earth government is the same way. If you can figure out your own defenses, you can come on in. Of course the police will protect you, but would that be enough? I'm a doctor, and I'm here to ship you out if you want to go."

"And I'm an officer of government, and I will arrest you if you do not go," said John Fisher.

"And I represent the Instrumentality, which does not declare its policy to anyone, least of all to outsiders. But it is my personal policy," said the Lord Redlady, holding out his hands and twisting his thumbs in a meaningless, grotesque, but somehow very threatening way, "to see that this boy gets a safe trip to Earth and a fair deal when he comes back here!"

"You'll protect him all the way!" cried Lavinia, looking very happy.

"All the way. As far as I can. As long as I live."

"That's pretty long," muttered Hopper. "Conceited little pommy cockahoop!"

"Watch your language, Hopper," said the Lord Redlady. "Rod?"

"Yes, sir?"

"Your answer?" The Lord Redlady was peremptory.

"I'm going," said Rod.

"What on Earth do you want?" said the Lord Redlady ceremoniously.

"A genuine Cape triangle."

"A what?" cried the Lord Redlady.

"A Cape triangle. A postage stamp."

"What's postage?" said the Lord Redlady, really puzzled.

"Payments on messages."

"But you do that with thumbprints or eyeprints!"

"No," said Rod, "I mean paper ones."

"Paper messages?" said the Lord Redlady, looking as though someone had mentioned grass battleships, hairless sheep, solid cast-iron women, or something else equally improbable. "Paper messages?" he repeated, and then he laughed, quite charmingly. "Oh!" he said, with a tone of secret discovery. "You mean antiquities . . . ?"

"Of course," said Rod. "Even before Space itself."

"Earth has a lot of antiquities, and I am sure you will be welcome to study them or to collect them. That will be perfectly all right. Just don't do any of the wrong things, or you will be in real trouble."

"What are the wrong things?" said Rod.

"Buying real people, or trying to. Shipping religion from one planet to another. Smuggling underpeople."

"What's religion?" said Rod.

"Later, later," said the Lord Redlady. "You'll learn everything later. Doctor, you take over."

Wentworth stood very carefully so that his head did not touch the ceiling. He had to bend his neck a little. "We have two boxes, Rod."

When he spoke, the door whirred in its tracks and showed them a small room beyond. There was a large box like a coffin and a very small box, like the kind that women have around the house to keep a single party-going bonnet in.

"There will be criminals, and wild governments, and conspirators, and adventurers, and just plain good people gone wrong at the thought of your wealth—there will be all these waiting for you to kidnap you or rob or even kill you—"

"Why kill me?"

"To impersonate you and try to get your money," said the doctor. "Now look. This is your big choice. If you take the big box, we can put you in a sailship convoy and you will get there in several hundred or thousand years. But you will get there, ninety-nine point ninety-nine percent. Or we can send the big box on the regular planoforming ships, and somebody will steal you. Or we scun you down and put you in the little box."

"*That* little box?" cried Rod.

"Scunned. You've scunned sheep, haven't you?"

"I've heard of it. But a man, no. Dehydrate my body, pickle my head, and freeze the whole mucking mess?" cried Rod.

"That's it. Too bloody right!" cried the doctor cheerfully. "That'll give you a real chance of getting there alive."

"But who'll put me together? I'd need my own doctor—" His voice quavered at the unnaturalness of the risk, not at the mere chanciness and danger of it.

"Here," said the Lord Redlady, "is your doctor, already trained."

"I am at your service," said the little Earth-animal, the "monkey," with a small bow to the assembled company. "My name is A'gentur and I have been conditioned as a physician, a surgeon and a barber."

The women had gasped. Hopper and Bill stared at the little animal in horror.

"You're an underperson!" yelled Hopper. "We've never let the crutting things loose on Norstrilia."

"I'm not an underperson. I'm an animal. Conditioned to—" The monkey jumped. Hopper's heavy knife twanged like a musical instrument as it clung to the softer steel of the wall. Hopper's other hand held a long thin knife, ready to reach Redlady's heart.

The left hand of the Lord Redlady flashed straight forward. Something in his hand glowed silently, terribly. There was a hiss in the air.

Where Hopper had been, a cloud of oily thick smoke, stinking of burning meat, coiled slowly toward the ventilators. Hopper's clothing and personal belongings, including one false tooth, lay on the chair in which he had been sitting. They were undamaged. His drink stood on the floor beside the chair, forever to remain unfinished.

The doctor's eyes gleamed as he stared strangely at Redlady.

"Noted and reported to the Old North Australian Navy."

"I'll report it too," said the Lord Redlady, ". . . as the use of weapons on diplomatic grounds."

"Never mind," said John Fisher to the hundredth, not angry at all, but just pale and looking a little ill. Violence did not frighten him, but decision did. "Let's get on with it. Which box, big or little, boy?"

The workwoman Eleanor stood up. She had said nothing but now she dominated the scene. "Take him in there, girls," she said, "and wash him like you would for the Garden of Death. I'll wash myself in there. You see," she added, "I've always wanted to see the blue skies on Earth, and wanted to swim in a house that ran around on the big big waters. I'll take your big box, Rod, and if I get through alive, you will owe me some treats on Earth. You take the little box, Roddy, take the little box. And that little tiny doctor with the fur on him. Rod, I trust him."

Rod stood up.

Everybody was looking at him and at Eleanor.

"You agree?" said the Lord Redlady.

He nodded.

"You agree to be scunned and put in the little box for instant shipment to Earth?"

He nodded again.

"You will pay all the extra expenses?"

He nodded again.

The doctor said,

"You authorize me to cut you up and reduce you down, in the hope that you may be reconstituted on Earth?"

Rod nodded to him, too.

"Shaking your head isn't enough," said the doctor. "You have to agree for the record."

"I agree," said Rod quietly.

Aunt Doris and Lavinia came forward to lead him into the dressing room and shower room. Just as they reached for his arms, the doctor patted Rod on the back with a quick strange motion. Rod jumped a little.

"Deep hypnotic," said the doctor. "You can manage his body all right, but the next words he utters will be said, luck willing, on Old Earth itself."

The women were wide-eyed, but they led Rod forward to be cleaned for the operations and the voyage.

The doctor turned to the Lord Redlady and to John Fisher, the Financial Secretary.

"A good night's work," he said. "Pity about that man, though."

Bill sat still, frozen with grief in his chair, staring at Hopper's empty clothing in the chair next to him.

The console tinkled, "Twelve hours, Greenwich mean time. No adverse weather reports from the channel coast or from Meeya Meefla or Earthport building. All's well!"

The Lord Redlady served drinks to the Misters. He did not even offer one to Bill. It would have been no use, at this point.

From beyond the door, where they were cleaning the body, clothes and hair of the deeply hypnotized Rod, Lavinia and Aunt Doris unconsciously reverted to the ceremony of the Garden of Death and lifted their voices in a sort of plainsong chant:

*Out in the Garden of Death, our young*
*Have tasted the valiant taste of fear.*
*With muscular arm and reckless tongue,*
*They have won, and lost, and escaped us here.*


The three men listened for a few moments, attentively. From the other washroom there came the sounds
of the workwoman Eleanor, washing herself, alone and
unattended, for a long voyage and a possible death.

The Lord Redlady heaved a sigh. "Have a drink,
Bill. Hopper brought it on himself."

Bill refused to speak to them but he held forth
his glass.

The Lord Redlady filled that and the others. He
turned to John Fisher to the hundredth and said:

"You're shipping him?"

"Who?"

"The boy."

"I thought so."

"Better not," said the Lord Redlady.

"You mean—danger?"

"That's only half the word for it," said the Lord
Redlady. "You can't possibly plan to offload him at
Earthport. Put him into a good medical station. There's
an old one, still good, on Mars, if they haven't closed
it down. I know Earth. Half the people of Earth will
be waiting to greet him and the other half will be
waiting to rob him."

"You represent the Earth government, Sir and
Commissioner," said John Fisher. "That's a rum way
to talk about your own people."

"They are not that way all the time," laughed Redlady. "Just when they're in heat. Sex hasn't a chance

to compare with money when it comes to the human race on Earth. They all think that they want power and freedom and six other impossible things. I'm not speaking for the Earth government when I say this. Just for myself."

"If we don't ship him, who will?" demanded Fisher.

"The Instrumentality."

"The Instrumentality? You don't conduct commerce. How can you?"

"We don't conduct commerce, but we do meet emergencies. I can flag down a long-jump cruiser and he'll be there months before anybody expects him."

"Those are warships. You can't use one for passengers!"

"Can't I?" said the Lord Redlady, with a smile.

"The Instrumentality would—?" said Fisher, with a puzzled smile. "The cost would be tremendous. How will you pay for it? It'd be hard to justify."

"*He* will pay for it. Special donation from him for special service. One megacredit for the trip."

The Financial Secretary whistled. "That's a fearful price for a single trip. You'd want SAD money and not surface money, I suppose?"

"No. FOE money."

"Hot buttered moonbeams, man! That's a thousand times the most expensive trip that any person has ever had."

The big doctor had been listening to the two of them. "Mister and Owner Fisher," he said, "I recommend it."

"You?" cried John Fisher angrily. "You're a Norstrilian and you want to rob this poor boy?"

"Poor boy?" snorted the doctor. "It's not that. The

trip's no good if he's not alive. Our friend here is extravagant but his ideas are sound. I suggest one amendment."

"What's that?" said the Lord Redlady quickly.

"One and a half megacredits for the round trip. If he is well and alive and with the same personality, apart from natural causes. But note this. One kilocredit only if you deliver him on Earth dead."

John Fisher rubbed his chin. His suspicious eyes looked down at Redlady, who had taken a seat, and looked up at the doctor, whose head was still bumping the ceiling.

A voice behind him spoke.

"Take it, Mister Financial Secretary. The boy won't use money if he's dead. You can't fight the Instrumentality, you can't be reasonable with the Instrumentality, and you can't buy the Instrumentality. With what they've been taking off us all these thousands of years, they've got more stroon than we do. Hidden away somewhere. You, there!" said Bill rudely to the Lord Redlady. "Do you have any idea what the Instrumentality is worth?"

The Lord Redlady creased his brow. "Never thought of it. I suppose it must have a limit. But I never thought of it. We do have accountants, though."

"See," said Bill. "Even the Instrumentality would hate to lose money. Take the doctor's bid, Redlady. Take him up on it, Fisher." His use of their surnames was an extreme incivility, but the two men were convinced.

"I'll do it," said Redlady. "It's awfully close to writing insurance, which we are not chartered to do. I'll write it in as his emergency clause."

"I'll take it," said John Fisher. "It's got to be a thousand years until another Norstrilian Financial Secretary pays money for a ticket like this, but it's worth it. To him. I'll square it in his accounts to our planet."

"I'll witness it," said the doctor.

"No, you won't," said Bill savagely. "The boy has one friend here. That's me. Let *me* do it."

They stared at him, all three.

He stared back.

He broke. "Sirs and Misters, please let me be the witness."

The Lord Redlady nodded and opened the console. He and John Fisher spoke the contract into it. At the end Bill shouted his full name as witness.

The two women brought Rod McBan, mother-naked, into the room. He was immaculately clean and he stared ahead as though he were in an endless dream.

"That's the operating room," said the Lord Redlady. "I'll spray us all with antiseptic, if you don't mind."

"Of course," said the doctor. "You must."

"You're going to cut him up and boil him down— here and now?" cried Aunt Doris.

"Here and now," said the Lord Redlady, "if the doctor approves. The sooner he goes, the better chance he has of coming through the whole thing alive."

"I consent," said the doctor. "I approve."

He started to take Rod by the hand, leading him toward the room with the long coffin and the small box. At some sign from Redlady, the walls had opened up to show a complete surgical theater.

"Wait a moment," said the Lord Redlady. "Take your colleague."

"Colleague?" said the giant.

"A'gentur," said Redlady. "It'll be he who puts Rod together again."

"Of course," said the doctor.

The monkey had jumped out of his basket when he heard his name mentioned.

Together, the giant and the monkey led Rod into the little gleaming room. They closed the door behind them.

The ones who were left behind sat down nervously.

"Mister and Owner Redlady," said Bill, "since I'm staying, could I have some more of that drink?"

"Of course, Sir and Mister," said the Lord Redlady, not having any idea of what Bill's title might be.

There were no screams from Rod, no thuds, no protest. There was the cloying sweet horror of unknown medicines creeping through the airvents. The two women said nothing as the group of people sat around. Eleanor, wrapped in an enormous towel, came and sat with them. In the second hour of the operations on Rod, Lavinia began sobbing.

She couldn't help it.

# Traps, Fortunes and Watchers

We all know that no communications systems are leakproof. Even inside the far-reaching communications patterns of the Instrumentality, there were soft spots, rotten points, garrulous men. The MacArthur-McBan computer, sheltered in the Palace of the Governor of Night, had had time to work out abstract economics and weather patterns, but the computer had not tasted human love or human wickedness. All the messages concerning Rod's speculation in the forward santaclara crop and stroon export had been sent in the clear. It was no wonder that on many worlds, people saw Rod as a chance, an opportunity, a victim, a benefactor, or an enemy.

For we all know the old poem:

*Luck is hot and people funny.*
*Everybody's fond of money.*
*Lose a chance and sell your mother.*
*Win the pot and buy another.*
*Other people fall and crash:*
*You may get the ton of cash!*

It applied in this case too. People ran hot and cold with the news.

## On Earth, Same Day, within Earthport Itself

Commissioner Teadrinker tapped his teeth with a pencil.

Four megacredits FOE money already and more, much more to come.

Teadrinker lived in a fever of perpetual humiliation. He had chosen it. It was called "the honorable disgrace" and it applied to ex-Lords of the Instrumentality who chose long life instead of service and honor. He was a thousandmorer, meaning that he had traded his career, his reputation, and his authority for a long life of one thousand or more years. (The Instrumentality had learned, long ago, that the best way to protect its members from temptation was to tempt them itself. By offering "honorable disgrace" and low, secure jobs within the Instrumentality to those Lords who might be tempted to trade long life for their secrets, it kept its own potential defectors. Teadrinker was one of these.)

He saw the news and he was a skilled wise man. He could not do anything to the Instrumentality with money, but money worked wonders on Earth. He could buy a modicum of honor. Perhaps he could even have the records falsified and get married again. He flushed slightly, even after hundreds of years, when he remembered his first wife blazing at him when she saw his petition for long life and honorable disgrace: "Go ahead and live, you fool. Live and watch me die without you, inside the decent four hundred years which everybody else has if they work for it and want it. Watch your children die, watch your friends die, watch all your hobbies and ideas get out of date. Go along, you horrible little man, and let me die like a human being!"

A few megacredits could help that.

Teadrinker was in charge of incoming visitors. His underman, the cattle-derived B'dank, was custodian of the scavenger spiders—half-tame one-ton insects which stood by for emergency work if the services of the tower failed. He wouldn't need to have this Norstrilian merchant very long. Just long enough for a recorded order and a short murder.

Perhaps not. If the Instrumentality caught him, it would be dream-punishments, things worse than Shayol itself.

Perhaps yes. If he succeeded, he would escape a near immortality of boredom and could have a few decades of juicy fun instead.

He tapped his teeth again.

"Do nothing, Teadrinker," he said to himself, "but think, think, think. Those spiders look as though they might have possibilities."

## On Viola Siderea, at the Council of the Guild of Thieves

"Put two converted police cruisers in orbit around the Sun. Mark them for charter or sale, so that we won't run into the police.

"Put an agent into every liner which is Earthbound within the time stated.

"Remember, we don't want the man. Just his luggage. He's sure to be carrying a half-ton or so of stroon. With that kind of fortune, we could pay off

all the debts we gathered with that Bozart business.
Funny we never heard from Bozart. Nothing.

"Put three senior thieves in Earthport itself. Make
sure that they have fake stroon, diluted down to about
one-thousandth, so that they can work the luggage
switch if they have the chance.

"I know all this costs money, but you have to
spend money to get it. Agreed, gentlemen of the
larcenical arts?"

There was a chorus of agreement around the table,
except for one old, wise thief who said,

"You know my views."

"Yes," said the chairman, with toneless polite hatred,
"we know your views. Rob corpses. Clean out wrecks.
Become human hyenas instead of human wolves."

With unexpected humor the old man said, "Crudely
put. But correct. And safer."

"Do we need to vote?" said the chairman, looking
around the table.

There was a chorus of nos.

"Carried, then," said the presiding chief. "Hit hard,
and hit for the small target, not the big one."


## Ten Kilometers Below the Surface of the Earth

"He is coming, father! He is coming."

"Who is coming?" said the voice, like a great drum
resounding.

E'lamelanie said it as though it were a prayer: "The
blessed one, the appointed one, the guarantor of our
people, the new messenger on whom the robot, rat
and Copt agreed. With money he is coming, to help

us, to save us, to open to us the light of day and the vaults of heaven."

"You are blasphemous," said the E'telekeli.

The girl fell into a hush. She not only respected her father. She worshipped him as her personal religious leader. His great eyes blazed as though they could see through thousands of meters of dirt and rock and still see beyond into the deep of space. Perhaps he could see that far . . . Even his own people were never sure of the limits of his power. His white face and white feathers gave his penetrating eyes a miraculously piercing capacity.

Calmly, rather kindly, he added, "My darling, you are wrong. We simply do not know who this man McBan really is."

"Couldn't it be written?" she pleaded. "Couldn't it be promised? That's the direction of space from which the robot, the rat and the Copt sent back our very special message, 'From the uttermost deeps one shall come, bringing uncountable treasure and a sure delivery.' So it might be now! Mightn't it?"

"My dear," he responded, "you still have a crude idea of real treasure if you think it is measured in megacredits. Go read The Scrap of the Book, then think, and then tell me what you have thought. But meanwhile—no more chatter. We must not excite our poor oppressed people."

## Ruth, on the Beach Near Meeya Meefla

On this day Ruth thought nothing at all of Norstrilia or treasures. She was trying to do watercolors of the breakers and they came out very badly indeed. The real ones kept on being too beautiful and the water colors looked like watercolors.

## The Temporary Council of the Commonwealth of Old North Australia

"All the riffraff of all the worlds. They're all going to make a run for that silly boy of ours."

"Right."

"If he stays here, they'll come here."

"Right."

"Let's let him go to Earth. I have a feeling that little rascal Redlady will smuggle him out tonight and save us the trouble."

"Right."

"After a while it will be all right for him to come back. He won't spoil our hereditary defense of looking stupid, I'm afraid he's bright but by Earth standards he's just a yokel."

"Right."

"Should we send along twenty or thirty more Rod McBans and get the attackers really loused up?"

"No."

"Why not, Sir and Owner?"

"Because it would look clever. We rely on never looking clever. I have the next best answer."

"What's that?"

"Suggest to all the really rum worlds we know that a good impersonator could put his hands on the McBan money. Make the suggestion so that they would not know that we had originated it. The starlanes will be full of Rod McBans, complete with phony Norstrilian accents, for the next couple of hundred years. And no one will suspect that we set them up to it. Stupid's the word, mate, stupid. If they ever think we're clever, we're for it!" The speaker sighed: "How do the bloody fools suppose our forefathers got off Paradise VII if they weren't clever? How can they think we'd hold this sharp little monopoly for thousands of years? They're stupid not to think about it, but let's not make them think. Right?"

"Right."

# The Nearby Exile

Rod woke with a strange feeling of well-being. In a corner of his mind there were memories of pandemonium—knives, blood, medicine, a monkey working as surgeon. Rum dreams! He glanced around and immediately tried to jump out of bed.

The whole world was on fire!

Bright blazing intolerable fire, like a blowtorch.

But the bed held him. He realized that a loose comfortable jacket ended in tapes and that the tapes were anchored in some way to the bed.

"Eleanor!" he shouted. "Come here."

He remembered the mad bird attacking him, Lavinia transporting him to the cabin of the sharp Earthman, Lord Redlady. He remembered medicines and fuss. But this—what was this?

When the door opened, more of the intolerable light poured in. It was as though every cloud had been stripped from the sky of Old North Australia, leaving only the blazing heavens and the fiery sun. There were people who had seen that happen, when the weather machines occasionally broke down and let a hurricane cut a hole in the clouds, but it had certainly not happened in his time, or in his grandfather's time.

The man who entered was pleasant, but he was
no Norstrilian. His shoulders were slight, he did not
look as though he could lift a cow, and his face
had been washed so long and so steadily that it
looked like a baby's face. He had an odd medical-
looking suit on, all white, and his face combined
the smile and the ready professional sympathy of a
good physician.

"We're feeling better, I see," said he.

"Where on Earth am I?" asked Rod. "In a satel-
lite? It feels odd."

"You're not on Earth, man."

"I know I'm not. I've never been there. Where's
this place?"

"Mars. The Old Star Station. I'm Jeanjacques
Vomact." Rod mumbled the name so badly the other
man had to spell it out for him. When that was
straightened out, Rod came back to the subject.

"Where's Mars? Can you untie me? When's that
light going to go off?"

"I'll untie you right now," said Doctor Vomact,
"but stay in bed and take it easy until we've given
you some food and taken some tests. The light—that's
sunshine. I'd say it's about seven hours, local time,
before it goes off. This is late morning. Don't you
know what Mars is? It's a planet."

"New Mars, you mean," said Rod proudly, "the
one with the enormous shops and the zoological
gardens."

"The only shops we have here are the cafeteria and
the PX. New Mars? I've heard of that place somewhere.
It does have big shops and some kind of an animal
show. Elephants you can hold in your hand. They've

got those too. This isn't that place at all. Wait a sec,
I'll roll your bed to the window."

Rod looked eagerly out of the window. It was
frightening. A naked, dark sky did not have a cloud
in sight. A few holes showed in it here and there.
They almost looked like the "stars" which people saw
when they were in spaceship transit from one cloudy
planet to another. Dominating everything was a single
explosive horrible light, which hung high and steady
in the sky without ever going off. He found himself
cringing for the explosion, but he could tell, from the
posture of the doctor next to him, that the doctor was
not in the least afraid of that chronic hydrogen bomb,
whatever it might turn out to be. Keeping his voice
level and trying not to sound like a boy, he said,

"What's that?"

"The Sun."

"Don't cook my book, mate. Give me the straight
truth. Everybody calls his star a sun. What's this one?"

"The Sun. The original Sun. The Sun of Old Earth
itself. Just as this is plain Mars. Not even Old Mars.
Certainly not New Mars. This is Earth's neighbor."

"That thing never goes off, goes up—boom!—or
goes down?"

"The Sun, you mean?" said Doctor Vomact. "No, I
should think not. I suppose it looked that way to your
ancestors and mine half a million years ago, when we
were all running around naked on Earth." The doctor
busied himself as he talked. He chopped the air with
a strange-looking little key, and the tapes fell loose.
The mittens dropped off Rod's hands. Rod looked at
his own hands in the intense light and saw that they
seemed strange. They looked smooth and naked and

clean, like the doctor's own hands. Weird memories began to come back to him, but his handicap about spieking and hiering telepathically had made him cautious and sensitive, so he did not give himself away.

"If this is old, old Mars, what are you doing, talking the Old North Australian language to me? I thought my people were the only ones in the universe who still spoke Ancient Inglish." He shifted proudly but clumsily over to the Old Common Tongue: "You see, the Appointed Ones of my family taught me this language as well. I've never been offworld before."

"I speak your language," said the doctor, "because I learned it. I learned it because you paid me, very generously, to learn it. In the months that we have been reassembling you, it's come in handy. We just let down the portal of memory and identity today, but I've talked to you for hundreds of hours already."

Rod tried to speak.

He could not utter a word. His throat was dry and he was afraid that he might throw up his food—if he had eaten any.

The doctor put a friendly hand on his arm. "Easy, Mister and Owner McBan, easy now. We all do that when we *come out.*"

Rod croaked, "*I've been dead? Dead? Me?*"

"Not exactly dead," said the doctor, "but close to it."

"The box—that little box!" cried Rod.

"What little box?"

"Please, Doctor—the one I came in?"

"That box wasn't so little," said Doctor Vomact. He squared his hands in the air and made a shape about the size of the little ladies' bonnet-box which Rod had seen in the Lord Redlady's private operating room. "It

was this big. Your head was full natural size. That's
why it's been so easy and so successful to bring you
back to normality in such a hurry."

"And Eleanor?"

"Your companion? She made it, too. Nobody inter-
cepted the ship."

"You mean the rest is true, too? I'm still the richest man in the universe? And I'm gone, gone from
home?" Rod would have liked to beat the bedspread,
but did not.

"I am glad," said Doctor Vomact, "to see you express
so much feeling about your situation. You showed a
great deal when you were under the sedatives and
hypnotics, but I was beginning to wonder how we
could help you realize your true position when you
came back, as you have, to normal life. Forgive me
for talking this way. I sound like a medical journal.
It's hard to be friends with a patient, even when one
really likes him . . ."

Vomact was a small man, a full head shorter than
Rod himself, but so gracefully proportioned that he
did not look stunted or little. His face was thin, with
a mop of ungovernable black hair which fell in all
directions. Among Norstrilians, this fashion would
have been deemed eccentric; to judge by the fact that
other Earthmen let their hair grow wild and long, it
must have been an Earth fashion. Rod found it foolish but not repulsive.

It was not Vomact's appearance which caused the
impression. It was the personality which tingled out
of every pore. Vomact could become calm when he
knew, from his medical wisdom, that kindness and
tranquility were in order, but these qualities were

not usual to him. He was vivacious, moody, lively, talkative to an extreme, but he was sensitive enough to the person to whom he was talking: he never became a bore. Even among Norstrilian women, Rod had never seen a person who expressed so much, so fluently. When Vomact talked, his hands were in constant motion—outlining, describing, clarifying the points which he described. When he talked he smiled, scowled, raised his eyebrows in questioning, stared with amazement, looked aside in wonder. Rod was used to the sight of two Norstrilians having a long telepathic conversation, spieking and hiering one another as their bodies reposed, comfortable and immobile, while their minds worked directly on one another. To do all this with the speaking voice—that, to a Norstrilian, was a marvel to hear and behold. There was something graceful and pleasant about the animation of this Earth doctor which stood in complete contrast to the quick dangerous decisiveness of the Lord Redlady. Rod began to think that if Earth were full of people, all of them like Vomact, it must be a delightful but confusing place. Vomact once hinted that his family was unusual, so that even in the long weary years of perfection, when everyone else had numbers, they kept their family name secret but remembered.

One afternoon Vomact suggested that they walk across the Martian plain a few kilometers to the ruins of the first human settlement on Mars. "We have to talk," said he, "but it is easy enough to talk through these soft helmets. The exercise will do you good. You're young and you will take a lot of conditioning."

Rod agreed.

Friends they became in the ensuing days.

Rod found that the doctor was by no means as young as he looked, just ten years or so older than himself. The doctor was a hundred and ten years old, and had gone through his first rejuvenation just ten years before. He had two more and then death, at the age of four hundred, if the present schedule were kept for Mars.

"You may think, Mister McBan, that you are an upset, wild type yourself. I can promise you, young bucko, that Old Earth is such a happy mess these days that they will never notice you. Haven't you heard about the Rediscovery of Man?"

Rod hesitated. He had paid no attention to the news himself, but he did not want to discredit his home planet by making it seem more ignorant than it really was. "Something about language, wasn't it? And length of life, too? I never paid much attention to offplanet news, unless it was technical inventions or big battles. I think some people in Old North Australia have a keen interest in Old Earth itself. What was it, anyhow?"

"The Instrumentality finally took on a big plan. Earth had no dangers, no hopes, no rewards, no future except endlessness. Everybody stood a thousand-to-one chance of living the four hundred years which was allotted for persons who earned the full period by keeping busy—"

"Why didn't everybody do it?" interrupted Rod.

"The Instrumentality took care of the shorties in a very fair way. If offered them wonderfully delicious and exciting vices when they got to be about seventy. Things that combined electronics, drugs and sex in the subjective mind. Anybody who didn't have a lot of work to do ended up getting 'the blissfuls' and eventually died of sheer fun. Who wants to take time for mere hundred-years' renewals when they can have five or six thousand years of orgies and adventures every single night?"

"Sounds horrible to me," said Rod. "We have our Giggle Rooms, but people die in them right away. They don't mess around, dying among their neighbors. Think of the awful interaction you must get with the normals."

Doctor Vomact's face clouded over with anger and grief. He turned away and looked over the endless Martian plains. Dear blue Earth hung friendlily in the sky. He looked up at the star of Earth as though he hated it and he said to Rod, his face still turned away,

"You may have a point there, Mister McBan. My mother was a shortie and after she gave up, my father went too. And I'm a normal. I don't suppose I'll get over what it did to me. They weren't my real parents, of course—there was nothing that dirty in my family—but they were my final adopters. I've always thought that you Old North Australians were crazy, rich barbarians for killing off your teen-agers if they didn't jump enough or something crude like that, but I'll admit that you're clean barbarians. You don't make yourselves live with the sweet sick stink of death inside your own apartments . . ."

"What's an apartment?"

"What we live in."

"You mean a house," said Rod.

"No, an apartment is part of a house. Two hundred thousand of them sometimes make up one big house."

"You mean," said Rod, "there are two hundred thousand families all in one enormous living room? The room must be kilometers long."

"No, no, no!" said the doctor, laughing a little. "Each apartment has a separate living room with sleep sections that come out of the walls, an eating section, a washroom for yourself and your visitors that might come to have a bath with you, a garden room, a study room, and a personality room."

"What's a personality room?"

"That," said the doctor, "is a little room where we do things that we don't want our own families to watch."

"We call that a bathroom," said Rod.

The doctor stopped in their walk. "That's what makes it so hard to explain to you what Earth is doing. You're fossils, that's what you are. You've had the old language of Inglish, you keep your family system and your names, you've had unlimited life—"

"Not unlimited," said Rod, "just long. We have to work for it and pay for it with tests."

The doctor looked sorry. "I didn't mean to criticize you. You're different. Very different from what Earth has been. You would have found Earth inhuman. Those apartments we were talking about, for example. Two-thirds of them empty. Underpeople moving into the basements. Records lost; jobs forgotten. If we didn't make such good robots, everything would have fallen to pieces at the same time." He looked at Rod's face. "I can see you don't understand me. Let's take a practical case. Can you imagine killing me?"

"No," said Rod. "I like you."

"I don't mean that. Not the real us. Suppose you

didn't know who I was and you found me intruding on your sheep or stealing your stroon."

"You couldn't steal my stroon. My government processes it for me and you couldn't get near it."

"All right, all right, not stroon. Just suppose I came from off your planet without a permit. How would you kill me?"

"I wouldn't kill you. I'd report it to the police."

"Suppose I drew a weapon on you?"

"Then," said Rod, "you'd get your neck broken. Or a knife in your heart. Or a minibomb somewhere near you."

"There!" said the doctor, with a broad grin.

"There what?" said Rod.

"You know how to kill people, should the need arise."

"All citizens know how," said Rod, "but that doesn't mean they do it. We're not bushwhacking each other all the time, the way I heard some Earth people thought we did."

"Precisely," said Vomact. "And that's what the Instrumentality is trying to do for all mankind today. To make life dangerous enough and interesting enough to be real again. We have diseases, dangers, fights, chances. It's been wonderful."

Rod looked back at the group of sheds they had left. "I don't see any signs of it here on Mars."

"This is a military establishment. It's been left out of the Rediscovery of Man until the effects have been studied better. We're still living perfect lives of four hundred years here on Mars. No danger, no change, no risk."

"How do you have a name, then?"

"My father gave it to me. He was an official Hero of

the Frontier Worlds who came home and died a shortie. The Instrumentality let people like that have names before they gave the privilege to everybody."

"What are you doing here?"

"Working." The doctor started to resume their walk. Rod did not feel much awe of him. He was such a shamelessly talkative person, the way most Earth men seemed to be, that it was hard not to be at ease with him.

Rod took Vomact's arm, gently. "There's more to it—"

"You know it," said Vomact. "You have good perceptions. Should I tell you?"

"Why not?" said Rod.

"You're my patient. It might not be fair to you."

"Go ahead," said Rod. "You ought to know I'm tough."

"I'm a criminal," said the doctor.

"But you're alive," said Rod. "In my world we kill criminals or we send them offplanet."

"I'm offplanet," said Vomact. "This isn't my world. For most of us here on Mars, this is a prison, not a home."

"What did you do?"

"It's too awful . . ." said the doctor. "I'm ashamed of it myself. They have sentenced me to conditional conditional."

Rod looked at him quickly. Momentarily he wondered whether he might be the victim of some outrageous deadpan joke. The doctor was serious; his face expressed bewilderment and grief.

"I revolted," said the doctor, "without knowing it. People can say anything they want on Earth, and they can print up to twenty copies of anything they need to print, but beyond that it's mass communications. Against the law. When the Rediscovery of Man

came, they gave me the Spanish language to work
on. I used a lot of research to get out *La Prensa*.
Jokes, dialogues, imaginary advertisements, reports of
what had happened in the ancient world. But then I
got a bright idea. I went down to Earthport and got
the news from incoming ships. What was happening
here. What was happening there. You have no idea,
Rod, how interesting mankind is! And the things we
do . . . so strange, so comical, so pitiable. The news
even comes in on machines, all marked 'official use
only.' I disregarded that and I printed up one issue
with nothing but truth in it—a real issue, all facts.

"*I printed real news.*

"Rod, the roof fell in. All persons who had been
reconditioned for Spanish were given stability tests.
I was asked, did I know the law? Certainly, said I, I
knew the law. No mass communications except within
government. News is the mother of opinion, opinion
the cause of mass delusion, delusion the source of war.
The law was plain and I thought it did not matter. I
thought it was just an old law.

"I was wrong, Rod, wrong. They did not charge me
with violating the news laws. They charged me with
revolt—against the Instrumentality. They sentenced me
to death, immediately. Then they made it conditional,
conditional on my going offplanet and behaving well.
When I got here, they made it double conditional. If
my act has no bad results. *But I can't find out.* I can
go back to Earth any time. That part is no trouble.
If they think my misdeed still has effect, they will
give me the dream punishments or send me off to
that awful planet somewhere. If they think it doesn't
matter, they will restore my citizenship with a laugh.

But they don't know the worst of it. My underman learned Spanish and the underpeople are keeping the newspaper going very secretly. I can't even imagine what they will do to me if they ever find out what has gone wrong and know that it was me who started it all. Do you think I'm wrong, Rod?"

Rod stared at him. He was not used to judging adults, particularly not at their own request. In Old North Australia, people kept their distance. There were fitting ways for doing everything, and one of the most fitting things was to deal only with people of your own age group.

He tried to be fair, to think in an adult way, and he said, "Of course I think you're wrong, Mister and Doctor Vomact. But you're not very wrong. None of us should trifle with war."

Vomact seized Rod's arm. The gesture was hysterical, almost ugly. "Rod," he whispered, very urgently, "you're rich. You come from an important family. Could you get me into Old North Australia?"

"Why not?" said Rod. "I can pay for all the visitors I want."

"No, Rod, I don't mean that. As an immigrant."

It was Rod's turn to become tense. "Immigrant?" he said. "The penalty for immigration is death. We're killing our own people right now, just to keep the population down. How do you think we could let outsiders settle with us? And the stroon. What about that?"

"Never mind, Rod," said Vomact. "I won't bother you again. I won't mention it again. It's a weary thing, to live many years with death ready to open the next door, ring the next bell, be on the next page of the message file. I haven't married. How could I?" With a whimsical turn of his vivacious mind and face, he was off on a cheerful track. "I have a medicine, Rod, a medicine for doctors, even for rebels. Do you know what it is?"

"A tranquilizer?" Rod was still shocked at the indecency of anyone mentioning immigration to a Norstrilian. He could not think straight.

"Work," said the little doctor. "That's my medicine."

"Work is always good," said Rod, feeling pompous at the generalization. The magic had gone out of the afternoon.

The doctor felt it too. He sighed. "I'll show you the old sheds which men from Earth first built. And then I'll go to work. Do you know what my main work is?"

"No," said Rod, politely.

"You," said Doctor Vomact, with one of his sad gay mischievous smiles. "You're well, but I've got to make you more than well. I've got to make you kill-proof."

They had reached the sheds.

The ruins might be old but they were not very impressive. They looked something like the homes on the more modest stations back on Norstrilia.

On their way back Rod said, very casually,

"What are you going to do to me, Sir and Doctor?"

"Anything you want," said Vomact lightly.

"Really, now. What?"

"Well," said Vomact, "the Lord Redlady sent along a whole cube of suggestions. Keep your personality. Keep your retinal and brain images. Change your appearance. Change your workwoman into a young man who looks just like your description."

"You can't do that to Eleanor. She's a citizen."

"Not here, not on Mars, she isn't. She's your baggage."

"But her legal rights!"

"This is Mars, Rod, but it's Earth territory. Under Earth law. Under the direct control of the Instrumentality. We can do these things all right. The hard thing is this: Would you consent to passing for an underman?"

"I never saw one. How would I know?" said Rod.

"Could you stand the shame of it?"

Rod laughed, by way of an answer.

Vomact sighed. "You're funny people, you Norstrilians. I'd rather die than be mistaken for an underman. The disgrace of it, the contempt! But the Lord Redlady said that you could walk into Earth as free as a breeze if we made you pass for a cat-man. I might as well tell you, Rod. Your wife is already here."

Rod stopped walking. "My wife? I have no wife."

"Your cat-wife," said the doctor. "Of course it isn't real marriage. Underpeople aren't allowed to have it. But they have a companionship which looks something like marriage and we sometimes slip and call them husband and wife. The Instrumentality has already sent a cat-girl out to be your 'wife.' She'll travel back to Earth with you from Mars. You'll just be a pair of lucky cats who've been doing dances and acrobatics for the bored station personnel here."

"And Eleanor?"

"I suppose somebody will kill her, thinking it's you. That's what you brought her for, isn't it? Aren't you rich enough?"

"No, no, no," said Rod, "nobody is that rich. We have to think of something else."

They spent the entire walk making new plans which would protect Eleanor and Rod both.

As they entered the shedport and took off their helmets, Rod said,

"This wife of mine, when can I see her?"

"You won't overlook her," said Vomact. "She's as wild as fire and twice as beautiful."

"Does she have a name?"

"Of course she does," said the doctor. "They all do."

"What is it, then?"

"C'mell."

# Hospitality and Entrapment

People waited, here and there. If there had been worldwide news coverage, the population would have converged on Earthport with curiosity, passion, or greed. But *news* had been forbidden long before; people could know only the things which concerned them personally; the centers of Earth remained undisturbed. Here and there, as Rod made his trip from Mars to Earth, there were anticipations of the event. Overall, the world of Old Old Earth remained quiet, except for the perennial bubble of its inward problems.

## On Earth, The Day of Rod's Flight, Within Earthport Itself

"They shut me out of the meeting this morning, when I'm in charge of visitors. That means that something is in the air," said Commissioner Teadrinker to his underman, B'dank.

B'dank, expecting a dull day, had been chewing his cud while sitting on his stool in the corner. He knew far more about the case than did his master, and he had learned his additional information from the secret sources of the underpeople, but he was resolved to betray nothing, to express nothing. Hastily he swallowed his cud and said, in his reassuring, calm bull voice:

"There might be some other reason, Sir and Master. If they were considering a promotion for you, they would leave you out of the meeting. You certainly deserve a promotion, Sir and Master."

"Are the spiders ready?" asked Teadrinker crossly.

"Who can tell the mind of a giant spider?" said B'dank calmly. "I talked to the foreman-spider for three hours yesterday with sign language. He wants twelve cases of beer. I told him I would give him more—he could have ten. The poor devil can't count, though he thinks he can, so he was pleased at having outbargained me. They will take the person you designate to the steeple of Earthport and they will hide that person so that the human being cannot be found for many hours. When I appear with the cases of beer, they will give me the person. I will then jump out of a window, holding the person in my arms. There are so few people who go down the outside of Earthport that they may not notice me at all. I will take the person to the ruined palace directly under Alpha Ralpha Boulevard, the one which you showed me, Sir and Master, and there I will keep the person in good order until you come and do the things which you have to do."

Teadrinker looked across the room. The big, florid, handsome face was so exasperatingly calm that it annoyed him. Teadrinker had heard that bull-men, because of their cattle origin, were sometimes subject to fits of uncontrollable frantic rage, but he had never seen the least sign of any such phenomenon in B'dank. He snapped,

"Aren't you worried?"

"Why should I worry, Sir and Master? You are doing the worrying for both of us."

"Go fry yourself!"

"That is not an operational instruction," said B'dank. "I suggest that the master eat something. That will calm his nerves. Nothing at all will happen today, and it is very hard for true men to wait for nothing at all. I have seen many of them get upset."

Teadrinker gritted his teeth at this extreme reasonableness. Nevertheless, he took a dehydrated banana out of his desk drawer and began chewing on it.

He looked sharply across at B'dank. "Do you want one of these things?"

B'dank slid off his chair with surprisingly smooth agility; he was at the desk, his enormous ham-sized hand held out, before he said,

"Yes, indeed, sir. I love bananas."

Teadrinker gave him one and then said, fretfully,

"Are you sure of the fact you never met the Lord Redlady?"

"Sure as any underman can be," said B'dank, munching the banana. "We never really know what has been put into our original conditioning, or who put it there. We're inferior and we're not supposed to know. It is forbidden even to inquire."

"So you admit that you might be a spy or agent of the Lord Redlady?"

"I might be, sir, but I do not feel like it."

"Do you know who Redlady is?"

"You have told me, sir, that he is the most dangerous human being in the whole galaxy."

"That's right," said Teadrinker, "and if I am running

into something which the Lord Redlady has set up, I might as well cut up my throat before I start."

"It would be simpler, sir," said B'dank, "not to kidnap this Rod McBan at all. That is the only element of danger. If you did nothing, things would go on as they always have gone on—quietly, calmly."

"That's the horror and anxiety of it! They *do* always go on. Don't you think I want to get out of here, to taste power and freedom again?"

"You say so, sir," said B'dank, hoping that Teadrinker would offer him one more of those delicious dried bananas.

Teadrinker, distracted, did not.

He just walked up and down his room, desperate with the torment of hope, danger and delay.

## Antechamber of the Bell and Bank

The Lady Johanna Gnade was there first. She was clean, well dressed, alert. The Lord Jestocost, who followed her in, wondered if she had any personal life at all. It was bad manners, among the Chiefs of the Instrumentality, to inquire into another Chief's personal affairs, even though the complete personal histories of each of them, kept up to the day and minute, was recorded in the computer cabinet in the corner. Jestocost knew, because he had peeped his own record, using another Chief's name, just so that he could see whether several minor illegalities of his had been recorded; they had been, all except for the biggest one—his deal with the cat-girl C'mell—which he had successfully kept off the recording screens.

(The record simply showed him having a nap at the time.) If the Lady Johanna had any secrets, she kept them well.

"My Sir and Colleague," said she, "I suspect you of sheer inquisitiveness—a vice most commonly attributed to women."

"When we get as old as this, my lady, the differences in character between men and women become imperceptible. If, indeed, they ever existed in the first place. You and I are bright people and we each have a good nose for danger or disturbance. Isn't it likely we would both look up somebody with the impossible name of Roderick Frederick Ronald Arnold William MacArthur McBan to the hundred-and-fifty-first generation? See—I memorized all of it! Don't you think that was rather clever of me?"

"Rather," said she, in a tone which implied she didn't.

"I'm expecting him this morning."

"You are?" she asked, on a rising note which implied that there was something improper about his knowledge. "There's nothing about it in the messages."

"That's it," said the Lord Jestocost, smiling. "I arranged for Mars solar radiation to be carried two extra decimals until he left. This morning it's back down to three decimals. That means he's coming. Clever of me, wasn't it?"

"Too clever," she said. "Why ask me? I never thought you valued my opinion. Anyhow, why are you taking all these pains with the case? Why don't you just ship him out so far that it would take him a long lifetime, even with stroon, to get back here again?"

He looked at her evenly until she flushed. He said nothing.

"My—my comment was improper, I suppose," she stammered. "You and your sense of justice. You're always putting the rest of us in the wrong."

"I didn't mean to," he said mildly, "because I am just thinking of Earth. Did you know he owns this tower?"

"Earthport?" she cried. "Impossible."

"Not at all," said Jestocost. "I myself sold it to his agent ten days ago. For forty megacredits FOE money. That's more than we happen to have on Earth right now. When he deposited it, we began paying him three percent a year interest. And that wasn't all he bought from me. I sold him that ocean too, right there, the one the ancients called Atlantic. And I sold him three hundred thousand attractive underwomen trained in various tasks, together with the dower rights of seven hundred human women of appropriate ages."

"You mean you did all this to save the Earth treasury three megacredits a year?"

"Wouldn't you? Remember, this is FOE money."

She pursed her lips. Then she burst into a smile. "I never saw anyone else like you, my Lord Jestocost. You're the fairest man I ever knew and yet you never forget a little bit more in the way of earnings!"

"That's not the end of it," said he with a very crafty, pleased smile. "Did you read Amended (Reversionary) Schedule 711-19-13P, which you yourself voted for eleven days ago?"

"I looked at it," she said defensively. "We all

did. It was something to do with Earth funds and Instrumentality funds. The Earth representative didn't complain. We all passed it because we trusted you."

"Do you know what it means?"

"Frankly, not at all. Does it have anything to do with this rich old man, McBan?"

"Don't be sure," said the Lord Jestocost, "that he's old. He might be young. Anyhow, the tax schedule raises taxes on kilocredits very slightly. Megacredit taxes are divided evenly between Earth and the Instrumentality, provided that the owner is not personally operating the property. It comes to one percent a month. That's the very small type in the footnote at the bottom of the seventh page of rates."

"You—you mean—" she gasped with laughter, "that by selling the poor man the Earth you are not only cutting him out of three percent interest a year, but you're charging him twelve percent taxes. Blessed rockets, man, you're weird. I love you. You're the cleverest, most ridiculous person we ever had as a Chief of the Instrumentality!" From the Lady Johanna Gnade, this was lurid language indeed. Jestocost did not know whether to be offended or pleased.

Since she was in a rare good humor, he dared to mention his half-secret project to her.

"Do you think, my lady, that if we have all this unexpected credit, we could waste a little of our stroon imports?"

Her laugh stopped. "On what?" she said sharply.

"On the underpeople. For the best of them."

"Oh, no. Oh, no! Not for the animals, while there are still *people* who suffer. You're mad to think of it, my Lord."

"I'm mad," he said. "I'm mad all right. Mad—for justice. And this strikes me as simple justice. I'm not asking for equal rights. Merely for a little more justice for them."

"They're *underpeople*," she said blankly. "They're *animals*." As though this comment settled the matter altogether.

"You never heard, did you, my lady, of the dog named Joan?" His question held a wealth of allusion.

She saw no depth in it, said flatly, "No," and went back to studying the agenda for the day.


## Ten Kilometers Below the Surface of the Earth

The old engines turned like tides. The smell of hot oil was on them. Down here there were no luxuries. Life and flesh were cheaper than transistors; besides, they had much less radiation to be detected. In the groaning depths, the hidden and forgotten underpeople lived. They thought their chief, the E'telekeli, to be magical. Sometimes he thought so himself.

His white handsome face staring like a marble bust of immortality, his crumpled wings hugged closely to him in fatigue, he called to his first-egg child, the girl E'lamelanie,

"He comes, my darling."

"That one, father? The promised one."

"The rich one."

Her eyes widened. She was his daughter but she did not always understand his powers. "How do you know, father?"

"If I tell you the truth, will you agree to let me

erase it from your mind right away, so there will be no danger of betrayal?"

"Of course, father."

"No," said the marble-faced bird-man, "you must say the right words . . ."

"I promise, father, that if you fill my heart with the truth, and if my joy at the truth is full, that I will yield to you my mind, my whole mind without fear, hope, or reservation, and that I will ask you to take from my mind whatever truth or parts of the truth might hurt our kind of people, in the Name of the First Forgotten One, in the Name of the Second Forgotten One, in the Name of the Third Forgotten One, and for the sake of D'joan whom we all love and remember!"

He stood. He was a tall man. His legs ended in the enormous feet of a bird, with white talons shimmering like mother of pearl. His humanoid hands stood forth from the joints of his wings; with them he extended the prehistoric gesture of blessing over her head, while he chanted the truth in a ringing hypnotic voice,

"Let the truth be yours, my daughter, that you may be whole and happy with the truth. Knowing the truth, my daughter, know freedom and the right to forget!

"The child, my child, who was your brother, the little boy you loved . . ."

"Yeekasoose!" she said, her voice trance-like and childish.

"E'ikasus, whom you remember, was changed by me, his father, into the form of a small ape-man, so that the true people mistook him for an animal, not an underperson. They trained him as a surgeon and sent him to the Lord Redlady. He came with this young man McBan to Mars, where he met C'mell, whom I recommended to the Lord Jestocost for confidential errands. They are coming back with this man today. He has already bought the Earth, or most of it. Perhaps he will do us good. Do you know what you should know, my daughter?"

"Tell me, father, tell me. *How* do you know?"

"Remember the truth, girl, and then lose it! The messages come from Mars. We cannot touch the Big Blink or the message-coding machines, but each recorder has his own style. By a shift in the pace of his work, a friend can relay moods, emotions, ideas, and sometimes names. They have sent me words like 'riches, monkey, small, cat, girl, everything, good' by the pitch and speed of their recording. The human messages carry ours and no cryptographer in the world can find them.

"Now you know, and you will now now now *now* forget!"

He raised his hands again.

E'lamelanie looked at him normally with a happy smile. "It's so sweet and funny, daddy, but I know I've just forgotten something good and wonderful!"

Ceremonially he added, "Do not forget Joan."

Formally she responded, "I shall never forget Joan."

# The High Sky Flying

Rod walked to the edge of the little park. This was utterly unlike any ship he had ever seen or heard about in Norstrilia. There was no noise, no cramping, no sign of weapons—just a pretty little cabin which housed the controls, the Go-Captain, the Pinlighters, and the Stop-Captain, and then a stretch of incredible green grass. He had walked on this grass from the dusty ground of Mars. There was a puff and a whisper. A false blue sky, very beautiful, covered him like a canopy.

He felt strange. He had whiskers like a cat, forty centimeters long, growing out of his upper lip, about twelve whiskers to each side. The doctor had colored his eyes with bright green irises. His ears reached up to a point. He looked like a cat-man and he wore the professional clothing of an acrobat; C'mell did too.

He had not gotten over C'mell.

She made every woman in Old North Australia look like a sack of lard. She was lean, limber, smooth, menacing and beautiful; she was soft to the touch, hard in her motions, quick, alert, and cuddlesome. Her red hair blazed with the silkiness of animal fire. She spoke with a soprano which tinkled like wild bells. Her ancestors and ancestresses had been bred to produce the most seductive girl on Earth. The task had succeeded. Even in repose, she was voluptuous. Her wide hips and sharp eyes invited the masculine passions. Her catlike dangerousness challenged every man whom she met. The true men who looked at her knew that she was a cat, and still could not keep their eyes off her. Human women treated her as though she were something disgraceful. She traveled as an acrobat, but she had already told Rod McBan confidentially that she was by profession a "girlygirl," a female animal, shaped and trained like a person to serve as hostess to offworld visitors, required by law and custom to invite their love, while promised the penalty of death if she accepted it.

Rod liked her, though he had been painfully shy with her at first. There was no side to her, no posh, no swank. Once she got down to business, her incredible body faded part way into the background, though with the sides of his eyes he could never quite forget it. It was her mind, her intelligence, her humor and good humor, which carried them across the hours and days they spent together. He found himself trying to impress her that he was a grown man, only to discover that in the spontaneous, sincere affections of her quick cat heart she did not care in the least what his status was. He was simply her partner and they had work to do together. It was his job to stay alive and it was her job to keep him alive.

Doctor Vomact had told him not to speak to the other passengers, not to say anything to each other, and to call for silence if any of them spoke.

There were ten other passengers who stared at one another in uncomfortable amazement.

Ten in number, they were.

All ten of them were Rod McBan.

Ten identical Roderick Frederick Ronald Arnold William MacArthur McBans to the one hundred and fifty-first, all exactly alike. Apart from C'mell herself and the little monkey-doctor, A'gentur, the only person on the ship who was *not* Rod McBan was Rod McBan himself. He had become the cat-man. The others seemed, each by himself, to be persuaded that he alone was Rod McBan and that the other nine were parodies. They watched each other with a mixture of gloom and suspicion mixed with amusement, just as the real Rod McBan would have done, had he been in their place.

"One of them," said Doctor Vomact in parting, "is your companion Eleanor from Norstrilia. The other nine are mouse-powered robots. They're all copied from you. Good, eh?" He could not conceal his professional satisfaction.

And now they were all about to see Earth together.

C'mell took Rod to the edge of the little world and said gently, "I want to sing 'The Tower Song' to you, just before we shut down on the top of Earthport." And in her wonderful voice she sang the strange little old song,

*And oh! my love, for you.*
*High birds crying, and a*
*High sky flying, and a*
*High wind driving, and a*
*High heart striving, and a*
*High brave place for you!*

Rod felt a little funny, standing there, looking at nothing, but he also felt pleasant with the girl's head against his shoulder and his arm enfolding her. She seemed not only to need him, but to trust him very deeply. She did not feel adult—not self-important and full of unexplained business. She was merely a girl, and for the time *his* girl. It was pleasant and it gave him a strange foretaste of the future.

The day might come when he would have a permanent girl of his own, facing not a day, but life, not a danger, but destiny. He hoped that he could be as relaxed and fond with that future girl as he was with C'mell.

C'mell squeezed his hand, as though in warning.

He turned to look at her but, she stared ahead and nodded with her chin.

"Keep watching," she said, "straight ahead. Earth."

He looked back at the blank artificial sky of the ship's force-field. It was a monotonous but pleasant blue, conveying depths which were not really there.

The change was so fast that he wondered whether he had really seen it.

In one moment the clear flat blue.

Then the false sky splashed apart as though it had literally been slashed into enormous ribbons, ribbons in their turn becoming blue spots and disappearing.

Another blue sky was there—Earth's.

Manhome.

Rod breathed deeply. It was hard to believe. The sky itself was not so different from the false sky which had surrounded the ship on its trip from Mars, but there was an aliveness and wetness to it, unlike any other sky he had ever heard about.

It was not the sight of the Earth which surprised him—it was the smell. He suddenly realized that Old North Australia must smell dull, flat, dusty to Earthmen. This Earth air smelled alive. There were the odors of plants, of water, of things which he could not even guess. The air was coded with a million years of memory. In this air his people had swum to manhood, before they conquered the stars. The wetness was not the cherished damp of one of his covered canals. It was wild free moisture which came laden with the indications of things living, dying, sprawling, squirming, loving with an abundance which no Norstrilian could understand. No wonder the descriptions of Earth had always seemed fierce and exaggerated! What was stroon that men would pay water for it—water, the giver and carrier of life. This *was* his home, no matter how many generations his people had lived in the twisted hells of Paradise VII or the dry treasures of Old North Australia. He took a deep breath, feeling the plasma of Earth pour into him, the quick effluvium which had made man. He smelled Earth again—it would take a long lifetime, even with stroon, before a man could understand all these odors which came all the way up to the ship, which hovered, as planoforming ships usually did not, twenty-odd kilometers above the surface of the planet.

There was something strange in this air, something sweet-clear to the nostrils, refreshing to the spirit. One great beautiful odor overrode all the others. What could it be? He sniffed and then said, very clearly, to himself,

"Salt!"

C'mell reminded him that he was beside her.

"Do you like it, C'rod?"

"Yes, yes, it's better than—" Words failed him. He looked at her. Her eager, pretty, comradely smile made him feel that she was sharing every milligram of his delight. "But why," he asked, "do you waste salt on the air? What good does it do?"

"Salt?"

"Yes—in the air. So rich, so wet, so salty. Is it to clean the ship some way that I do not understand?"

"Ship? We're not on the ship, C'rod. This is the landing roof of Earthport."

He gasped.

No ship? There was not a mountain on Old North Australia more than six kilometers above MGL—mean ground level—and those mountains were all smooth, worn, old, folded by immense eons of wind into a gentle blanketing that covered his whole home world.

He looked around.

The platform was about two hundred meters long by one hundred wide.

The ten "Rod McBans" were talking to some men in uniform. Far at the other side a steeple rose into eye-catching height—perhaps a whole half-kilometer. He looked down.

There it was—Old Old Earth.

The treasure of water reached before his very eyes—water by the millions of tons, enough to feed a galaxy of sheep, to wash an infinity of men. The water was broken by a few islands on the far horizon to the right.

"Hesperides," said C'mell, following the direction of his gaze. "They came up from the sea when the Daimoni built this for us. For people, I mean. I shouldn't say 'us.'"

He did not notice the correction. He stared at the sea. Little specks were moving in it, very slowly. He pointed at one of them with his finger and asked C'mell,

"Are those wethouses?"

"What did you call them?"

"Houses which are wet. Houses which sit on water. Are those some of them?"

"Ships," she said, not spoiling his fun with a direct contradiction. "Yes, those are ships."

"Ships?" he cried. "You'd never get one of those into space. Why call them ships then?"

Very gently C'mell explained, "People had ships for water before they had ships for space. I think the Old Common Tongue takes the word for space vessel from the things you are looking at."

"I want to see a city," said Rod. "Show me a city."

"It won't look like much from here. We're too high up. Nothing looks like much from the top of Earthport. But I can show you, anyhow. Come over here, dear."

When they walked away from the edge, Rod realized that the little monkey was still with them. "What are you doing here with us?" asked Rod, not unkindly.

The monkey's preposterous little face wrinkled into a knowing smile. The face was the same as it had been before, but the expression was different—more assured, more clear, more purposive than ever before. There was even humor and cordiality in the monkey's voice.

"We animals are waiting for the people to finish their entrance."

We animals? thought Rod. He remembered his furry

head, his pointed ears, his cat-whiskers. No wonder he felt at ease with this girl and she with him.

The ten Rod McBans were walking down a ramp, so that the floor seemed to be swallowing them slowly from the feet up. They were walking in single file, so that the head of the leading one seemed to sit bodiless on the floor, while the last one in line had lost nothing more than his feet. It was odd indeed.

Rod looked at C'mell and A'gentur and asked them frankly, "When people have such a wide, wet, beautiful world, all full of life, why should they kill me?"

A'gentur shook his monkey head sadly, as though he knew full well, but found the telling of it inexpressibly wearisome and sad.

C'mell answered, "You are who you are. You hold immense power. Do you know that this tower is yours?"

"Mine!" he cried.

"You've bought it, or somebody bought it for you. Most of that water is yours, too. When you have things that big, people ask you for things. Or they take them from you. Earth is a beautiful place but I think it is a dangerous place, too, for offworlders like you who are used to just one way of life. You have not caused all the crime and meanness in the world, but it's been sleeping and now wakes up for you."

"Why for me?"

"Because," said A'gentur, "you're the richest person who has ever touched this planet. You own most of it already. Millions of human lives depend on your thoughts and your decisions."

They had reached the opposite side of the top platforms. Here, on the land side, the rivers were

all leaking badly. Most of the land was covered with
steamclouds, such as they saw on Norstrilia when a
covered canal burst out of its covering. These clouds
represented incalculable treasures of rain. He saw that
they parted at the foot of the tower.

"Weather machines," said C'mell. "The cities are
all covered with weather machines. Don't you have
weather machines in Old North Australia?"

"Of course we do," said Rod, "but we don't waste
water by letting it float around in the open air like that.
It's pretty, though. I guess the extravagance of it makes
me feel critical. Don't you Earth people have anything
better to do with your water than to leave it lying on
the ground or having it float over open land?"

"We're not Earth people," said C'mell. "We're
underpeople. I'm a cat-person and he's made from
apes. Don't call us people. It's not decent."

"Fudge!" said Rod. "I was just asking a question
about Earth, not pestering your feelings when—"

He stopped short.

They all three spun around.

Out of the ramp there came something like a mowing machine. A human voice, a man's voice, screamed
from within it, expressing rage and fear.

Rod started to move forward.

C'mell held his arm, dragging back with all her weight.
"No! Rod, no! No!"

A'gentur slowed him down better by jumping into his
face, so that Rod suddenly saw nothing but a universe
of brown belly-fur and felt tiny hands gripping his hair
and pulling it. He stopped and reached for the monkey.
A'gentur anticipated him and dropped to the ground
before Rod could hit him.

The machine was racing up the outside of the steeple and almost disappearing into the sky above. The voice had become thin.

Rod looked at C'mell. "All right. What was it? What's happening?"

"That's a spider, a giant spider. It's kidnapping or killing Rod McBan."

"Me?" keened Rod. "It'd better not touch me. I'll tear it apart."

"*Sh-h-h!*" said C'mell.

"Quiet!" said the monkey.

"Don't '*sh-h-h*' me and don't 'quiet' me," said Rod. "I'm not going to let that poor blighter suffer on my account. Tell that thing to come down. What is it, anyhow, this spider? A robot?"

"No," said C'mell, "an insect."

Rod was narrowing his eyes, watching the mowing machine which hung on the outside of the tower. He could barely see the man within its grip. When C'mell said "insect," it triggered something in his mind. Hate. Revulsion. Resistance to dirt. Insects on Old North Australia were small, serially numbered and licensed. Even at that, he felt them to be his hereditary enemies. (Somebody had told him that Earth insects had done terrible things to the Norstrilians when they lived on Paradise VII.) Rod yelled at the spider, making his voice as loud as possible,

"You—come—down!"

The filthy thing on the tower quivered with sheer smugness and seemed to bring its machine-like legs closer together, settling down to be comfortable.

Rod forgot he was supposed to be a cat.

He gasped for air. Earth air was wet but thin. He

closed his eyes for a moment or two. He thought hate, hate, hate for the insect. Then he shrieked telepathically, louder than he had ever shrieked at home:

hate-spit-spit-vomit!
dirt, dirt, dirt,
explode!
crush!
ruin!
stink, collapse, putrefy, disappear!
hate-hate-hate!

The fierce red roar of his inarticulate spieking hurt even him. He saw the little monkey fall to the ground in a dead faint. C'mell was pale and looked as though she might throw up her food.

He looked away from them and up at the "spider." Had he reached it?

He had.

Slowly, slowly, the long legs moved out in spasm, releasing the man, whose body flashed downward. Rod's eyes followed the movement of "Rod McBan" and he cringed when a wet crunch let him know that the duplicate of his own body had been splashed all over the hard deck of the tower, a hundred meters away. He glanced back up at the "spider." It scrabbled for purchase on the tower and then cartwheeled downward. It too hit the deck hard and lay there dying, its legs twitching as its personality slipped into its private, everlasting night.

Rod gasped. "Eleanor. Oh, maybe that's Eleanor!" His voice wailed. He started to run to the facsimile of his human body, forgetting that he was a cat-man.

C'mell's voice was as sharp as a howl, though low in tone. "Shut up! Shut up! Stand still! Close your mind! Shut up! We're dead if you don't shut up!"

He stopped, stared at her stupidly. Then he saw she was in mortal earnest. He complied. He stopped moving. He did not try to talk. He capped his mind, closed himself against telepathy until his brainbox began to ache. The little monkey, A'gentur, was crawling up off the floor, looking shaken and sick. C'mell was still pale.

Men came running up the ramp, saw them, and headed toward them.

There was the beat of wings in the air.

An enormous bird—no, it was an ornithopter—landed with its claws scratching the deck. A uniformed man jumped out and cried,

"Where is he?"

"He jumped over!" C'mell shouted.

The man started to follow the direction of her gesture and then cut sharply back to her.

"Fool!" he said. "People can't jump off here. The barrier would hold ships in place. What did you see?"

C'mell was a good actress. She pretended to be getting over shock and gasping for words. The uniformed man looked at her haughtily.

"Cats," he said, "and a monkey. What are you doing here? Who are you?"

"Name C'mell, profession, girlygirl, Earthport staff, commanded by Commissioner Teadrinker. This—boyfriend, no status, name C'roderick, cashier in night bank down below. Him?" She nodded at A'gentur. "I don't know much about him."

"Name A'gentur. Profession, supplementary surgeon.

Status, animal. I'm not an underperson. Just an animal. I came in on the ship from Mars with the dead man there and some other true men who looked like him, and they went down first—"

"Shut up," said the uniformed man. He turned to the approaching men and said, "Honored Subchief, Sergeant 387 reporting. The user of the telepathic weapon has disappeared. The only things here are these two cat-people, not very bright, and a small monkey. They can talk. The girl says she saw somebody get off the tower."

The subchief was a tall redhead with a uniform even handsomer than the sergeant's. He snapped at C'mell, "How did he do it?"

Rod knew C'mell well enough by now to recognize the artfulness of her becoming confused, feminine and incoherent—in appearance. Actually, she was in full control of the situation. Said she, babbling:

"He jumped, I think. I don't know how."

"That's impossible," said the subchief. "Did you see where he went?" he barked at Rod McBan.

Rod gasped at the suddenness of the question: besides, C'mell had told him to keep quiet. Between these two peremptories, he said, "Er—ah—oh—you see—"

The little monkey-surgeon interrupted drily, "Sir and Master Subchief, that cat-man is not very bright. I do not think you will get much out of him. Handsome but stupid. Strictly breeding stock—"

Rod gagged and turned a little red at these remarks, but he could tell from the hooded quick glare which C'mell shot him that she wanted him to go on being quiet.

She cut in. "I did notice one thing, Master. It might matter."

"By the Bell and Bank, animal! Tell me!" cried the subchief. "Stop deciding what I ought to know!"

"The strange man's skin was lightly tinged with blue."

The subchief took a step back. His soldiers and the sergeant stared at him. In a serious, direct way he said to C'mell, "Are you *sure?*"

"No, my Master. I just thought so."

"You saw just one?" barked the subchief.

Rod, overacting the stupidity, held up four fingers.

"That idiot," cried the subchief, "thinks he saw four of them. Can he count?" he asked C'mell.

C'mell looked at Rod as though he were a handsome beast with not a brain in his head. Rod looked back at her, deliberately letting himself feel stupid. This was something which he did very well, since by neither hiering nor spieking at home, he had had to sit through interminable hours of other people's conversation when he was little, never getting the faintest idea of what it was all about. He had discovered very early that if he sat still and looked stupid, people did not bother him by trying to bring him into the conversation, turning their voices on and braying at him as though he were deaf. He tried to simulate the familiar old posture and was rather pleased that he could make such a good showing with C'mell watching him. Even when she was seriously fighting for their freedom and playing girl all at once, her corona of blazing hair made her shine forth like the sun of Earth itself; among all these people on the platform, her beauty and her intelligence made her stand out,

cat though she was. Rod was not at all surprised that
he was overlooked, with such a vivid personality next
to him; he just wished that he could be overlooked a
little more, so that he could wander over idly and see
whether the body was Eleanor's or one of the robots'.
If Eleanor had already died for him, in her first few
minutes of the big treat of seeing Earth, he felt that
he would never forgive himself as long as he lived.

The talk about the blue men amused him deeply.
They existed in Norstrilian folklore, as a race of
faraway magicians who, through science or hypnotism, could render themselves invisible to other men
whenever they wished. Rod had never talked with
an Old North Australian security officer about the
problem of guarding the stroon treasure from attacks
by invisible men, but he gathered, from the way
people told stories of blue men, that they had either
failed to show up on Norstrilia or that the Norstrilian authorities did not take them very seriously. He
was amazed that the Earth people did not bring in
a couple of first-class telepaths and have them sweep
the deck of the tower for every living thing, but to
judge by the chatter of voices that was going on, and
the peering with eyes which occurred, Earth people
had fairly weak senses and did not get things done
promptly and efficiently.

The question about Eleanor was answered for
him.

One of the soldiers joined the group, waited after
saluting, and was finally allowed to interrupt C'mell's
and A'gentur's endless guessing as to how many blue
men there might have been on the tower, if there
had been any at all.

The subchief nodded at the soldier, who said,

"Beg to report, Sir and Subchief, the body is not a body. It is just a robot which looks like a person."

The day brightened immeasurably within Rod's heart. Eleanor was safe, somewhere further down in this immense tower.

The comment seemed to decide the young officer. "Get a sweeping machine and a looking dog," he commanded the sergeant, "and see to it that this whole area is swept and looked down to the last square millimeter."

"It is done," said the soldier.

Rod thought this an odd remark, because nothing at all had been done yet.

The subchief issued another command: "Turn on the kill-spotters before we go down the ramp. Any identity which is not perfectly clear must be killed automatically by the scanning device. Including us," he added to his men. "We don't want any blue men walking right down into the tower among us."

C'mell suddenly and rather boldly stepped up to the officer and whispered in his ear. His eyes rolled as he listened, he blushed a little, and then changed his orders: "Cancel the kill-spotters. I want this whole squad to stand body-to-body. I'm sorry, men, but you're going to have to touch these underpeople for several minutes. I want them to stand so close to us that we can be sure there is nobody extra sneaking into our group."

(C'mell later told Rod that she had confessed to the young officer that she might be a mixed type, part human and part animal, and that she was the special girlygirl of two off-Earth magnates of the

Instrumentality. She said she *thought* that she had a definite identity but was not sure, and that the kill-spotters might destroy her if she did not yield a correct image as she went past them. They would, she told Rod later, have caught any underman passing as a man, or any man passing as an underman, and would have killed the victim by intensifying the magnetic layout of his own organic body. These machines were dangerous things to pass, since they occasionally killed normal, legitimate people and underpeople who merely failed to provide a clear focus.)

The officer took the left forward corner of the living rectangle of people and underpeople. They formed tight ranks. Rod felt the two soldiers next to him shudder as they came into contact with his "cat" body. They kept their faces averted from him as though he smelled bad for them. Rod said nothing; he just looked forward and kept his expression pleasantly stupid.

What followed next was surprising. The men walked in a strange way, all of them moving their left legs in unison, and then their right legs. A'gentur could not possibly do this, so with a nod of the sergeant's approval, C'mell picked him up and carried him close to her bosom. Suddenly, weapons flared.

*These,* thought Rod, *must be cousins of the weapons which the Lord Redlady carried a few weeks ago, when he landed his ship on my property.* (He remembered Hopper, his knife quivering like the head of a snake, threatening the life of the Lord Redlady; and he remembered the sudden silent burst, the black oily smoke, and the gloomy Bill looking at the chair where his pal had existed a moment before.)

These weapons showed a little light, just a little, but their force was betrayed by the buzzing of the floor and the agitation of the dust.

"Close in, men! Right up to your own feet! Don't let a blue man through!" shouted the subchief.

The men complied.

The air began to smell funny and burned.

The ramp was clear of life except for their own.

When the ramp swung around a corner, Rod gasped.

This was the most enormous room he had ever seen. It covered the entire top of Earthport. He could not even begin to guess how many hectares it was, but a small farm could have been accommodated on it. There were few people there. The men broke ranks at a command of the subchief. The officer glared at the cat-man Rod, the cat-girl C'mell and the ape A'gentur.

"You stand right where you are till I come back!"

They stood, saying nothing.

C'mell and A'gentur took the place for granted.

Rod stared as though he would drink up the world with his eyes. In this one enormous room, there was more antiquity and wealth than all Old North Australia possessed. Curtains of an incredibly rich material shimmered down from the thirty-meter ceiling; some of them seemed to be dirty and in bad repair, but any one of them, after paying the twenty million percent import duty, would cost more than any Old North Australian could afford to pay. There were chairs and tables here and there, some of them good enough to deserve a place in the Museum of Man on New Mars. Here they were merely used. The people did not seem any the happier for having all this wealth around them. For the first time, Rod got a glimpse of what the spartan self-imposed poverty had done to make life worthwhile at home. His people did not have much, when they could have chartered endless argosies of treasure, inbound from all worlds to their own planet, in exchange for the life-prolonging stroon. But if they had been heaped with treasure they would have appreciated nothing and would have ended up possessing nothing. He thought of his own little collection of hidden antiquities. Here on Earth it would not have filled a dustbin, but in the Station of Doom it would afford him connoisseurship as long as he lived.

The thought of his home made him wonder what Old Hot and Simple, the Hon. Sec., might be doing with his adversary on Earth. "It's a long, long way to reach here!" he thought to himself.

C'mell drew his attention by plucking at his arm.

"Hold me," commanded she, "because I am afraid I might fall down and Yeekasoose is not strong enough to hold me."

Rod wondered who Yeekasoose might be, when only the little monkey A'gentur was with them; he also wondered why C'mell should need to be held. Norstrilian discipline had taught him not to question orders in an emergency. He held her.

She suddenly slumped as though she had fainted or had gone to sleep. He held her with one arm and with his free hand he tipped her head against his shoulder so that she would look as though she were weary and affectionate, not unconscious. It was pleasant to hold her little female body, which felt fragile and delicate beyond belief. Her hair, disarrayed and windblown, still carried the smell of the salty sea air which had so surprised him an hour ago. She herself, he thought, was the greatest treasure of Earth which he had yet seen. But suppose he did have her? What could he do with her in Old North Australia? Underpeople were completely forbidden, except for military uses under the exclusive control of the Commonwealth government. He could not imagine C'mell directing a mowing machine as she walked across a giant sheep, shearing it. The idea of her sitting up all night with a lonely or frightened sheep-monster was itself ridiculous. She was a playgirl, an ornament in human form; for such as her, there was no place under the comfortable grey skies of home. Her beauty would fade in the dry air; her intricate mind would turn sour with the weary endlessness of a farm culture: property, responsibility, defense, self-reliance, sobriety. New Melbourne would look like a collection of rude shacks to her.

He realized that his feet were getting cold. Up on the deck they had had sunlight to keep them warm, even though the chill salty wet air of Earth's marvelous "seas" was blowing against them. Here, inside, it was merely high and cold, while still wet; he had never encountered *wet* cold before, and it was a strangely uncomfortable experience.

C'mell came to and shook herself to wakefulness just as they saw the officer walking toward them from the other end of the immense room.

*Later, she told Rod what she had experienced when she lapsed into unconsciousness.*

*First, she had had a call which she could not explain. This had made her warn Rod. "Yeekasoose" was, of course E'ikasus, the real name of the "monkey" which he called A'gentur.*

*Then, as she felt herself swimming away into half-sleep with Rod's strong arm around her, she had heard trumpets playing, just two or three of them, playing different parts to the same intricate, lovely piece of music, sometimes in solos, sometimes together. If a human or robot telepath had peeped her mind while she listened to the music, the impression would have been that of a perceptive c'girl who had linked herself with one of the many telepathic entertainment channels which filled the space of Earth itself.*

*Last, there came the messages. They were not encoded in the music in any way whatever. The music caused the images to form in her mind because she was C'mell, herself, unique, individual. Particular fugues or even individual notes reached into her memory and emotions, causing her mind to bring up old, half-forgotten associations. First she thought of "High birds flying . . ." as in the song which she had sung to Rod. Then she saw eyes, piercing eyes which blazed with knowledge while they stayed moist with humility. Then she smelled the strange odors of Downdeep-downdeep, the work-city where the underpeople maintained the civilization on the surface and where some illegal underpeople lurked, overlooked by the authority of Man. Finally she saw Rod himself, striding off the deck with his loping Norstrilian walk. It added up simply. She was to bring Rod to the forgotten, forlorn, forbidden chambers of the Nameless One, and to do so promptly. The music in her head stopped, and she woke up.*

The officer arrived.

He looked at them inquisitively and angrily. "This whole business is funny. The Acting Commissioner does not believe that there are any blue men. We've all heard of them. And yet we know somebody set off a telepathic emotion-bomb. That rage! Half the people in this room fell down when it went off. Those weapons are completely prohibited for use inside the Earth's atmosphere."

He cocked his head at them.

C'mell remained prudently silent, Rod practiced looking thoroughly stupid, and A'gentur looked like a bright, helpless little monkey.

"Funnier still," said the officer, "the Acting Commissioner got orders to let you go. He got them while he was chewing me out. How does anybody know that you underpeople are here? Who are you, anyhow?"

He looked at them with curiosity for a minute, but then the curiosity faded with the pressure of his lifelong habits.

He snapped, "Who cares? Get along. Get out. You're underpeople and you're not allowed to stand in this room, anyhow."

He turned his back on them and walked away.

"Where are we going?" whispered Rod, hoping C'mell would say that he could go down to the surface and see Old Earth itself.

"Down to the bottom of the world, and then—" she bit her lip ". . . and then, much further down. I have instructions."

"Can't I take an hour and look at Earth?" asked Rod. "You stay with me, of course."

"When death is jumping around us like wild sparks? Of course not. Come along, Rod. You'll get your freedom some time soon, if somebody doesn't kill you first. Yeekasoose, you lead the way!"

They walked toward a dropshaft.

When Rod looked down it, the sight made him dizzy. Only the sight of people floating up and down in it made him realize that this was some Earth device which his people did not have in Old North Australia.

"Take a belt," said C'mell quietly. "Do it as though you were used to it."

He looked around. Only after she had taken a canvas belt, about fifteen centimeters wide, and was cinching it to her waist, did he see what she meant. He took one too and put it on. They waited while A'gentur ran up and down the racks of belts, looking for one small enough to fit him. C'mell finally helped him by taking one of normal size and looping it around his waist twice before she hooked it.

"Magnetic," she murmured. "For the dropshafts."

They did not take the main dropshaft.

"That's for people only," said C'mell.

The underpeople dropshaft was the same, except that it did not have the bright lights, the pumping of fresh air, the labeling of the levels, and the entertaining pictures to divert the passengers as they went up and down. This dropshaft, moreover, seemed to have more cargo than people in it. Huge boxes, bales, bits of machines, furniture and inexplicable bundles, each tied with magnetic belts and each guided by an underperson, floated up and down in the mysterious ever busy traffic of Old Earth.

# Discourses and Recourses

Rod McBan, disguised as a cat, floated down the dropshaft to the strangest encounter which could have befallen any man of his epoch. C'mell floated down beside him. She clenched her skirt between her knees, so that it would not commit immodesties. A'gentur, his monkey hand lightly on C'mell's shoulder, loved her soft red hair as it stood and moved with the updraft which they themselves created; he looked forward to becoming E'ikasus again and he admired C'mell deeply, but love between the different strains of underpeople was necessarily platonic. Physiologically they could not breed outside their own stock, and emotionally they found it hard to mesh deeply with the empathic needs of another form of life, however related it might be. E'ikasus therefore very truly and deeply wanted C'mell for his friend, and nothing more.

While they moved downward in relative peace, other people were concerned about them on various worlds.

## Old North Australia, Administrative Offices of the Commonwealth, The Same Day

"You, former Hon. Sec. of this government, are charged with going outside the limits of your onseckish duties and of attempting to commit mayhem or murder upon the person of one of Her Absent Majesty's subjects, the said subject being Roderick Frederick Ronald Arnold William MacArthur McBan to the one-hundred-and-fifty-first generation; and you are further charged with the abuse of an official instrument of this Commonwealth government in designing and encompassing the said unlawful purpose, to wit, one mutated sparrow, serial number 0919487, specialty number 2328525, weighing forty-one kilograms, and having a monetary value of 685 minicredits. What say you?"

Houghton Syme CXLIX buried his face in his hands and sobbed.

## The Cabin of the Station of Doom, At the Same Time

"Aunt Doris, he's dead, he's dead, he's dead. I feel it."

"Nonsense, Lavinia. He may be in trouble and we might not know. But with all that money, the government or the Instrumentality would use the Big Blink to send word of the change in status of this property. I don't mean to sound cold-hearted, girl, but when there is this much property at stake, people act rapidly."

"He is *so* dead."

Doris was not one to discount the telepathic arts.

She remembered how the Australians had gotten off the incarnate fury of Paradise VII. She went over to the cupboard and took from it a strangely tinted jar. "Do you know what this is?" said she to Lavinia.

The girl forced a smile past her desperate inward feelings. "Yes," she said. "Ever since I was no bigger than a mini-elephant, people have told me that jar was 'do not touch.'"

"Good girl, then, if you haven't touched it!" said Aunt Doris drily. "It's a mixture of stroon and Paradise VII honey."

"Honey?" cried Lavinia. "I thought no one ever went back to that horrible place."

"Some do," said Aunt Doris. "It seems that some Earth forms have taken over and are still living there. Including bees. The honey has powers on the human mind. It is a strong hypnotic. We mix it with stroon to make sure it is safe."

Aunt Doris put a small spoon into the jar, lifted, spun the spoon to pick up the threads of heavy honey, and handed the spoon to Lavinia. "Here," said she, "take this and lick it off. Swallow it all down."

Lavinia hesitated and then obeyed. When the spoon was clean she licked her lips and handed the clean spoon back to Aunt Doris, who put it aside for washing up.

Aunt Doris ceremoniously put the jar back on the high shelf of the cupboard, locked the cupboard, and put the key in the pocket of her apron.

"Let's sit outside," said she to Lavinia.

"When's it going to happen?"

"When's what going to happen?"

"The trance—the visions—whatever this stuff brings on?"

Doris laughed her weary rational laugh. "Oh, that! Sometimes nothing at all happens. In any event, it won't hurt you, girl. Let's sit on the bench. I'll tell you if you start looking strange to me."

They sat on the bench, doing nothing. Two police ornithopters, flying just under the forever grey clouds, quietly watched the Station of Doom. They had been doing this ever since Rod's computer showed him how to win all that money: the fortune was still piling up, almost faster than it could be computed. The bird-engines were lazy and beautiful as they flew. The operators had synchronized the flapping of the two sets of wings, so that they looked like rukhs doing a ballet. The effect caught the eyes of both Lavinia and Aunt Doris.

Lavinia suddenly spoke in a clear, sharp, demanding voice, quite unlike her usual tone: "It's all mine, isn't it?"

Doris breathed softly, "What, my dear?"

"The Station of Doom. I'm one of the heiresses, anyhow, aren't I?" Lavinia pursed her lips in a proud prim smug smile which would have humiliated her if she had been in her right mind.

Aunt Doris said nothing. She nodded silently.

"If I marry Rod I'll be Missus and Owner McBan, the richest woman who ever lived. But if I do marry him, he'll hate me, because he'll think it's for his money and his power. But I've loved Rod, loved him specially because he couldn't hier or spiek. I've always known that he would need me someday, not like my Daddy, singing his crazy sad proud songs forever and ever! But how can I marry him now . . . ?"

Whispered Doris, very gently, very insinuatingly:

"Look for Rod, my dear. Look for Rod in that part of your mind which thought he was dead. Look for Rod, Lavinia, look for Rod."

Lavinia laughed happily, and it was the laugh of a small child.

She stared at her feet, at the sky, at Doris—looking right through her.

Her eyes seemed to clear. When she spoke, it was in her normal adult voice:

"I see Rod. Someone has changed him into a cat-man, just like the pictures we've seen of underpeople. And there's a girl with him—a girl, Doris—and I can't be jealous of him being with her. She is the most beautiful thing that ever lived on any world. You ought to see her hair, Doris. You ought to see her hair. It is like a bushel of beautiful fire. Is that Rod? I don't know. I can't tell. I can't see." She sat on the bench, looking straight at Doris and seeing nothing, but weeping copiously.

Aunt Doris started to get up; it was about time for the poor thing to be led to her bed, so that she could sleep off the hypnotic of Paradise VII.

But Lavinia spoke again. "I see them too."

"Who?" said Aunt Doris, not much interested, now that they had found their information about Rod. Doris never mentioned the matter to any masculine person, but she was a deeply superstitious person who found great satisfaction in tampering with the preternatural, but even in these ventures she kept the turn of mind, essentially practical, which had characterized her whole life. Thus, when Lavinia stumbled on the greatest secret of the contemporary universe, she made no note of it. She told no one about it, then or later.

Lavinia insisted, "I see the proud pale people with strong hands and white eyes. The ones who built the palace of the Governor of Night."

"That's nice," said Aunt Doris, "but it is time for your nap . . ."

"Goodbye, dear people . . ." said Lavinia, a little drunkenly.

*She had glimpsed the Daimoni in their home world.*

Aunt Doris, unheeding, stood up and took Lavinia's arm, leading her away to rest. Nothing remained of the Daimoni, except for a little song which Lavinia found herself making up a few weeks later, not knowing whether she had dreamed some such thing or had read it in a book:

*Oh, you will see, you will see*
*Them striding fair, oh fair and free!*
*Down garden paths of silver grass*
*Past flowing rivers,*
*Their hair pushed back*
*By fingers of the wind.*
*And you will know them*
*By their blank white faces,*
*Expressionless, removed,*
*All lines smoothed,*
*As they stride on in the night*
*Toward their unimaginable goals. . . .*

Thus came news of Rod, unreported, unrepeated; thus passed the glimpse of the Daimoni in their star-hidden home.

## At the Beach of Meeya Meefla, The Same Day

"Father, you can't be here. You never come here!"

"But I have," said Lord William Not-from-here. "And it's important."

"Important?" laughed Ruth. "Then it's not me. I'm not important. Your work up there is." She looked toward the rim of the Earthport, which floated, distinct and circular, beyond the crests of some faraway clouds.

The overdressed lord squatted incongruously on the sand.

"Listen, girl," said he slowly and emphatically, "I've never asked much of you but I am asking now."

"Yes, father," she said, a little frightened by this totally unaccustomed air: her father was usually playfully casual with her, and equally usually forgot her ten seconds after he got through talking to her.

"Ruth, you know we are Old North Australians?"

"We're rich, if that's what you mean. Not that it matters, the way things go."

"I'm not talking about riches now, I'm talking about home, and I mean it!"

"Home? We never had a home, father."

"Norstrilia!" he snarled at her.

"I never saw it, father. Nor did you. Nor your father. Nor great-grandpa. What are you talking about?"

"We can go home again!"

"Father, what's happened? Have you lost your mind? You've always told me that our family bought out and could never go back. What's happened now? Have they changed the rules? I'm not even sure I want to go there, anyhow. No water, no beaches, no cities. Just a dry dull planet with sick sheep and a lot of immortal farmers who go around armed to the teeth!"

*"Ruth, you can take us back!"*

She jumped to her feet and slapped the sand off her bottom. She was a little taller than her father; though he was an extremely handsome, aristocratic-looking man, she was an even more distinctive person. It would be obvious to anyone that she would never lack for suitors or pursuers.

"All right, father. You always have schemes. Usually it's antique money. This time I'm mixed up with it somehow, or you wouldn't be here. Father, just what do you want me to do?"

"To marry. To marry the richest man who has ever been known in the universe."

"Is that all?" she laughed. "Of course I'll marry him. I've never married an offworlder before. Have you made a date with him?"

"You don't understand, Ruth. This isn't Earth marriage. In Norstrilian law and custom you marry only one man, you marry only once, and you stay married to him for as long as you live."

A cloud passed over the sun. The beach became cooler. She looked at her father with a funny mixture of sympathy, contempt, and curiosity.

"That," she said, "is a cat of another breed. I'll have to see him first . . ."

## The Assistant Commissioner's Office, Top of Earthport, Four Hours Later

"Don't tell me there's nothing. Or make up stories about the blue men. You go back to that top deck and take it apart, molecule by molecule, until you find out where that brainbomb went off!"

"But, sir—"

"Don't but me! I've been in battle and you haven't. I know a bomb when I feel one. The blasted thing still gives me a headache. Now you take your men back up to that top deck and find out where that bomb went off."

"Yes, sir," said the young subchief gloomily, never thinking for a moment that he would have the least success in his mission. He saluted dispiritedly.

When he met his men at the door, he gave them an almost imperceptible shake of his head. In consequence, he and his men were the sorriest collection of slouching scarecrows ever seen at Earthport as they trudged their weary way up the ramp to the top deck of Earthport.

## Antechamber of the Bell and Bank, The Same Time

"We got the bull-man, B'dank, but somehow he escaped. Probably he is down in the sewers, hiding out. I haven't got the heart to send the police after him. He won't last long, down there. And it would make a fuss if I pardoned him. You might agree with me, but the rest of the Council wouldn't."

"And Commissioner Teadrinker, my Lord? What are you going to do about him? That's sticky wicket, my Lord. He's a former Lord of the Instrumentality. We can't have people like that committing crimes." The Lady Johanna Gnade was emphatic.

"I have the punishment for him," said Jestocost, with a bland smile.

"Oblivion and reconditioning?" said the Lady Johanna. "He's basically talented material."

"Nothing that simple."

"What, my Lord?"

"Nothing."

"What do you mean, 'nothing,' Jestocost? It does not make sense." The Lady Johanna let a rare note of petulance come into her voice.

"I meant what I said, my Lady. Nothing. He knows that I know something. The spider is dead. The robot is demolished. Nine other Rod McBans are causing a bit of chaos in the lower city. But Teadrinker doesn't know that I know everything. I have my own sources."

"We know you pride yourself on that," said the Lady Johanna, with a charming wry smile. "We also know that you like to keep individual secrets from the rest of us. We put up with it, my Lord, because we love you and trust you, but it could be a very dangerous practice if it were carried out by other persons, less judicious than you, or less skillful. And it could even be dangerous if—" She hesitated, looked at him appraisingly, and then went on, "—if, my Lord, you lost your shrewdness, or died suddenly."

"I haven't," said he crisply, dismissing the subject.

"You haven't told me what you are going to do with Teadrinker."

"Nothing, I said," said Jestocost a little crossly. "I'm going to do nothing at all and let him wait for me to bring destruction down on him. If he begins to think that I have forgotten, I will find some little way of reminding him that somebody or something is on his trail. Teadrinker is going to be a very unhappy man before I get through with him."

"That sounds inhumane, my Lord. He might appeal."

"And be tried for murder?"

She gave up. "Your ways are new, my Lord. You have seen your way into the Rediscovery of Man. Letting people suffer. Letting things go wrong. I was brought up on the old philosophy—if you see wrong, right it."

"And I saw," said Jestocost, "that we were dying of perfection."

"I suppose you're right," said she wearily. "You have this rich man covered, I suppose?"

"As well as I can manage," said Jestocost.

"That's perfect, then," said she with an air of finality. "I just hope you haven't gotten him mixed up with that queer hobby of yours."

"Queer hobby?" said Jestocost in a courtly fashion, with a lift of his eyebrows.

"Underpeople," she said with a tone of disgust. "*Underpeople.* I like you, Jestocost, but your fussing about those animals sometimes makes me sick."

He did not argue. He stood very still and looked at her. She knew he was avoiding a provocation. He was her senior, so she offered him a very slight curtsey and left the room.

## Antechamber of the Bell and Bank, Ten Minutes Later

A bear-woman, complete with starched cap and nurse's uniform, pushed the wheelchair of the Lord Crudelta into the room. Jestocost looked up from the situation shows which he had been watching. When he saw who it was, he offered Crudelta a deep bow indeed. The bear-woman, flustered by this famous place and all the great dignitaries whom she was meeting, spoke up in a singularly high voice, begging:

"My Lord and Master Crudelta, may I leave you here?"

"Yes. Go. I will call for you later. Go to the bathroom on your way out. It's on the right."

"My Lord—!" she gasped with embarrassment.

"You wouldn't have dared if I hadn't told you. I've been watching your mind for the last half-hour. Now go along."

The bear-woman fled with a rustle of her starched skirts.

When Crudelta looked directly at him, Jestocost gave him a very deep bow. In lifting his eyes he looked directly into the face of the old, old man and said, with something near pride in his voice,

"Still up to your old tricks, my Lord and Colleague Crudelta!"

"And you to yours, Jestocost. How are you going to get that boy out of the sewers?"

"What boy? What sewers?"

"Our sewers. The boy you sold this tower to."

For once, Jestocost was flabbergasted. His jaw

dropped. Then he collected himself and said, "You're a knowledgeable man, my Lord Crudelta."

"That I am," said Crudelta, "and a thousand years older than you, to boot. That was my reward for coming back from the Nothing-at-all."

"I know that, sir." Jestocost's full, pleasant face did not show worry, but he studied the old man across from him with extreme care. In his prime, the Lord Crudelta had been the greatest of the Lords of the Instrumentality, a telepath of whom the other Lords were always a little afraid, because he picked minds so deftly and quickly that he was the best mental pickpocket who had ever lived. A strong conservative, he had never opposed a specific policy because it ran counter to his general appetites. He had, for example, carried the vote for the Rediscovery of Man by coming out of retirement and tongue-lashing the whole Council into a corner with his vehement support for reform. Jestocost had never liked him—who could like a rapier tongue, a mind of unfathomable brilliance, a cold old ego which neither offered nor asked companionship? Jestocost knew that if the old man had caught on to the Rod McBan adventure, he might be on the trail of Jestocost's earlier deal with—no, no, no! don't think it here, not with those eyes watching.

"I know about that, too," said the old old man.

"What?"

"The secret you are trying most of all to hide."

Jestocost stood submissive, waiting for the blow to fall.

The old man laughed. Most people would have expected a cackle from that handsome fresh young

face with the withered spidery body. They would
have been fooled. The laugh was full-bodied, genuine
and warm.

"Redlady's a fool," said Crudelta.

"I think so too," said Jestocost, "but what are your
reasons, my Lord and Master?"

"Sending that young man off his own planet when
he has so much wealth and so little experience."

Jestocost nodded, not wanting to say anything until
the old man had made his line of attack plain.

"I like your idea, however," said the Lord Crudelta.
"Sell him the Earth and then tax him for it. But what
is your ultimate aim? Making him Emperor of the
Planet Earth, in the old style? Murdering him? Driving him mad? Having the cat-girl of yours seduce him
and then send him home a bankrupt? I admit I have
thought of all these too, but I didn't see how any of
them would fit in with your passion for justice. But
there's one thing you can't do, Jestocost. You can't sell
him the planet Earth and then have him stay here
and manage it. He might want to use this tower for
his residence. That would be too much. I am too
old to move out. And he mustn't roll up that ocean
out there and take it home for a souvenir. You've all
been very clever, my Lord—clever enough to be fools.
You have created an unnecessary crisis. What are you
going to get out of it?"

Jestocost plunged. The old man must have picked
his own mind. Nowhere else could he have put all
the threads of the case together. Jestocost decided
on the truth and the whole truth. He started with
the day that the Big Blink rang in the enormous
transactions in stroon futures, financial gambles which

soon reached out of the commodity markets of Old
North Australia and began to unbalance the economy
of all the civilized worlds. He started to explain who
Redlady was—

"Don't tell me that," cried the Lord Crudelta. "It
was I who caught him, sentenced him to death, and
then argued to have the sentence set aside. He's not
a bad man, but he's a sly one, that he is. He's smart
enough to be an utter and complete fool when he
gets wound up in his logical plots. I'll wager you a
minicredit to a credit that he has already murdered
somebody by now. He always does. He has a taste for
theatrical violence. But go back to your story. Tell me
what you plan to do. If I like it, I will help you. If I
don't like it, I will have the whole story before a plenum of the Council this very morning, and you know
that they will tear your bright idea to shreds. They
will probably seize the boy's property, send him to a
hospital, and have him come out speaking Basque as
a flamenco player. You know as well as I do that the
Instrumentality is very generous with other people's
property, but pretty ruthless when it comes to any
threat directed against itself. After all, I was one of
the men who wiped out Raumsog."

Jestocost began to talk very quietly, very calmly.
He spoke with the assurance of an accountant who,
books in order, is explaining an intricate point to his
manager. Old himself, he was a child compared to
the antiquity and wisdom of the Lord Crudelta. He
went into details, including the ultimate disposition of
Rod McBan. He even shared with the Lord Crudelta
his sympathies for the underpeople and his own very
secret, very quiet struggle to improve their position.

The only thing which he did not mention was the E'telekeli and the counter-brain which the under-people had set up in Downdeep-downdeep. If the old man knew it, he knew it, and Jestocost couldn't stop him, but if he did not know it, there was no point in telling him.

The Lord Crudelta did not respond with senile enthusiasm or childish laughter. He reverted, not to his childhood but to his maturity; with great dignity and force he said:

"I approve. I understand. You have my proxy if you need it. Call that nurse to come and get me. I thought you were a clever fool, Jestocost. You sometimes are. This time you are showing that you have a heart as well as a head. One thing more. Bring that doctor Vomact back from Mars soon, and don't torment Teadrinker too long, just for the sake of being clever. I might take it into my mind to torment you."

"And the ex-Lord Redlady?" asked Jestocost deferentially.

"Him, nothing. Nothing. Let him live his life. The Old North Australians might as well cut their political teeth on him."

The bear-woman rustled back into the room. The Lord Crudelta waved his hand. Jestocost bowed almost to the floor, and the wheelchair, heavy as a tank, creaked its way across the doorsill.

"That," said Jestocost, "could have been trouble!" He wiped his brow.

# The Road to the Catmaster

Rod, C'mell and A'gentur had had to hold the sides of the shaft several times as the traffic became heavy and large loads, going up or down, had to pass each other and them too. In one of these waits C'mell caught her breath and said something very swiftly to the little monkey. Rod, not heeding them, caught nothing but the sudden enthusiasm and happiness in her voice. The monkey's murmured answer made her plaintive and she insisted,

"But, Yeekasoose, you must! Rod's whole life could depend on it. Not just saving his life now, but having a better life for hundreds and hundreds of years."

The monkey was cross: "Don't ask me to think when I am hungry. This fast metabolism and small body just isn't enough to support real thinking."

"If it's food you want, have some raisins." She took a square of compressed seedless raisins out of one of her matching bags.

A'gentur ate them greedily but gloomily.

Rod's attention drifted away from them as he saw magnificent golden furniture, elaborately carved and inlaid with a pearlescent material, being piloted up the shaft by a whole troop of talkative dog-men. He

487

asked them where the furniture was going. When they did not answer him, he repeated his question in a more peremptory tone of voice, as befitted the richest Old North Australian in the universe. The tone of demand brought answers, but they were not the ones he was expecting. "Meow," said one dog-man. "Shut up, cat, or I'll chase you up a tree." "Not to your house, buster. Exactly what do you think you are—people?" "Cats are always nosy. Look at that one." The dog-foreman rose into sight; with dignity and kindness he said to Rod, "Cat-fellow, if you feel like talking, you may get marked surplus. Better keep quiet in the public dropshaft!" Rod realized that to these beings he was one of them, a cat made into a man, and that the underpeople workmen who served Old Earth had been trained not to chatter while working on the business of Man.

He caught the tail of C'mell's urgent whisper to A'gentur: ". . . and don't ask him. *Tell Him.* We'll risk the people zone for a visit to the Catmaster! *Tell Him.*"

A'gentur was panting with a rapid, shallow breath. His eyes seemed to protrude from their sockets and yet he was looking at nothing. He groaned as though with some inward effort. At last he lost his grip on the wall and would have floated slowly downward if C'mell had not caught him and cuddled him like a baby. C'mell whispered, eagerly,

"You reached Him?"

"Him," gasped the little monkey.

"Who?" asked Rod.

"Aitch Eye," said C'mell. "I'll tell you later." Of A'gentur she asked, "If you got Him, what did He say?"

"He said, 'E'ikasus, I do not say no. You are my

son. Take the risk if you think it wise.' And don't ask
me now, C'mell. Let me think a little. I have been
all the way to Norstrilia and back. I'm still cramped
in this little body. Do we have to do it now? Right
now? Why can't we go to Him"—and A'gentur nodded toward the depths below—"and find out what we
want Rod for, anyhow? Rod is a means, not an end.
Who really knows what to do with him?"

"What are you talking about?" said Rod.

Simultaneously C'mell snapped, "I know what we
are going to do with him."

"What?" said the little monkey, very tired again.

"We're going to let this boy go free, and let him
find happiness, and if he wants to give us his help,
we will take it and be grateful. But we are not going
to rob him. Not going to hurt him. That would be a
mean, dirty way to start being better creatures than
we are. If he knows who he is before he meets Him,
they can make sense." She turned to Rod and said
with mysterious urgency,

"Don't you want to *know* who you are?"

"I'm Rod McBan to the hundred and fifty-first,"
said he promptly.

"Sh-h-h," said she, "no names here. I'm not talking
about names. I'm talking about the deep insides of
you. Life itself, as it flows through you. Do you have
any idea who you are?"

"You're playing games," he said. "I know perfectly
well who I am, and where I live, and what I have. I
even know that right now I am supposed to be a cat-man
named C'roderick. What else is there to know?"

"You men!" she sobbed at him. "You men! Even
when you're people, you're so dense that you can't

understand a simple question. I'm not asking you your name or your address or your label or your greatgrandfather's property. I'm asking about *you*, Rod, the only one that will ever live, no matter how many numbers your grandsons may put after their names. You're not in the world just to own a piece of property or to handle a surname with a number after it. You're *you*. There's never been another you. There will never be another one, after you. What does this 'you' want?"

Rod glanced down at the walls of the tunnel, which seemed to turn—oh, so far below—very gently to the north. He looked up at the little rhomboids of light cast on the tunnel walls by the landing doors into the various levels of Earthport. He felt his own weight tugging gently at his hand as he held to the rough surface of the vertical shaft, supported by his belt. The belt itself felt uncomfortable about his middle; after all, it was supporting most of his weight, and it squeezed him. *What do I want?* thought he. *Who am I that I should have a right to want anything? I am Rod McBan CLI, the Mister and Owner of the Station of Doom. But I'm also a poor freak with bad telepathy who can't even spiek or hier rightly.*

C'mell was watching him as clinically as a surgeon, but he could tell from her expression that she was not trying to peep his mind.

He found himself speaking almost as wearily as had A'gentur, who was also called something like "Yeeka-soose," and who had strange powers for a little monkey:

"I don't suppose I want anything much, C'mell, except that I should like to spiek and hier correctly, like other people on my native world."

She looked at him, her expression showing intense sympathy and the effort to make a decision.

A'gentur interrupted with his high clear monkey voice, "Say that to me, Sir and Master."

Rod repeated: "I don't really want anything. I would like to spiek and hier because other people are fussing at me about it. And I would like to get a Cape of Good Hope twopenny triangular blue stamp while I am still on Earth. But that's about all. I guess there's nothing I really want."

The monkey closed his eyes and seemed to fall asleep again; Rod suspected it was some kind of telepathic trance.

C'mell hooked A'gentur on an old rod which protruded from the surface of the shaft. Since he weighed only a few grams, there was no noticeable pull on the belt. She seized Rod's shoulder and pulled him over to her.

"Rod, listen! Do you want to know who you are?"

"I don't know," said he. "I might be miserable."

"Not if you *know* who you are!" she insisted.

"I might not like me," said Rod. "Other people don't and my parents died together when their ship went milky out in space. I'm not normal."

"For God's sake, Rod!" she cried.

"Who?" said he.

"Forgive me, father," said she, speaking to no one in sight.

"I've heard that name, before, somewhere," said Rod. "But let's get going. I want to get to this mysterious place you are taking me and then I want to find out about Eleanor."

"Who's that?"

"My servant. She's disguised as me, taking risks for me, along with eight robots. It's up to me to do what I can for her. Always."

"But she's your *servant,*" said C'mell. "She serves you. Almost like being an underperson, like me."

"She's a person," said Rod, stubbornly. "We have no underpeople in Norstrilia, except for a few in government jobs. But she's my friend."

"Do you want to marry her?"

"Great sick sheep, girl! Are you barmy? No!"

"Do you want to marry anybody?"

"At sixteen?" he cried. "Anyhow, my family will arrange it." The thought of plain honest devoted Lavinia crossed his mind, and he could not help comparing her to this wild voluptuous creature who floated beside him in the tunnel as the traffic passed them going up and down. With near weightlessness, C'mell's hair floated like a magic flower around her head. She had been brushing it out of her eyes from time to time. He snorted, "Not Eleanor."

When he said this, another idea crossed the mind of the beautiful cat-girl.

"You know what I am, Rod," said she, very seriously.

"A cat-girl from the planet Earth. You're supposed to be my wife."

"That's right," she said, with an odd intonation in her voice. "Be it, then!"

"What?" said Rod.

"My husband," she said, her voice catching slightly. "Be my husband, if it will help you to find you."

She stole a quick glance up and down the shaft. There was nobody near.

"*Look, Rod, look!*" She spread the opening of her

dress down and aside. Even with the poor light, to which his eyes had become accustomed, he could see the fine tracery of veins in her delicate chest and her young, pear-shaped breasts. The aureoles around the nipples were a clear, sweet, innocent pink; the nipples themselves were as pretty as two pieces of candy. For a moment there was pleasure and then a terrible embarrassment came over him. He turned his face away and felt horribly self-conscious. What she had done was interesting but it wasn't *nice*.

When he dared to glance at her, she was still studying his face.

"I'm a girlygirl, Rod. This is my business. And you're a cat, with all the rights of a tomcat. Nobody can tell the difference, here in this tunnel. *Rod, do you want to do anything?*"

Rod gulped and said nothing.

She swept her clothing back into place. The strange urgency left her voice. "I guess," she said, "that that left me a little breathless. I find you pretty attractive, Rod. I find myself thinking, 'What a pity he is not a cat.' I'm over it now."

Rod said nothing.

A bubble of laughter came into her voice, along with something mothering and tender, which tugged at his heartstrings. "Best of all, Rod, I didn't mean it. Or maybe I did. I had to give you a chance before I felt that I really knew you. Rod, I'm one of the most beautiful girls on Old Earth itself. The Instrumentality uses me for that very reason. We've turned you into a cat and offered you me, and you won't have me. Doesn't that suggest that you don't know who you are?"

"Are you back on that?" said Rod. "I guess I just don't understand girls."

"You'd better, before you're through with Earth," she said. "Your agents have bought a million of them for you, out of all that stroon money."

"People or underpeople?"

"Both!"

"Let them bug sheep!" he cried. "I had no part in ordering them. Come on, girl. This is no place for a boudoir conversation!"

"Where on Earth did you learn that word?" she laughed.

"I read books. Lots of books. I may look like a peasant to you Earth people, but I know a lot of things."

"Do you trust me, Rod?"

He thought of her immodesty, which still left him a little breathless. The Old North Australian humor reasserted itself in him, as a cultural characteristic and not just as an individual one: "I've seen a lot of you, C'mell," said he with a grin. "I suppose you don't have many surprises left. All right, I trust you. Then what?"

She studied him closely.

"I'll tell you what E'ikasus and I were discussing."

"Who?"

"Him." She nodded at the little monkey.

"I thought his name was A'gentur."

"Like yours is C'rod!" she said.

"He's not a monkey?" asked Rod.

She looked around and lowered her voice. "He's a bird," she said solemnly, "and he's the second most important bird on Earth."

"So what?" said Rod.

"He's in charge of your destiny, Rod. Your life or your death. Right now."

"I thought," he whispered back, "that that was up to the Lord Redlady and somebody named Jestocost on Earth."

"You're dealing with other powers, Rod—powers which keep themselves secret. They want to be friends with you. And I think," she added in a complete non sequitur, "that we'd better take the risk and go."

He looked blank and she added,

"To the Catmaster."

"They'll do something to me there."

"Yes," she said. Her face was calm, friendly, and even. "You will die, maybe—but not much chance. Or you might go mad—there's always the possibility. Or you will find all the things you want—that's the likeliest of all. I have been there, Rod. I myself have been there. Don't you think that I look like a happy, busy girl, when you consider that I'm really just an animal with a rather low-down job?"

Rod studied her. "How old are you?"

"Thirty next year," she said, inflexibly.

"For the first time?"

"For us animal-people there is no second time, Rod. I thought you knew that."

He returned her gaze. "If you can take it," said he, "I can too. Let's go."

She lifted A'gentur or E'ikasus, depending on which he really was, off the wall, where he had been sleeping like a marionette between plays. He opened his exhausted little eyes and blinked at her.

"You have given us our orders," said C'mell. "We are going to the Department Store."

"I have," he said, crossly, coming much more awake. "I don't remember it!"

She laughed, "Just through me, E'ikasus!"

"That name!" he hissed. "Don't get foolhardy. Not in a public shaft."

"All right, A'gentur," she responded, "but do you approve?"

"Of the decision?"

She nodded.

The little monkey looked at both of them. He spoke to Rod, "If she gambles her life and yours, not to mention mine—if she takes chances to make you much, much happier, are you willing to come along?"

Rod nodded in silent agreement.

"Let's go, then," said the monkey-surgeon.

"Where are we going?" asked Rod.

"Down into Earthport City. Among all the people. Swarms and swarms of them," said C'mell, "and you will get to see the everyday life of Earth, just the way that you asked at the top of the tower, an hour ago."

"A year ago, you mean," said Rod. "So much has happened!" He thought of her young naked breasts and the impulse which had made her show them to him, but the thought did not make him excited or guilty; he felt friendly, because he sensed in their whole relationship a friendliness much more fervent than sex itself.

"We are going to a store," said the sleepy monkey.

"A commissary. For things? What for?"

"It has a nice name," said C'mell, "and it is run by a wonderful person. The Catmaster himself. Five hundred some years old, and still allowed to live by virtue of the legacy of the Lady Goroke."

"Never heard of her," said Rod. "What's the name?"

"The Department Store of Hearts' Desires," said C'mell and E'ikasus simultaneously.

The trip was a vivid, quick dream. They had only a few hundred meters to fall before they reached ground level.

They came out on the people-street. A robot-policeman watched them from a corner.

Human beings in the costumes of a hundred historical periods were walking around in the warm, wet air of Earth. Rod could not smell as much salt in the air as he had smelled at the top of the tower, but down here in the city it smelled of more people than he had ever even imagined in one place. Thousands of individuals, hundreds and thousands of different kinds of foods, the odors of robots, of underpeople and of other things which seemed to be unmodified animals.

"This is the most interesting-smelling place I have ever been," said he to C'mell.

She glanced at him idly. "That's nice. You can smell like a dog-man. Most of the real people I have known couldn't smell their own feet. Come on though, C'roderick—*remember who you are!* If we're not tagged and licensed for the surface, we'll get stopped by that policeman in one minute or less."

She carried E'ikasus and steered Rod with a pressure on his elbow. They came to a ramp which led to an underground passage, well illuminated. Machines, robots and underpeople were hurrying back and forth along it, busy with the commerce of Earth.

Rod would have been completely lost if he had

been without C'mell. Though his miraculous broad-
band hiering, which had so often surprised him at
home, had not returned during his few hours on Old
Earth, his other senses gave him a suffocating awareness of the huge number of people around him and
above him. (He never realized that there were times,
long gone, when the cities of Earth had populations
which reached the tens of millions; to him, several
hundred thousand people, and a comparable number
of underpeople, was a crowd almost beyond all measure.) The sounds and smells of underpeople were
subtly different from those of people; some of the
machines of Earth were bigger and older than anything
which he had previously imagined; and above all, the
circulation of water in immense volumes, millions
upon millions of gallons, for the multiple purposes
of Earthport—sanitation, cooling, drinking, industrial
purposes—made him feel that he was not among a
few buildings, which he would have called a city in
Old North Australia, but that he himself had become
a blood-cell thrusting through the circulatory system
of some enormous composite animal, the nature of
which he imperfectly understood. This city was alive
with a sticky, wet, complicated aliveness which he had
hitherto not even imagined to be possible. Movement
characterized it. He suspected that the movement went
on by night and day, that there was no real cessation to it, that the great pumps thrust water through
feeder pipes and drains whether people were awake
or not, that the brains of this organization could be
no one place, but had to comprise many sub-brains,
each committed and responsible for its particular
tasks. No wonder underpeople were needed! It would

be boredom and pain, even with perfected automation, to have enough human supervisors to reconnect the various systems if they had breakdowns inside themselves or at their interconnections. Old North Australia had vitality, but it was the vitality of open fields, few people, immense wealth, and perpetual military danger; this was the vitality of the cesspool, of the compost heap, but the rotting, blooming, growing components were not waste material but human beings and near-human beings. No wonder that his forefathers had fled the cities as they had been. They must have been solid plague to free men. And even Old Original Australia, somewhere here on Earth, had lost its openness and freedom in order to become the single giant city-complex of Aojou Nanbien. It must, Rod thought with horror, have been a thousand times the size of this city of Earthport. (He was wrong, because it was one hundred fifty thousand times the size of Earthport before it died. Earthport had only about two hundred thousand permanent residents when Rod visited it, with an additional number walking in from the nearer suburbs, the outer suburbs still being ruined and abandoned, but Australia—under the name of Aojou Nanbien—had reached a population of thirty billion before it died, and before the Wild Ones and the Menschenjäger had set to work killing off the survivors.)

Rod was bewildered, but C'mell was not.

She had put A'gentur down, over his whined monkeylike protest. He trotted unwillingly beside them.

With the impudent knowledgeability of a true city girl, she had led them to a cross-walk from which a continuous whistling roar came forth. By writing,

by picture, and by loudspeaker, the warning system
repeated: KEEP OFF. FREIGHT ONLY. DANGER. KEEP
OFF. She had snatched up A'gentur-E'ikasus, grabbed
Rod by the arm, and jumped with them onto a series
of rapidly moving airborne platforms. Rod, startled
by the suddenness with which they had found the
trackway, shouted to ask what it was:

"Freight? What's that?"

"Things. Boxes. Foods. This is the Central Trackway. No sense in walking six kilometers when we can
get this. Be ready to jump off with me when I give
you the sign!"

"It *feels* dangerous," he said.

"It isn't," said she, "not if you're a cat."

With this somewhat equivocal reassurance, she let
them ride. A'gentur could not care less. He cuddled
his head against her shoulder, wrapped his long,
gibbon-like arms around her upper arm, and went
soundly to sleep.

C'mell nodded at Rod.

"Soon now!" she called, judging their distance by
landmarks which he found meaningless. The landing points had flat, concrete-lined areas where the
individual flat cars, rushing along on their river of
air, could be shunted suddenly to the side for loading or unloading. Each of these loading areas had a
number, but Rod had not even noticed at what point
they had gotten on. The smells of the underground
city changed so much as they moved from one district
to another that he was more interested in odors than
in the numbers on the platforms.

She pinched his upper arm very sharply as a sign
that he should get ready.

They jumped.

He staggered across the platform until he caught himself up against a large vertical crate marked *Algonquin Paper Works—Credit Slips, Miniature—2mm.* C'mell landed as gracefully as if she had been acting a rehearsed piece of acrobatics. The little monkey on her shoulder stared with wide bright eyes.

"This," said the monkey A'gentur-E'ikasus firmly and contemptuously, "is where all the people play at working. I'm tired, I'm hungry, and my body sugar is low." He curled himself tight against C'mell's shoulder, closed his eyes, and went back to sleep.

"He has a point," said Rod. "Could we eat?"

C'mell started to nod and then caught herself short—"You're a cat."

He nodded. Then he grinned. "I'm hungry, anyhow. And I need a sandbox."

"Sandbox?" she asked, puzzled.

"An awef," he said very clearly, using the Old North Australian term.

"Awef?"

It was his turn to get embarrassed. He said it in full: "An animal waste evacuation facility."

"You mean a johnny," she cried. She thought a minute and then said, "Fooey."

"What's the matter?" he asked.

"Each kind of underpeople has to use its own. It's death if you don't use one and it's death if you use the wrong one. The cat one is four stations back on this underground trackway. Or we can walk back on the surface. It would only be a half hour."

He said something rude to Earth. She wrinkled her brow.

"All I said was, 'Earth is a large healthy sheep.' That's not so dirty." Her good humor returned.

Before she could ask him another question he held up a firm hand. "I am not going to waste a half hour. You wait here." He had seen the universal sign for "men's room" at the upper level of the platform. Before she could stop him he had gone into it. She caught her hand up to her mouth, knowing that the robot police would kill him on sight if they found him in the wrong place. It would be such a ghastly joke if the man who owned the Earth were to die in the wrong toilet.

As quick as thought she followed him, stopping just outside the door to the men's room. She dared not go in; she trusted that the place was empty when Rod entered it, because she had heard no boom of a slow, heavy bullet, none of the crisp buzzing of a burner. Robots did not use toilets, so they went in only when they were investigating something. She was prepared to distract any man living if he tried to enter that toilet, by offering him the combination of an immediate seduction or a complimentary and unwanted monkey.

A'gentur had awakened.

"Don't bother," he said. "I called my father. Anything approaching that door will fall asleep."

An ordinary man, rather tired and worried-looking, headed for the men's room. C'mell was prepared to stop him at any cost, but she remembered what A'gentur-E'ikasus had told her, so she waited. The man reeled as he neared them. He stared at them, saw that they were underpeople, looked on through them as though they were not there. He took two more steps toward the door and suddenly reached out his hands as if he were going blind. He walked into the wall two meters from the door, touched it firmly and blindly with his hands, and crumpled gently to the floor, where he lay snoring.

"My dad's good," said A'gentur-E'ikasus. "He usually leaves real people alone, but when he must get them, he gets them. He even gave that man the distinct memory that he mistakenly took a sleeping pill when he was reaching for a pain-killer. When the human wakes up, he will feel foolish and will tell no one of his experience."

Rod came out of the ever-so-dangerous doorway. He grinned at them boyishly and did not notice the crumpled man lying beside the wall. "That was easier than turning back, and nobody noticed me at all. See, I saved you a lot of trouble, C'mell!"

He was so proud of his foolhardy adventure that she did not have the heart to blame him. He smiled widely, his cat-whiskers tipping as he did so. For a moment, just a moment, she forgot that he was an important person and a real man to boot: he was a boy, and mighty like a cat, but all boy in his satisfaction, his wanton bravery, his passing happiness with vainglory. For a second or two she loved him. Then she thought of the terrible hours ahead, and of how he would go home, rich and scornful, to his all-people planet. The moment of love passed but she still liked him very much.

"Come along, young fellow. You can eat. You are going to eat cat food since you are C'roderick, but it's not so bad."

He frowned. "What is it? Do you have fish here?

I tasted fish one time. A neighbor bought one. He traded two horses for it. It was delicious."

"He wants fish," she cried to E'ikasus.

"Give him a whole tuna for himself," grumbled the monkey. "My blood sugar is still low. I need some pineapple."

C'mell did not argue. She stayed underground and led them into a hall which had a picture of dogs, cats, cattle, pigs, bears, and snakes above the door; that indicated the kinds of people who could be served there. E'ikasus scowled at the sign but he rode C'mell's shoulder in.

"This gentleman," said C'mell, speaking pleasantly to an old bear-man who was scratching his belly and smoking a pipe, all at the same time, "has forgotten his credits."

"No food," said the bear-man. "Rules. He can drink water, though."

"I'll pay for him," said C'mell.

The bear-man yawned. "Are you sure that he won't pay you back? If he does, that is private trading and it is punished by death."

"I know the rules," said C'mell. "I've never been disciplined yet."

The bear looked her over critically. He took his pipe out of his mouth and whistled. "No," said he, "and I can see that you won't be. What are you, anyhow? A model?"

"A girlygirl," said C'mell.

The bear-man leapt from his stool with astonishing speed. "Cat-madame!" he cried. "A thousand pardons. You can have anything in the place. You come from the top of Earthport? You know the Lords of the

Instrumentality personally? You would like a table roped off with curtains? Or should I just throw everybody else out of here and report to my Man that we have a famous, beautiful slave from the high places?"

"Nothing that drastic," said C'mell. "Just food."

"Wait a bit," said A'gentur-E'ikasus. "If you're offering specials, I'll have two fresh pineapples, a quarter-kilo of ground fresh coconut, and a tenth of a kilo of live insect grubs."

The bear-man hesitated. "I was offering things to the cat-lady, who serves the mighty ones, not to you, monkey. But if the lady desires it, I will send for those things." He waited for C'mell's nod, got it, and pushed a button for a low-grade robot to come. He turned to Rod McBan. "And you, cat-gentleman, what would you like?"

Before Rod could speak, C'mell said, "He wants two sailfish steaks, fried potatoes, Waldorf salad, an order of ice cream, and a large glass of orange juice."

The bear-man shuddered visibly. "I've been here for years and that is the most horrible lunch I ever ordered for a cat. I think I'll try it myself."

C'mell smiled the smile which had graced a thousand welcomes.

"I'll just help myself from the things you have on the counters. I'm not fussy."

He started to protest but she cut him short with a graceful but unmistakable wave of the hand. He gave up.

They sat at a table.

A'gentur-E'ikasus waited for his combination monkey and bird lunch. Rod saw an old robot, dressed in a prehistoric tuxedo jacket, ask a question of the

bear-man, leave one tray at the door, and bring another
tray to him. The robot whipped off a freshly starched
napkin. There was the most beautiful lunch Rod
McBan had ever seen. Even at a state banquet, the
Old North Australians did not feed their guests like
that. Just as they were finishing, the bear-cashier came
to the table and asked,

"Your name, cat-madame? I will charge these lunches
to the government."

"C'mell, servant to Teadrinker, subject to the Lord
Jestocost, a Chief of the Instrumentality."

The bear's face had been epilated, so that they
could see him pale.

"*C'mell,*" he whispered. "*C'mell!* Forgive me, my
Lady. I have never seen you before. You have blessed
this place. You have blessed my life. You are the friend
of all underpeople. Go in peace."

C'mell gave him the bow and smile which a reigning
empress might give to an active Lord of the Instrumentality. She started to pick up the monkey but he
scampered on ahead of her. Rod was puzzled. As the
bear-man bowed him out, he asked,

"C'mell. You are famous?"

"In a way," she said. "But only among the Underpeople." She hurried them both toward a ramp. They
reached daylight at last, but even before they came
to the surface, Rod's nose was assaulted by a riot of
smells—foods frying, cakes baking, liquor spilling its
pungency on the air, perfumes fighting with each other
for attention, and, above all, the smell of old things:
dusty treasures, old leathers, tapestries, the echo-smells
of people who had died a long time ago.

C'mell stopped and watched him. "You're smelling

things again? I must say, you have a better nose than any human being I ever met before. How does it smell to you?"

. "Wonderful," he gasped. "Wonderful. Like all the treasures and temptations of the universe spilled out into one little place."

"It's just the Thieves' Market of Paris."

"There are thieves on Earth? Open ones, like on Viola Siderea?"

"Oh, no," she laughed. "They would die in a few days. The Instrumentality would catch them. These are just people, playing. The Rediscovery of Man found some old institutions, and an old market was one of them. They make the robots and underpeople find things for them and then they pretend to be ancient, and make bargains with each other. Or they cook food. Not many real people ever cook food these days. It's so funny that it tastes good to them. They all pick up money on their way in. They have barrels of it at the gate. In the evening, or when they leave, they usually throw the money in the gutter, even though they should really put it back in the barrel. It's not money we underpeople could use. We go by numbers and computer cards," she sighed. "I could certainly use some of that extra money."

"And underpeople like you—like us—" said Rod, "what do we do in the market?"

"Nothing," she whispered. "Absolutely nothing. We can walk through if we are not too big and not too small and not too dirty and not too smelly. And even if we are all right, we must walk right through without looking directly at the real people and without touching anything in the market."

"Suppose we do?" asked Rod defiantly.

"The robot police are there, with orders to kill on sight when they observe an infraction. Don't you realize, C'rod," she sobbed at him, "that there are millions of us in tanks, way below in Downdeep-downdeep, ready to be born, to be trained, to be sent up here to serve Man? We're not scarce at all, C'rod, we're not scarce at all!"

"Why are we going through the market then?"

"It's the only way to the Catmaster's store. We'll be tagged. Come along."

Where the ramp reached the surface, four bright-eyed robots, their blue enamel bodies shining and their milky eyes glowing, stood at the ready. Their weapons had an ugly buzz to them and were obviously already off the "safety" mark. C'mell talked to them quietly and submissively. When the robot-sergeant led her to a desk, she stared into an instrument like binoculars and blinked when she took her eyes away. She put her palm on a desk. The identification was completed. The robot sergeant handed her three bright disks, like saucers, each with a chain attached. Wordlessly she hung them around her own neck, Rod's neck, and A'gentur's. The robots let them pass. They walked in demure single file through the place of beautiful sights and smells. Rod felt that his eyes were wet with tears of rage. "I'll buy this place," he thought to himself, "if it's the only thing I'll ever buy."

C'mell had stopped walking.

Rod looked up, very carefully.

There was the sign: THE DEPARTMENT STORE OF HEARTS' DESIRES. A door opened. A wise old cat-person's face looked out, stared at them, snapped, "No underpeople!" and slammed the door. C'mell rang the doorbell a second time. The face reappeared, more puzzled than angry.

"Business," she whispered, "of the Aitch Eye."

The face nodded and said, "In, then. Quick!"

# The Department Store of Hearts' Desires

Once inside, Rod realized that the store was as rich as the market. There were no other customers. After the outside sounds of music, laughter, frying, boiling, things falling, dishes clattering, people arguing, and the low undertone of the ever-ready robot weapons buzzing, the quietness of the room was itself a luxury, like old, heavy velvet. The smells were no less variegated than those on the outside, but they were different, more complicated, and many more of them were completely unidentifiable.

One smell he was sure of: fear, human fear. It had been in this room not long before.

"Quick," said the old cat-man. "I'm in trouble if you don't get out soon. What is your business?"

"I'm C'mell," said C'mell.

He nodded pleasantly, but showed no sign of recognition. "I forget people," he said.

"This is A'gentur." She indicated the monkey.

The old cat-man did not even look at the animal.

C'mell persisted, a note of triumph coming into her voice: "You may have heard of him under his real name, E'ikasus."

The old man stood there, blinking, as though he were taking it in. "Yeekasoose? With the letter E?"

"Transformed," said C'mell inexorably, "for a trip all the way to Old North Australia and back."

"Is this true?" said the old man to the monkey.

E'ikasus said calmly, "I am the son of Him of whom you think."

The old man dropped to his knees, but did so with dignity:

"I salute you, E'ikasus. When you next think-with your father, give him my greetings and ask from him his blessing. I am C'william, the Catmaster."

"You are famous," said E'ikasus tranquilly.

"But you are still in danger, merely being here. I have no license for underpeople!"

C'mell produced her trump. "Catmaster, your next guest. This is no c'man. He is a true man, an off-worlder, and he has just bought most of the planet Earth."

C'william looked at Rod with more than ordinary shrewdness. There was a touch of kindness in his attitude. He was tall for a cat-man; few animal features were left to him, because old age, which reduces racial and sexual contrasts to mere memories, had wrinkled him into a uniform beige. His hair was not white, but beige too; his few cat-whiskers looked old and worn. He was garbed in a fantastic costume which—Rod later learned—consisted of the court robes of one of the Original Emperors, a dynasty which had prevailed for many centuries among the further stars. Age was upon him, but wisdom was too; the habits of life, in his case, had been cleverness and kindness, themselves unusual in combination. Now very old, he was reaping the harvest of his years. He had done well with the thousands upon thousands of days behind him, with the result that age had brought a curious joy into his manner, as though each experience meant one more treat before the long bleak dark closed in. Rod felt himself attracted to this strange creature, who looked at him with such penetrating and very personal curiosity, and who managed to do so without giving offense.

The Catmaster spoke in very passable Norstrilian: "I know what you are thinking, Mister and Owner McBan."

"You can hier me?" cried Rod.

"Not your thoughts. Your face. It reads easily. I am sure that I can help you."

"What makes you think I need help?"

"All things need help," said the old c'man briskly, "but we must get rid of our other guests first. Where do you want to go, excellent one? And you, cat-madame?"

"Home," said E'ikasus. He was tired and cross again. After speaking brusquely, he felt the need to make his tone more civil. "This body suits me badly, Catmaster."

"Are you good at falling?" said the Catmaster. "Free fall?"

The monkey grinned. "With this body? Of course. Excellent. I'm tired of it."

"Fine," said the Catmaster. "You can drop down my waste chute. It falls next to the forgotten palace where the great wings beat against time."

The Catmaster stepped to one side of the room. With only a nod at C'mell and Rod, followed by a brief "See you later," the monkey watched as the Catmaster opened a manhole cover, leaped trustingly into the complete black depth which appeared, and was gone. The Catmaster replaced the cover carefully.

He turned to C'mell.

She faced him truculently, the defiance of her posture oddly at variance with the innocent voluptuousness of her young female body. "I'm going nowhere."

"You'll die," said the Catmaster. "Can't you hear their weapons buzzing just outside the door? You know what they do to us underpeople. Especially to us cats. They use us, but do they trust us?"

"I know one who does . . ." she said. "The Lord Jestocost could protect me, even here, just as he protects you, far beyond your limit of years."

"Don't argue it. You will make trouble for him with the other real people. Here, girl, I will give you a tray to carry with a dummy package on it. Go back to the underground and rest in the commissary of the bear-man. I will send Rod to you when we are through."

"Yes," she said hotly, "but will you send him alive or dead?"

The Catmaster rolled his yellow eyes over Rod. "Alive," he said. "This one—alive. I have predicted. Did you ever know me to be wrong? Come on, girl, out the door with you."

C'mell let herself be handed a tray and a package, taken seemingly at random. As she left Rod thought of her with quick desperate affection. She was his closest link with Earth. He thought of her excitement and of how she had bared her young breasts to him, but now the memory, instead of exciting him, filled him with tender fondness instead. He blurted out, "C'mell, will you be all right?"

She turned around at the door itself, looking all woman and all cat. Her red wild hair gleamed like a hearth-fire against the open light from the doorway. She stood erect, as though she were a citizen of Earth and not a mere underperson or girlygirl. She held out her right hand clearly and commandingly while balancing the tray on her left hand. When he shook hands with her, Rod realized that her hand felt utterly human but very strong. With scarcely a break in her voice she said,

"Rod, goodbye. I'm taking a chance with you, but it's the best chance I've ever taken. You can trust the Catmaster, here in the Department Store of Hearts' Desires. He does strange things, Rod, but they're good strange things."

He released her hand and she left. C'william closed the door behind her. The room became hushed.

"Sit down for a minute while I get things ready. Or look around the room if you prefer."

"Sir Catmaster—" said Rod.

"No title, please. I am an underperson, made out of cats. You may call me C'william."

"C'william, please tell me first. I miss C'mell. I'm worried about her. Am I falling in love with her? Is that what falling in love means?"

"She's your wife," said the Catmaster. "Just temporarily and just in pretense, but she's still your wife. It's Earthlike to worry about one's mate. She's all right."

The old c'man disappeared behind a door which had an odd sign on it: HATE HALL.

Rod looked around.

The first thing, the very first thing, which he saw

was a display cabinet full of postage stamps. It was made of glass, but he could see the soft blues and the inimitable warm brick reds of his Cape of Good Hope triangular postage stamps. He had come to Earth and there they were! He peered through the glass at them. They were even better than the illustrations which he had seen back on Norstrilia. They had the temper of great age upon them and yet, somehow, they seemed to freight with them the love which men, living men now dead, had given them for thousands and thousands of years. He looked around, and saw that the whole room was full of odd riches. There were ancient toys of all periods, flying toys, copies of machines, things which he suspected were trains. There was a two-story closet of clothing, shimmering with embroidery and gleaming with gold. There was a bin of weapons, clean and tidy—models so ancient that he could not possibly guess what they had been used for, or by whom. Everywhere, there were buckets of coins, usually gold ones. He picked up a handful. They had languages he could not even guess at and they showed the proud imperious faces of the ancient dead. Another cabinet was one which he glanced at and then turned away from, shocked and yet inquisitive: it was filled with indecent souvenirs and pictures from a hundred periods of men's history, images, sketches, photographs, dolls and models, all of them portraying grisly, comical, sweet, friendly, impressive or horrible versions of the many acts of love. The next section made him pause utterly. Who would have ever wanted these things? Whips, knives, hoods, leather corsets. He passed on, very puzzled.

The next section stopped him breathless. It was

full of old books, genuine old books. There were a
few framed poems, written very ornately. One had
a scrap of paper attached to it, reading simply, "My
favorite." Rod looked down to see if he could make
it out. It was ancient Inglish and the odd name was
"E.Z.C. Judson, Ancient American, A.D. 1823–1866."
Rod understood the words of the poem but he did
not think that he really got the sense of it. As he
read it, he had the impression that a very old man,
like the Catmaster, must find in it a poignancy which
a younger person would miss:

> Drifting in the ebbing tide,
> Slow but sure I onward glide—
>     Dim the vista seen before,
> Useless now to look behind—
> Drifting on before the wind
>     Toward the unknown shore.

> Counting time by ticking clock,
> Waiting for the final shock—
>     Waiting for the dark forever—
> Oh, how slow the moments go!
> None but I, meseems, can know
>     How close the tideless river!

Rod shook his head as if to get away from the
cobwebs of an irrecoverable tragedy. "Maybe," he
thought to himself, "that's the way people felt about
death when they did not die on schedule, the way
most worlds have it, or if they do not meet death a
few times ahead of time, the way we do in Norstrilia. They must have felt pretty sticky and uncertain."

Another thought crossed his mind and he gasped at the utter cruelty of it. "They did not even have Unselfing Grounds that far back! Not that we need them any more, but imagine just sliding into death, helpless, useless, hopeless. Thank the Queen we don't do that!"

He thought of the Queen, who might have been dead for more than fifteen thousand years, or who might be lost in space, the way many Old North Australians believed, and sure enough! there was her picture, with the words "Queen Elizabeth II." It was just a bust, but she was a pretty and intelligent-looking woman, with something of a Norstrilian look to her. She looked smart enough to know what to do if one of her sheep caught fire or if her own child came, blank and giggling, out of the traveling vans of the Garden of Death, as he himself would have done had he not passed the survival test.

Next there were two glass frames, neatly wiped free of dust. They had matched poems by someone who was listed as "Anthony Bearden, Ancient American, A.D. 1913–1949." The first one seemed very appropriate to this particular place, because it was all about the ancient desires which people had in those days. It read:

*TELL ME, LOVE!*

*Time is burning and the world on fire.*
*Tell me, love, what you most desire.*
*Tell me what your heart has hidden.*
*Is it open or—forbidden?*

*If forbidden, think of days*
*Racing past in a roaring haze,*
*Shocked and shaken by the blast of fire . . .*
*Tell me, love, what you most desire.*

*Tell me, love, what you most desire.*
*Dainty foods and soft attire?*
*Ancient books? Fantastic chess?*
*Wine-lit nights? Love—more, or less?*

*Now is the only now of our age.*
*Tomorrow tomorrow will hold the stage.*
*Tell me, love, what you most desire!*
*Time is burning and the world on fire.*

The other one might almost have been written about his arrival on Earth, his not knowing what could happen or what should happen to him now.

## NIGHT, AND THE SKY UNFAMILIAR

*The stars of experience have led me astray.*
*A pattern of purpose was lost on my way.*
*Where was I going? How can I say?*
*The stars of experience have led me astray.*

There was a slight sound.

Rod turned around to face the Catmaster.

The old man was unchanged. He still wore the lunatic robes of grandeur, but his dignity survived even this *outré* effect.

"You like my poems? You like my things? I like them myself. Many men come in here to take things from me, but they find that title is vested in the Lord Jestocost, and they must do strange things to obtain my trifles."

"Are all these things genuine?" asked Rod, thinking that even Old North Australia could not buy out this shop if they were.

"Certainly not," said the old man. "Most of them are forgeries—wonderful forgeries. The Instrumentality lets me go to the robot-pits where insane or worn-out robots are destroyed. I can have my pick of them if they are not dangerous. I put them to work making copies of anything which I find in the museums."

"Those Cape triangles?" said Rod. "Are they real?"

"Cape triangles? You mean the letter stickers. They are genuine, all right, but they are not mine. Those are on loan from the Earth Museum until I can get them copied."

"I will buy them," said Rod.

"You will not," said the Catmaster. "They are not for sale."

"Then I will buy Earth and you and them too," said Rod.

"Roderick Frederick Ronald Arnold William MacArthur McBan to the one hundred and fifty-first, you will not."

"Who are you to tell me?"

"I have looked at one person and I have talked to two others."

"All right," said Rod. "Who?"

"I looked at the other Rod McBan, your workwoman Eleanor. She is a little mixed up about having a young man's body, because she is very drunk in the home of the Lord William Not-from-here and a beautiful young woman named Ruth Not-from-here is trying to make Eleanor marry her. She has no idea that she is dealing with another woman and Eleanor, in her copy of your proper body, is finding the experience exciting but terribly confusing. No harm will come of it, and your Eleanor is perfectly safe. Half the rascals of Earth have converged on the Lord William's house, but he has a whole battalion from the Defense Fleet on loan around the place, so nothing is going to happen, except that Eleanor will have a headache and Ruth will have a disappointment."

Rod smiled. "You couldn't have told me anything better. Who else did you talk to?"

"The Lord Jestocost and John Fisher to the hundredth."

"Mister and Owner Fisher? He's here?"

"He's at his home. Station of the Good Fresh Joey. I asked him if you could have your heart's desire. After a little while, he and somebody named Doctor Wentworth said that the Commonwealth of Old North Australia would approve it."

"How did you ever pay for such a call?" cried Rod. "Those things are frightfully expensive."

"I didn't pay for it, Mister and Owner. *You* did. I charged it to your account, by the authority of your trustee, the Lord Jestocost. He and his forefathers have been my patrons for four hundred and twenty-six years."

"You've got your nerve," said Rod. "Spending my money when I was right here and not even asking me!"

"You are an adult for some purposes and a minor for other purposes. I am offering you the skills which keep me alive. Do you think any ordinary cat-man would be allowed to live as long as this?"

"No," said Rod. "Give me those stamps and let me go."

The Catmaster looked at him levelly. Once again there was the *personal* look on his face, which on Norstrilia would have been taken as an unpardonable affront; but along with the nosiness, there was an air of confidence and kindness which put Rod a little in awe of the man, underperson though he was. "Do you think that you could love these stamps when you get back home? Could they talk to you? Could they make you like yourself? Those pieces of paper are not your heart's desire. Something else is."

"What?" said Rod, truculently.

"In a bit, I'll explain. First, you cannot kill me. Second, you cannot hurt me. Third, if I kill you, it will be all for your own good. Fourth, if you get out of here, you will be a very happy man."

"Are you barmy, Mister?" cried Rod. "I can knock you flat and walk out that door. I don't know what you are talking about."

"Try it," said the Catmaster levelly.

Rod looked at the tall withered old man with the bright eyes. He looked at the door, a mere seven or eight meters away. He did not want to try it.

"All right," he conceded, "play your pitch."

"I am a clinical psychologist. The only one on Earth and probably the only one on any planet. I got my knowledge from some ancient books when I was a kitten, being changed into a young man. I change people just a little, little bit. You know that the Instrumentality has surgeons and brains experts and all sorts of doctors. They can do almost anything with personality—anything but the light stuff . . . *That*, I do."

"I don't get it," said Rod.

"Would you go to a brain surgeon to get a haircut? Would you need a dermatologist to give you a bath? Of course not. I don't do heavy work. I just change people a little bit. It makes them happy. If I can't do anything with them, I give them souvenirs from this junkpile out here. The real work is in there. That's where you're going, pretty soon." He nodded his head at the door marked HATE HALL.

Rod cried out, "I've been taking orders from one stranger after another, all these long weeks since my computers and I made that money! Can't I ever do anything myself?"

The Catmaster looked at him with sympathy. "None of us can. We may think that we are free. Our lives are made for us by the people we happen to know, the places we happen to be, the jobs or hobbies which we happen to run across. Will I be dead a year from now? I don't know. Will you be back in Old North Australia a year from now, still only seventeen, but rich and wise and on your way to happiness? I don't know. You've had a run of good luck. Look at it that way. It's luck. And I'm part of the luck. If you get killed here, it will not be my doing but just the overstrain of your body against the devices which the Lady Goroke approved a long time ago—devices which the Lord Jestocost reports to the Instrumentality. He keeps them legal that way. I'm the only underman in the universe who is entitled to process real people in any way whatever without having direct human supervision. All I do is to develop people, like an Ancient Man developing a photograph from a piece of paper exposed to different grades of light. I'm not a hidden judge, like your men in the Garden of Death. It's going to be you against you, with me just helping, and when you come out you're going to be a different you—the same you, but a little better there, a little more flexible here. As a matter of fact, that cat-type body you're wearing is going to make your contest with yourself a little harder for me to manage. We'll do it, Rod. Are you ready?"

"Ready for what?"

"For the tests and changes there." The Catmaster nodded at the door marked HATE HALL.

"I suppose so," said Rod. "I don't have much choice."

"No," said the Catmaster, sympathetically and almost sadly, "not at this point, you don't. If you walk out that door, you're an illegal cat-man, in immediate danger of being buzzed down by the robot police."

"Please," said Rod, "win or fail, can I have one of these Cape triangles?"

The Catmaster smiled. "I promise you—if you want one, you shall have it." He waved at the door: "Go on in."

Rod was not a coward, but it was with feet and legs of lead that he walked to the door. It opened by itself. He walked in, steady but afraid.

The room was dark with a darkness deeper than mere black. It was the dark of blindness, the expanse of cheek where no eye has ever been.

The door closed behind him and he swam in the dark, so tangible had the darkness become.

He felt blind. He felt as if he had never seen.

But he could hear.

He heard his own blood pulsing through his head.

He could smell—indeed, he was good at smelling.

And this air—this air—this air smelled of the open night on the dry plains of Old North Australia.

The smell made him feel little and afraid. It reminded him of his repeated childhoods, of the artificial drownings in the laboratories where he had gone to be reborn from one childhood to another.

He reached out his hands.

Nothing.

He jumped gently. No ceiling.

Using a fieldman's trick familiar from times of dust storms, he dropped lightly to his hands and feet. He scuttled crabwise on two feet and one hand, using the other hand as a shield to protect his face. In a very few meters he found the wall. He followed the wall around.

Circular.

This was the door.

Follow again.

With more confidence, he moved fast. Around, around, around. He could not tell whether the floor was asphalt or some kind of rough worn tile.

Door again.

A voice spieked to him.

Spieked! *And he heard it.*

He looked upward into the nothing which was bleaker than blindness, almost expecting to see the words in letters of fire, so clear had they been.

The voice was Norstrilian and it said,

*Rod McBan is a man, man, man.*

*But what is man?*

*(Immediate percussion of crazy, sad laughter.)*

Rod never noticed that he reverted to the habits of babyhood. He sat flat on his rump, legs spread out in front of him at a ninety-degree angle. He put his hands a little behind him and leaned back, letting the weight of his body push his shoulders a little bit upward. He knew the ideas that would follow the words, but he never knew why he so readily expected them.

Light formed in the room, as he had been sure it would.

The images were little, but they looked real.

Men and women and children, children and women and men marched into his vision and out again.

They were not freaks; they were not beasts; they were not alien monstrosities begotten in some outside universe; they were not robots; they were not underpeople; they were all hominids like himself, kinsmen in the Earthborn races of men.

First came people like Old North Australians and Earth people, very much alike, and both similar to the ancient types, except that Norstrilians were pale beneath their tanned skins, bigger, and more robust.

Then came Daimoni, white-eyed pale giants with a magical assurance, whose very babies walked as though they had already been given ballet lessons.

Then heavy men, fathers, mothers, infants swimming on the solid ground from which they would never arise.

Then rainmen from Amazonas Triste, their skins hanging in enormous folds around them, so that they looked like bundles of wet rags wrapped around monkeys.

Blind men from Olympia, staring fiercely at the world through the radars mounted on their foreheads.

Bloated monster-men from abandoned planets—people as bad off as his own race had been after escaping from Paradise VII.

And still more races.

People he had never heard of.

Men with shells.

Men and women so thin that they looked like insects.

A race of smiling, foolish giants, lost in the irreparable hebephrenia of their world. (Rod had the feeling that they were shepherded by a race of devoted dogs, more intelligent than themselves, who cajoled them into breeding, begged them to eat, led them to sleep. He saw no dogs, only the smiling unfocused fools, but the feeling *dog, good dog!* was somehow very near.)

A funny little people who pranced with an indefinable deformity of gait.

Water-people, the clean water of some unidentified world pulsing through their gills.

And then—

More people, still, but hostile ones. Lipsticked hermaphrodites with enormous beards and fluting voices. Carcinomas which had taken over men. Giants rooted in the Earth. Human bodies crawling and weeping as they crept through wet grass, somehow contaminated themselves and looking for more people to infect.

Rod did not know it, but he growled.

He jumped into a squatting position and swept his hands across the rough floor, looking for a weapon.

These were not men—they were enemies!

Still they came. People who had lost eyes, or who had grown fire-resistant, the wrecks and residues of abandoned settlements and forgotten colonies. The waste and spoilage of the human race.

And then—

Him.

Himself.

The child Rod McBan.

And voices, Norstrilian voices calling: "He can't hier. He can't spiek. He's a freak. He's a freak. He can't hier. He can't spiek."

And another voice: "His poor parents!"

The child Rod disappeared and there were his parents again. Twelve times taller than life, so high that he had to peer up into the black absorptive ceiling to see the underside of their faces.

The mother wept.

The father sounded stern.

The father was saying, "It's no use. Doris can watch him while we're gone, but if he isn't any better, we'll turn him in."

"Kill him?" shrieked the woman. "Kill my baby? Oh, no! No!"

The calm, loving, horrible voice of the man, "Darling, spiek to him yourself. He'll never hier. Can that be a Rod McBan?"

Then the woman's voice, sweet-poisonous and worse than death, sobbing agreement with her man against her son.

"I don't know, Rod. I don't know. Just don't tell me about it."

He *had* hiered them, in one of his moments of wild penetrating hiering when everything telepathic came in with startling clarity. He had hiered them when he was a baby.

The real Rod in the dark room let out a roar of
fear, desolation, loneliness, rage, hate. This was the
telepathic bomb with which he had so often startled
or alarmed the neighbors, the mind-shock with which
he had killed the giant spider in the tower of Earthport far above him.

But this time, the room was closed.

His mind roared back at itself.

Rage, loudness, hate, raw noise poured into him
from the floor, the circular wall, the high ceiling.

He cringed beneath it and as he cringed, the sizes
of the images changed. His parents sat in chairs,
chairs. They were little, little. He was an almighty
baby, so enormous that he could scoop them up with
his right hand.

He reached to crush the tiny loathsome parents
who had said, "Let him die."

To crush them, but they faded first.

Their faces turned frightened. They looked wildly
around. Their chairs dissolved, the fabric falling to a
floor which in turn looked like storm-eroded cloth.
They turned for a last kiss and had no lips. They
reached to hug each other and their arms fell off.
Their spaceship had gone milky in mid-trip, dissolving into traceless nothing. And he, he, he himself
had seen it!

The rage was followed by tears, by a guilt too deep
for regret, by a self-accusation so raw and wet that it
lived like one more organ inside his living body.

He wanted nothing.

No money, no stroon, no Station of Doom. He
wanted no friends, no companionship, no welcome,
no house, no food. He wanted no walks, no solitary

discoveries in the field, no friendly sheep, no treasures in the gap, no computer, no day, no night, no life.

He wanted nothing, and he could not understand death.

The enormous room lost all light, all sound, and he did not notice it. His own naked life lay before him like a freshly dissected cadaver. It lay there and it made no sense. There had been many Roderick Frederick Ronald Arnold William MacArthur McBans, one hundred and fifty of them in a row, but he—151! 151! 151!—was not one of them, not a giant who had wrestled treasure from the sick Earth and hidden sunshine of the Norstrilian plains. It wasn't his telepathic deformity, his spieklessness, his brain deafness to hiering. It was himself, the "Me-subtile" inside him, which was wrong, all wrong. He was the baby worth killing, who had killed instead. He had hated mama and papa for their pride and their hate: when he hated them, they crumpled and died out in the mystery of space, so that they did not even leave bodies to bury.

Rod rose to his feet. His hands were wet. He touched his face and he realized that he had been weeping with his face cupped in his hands.

Wait.

There was something.

There was one thing he wanted. He wanted Houghton Syme not to hate him. Houghton Syme could hier and spiek, but he was a shortie, living with the sickness of death lying between himself and every girl, every friend, every job he had met. And he, Rod, had mocked that man, calling him Old Hot and Simple. Rod might be worthless but he was not as bad off as Houghton Syme, the Hon. Sec. Houghton Syme was at least trying to be a man, to live his miserable scrap of life, and all Rod had ever done was to flaunt his wealth and near-immortality before the poor cripple who had just one hundred and sixty years to live. Rod wanted only one thing—to get back to Old North Australia in time to help Houghton Syme, to let Houghton Syme know that the guilt was his, Rod's, and not Syme's. The Onseck had a bit of a life and he deserved the best of it.

Rod stood there, expecting nothing.

He had forgiven his last enemy.

He had forgiven himself.

The door opened very matter-of-factly and there stood the Catmaster, a quiet wise smile upon his face,

"You can come out now, Mister and Owner McBan; and if there is anything in this outer room which you want, you may certainly have it."

Rod walked out slowly. He had no idea how long he had been in Hate Hall.

When he emerged, the door closed behind him.

"No, thanks, cobber. It's mighty friendly of you, but I don't need anything much, and I'd better be getting back to my own planet."

"Nothing?" said the Catmaster, still smiling very attentively and very quietly.

"I'd like to hier and spiek, but it's not very important."

"This is for you," said the Catmaster. "You put it in your ear and leave it there. If it itches or gets dirty, you take it out, wash it, and put it back in. It's not a rare device, but apparently you don't have them on your planet." He held out an object no larger than the kernel of a ground-nut.

Rod took it absently and was ready to put it into his pocket, not into his ear, when he saw that the smiling attentive face was watching, very gently but very alertly. He put the device into his ear. It felt a little cold.

"I will now," said the Catmaster, "take you to C'mell, who will lead you to your friends in Downdeep-downdeep. You had better take this blue two-penny Cape of Good Hope postage stamp with you. I will report to Jestocost that it was lost while I attempted to copy it. That is slightly true, isn't it?"

Rod started to thank him absent-mindedly and then—

Then, with a thrill which sent gooseflesh all over his neck, back and arms, he realized that the Catmaster had not moved his lips in the slightest, had not pushed air through his throat, had not disturbed the air with the pressure of noise. The Catmaster had spieked to Rod, and Rod had hiered him.

Thinking very carefully and very clearly, but closing his lips and making no sound whatever, Rod thought,

"Worthy and gracious Catmaster, I thank you for the ancient treasure of the old Earth stamp. I thank you even more for the hiering-spieking device which I am now testing. Will you please extend your right hand to shake hands with me, if you can actually hier me now?"

The Catmaster stepped forward and extended his hand.

Man and underman, they faced each other with a kindness and gratitude which was so poignant as to be very close to grief.

Neither of them wept. Neither.

They shook hands without speaking or spieking.

# Everybody's Fond Of Money

While Rod McBan was going through his private ordeal at the Department Store of Hearts' Desires, other people continued to be concerned with him and his fate.

## A Crime of Public Opinion

A middle-aged woman, with a dress which did not suit her, sat uninvited at the table of Paul, a real man once acquainted with C'mell.

Paul paid no attention to her. Eccentricities were multiplying among people these days. Being middle-aged was a matter of taste, and many human beings, after the Rediscovery of Man, found that if they let themselves become imperfect, it was a more comfortable way to live than the old way—the old way consisting of aging minds dwelling in bodies condemned to the perpetual perfection of youth.

"I had flu," said the woman. "Have you ever had flu?"

"No," said Paul, not very much interested.

"Are you reading a newspaper?" She looked at

his newspaper, which had everything except news in it.

Paul, with the paper in front of him, admitted that he was reading it.

"Do you like coffee?" said the woman, looking at Paul's cup of fresh coffee in front of him.

"Why would I order it if I didn't?" said Paul brusquely, wondering how the woman had ever managed to find so unattractive a material for her dress. It was yellow sunflowers on an off-red background.

The woman was baffled, but only for a moment.

"I'm wearing a girdle," she said. "They just came on sale last week. They're very, very ancient, and very authentic. Now that people can be fat if they want to, girdles are the rage. They have spats for men, too. Have you bought your spats yet?"

"No," said Paul flatly, wondering if he should leave his coffee and newspaper.

"What are you going to do about that man?"

"What man?" said Paul, politely and wearily.

"The man who's bought the Earth."

"Did he?" said Paul.

"Of course," said the woman. "Now he has more power than the Instrumentality. He could do anything he wants. He can give us anything we want. If he wanted to, he could give *me* a thousand-year trip around the universe."

"Are you an official?" said Paul sharply.

"No," said the woman, taken a little aback.

"Then how do you know these things?"

"*Everybody* knows them. Everybody." She spoke firmly and pursed her mouth at the end of the sentence.

"What are you going to do about this man? Rob him? Seduce him?" Paul was sardonic. He had had an unhappy love affair which he still remembered, a climb to the Abba-dingo over Alpha Ralpha Boulevard which he would never repeat, and very little patience with fools who had never dared and never suffered anything.

The woman flushed with anger. "We're all going to his hostel at twelve today. We're going to shout and shout until he comes out. Then we're going to form a line and make him listen to what each one of us wants."

Paul spoke sharply: "Who organized this?"

"I don't know. Somebody."

Paul spoke solemnly. "You're a human being. You have been trained. What is the Twelfth Rule?"

The woman turned a little pale but she chanted, as if by rote: "'Any man or woman who finds that he or she forms and shares an unauthorized opinion with a large number of other people shall report immediately for therapy to the nearest subchief.' But that doesn't mean me . . . ?"

"You'll be dead or scrubbed by tonight, madam. Now go away and let me read my paper."

The woman glared at him, between anger and tears. Gradually fear came over her features. "Do you really think what I was saying is unlawful?"

"Completely," said Paul.

She put her pudgy hands over her face and sobbed. "Sir, sir, can you—can you please help me find a subchief? I'm afraid I do need help. But I've dreamed so much, I've hoped so much. A man from the stars. But you're right, sir. I don't want to die or get blanked out. Sir, please help me!"

Moved by both impatience and compassion, Paul

left his paper and his coffee. The robot waiter hurried up to remind him that he had not paid. Paul walked over to the sidewalk where there were two barrels full of money for people who wished to play the games of ancient civilization. He selected the biggest bill he could see, gave it to the waiter, waited for his change, gave the waiter a tip, received thanks, and threw the change, which was all coins, into the barrel full of metal money. The woman had waited for him patiently, her blotched face sad.

When he offered her his arm, in the old-French manner, she took it. They walked a hundred meters, more or less, to a public visiphone. She half-cried, half-mumbled as she walked along beside him, with her uncomfortable, ancient spiked-heel feminine shoes:

"I used to have four hundred years. I used to be slim and beautiful. I liked to make love and I didn't think very much about things, because I wasn't very bright. I had had a lot of husbands. Then this change came along, and I felt useless, and I decided to be what I felt like—fat, and sloppy, and middle-aged, and bored. And I have succeeded too much, just the way two of my husbands said. And that man from the stars, he has all power. He can change things."

Paul did not answer her, except to nod sympathetically.

At the visiphone he stood until a robot appeared. "A subchief," he said. "Any subchief."

The image blurred and the face of a very young man appeared. He stared earnestly and intently while Paul recited his number, grade, neo-national assignment, quarters number and business. He had to state the business twice, "Criminal public opinion."

The subchief snapped, not unpleasantly, "Come on in, then, and we'll fix you up."

Paul was so annoyed at the idea that *he* would be suspected of criminal public opinion, "any opinion shared with a large number of other people, other than material released and approved by the Instrumentality and the Earth Government," that he began to spiek his protest into the machine.

"Vocalize, man and citizen! These machines don't carry telepathy."

When Paul got through explaining, the youngster in uniform looked at him critically but pleasantly, saying,

"Citizen, you've forgotten something yourself."

"Me?" gasped Paul. "I've done nothing. This woman just sat down beside me and—"

"Citizen," said the subchief, "what is the last half of the Fifth Rule for All Men?"

Paul thought a moment and then answered, "The services of every person shall be available, without delay and without charge, to any other true human being who encounters danger or distress." Then his own eyes widened and he said, "You want me to do this myself?"

"What do you think?" said the subchief.

"I can," said Paul.

"Of course," said the subchief. "You are normal. You remember the braingrips."

Paul nodded.

The subchief waved at him and the image faded from the screen.

The woman had seen it all. She, too, was prepared. When Paul lifted his hands for the traditional hypnotic gestures, she locked her eyes upon his hands. She made the responses as they were needed. When he had brainscrubbed her right there in the open street, she shambled off down the walkway, not knowing why tears poured down her cheeks. She did not remember Paul at all.

For a moment of crazy whimsy, Paul thought of going across the city and having a look at the wonderful man from the stars. He stared around absently, thinking. His eye caught the high thread of Alpha Ralpha Boulevard, soaring unsupported across the heavens from faraway ground to the mid-height of Earthport: he remembered himself and his own personal troubles. He went back to his newspaper and a fresh cup of coffee, helping himself to money from the barrel, this time, before he entered the restaurant.

## On a Yacht Off Meeya Meefla

Ruth yawned as she sat up and looked at the ocean. She had done her best with the rich young man.

The false Rod McBan, actually a reconstructed Eleanor, said to her:

"This is right nice."

Ruth smiled languidly and seductively. She did not know why Eleanor laughed out loud.

The Lord William Not-from-here came up from below the deck. He carried two silver mugs in his hands. They were frosted.

"I am glad," said he unctuously, "that you young people are happy. These are mint juleps, a very ancient drink indeed."

He watched as Eleanor sipped hers and then smiled. He smiled too. "You like it?"

Eleanor smiled right back at him. "Beats washing dishes, it does!" said "Rod McBan" enigmatically.

The Lord William began to think that the rich young man was odd indeed.

## Antechamber of the Bell and Bank

The Lord Crudelta commanded, "Send Jestocost here!" The Lord Jestocost was already entering the room. "What's happened on that case of the young man?"

"Nothing, Sir and Senior."

"Tush. Bosh. Nonsense. Rot." The old man snorted. "Nothing is something that doesn't happen at all. He has to be somewhere."

"The original is with the Catmaster, at the Department Store."

"Is that safe?" said the Lord Crudelta. "He might get to be too smart for us to manage. You're working some scheme again, Jestocost."

"Nothing but what I told you, Sir and Senior."

The old man frowned. "That's right. You *did* tell me. Proceed. But the others?"

"Who?"

"The decoys?"

The Lord Jestocost laughed aloud. "Our colleague, the Lord William, has almost betrothed his daughter to Mister McBan's workman, who is temporarily a 'Rod McBan' herself. All parties are having fun with no harm done. The robots, the eight survivors, are going around Earthport city. They are enjoying themselves as much as robots ever do. Crowds are gathering and asking for miracles. Pretty harmless."

"And the Earth economy? Is it getting out of balance?"

"I've set the computers to work," said the Lord Jestocost, "finding every tax penalty that we ever imposed on anybody. We're several megacredits ahead."

"FOE money."

"FOE money, Sir."

"You're not going to ruin him?" said Crudelta.

"Not at all, Sir and Senior," cried the Lord Jestocost. "I am a kind man."

The old man gave him a low dirty smile. "I've seen your kindness before, Jestocost, and I would rather have a thousand worlds for an enemy than have you be my friend! You're devious, you're dangerous, and you are tricky."

Jestocost, much flattered by this comment, said formally, "You do an honest official a great injustice, Sir and Senior."

The two men just smiled at each other: they knew each other well.

## Ten Kilometers Below the Surface of the Earth

The E'telekeli stood from the lectern at which he had been praying.

His daughter was watching him immovably from the doorway.

He spieked to her, "What's wrong, my girl?"

"I saw his mind, father, I saw it for just a moment

as he left the Catmaster's place. He's a rich young man from the stars, he's a nice young man, he has bought Earth, but he is not the man of the Promise."

"You expected too much, E'lamelanie," spieked her father.

"I expected hope," she spieked to him. "Is hope a crime among us underpeople? What Joan foresaw, what the Copt promised—where are they, father? Shall we never see daylight or know freedom?"

"True men are not free either," spieked the E'telekeli. "They too have grief, fear, birth, old age, love, death, suffering and the tools of their own ruin. Freedom is not something which is going to be given us by a wonderful man beyond the stars. Freedom is what you do, my dear, and what I do. Death is a very private affair, my daughter, and life—when you get to it—is almost as private."

"I know, father," she spieked. "I know. I know. I know." (But she didn't.)

"You may not know it, my darling," spieked the great bird-man, "but long before these people built cities, there were others in the Earth—the ones who came after the Ancient World fell. They went far beyond the limitations of the human form. They conquered death. They did not have sickness. They did not need love. They sought to be abstractions lying outside of time. And they died, E'lamelanie—they died terribly. Some became monsters, preying on the remnants of true men for reasons which ordinary men could not even begin to understand. Others were like oysters, wrapped up in their own sainthood. They had all forgotten that humanness is itself imperfection and corruption, that what is perfect is no longer understandable. We have

the Fragments of the Word, and we are truer to the
deep traditions of people than people themselves
are, but we must never be foolish enough to look
for perfection in this life or to count on our own
powers to make us really different from what we are.
You and I are animals, darling, not even real people,
but people do not understand the teaching of Joan,
that whatever *seems* human *is human*. It is the word
which quickens, not the shape or the blood or the
texture of flesh or hair or feathers. And there is that
power which you and I do not name, but which we
love and cherish because we need it more than do the
people on the surface. Great beliefs always come out
of the sewers of cities, not out of the towers of the
ziggurats. Furthermore, we are discarded animals, not
used ones. All of us down here are the rubbish which
mankind has thrown away and has forgotten. We have
a great advantage in this, because we know from the
very beginning of our lives that we are worthless. And
why are we worthless? Because a higher standard and
a higher truth says that we are—the conventional law
and the unwritten customs of mankind. But I feel love
for you, my daughter, and you have love for me. We
know that everything which loves has a value in itself,
and that therefore this worthlessness of underpeople
is wrong. We are forced to look beyond the minute
and the hour to the place where no clocks work and
no day dawns. There is a world outside of time, and
it is to that which we appeal. I know that you have
a love for the devotional life, my child, and I com-
mend you for it, but it would be a sorry faith which
waited for passing travelers or which believed that a
miracle or two could set the nature of things right

and whole. The people on the surface think they have gone beyond the old problems, because they do not have buildings which they call churches or temples, and they do not have professional religious men within their communities. But the higher power and the large problems still wait for all men, whether men like it or not. Today, Believing among mankind is a ridiculous hobby, tolerated by the Instrumentality because the Believers are unimportant and weak, but mankind has moments of enormous passion which will come again and in which we will share. So don't you wait for your hero beyond the stars. If you have a good devotional life within you, it is already here, waiting to be watered by your tears and ploughed up by your hard, clear thoughts. And if you don't have a devotional life, there are good lives outside.

"Look at your brother, E'ikasus, who is now resuming his normal shape. He let me put him in animal form and send him out among the stars. He took risks without committing the impudence of enjoying risk. It is not necessary to do your duty joyfully—just to do it. Now he has homed to the old lair and I know he brings us good luck in many little things, perhaps in big things. Do you understand, my daughter?"

She said that she did, but there was still a wild blank disappointed look in her eyes as she said it.


## A Police-Post on the Surface, Near Earthport

"The robot sergeant says he can do no more without violating the rule against hurting human beings." The subchief looked at his chief, licking his chops for a chance to get out of the office and to wander among the vexations of the city. He was tired of viewscreens, computers, buttons, cards, and routines. He wanted a raw life and high adventure.

"Which offworlder is this?"

"Tostig Amaral, from the planet of Amazonas Triste. He has to stay wet all the time. He is just a licensed trader, not an honored guest of the Instrumentality. He was assigned a girlygirl and now he thinks she belongs to him."

"Send the girlygirl to him. What is she, mouse-derived?"

"No, a c'girl. Her name is C'mell and she has been requisitioned by the Lord Jestocost."

"I know all about that," said the chief, wishing that he really did. "She's now assigned to that Old North Australian who has bought most of this planet, Earth."

"But this hominid wants her, just the same!" The subchief was urgent.

"He can't have her, not if a Lord of the Instrumentality commands her services."

"He is threatening to fight. He says he will kill people."

"Hmm. Is he in a room?"

"Yes, Sir and Chief."

"With standard outlets?"

"I'll look, Sir." The subchief twisted a knob and an electronic design appeared on the left-hand screen in front of him. "Yes, sir, that's it."

"Let's have a look at him."

"He got permission, sir, to run the fire sprinkler system all the time. It seems he comes from a rain-world."

"Try, anyhow."

"Yes, sir." The subchief whistled a call to the board. The picture dissolved, whirled, and resolved itself into the image of a dark room. There seemed to be a bundle of wet rags in one corner, out of which a well-shaped human hand protruded.

"Nasty type," said the chief, "and probably poisonous. Knock him out for exactly one hour. We'll be getting orders meanwhile."

## On an Earth-Level Street Under Earthport

Two girls talking.

". . . and I will tell you the biggest secret in the whole world, if you will never, never tell anyone."

"I'll bet it's not much of a secret. You don't have to tell me."

"I'll never tell you then. Never."

"Suit yourself."

"Really, if you even suspected it, you would be mad with curiosity."

"If you want to tell me, you can tell me."

"But it's a *secret*."

"All right, I'll never tell anybody."

"That man from the stars. He's going to marry me."

"*You?* That's ridiculous."

"Why is it so ridiculous? He's bought my dower rights already."

"I know it's ridiculous. There's something wrong."

"I don't see why you should think he doesn't like me if he has already bought my dower rights."

"Fool! I know it's ridiculous, because he has bought mine."

"*Yours?*"

"Yes."

"Both of us?"

"What for?"

"Search me."

"Maybe he is going to put us both in the same harem. Wouldn't that be romantic?"

"They don't have harems in Old North Australia. All they do is live like prudish old farmers and raise stroon and murder anybody at all that even gets near them."

"That sounds bad."

"Let's go to the police."

"You know, he's hurt our feelings. Maybe we can make him pay extra for buying our dower rights if he doesn't mean to use them."


## In Front of a Café


A man, drunk:

"I will get drunk every night and I will have musicians to play me to sleep and I will have all the money I need and it won't be that play money out of a barrel but it will be real money registered in the computer and I will make everybody do what I say and I know he will do it for me because my mother was named MacArthur in her genetic code before everybody got numbers and you have no call to laugh at me because his name really is MacArthur McBan the eleventh and I am probably the closest friend and relative he has on Earth . . ."

# Tostig Amaral

Rod McBan left the Department Store of Hearts' Desires simply, humbly; he carried a package of books, wrapped in dustproofing paper, and he looked like any other first-class cat-man messenger. The human beings in the market were still making their uproar, their smells of food, spices, and odd objects, but he walked so calmly and so straightforwardly through their scattered groups that even the robot police, weapons on the buzz, paid no attention to him.

When he had come across the Thieves' Market going the other way with C'mell and A'gentur, he had been ill at ease. As a Mister and Owner from Old North Australia, he had been compelled to keep his external dignity, but he had not felt ease within his heart. These people were strange, his destination had been unfamiliar, and the problems of wealth and survival lay heavy upon him.

Now, it was all different. Cat-man he might still be on the outside, but on the inside he once again felt his proper pride of home and planet.

And more.

He felt calm, down to the very tips of his nerve endings.

The hiering-spieking device should have alerted him, excited him: it did not. As he walked through the market, he noticed that very few of the Earth people were communicating with one another telepathically. They preferred to babble in their loud airborne language, of which they had not one but many kinds, with the Old Common Tongue serving as a referent to those who had been endowed with different kinds of ancient language by the processes of the Rediscovery of Man. He even heard Ancient Inglish, the Queen's Own Language, sounding remarkably close to his own spoken language of Norstrilian. These things caused neither stimulation nor excitement, not even pity. He had his own problems, but they were no longer the problems of wealth or of survival. Somehow he had confidence that a hidden, friendly power in the universe would take care of him, if he took care of others. He wanted to get Eleanor out of trouble, to disembarrass the Hon. Sec., to see Lavinia, to reassure Doris, to say a good goodbye to C'mell, to get back to his sheep, to protect his computer, and to keep the Lord Redlady away from his bad habit of killing other people lawfully on too slight an occasion for manslaughter.

One of the robot police, a little more perceptive than the others, watched this cat-man who walked with preternatural assurance through the crowds of men, but "C'roderick" did nothing but enter the market from one side, thread his way through it, and leave at the other side, still carrying his package; the robot turned away: his dreadful, milky eyes, always ready for disorder and death, scanned the marketplace again and again with fatigue-free vigilance.

Rod went down the ramp and turned right.

There was the underpeople commissary with the bear-man cashier. The cashier remembered him.

"It's been a long day, cat-sir, since I saw you. Would you like another special order of fish?"

"Where's my girl?" said Rod bluntly.

"C'mell?" said the bear-cashier. "She waited here a long time but then she went on and she left this message, 'Tell my man C'rod that he should eat before following me, but that when he has eaten he can either follow me by going to Upshaft Four, Ground Level, Hostel of the Singing Birds, Room Nine, where I am taking care of an offworld visitor, or he can send a robot to me and I will come to him.' Don't you think, cat-sir, that I've done well, remembering so complicated a message?" The bear-man flushed a little and the edge went off his pride as he confessed, for the sake of some abstract honesty, "Of course, that address part, I wrote that down. It would be very bad and very confusing if I sent you to the wrong address in people's country. Somebody might burn you down if you came into an unauthorized corridor."

"Fish, then," said Rod. "A fish dinner, please."

He wondered why C'mell, with his life in the balance, would go off to another visitor. Even as he thought this, he detected the mean jealousy behind it, and he confessed to himself that he had no idea of the terms, conditions, or hours of work required in the girlygirl business.

He sat dully on the bench, waiting for his food.

The uproar of Hate Hall was still in his mind, the pathos of his parents, those dying dissolving manikins, was bright within his heart, and his body throbbed with the fatigue of the ordeal. Idly he asked the bear-cashier, "How long has it been since I was here?"

The bear-cashier looked at the clock on the wall. "About fourteen hours, worthy cat."

"How long is that in real time?" Rod was trying to compare Norstrilian hours with Earth hours. He thought that Earth hours were one-seventh shorter, but he was not sure.

The bear-man was completely baffled. "If you mean galactic navigation time, dear guest, we never use that down here anyhow. Are there any other kinds of time?"

Rod realized his mistake and tried to correct it. "It doesn't matter. I am thirsty. What is lawful for under-people to drink? I am tired and thirsty, both, but I have no desire to become the least bit drunk."

"Since you are a c'man," said the bear-cashier, "I recommend strong black coffee mixed with sweet whipped cream."

"I have no money," said Rod.

"The famous cat-madame, C'mell your consort, has guaranteed payment for anything at all that you order."

"Go ahead, then."

The bear-man called a robot over and gave him the orders.

Rod stared at the wall, wondering what he was going to do with this Earth he had bought. He wasn't thinking very hard, just musing idly. A voice cut directly into his mind. He realized that the bear-man was spieking to him and that he could hier it.

"You are not an underman, Sir and Master."

"What?" spieked Rod.

"You hiered me," said the telepathic voice. "I am not going to repeat it. If you come in the sign of the Fish, may blessings be upon you."

"I don't know that sign," said Rod.

"Then," spieked the bear-man, "no matter who you are, may you eat and drink in peace because you are a friend of C'mell and you are under the protection of the One Who Lives in Downdeep."

"I don't know," spieked Rod. "I just don't know, but I thank you for your welcome, friend."

"I do not give such welcomes lightly," said the bear-man, "and ordinarily I would be ready to run away from anything as strange and dangerous and unexplained as yourself, but you bring with you the quality of peace, which made me think that you might travel in the fellowship of the sign of the Fish. I have heard that in that sign, people and underpeople remember the blessed Joan and mingle in complete comradeship."

"No," said Rod, "no. I travel alone."

His food and drink came. He consumed them quietly. The bear-cashier had given him a table and bench far from the serving tables and away from the other underpeople who dropped in, interrupting their tasks, eating in a hurry so that they could get back in a hurry. He saw one wolf-man, wearing the insignia of Auxiliary Police, who came to the wall, forced his identity-card into a slot, opened his mouth, bolted down five large chunks of red, raw meat, and left the commissary, all in less than one and one-half minutes. Rod was amazed but not impressed. He had too much on his mind.

At the desk he confirmed the address which C'mell had left, offered the bear-man a handshake, and went along to Upshaft Four. He still looked like a c'man and he carried his package alertly and humbly, as he had seen other underpeople behave in the presence of real persons.

He almost met death on the way. Upshaft Four was one-directional and was plainly marked, "People Only." Rod did not like the looks of it, as long as he moved in a cat-man body, but he did not think that C'mell would give him directions wrongly or lightly. (Later, he found that she had forgotten the phrase, "Special business under the protection of Jestocost, a chief of the Instrumentality," if he were to be challenged; but he did not know the phrase.)

An arrogant human man, wearing a billowing red cloak, looked at him sharply as he took a belt, hooked it and stepped into the shaft. When Rod stepped free, he and the man were on a level.

Rod tried to look like a humble, modest messenger, but the strange voice grated his ears:

"Just what do you think you are doing? This is a human shaft."

Rod pretended that he did not know it was himself whom the red-cloaked man was addressing. He continued to float quietly upward, his magnet-belt tugging uncomfortably at his waist.

A pain in the ribs made him turn suddenly, almost losing his balance in the belt.

"Animal!" cried the man. "Speak up or die."

Still holding his package of books, Rod said mildly, "I'm on an errand and I was told to go this way."

The man's senseless hostility gave caliber to his voice: "And who told you?"

"C'mell," said Rod absently.

The man and his companions laughed at that, and for some reason their laughter had no humor in it, just savagery, cruelty, and—way down underneath— something of fear. "Listen to that," said the man in a red cloak, "one animal says another animal told it to do something." He whipped out a knife.

"What are you doing?" cried Rod.

"Just cutting your belt," said the man. "There's nobody at all below us and you will make a nice red blob at the bottom of the shaft, cat-man. That ought to teach you which shaft to use."

The man actually reached over and seized Rod's belt. He lifted the knife to slash.

Rod became frightened and angry. His brain ran red. He spat thoughts at them—

pommy!
shortie!
Earthie
red dirty blue stinking little man,
die, puke, burst, blaze, die!

It all came out in a single flash, faster than he could control it. The red-cloaked man twisted oddly, as if in spasm. His two companions threshed in their belts. They turned slowly.

High above them, two women began screaming.

Further up a man was shouting, both with his voice and with his mind, "Police! Help! Police! Police! Brainbomb! Brainbomb! Help!"

The effort of his telepathic explosion left Rod feeling disoriented and weak. He shook his head and blinked his eyes. He started to wipe his face, only to hit himself on the jaw with the package of books, which he still carried. This aroused him a little. He looked at the three men. Redcloak was dead, his head at an odd angle. The other two seemed to be dead. One was floating upside down, his rump pointing upmost and the two limp legs swinging out at odd angles; the other was rightside up but had sagged in his belt. All three of them kept moving a steady ten meters a minute, right along with Rod.

There were strange sounds from above.

An enormous voice, filling the shaft with its volume, roared down: "Stay where you are! Police. Police. Police."

Rod glanced at the bodies floating upward. A corridor came by. He reached for the grip-bar, made it, and swung himself into the horizontal passage. He sat down immediately, not getting away from the Upshaft. He thought sharply with his new hiering. Excited, frantic minds beat all around him, looking for enemies, lunatics, crimes, aliens, anything strange.

Softly he began spieking to the empty corridor and to himself, "I am a dumb cat. I am the messenger C'rod. I must take the books to the gentleman from the stars. I am a dumb cat. I do not know much."

A robot, gleaming with the ornamental body-armor of Old Earth, landed at his cross-corridor, looked at Rod, and called up the shaft.

"Master, here's one. A c'man with a package."

A young subchief came into view, feet first as he managed to ride down the shaft instead of going up it. He seized the ceiling of the transverse corridor, gave himself a push and (once free of the shaft's magnetism) dropped heavily on his feet beside Rod. Rod hiered him thinking, "I'm good at this. I'm a good telepath. I clean things up fast. Look at this dumb cat."

Rod went on concentrating. "I'm a dumb cat. I have a package to deliver. I'm a dumb cat."

The subchief looked down at him scornfully. Rod felt the other's mind slide over his own in the rough equivalent of a search. He remained relaxed and tried to feel stupid while the other hiered him. Rod said nothing. The subchief flashed his baton over the package, eyeing the crystal knob at the end.

"Books," he snorted.

Rod nodded.

"You," said the bright young subchief, "you see bodies?" He spoke in a painfully clear, almost childish version of the Old Common Tongue.

Rod held up three fingers and then pointed upward.

"You, cat-man, you feel the brainbomb!"

Rod, beginning to enjoy the game, threw his head backward and let out a cattish yowl expressing pain. The subchief could not help clapping his hands over his ears. He started to turn away. "I can see what you think of it, cat-fellow. You're pretty stupid, aren't you?"

Still thinking low dull thoughts as evenly as he could, Rod said promptly and modestly, "Me smart cat. Very handsome too."

"Come along," said the subchief to his robot, disregarding Rod altogether.

Rod plucked at his sleeve.

The subchief turned back.

Very humbly Rod said, "Sir and Master, which way, Hostel of Singing Birds, Room Nine?"

"Mother of poodles!" cried the subchief. "I'm on a

murder case and this dumb cat asks *me* for directions."
He was a decent young man and he thought for a minute. "This way—" said he, pointing up the Upshaft—"it's
twenty more meters and then the third street over. But
that's 'people only.' It's about a kilometer over to the
steps for animals." He stood, frowning, and then swung
on one of his robots: "Wush', you see this cat!"

"Yes, master, a cat-man, very handsome."

"So you think he's handsome, too. He already thinks
so, so that makes it unanimous. He may be handsome,
but he's dumb. Wush', take this cat-man to the address
he tells you. Use the Upshaft by my authority. Don't
put a belt on him, just hug him."

Rod was immeasurably grateful that he had slipped
his shaftbelt off and left it negligently on the rack just
before the robot arrived.

The robot seized him around the waist with what
was literally a grip of iron. They did not wait for the
slow upward magnetic drive of the shaft to lift them.
The robot had some kind of a jet in his backpack and
lifted Rod with sickening speed to the next level. He
pushed Rod into the corridor and followed him.

"Where do you go?" said the robot, very plainly.

Rod, concentrating on feeling stupid just in case
someone might still be trying to hier his mind, said
slowly and stumblingly,

"Hostel of the Singing Birds, Room Nine."

The robot stopped still, as though he were communicating telepathically, but Rod's mind, though
alert, could catch not the faintest whisper of telepathic
communication. "Hot buttered sheep!" thought Rod.
"He's using radio to check the address with his headquarters right from here!"

Wush' appeared to be doing just that. He came to in a moment. They emerged under the sky, filled with Earth's own moon, the loveliest thing that Rod had ever seen. He did not dare to stop and enjoy the scenery, but he trotted lithely beside the robot-policeman.

They came down a road with heavy, scented flowers. The wet warm air of Earth spread the sweetness everywhere.

On their right there was a courtyard with copies of ancient fountains, a dining space now completely empty of diners, a robot-waiter in the corner, and many individual rooms opening on the plaza. The robot-policeman called to the robot-waiter,

"Where's number nine?"

The waiter answered him with a lifting of the hand and an odd twist of the wrist, twice repeated, which the robot-policeman seemed to understand perfectly well.

"Come along," he said to Rod, leading the way to an outside stairway which reached up to an outside balcony serving the second story of rooms. One of the rooms had a plain number nine on it.

Rod was about to tell the robot-policeman that he could see the number nine, when Wush', with officious kindness, took the doorknob and flung it open with a gesture of welcome to Rod.

There was the great cough of a heavy gun and Wush', his head blown almost completely off, clanked metallically to the iron floor of the balcony. Rod instinctively jumped for cover and flattened himself against the wall of the building.

A handsome man, wearing what seemed to be a

black suit, came into the doorway, a heavy-caliber
police pistol in his hand.

"Oh, there you are," said he to Rod, evenly enough.
"Come on in."

Rod felt his legs working, felt himself walking into
the room despite the effort of his mind to resist. He
stopped pretending to be a dumb cat. He dropped
the books on the ground and went back to thinking
like his normal Old North Australian self, despite
the cat body. It did no good. He kept on walking
involuntarily, and entered the room.

As he passed the man himself, he was conscious of
a sticky sweet rotten smell, like nothing he had ever
smelled before. He also saw that the man, though
fully clothed, was sopping wet.

He entered the room.

It was raining inside.

Somebody had jammed the fire-sprinkler system so
that a steady rain fell from the ceiling to the floor.

C'mell stood in the middle of the room, her glorious red hair a wet stringy mop hanging down her
shoulders. There was a look of concentration and
alarm on her face.

"I," said the man, "am Tostig Amaral. This girl said
that her husband would come with a policeman. I
did not think she was right. But she was right. With
a cat-husband there comes a policeman. I shoot the
policeman. He is a robot and I can pay the Earth
government for as many robots as I like. You are a
cat. I can kill you also, and pay the charges on you.
But I am a nice man, and I want to make love with
your little red cat over there, so I will be generous
and pay you something so that you can tell her she

is mine and not yours. Do you understand that, cat-man?"

Rod found himself released from the unexplained muscular bonds which had hampered his freedom.

"My Lord, my Master from afar," he said, "C'mell is an underperson. It is the law here that if an underperson and a person become involved in love, the underperson dies and the human person gets brainscrubbed. I am sure, my Master, that you would not want to be brainscrubbed by the Earth authorities. Let the girl go. I agree that you can pay for the robot."

Amaral glided across the room. His face was pale, petulant, human, but Rod saw that the black clothes were not clothes at all.

The "clothes" were mucous membranes, an extension of Amaral's living skin.

The pale face turned even more pale with rage.

"You're a bold cat-man to talk like that. My body is bigger than yours, and it is poisonous as well. We have had to live hard in the rain of Amazonas Triste, and we have mental and physical powers which you had better not disturb. If you will not take payment, go away anyhow. The girl is mine. What happens to her is my business. If I violate Earth regulations, I will destroy the c'girl and pay for her. Go away, or you die."

Rod spoke with deliberate calm and with calculated risk. "Citizen, I play no game. I am not a cat-man but a subject of Her Absent Majesty the Queen, from Old North Australia. I give you warning that it is a man you face, and no mere animal. Let that girl go."

C'mell struggled as though she were trying to speak, but could not.

Amaral laughed, "That's a lie, animal, and a bold one! I admire you for trying to save your mate. But she is mine. She is a girlygirl and the Instrumentality gave her to me. She is my pleasure. Go, bold cat! You are a good liar."

Rod took his last chance. "Scan me if you will."

He stood his ground.

Amaral's mind ran over his personality like filthy hands pawing naked flesh. Rod recoiled at the dirtiness and intimacy of being felt by such a person's thoughts, because he could sense the kinds of pleasure and cruelty which Amaral had experienced. He stood firm, calm, sure, just. He was not going to leave C'mell with this—this monster from the stars, man though he might be, of the old true human stock.

Amaral laughed. "You're a man, all right. A boy. A farmer. And you cannot hier or spiek except for the button in your ear. Get out, child, before I box your ears!"

Rod spoke: "Amaral, I herewith put you in danger."

Amaral did not reply with words.

His peaked sharp face grew paler and the folds of his skin dilated. They quivered, like the edges of wet, torn balloons. The room began to fill with a sickening sweet stench, as though it were a candy shop in which unburied bodies had died weeks before. There was a smell of vanilla, of sugar, of fresh hot cookies, of baked bread, of chocolate boiling in the pot; there was even a whiff of stroon. But as Amaral tensed and shook out his auxiliary skins each smell turned wrong, into a caricature and abomination of itself. The composite was hypnotic. Rod glanced at C'mell. She had turned completely white.

That decided him.

The calm which he had found with the Catmaster might be good, but there were moments for calm and other moments for anger.

Rod deliberately chose anger.

He felt fury rising in him as hot and quick and greedy as if it had been love. He felt his heart go faster, his muscles become stronger, his mind clearer. Amaral apparently had total confidence in his own poisonous and hypnotic powers, because he was staring straight forward as his skins swelled and waved in the air like wet leaves under water. The steady drizzle from the sprinkler kept everything penetratingly wet.

Rod disregarded this. He welcomed fury.

With his new hiering device, he focused on Amaral's mind, and only on Amaral's.

Amaral saw the movement of his eyes and whipped a knife into view.

"Man or cat, you're dying!" said Amaral, himself hot with the excitement of hate and collision.

Rod then spieked, in his worst scream—

beast, filth, offal—
spot, dirt, vileness,
wet, nasty—
die, die, die!

He was sure it was the loudest cry he had ever given. There was no echo, no effect. Amaral stared at him, the evil knife-point flickering in his hand like the flame atop a candle.

Rod's anger reached a new height.

He felt pain in his mind when he walked forward,

cramps in his muscles as he used them. He felt a real fear of the offworld poison which this man-creature might exude, but the thought of C'mell—cat or no cat—alone with Amaral was enough to give him the rage of a beast and the strength of a machine.

Only at the very last moment did Amaral realize Rod had broken loose.

Rod never could tell whether the telepathic scream had really hurt the wet-worlder or not, because he did something very simple.

He reached with all the speed of a Norstrilian farmer, snatched the knife from Amaral's hand, ripping folds of soft, sticky skin with it, and then slashed the other man from clavicle to clavicle.

He jumped back in time to avoid the spurt of blood.

The "wet black suit" collapsed as Amaral died on the floor.

Rod took the dazed C'mell by the arm and led her out of the room. The air on the balcony was fresh, but the murder-smell of Amazonas Triste was still upon him. He knew that he would hate himself for weeks, just from the memory of that smell.

There were whole armies of robots and police outside. The body of Wush' had been taken away.

There was silence as they emerged.

Then a clear, civilized, commanding voice spoke from the plaza below,

"Is he dead?"

Rod nodded.

"Forgive me for not coming closer. I am the Lord Jestocost. I know you, C'roderick, and I know who you really are. These people are all under my orders.

You and the girl can wash in the rooms below. Then you can run a certain errand. Tomorrow, at the second hour, I will see you."

Robots came close to them—apparently robots with no sense of smell, because the fulsome stench did not bother them in the least. People stepped out of their way as they passed.

Rod was able to murmur, "C'mell, are you all right?"

She nodded and she gave him a wan smile. Then she forced herself to speak. "You are brave, Mister McBan. You are even braver than a cat."

The robots separated the two of them.

Within moments Rod found little white medical robots taking his clothing off him gently, deftly, and quickly. A hot shower, with a smell of medication to it, was already hissing in the bath-stall. Rod was tired of wetness, tired of all this water everywhere, tired of wet things and complicated people, but he stumbled into the shower with gratitude and hope. He was still alive. He had unknown friends.

And C'mell. C'mell was safe.

"Is this," thought Rod, "what people call love?"

The clean stinging astringency of the shower drove all thoughts from his mind. Two of the little white robots had followed him in. He sat on a hot, wet wooden bench and they scrubbed him with brushes which felt as if they would remove his very skin.

Bit by bit, the terrible odor faded.

# Birds, Far Underground

Rod McBan was too weary to protest when the little white robots wrapped him in an enormous towel and led him into what looked like an operating room.

A large man, with a red-brown spade beard, very uncommon on Earth at this time, said,

"I am Doctor Vomact, the cousin of the other Doctor Vomact you met on Mars. I know that you are not a cat, Mister and Owner McBan, and it is only my business to check up on you. May I?"

"C'mell—" began Rod.

"She is perfectly all right. We have given her a sedative and for the time being she is being treated as though she were a human woman. Jestocost told me to suspend the rules in her case, and I did so, but I think we will both have trouble about the matter from some of our colleagues later on."

"Trouble?" said Rod. "I'll pay—"

"No, no, it's not payment. It's just the rule that damaged underpeople should be destroyed and not put in hospitals. Mind you, I treat them myself now and then, if I can do it on the sly. But now let's have a look at you."

"Why are we talking?" spieked Rod. "Didn't you know that I can hier now?"

Instead of getting a physical examination, Rod had a wonderful visit with the doctor, in which they drank enormous glasses of a sweet Earth beverage called *chai* by the ancient Parosski ones. Rod realized that between Redlady, the other Doctor Vomact on Mars, and the Lord Jestocost on Earth, he had been watched and guarded all the way through. He found that this Doctor Vomact was a candidate for a Chiefship of the Instrumentality, and he learned something of the strange tests required for that office. He even found that the doctor knew more than he himself did about his own financial position, and that the actuarial balances of Earth were sagging with the weight of his wealth, since the increase in the price of stroon might lead to shorter lives. The doctor and he ended by discussing the underpeople; he found that the doctor had just as vivid an admiration for C'mell as he himself did. The evening ended when Rod said,

"I'm young, Doctor and Sir, and I sleep well, but I'm never going to sleep again if you don't get that smell away from me. I can smell it inside my nose."

The doctor became professional. He said,

"Open your mouth and breathe right into my face!"

Rod hesitated and then obeyed.

"Great crooked stars!" said the doctor. "I can smell it too. There's a little bit in your upper respiratory system, perhaps a little even in your lungs. Do you need your sense of smell for the next few days?"

Rod said he did not.

"Fine," said the doctor. "We can numb that section of the brain and do it very gently. There'll be no residual damage. You won't smell anything for eight to ten days, and by that time the smell of Amaral will be gone.

Incidentally, you were charged with first-degree murder, tried, and acquitted, on the matter of Tostig Amaral."

"How could I be?" said Rod. "I wasn't even arrested."

"The Instrumentality computed it. They had the whole scene on tape, since Amaral's room has been under steady surveillance since yesterday. When he warned you that whether cat or man, you were dying, he finished the case against himself. That was a death threat and your acquittal was for self-defense."

Rod hesitated and then blurted out the truth, "And the men in the shaft?"

"The Lord Jestocost and Crudelta and I talked it over. We decided to let the matter drop. It keeps the police lively if they have a few unsolved crimes here and there. Now lie down, so I can kill off that smell."

Rod lay down. The doctor put his head in a clamp and called in robot assistants. The smell-killing process knocked him out, and when he awakened, it was in a different building. He sat up in bed and saw the sea itself. C'mell was standing at the edge of the water. He sniffed. He smelled no salt, no wet, no water, no Amaral. It was worth the change.

C'mell came to him. "My dear, my very dear, my Sir and Master but my very dear! You chanced your life for me last night."

"I'm a cat myself," laughed Rod.

He leaped from the bed and ran out to the water margin. The immensity of blue water was incredible. The white waves were separate, definable miracles, each one of them. He had seen the enclosed lakes of Norstrilia, but none of them did things like this.

C'mell had the tact to stay silent till he had seen his fill.

Then she broke the news.

"You own Earth. You have work to do. Either you stay here and begin studying how to manage your property, or you go somewhere else. Either way something a little bit sad is going to happen. Today."

He looked at her seriously, his pajamas flapping in the wet wind which he could no longer smell.

"I'm ready," he said. "What is it?"

"You lose me."

"Is that all?" he laughed.

C'mell looked very hurt. She stretched her fingers as though she were a nervous cat looking for something to claw.

"I thought—" said she, and stopped. She started again, "I thought—" She stopped again. She turned to look at him, staring fully, trustingly into his face. "You're such a young man, but you can do anything. Even among men you are fierce and decided. Tell me, Sir and Master, what—what do you wish?"

"Nothing much," he smiled at her, "except that I am buying you and taking you home. We can't go to Norstrilia unless the law changes, but we can go to New Mars. They don't have any rules there, none which a few tons of stroon won't get changed. C'mell, I'll stay cat. Will you marry me?"

She started laughing but the laughter turned into weeping. She hugged him and buried her face against his chest. At last she wiped her tears off on her arm and looked up at him:

"Poor silly me! Poor silly you! Don't you see it, Mister, I *am* a cat. If I had children, they would be cat-kittens, every one of them, unless I went every single week to get the genetic code recycled so that they would turn out underpeople. Don't you know that you and I can never marry—not with any real hope? Besides, Rod, there is the other rule. You and I cannot even see each other again from this sunset onward. How do you think the Lord Jestocost saved my life yesterday? How did he get me into a hospital to be flushed out of all those Amaral poisons? How did he break almost all the rules of the book?"

The brightness had gone out of Rod's day. "I don't know," he said dully.

"By promising them I would die promptly and obediently if there were any more irregularities. By saying I was a nice animal. A biddable one. My death is hostage for what you and I must do. It's not a law. It's something worse than a law—it's an agreement between the Lords of the Instrumentality."

"I see," said he, understanding the logic of it, but hating the cruel Earth customs which put C'mell and himself together, only to tear them apart.

"Let's walk down the beach, Rod," she said. "Unless you want your breakfast first of all . . ."

"Oh, no," he said. Breakfast! A flutty crupp for all the breakfasts on Earth!

She walked as though she had not a care in the world, but there was an undertone of meaning to her walk which warned Rod that she was up to something.

It happened.

First, she kissed him, with a kiss he remembered the rest of his life.

Then, before he could say a word, she spieked. But her spieking was not words or ideas at all. It was singing of a high wild kind. It was the music which

went along with her very own poem, which she had
sung to him atop Earthport:

> *And oh! my love, for you.*
> *High birds crying, and a*
> *High sky flying, and a*
> *High wind driving, and a*
> *High heart striving, and a*
> *High brave place for you!*

But it was not those words, not those ideas, even
though they seemed subtly different this time. She
was doing something which the best telepaths of Old
North Australia had tried in vain for thousands of years
to accomplish—she was transmitting the mathematical
and proportional essence of music right out of her
mind, and she was doing it with a clarity and force
which would have been worthy of a great orchestra.
The "high wind driving" fugue kept recurring.

He turned his eyes away from her to see the astonishing thing which was happening all around them.
The air, the ground, the sea were all becoming thick
with life. Fish flashed out of blue waves. Birds circled
by the multitude around them. The beach was thick
with little running birds. Dogs and running animals
which he had never seen before stood restlessly around
C'mell—hectares of them.

Abruptly she stopped her song.

With very high volume and clarity, she spat commands in all directions:

"Think of people."

"Think of this cat and me running away somewhere."

"Think of ships."

"Look for strangers."

"Think of things in the sky."

Rod was glad he did not have his broad-band hiering come on, as it sometimes had done at home. He was sure he would have gone dizzy with the pictures and the contradictions of it all.

She had grabbed his shoulders and was whispering fiercely into his ear:

"Rod, they'll cover us. Please make a trip with me, Rod. One last dangerous trip. Not for you. Not for me. Not even for mankind. For life, Rod. The Aitch Eye wants to see you."

"Who's the Aitch Eye?"

"He'll tell you the secret if you see him," she hissed. "Do it for me, then, if you don't trust my ideas."

He smiled. "For you, C'mell, yes."

"Don't even think, then, till you get there. Don't even ask questions. Just come along. Millions of lives depend on you, Rod."

She stood up and sang again, but the new song had no grief in it, no anguish, no weird keening from species to species. It was as cool and pretty as a music box, as simple as an assured and happy goodbye.

The animals vanished so rapidly that it was hard to believe that legions of them had so recently been there.

"That," said C'mell, "should rattle the telepathic monitors for a while. They are not very imaginative anyhow, and when they get something like this they write up reports about it. Then they can't understand their reports and sooner or later one of them asks me what I did. I tell them the truth. It's simple."

"What are you going to tell them this time?" he asked, as they walked back to the house.

"That I had something which I did not want them to hear."

"They won't take that."

"Of course not, but they will suspect me of trying to beg stroon for you to give to the underpeople."

"Do you want some, C'mell?"

"Of course not! It's illegal and it would just make me live longer than my natural life. The Catmaster is the only underperson who gets stroon, and he gets it by a special vote of the Lords."

They had reached the house. C'mell paused:

"Remember, we are the servants of the Lady Frances Oh. She promised Jestocost that she would order us to do anything that I asked her to. So she's going to order us to have a good, hearty breakfast. Then she is going to order us to look for something far under the surface of Earthport."

"She is? But why—"

"No questions, Rod." The smile she gave him would have melted a monument. He felt well. He was amused and pleased by the physical delight of hiering and spieking with the occasional true people who passed by. (Some underpeople could hier and spiek but they tried to conceal it, for fear that they would be resented.) He felt strong. Losing C'mell was a sad thing to do, but it was a whole day off; he began dreaming of things that he could do for her when they parted. Buying her the services of thousands of people for the rest of her life? Giving her jewelry which would be the envy of Earth mankind? Leasing her a private planoform yacht? He suspected these might not be legal, but they were pleasant to think about.

\*      \*      \*

Three hours later, he had no time for pleasant thoughts. He was bone-weary again. They had flown into Earthport city "on the orders of" their hostess, the Lady Oh, and they had started going down. Forty-five minutes of dropping had made his stomach very queasy. He felt the air go warm and stale and he wished desperately that he had not given up his sense of smell.

Where the dropshafts ended, the tunnels and the elevators began.

Down they went, where incredibly old machinery spun slowly in a spray of oil performing tasks which only the wildest mind could guess at.

In one room, C'mell had stopped and had shouted at him over the noise of engines:

"That's a pump."

It did not look obvious. Huge turbines moved wearily. They seemed to be hooked up to an enormous steam engine powered by nuclear fuel. Five or six brightly polished robots eyed them suspiciously as they walked around the machine, which was at least eighty meters long by forty-five high.

"And come here . . ." shouted C'mell.

They went into another room, empty and clean and quiet except for a rigid column of moving water which shot from floor to ceiling with no evidence of machinery at all. An underman, sloppily formed from a rat body, got up from his rocking chair when they entered. He bowed to C'mell as though she were a great lady but she waved him back to his chair.

She took Rod near the column of water and pointed to a shiny ring on the floor.

"That's the other pump. They do the same amount of work."

"What is it?" he shouted.

"Force-field, I guess. I'm not an engineer." They went on.

In a quieter corridor she explained that the pumps were both of them for the service of weather control. The old one had been running six or seven thousand years, and showed very little wear. When people had needed a supplementary one, they had simply printed it on plastic, set it in the floor, and turned it on with a few amps. The underman was there just to make sure that nothing broke down or went critical.

"Can't real people design things any more?" asked Rod.

"Only if they want to. Making them want to do things is the hard part now."

"You mean, they don't want to do anything?"

"Not exactly," said C'mell, "but they find that we are better than they are at almost anything. Real work, that is, not statesmanship like running the Instrumentality and the Earth Government. Here and there a real human being gets to work, and there are always offworlders like you to stimulate them and challenge them with new problems. But they used to have secure lives of four hundred years, a common language, and a standard conditioning. They were dying off, just by being too perfect. One way to get better would have been to kill off us underpeople, but they couldn't do that all the way. There was too much messy work to be done that you couldn't count on robots for. Even the best robot, if he's a computer linked to the mind of a mouse, will do fine routine, but unless he has a very complete human education, he's going to make some wild judgments which won't suit what people want. So they need underpeople. I'm still a cat underneath it all, but even the cats which are unchanged are pretty close relatives of human beings. They make the same basic choices between power and beauty, between survival and self-sacrifice, between common sense and high courage. So the Lady Alice More worked out this plan for the Rediscovery of Man. Set up the Ancient Nations, give everybody an extra culture besides the old one based on the Old Common Tongue, let them get mad at each other, restore some disease, some danger, some accidents, but average it out so that nothing is really changed."

They had come to a storeroom, the sheer size of which made Rod blink. The great reception hall at the top of Earthport had astounded him; this room was twice the size. The room was filled with extremely ancient cargoes which had not even been unpacked from their containers. Rod could see that some were marked outbound for worlds which no longer existed, or which had changed their names; others were inbound, but no one had unpacked them for five thousand years and more.

"What's all this stuff?"

"Shipping. Technological change. Somebody wrote it all off the computers, so they didn't have to think of it any more. This is the thing which underpeople and robots are searching, to supply the ancient artifacts for the Rediscovery of Man. One of our boys—rat stock, with a human I.Q. of 300—found something marked Musée National. It was the whole National Museum of the Republic of Mali, which had been put inside a mountain when the ancient wars became severe. Mali apparently was not a very important 'nation,' as they called those groupings, but it had the same language as France, and we were able to supply real material, almost everything that was needed to restore some kind of a French civilization. China has been hard. The Chinesians survived longer than any other nation, and they did their own grave robbing, so that we have found it impossible to reconstruct China before the age of space. We can't modify people into being Ancient Chinese."

Rod stopped, thunderstruck. "Can I talk to you here?"

C'mell listened with a faraway look on her face. "Not here. I feel the very weak sweep of a monitor across my mind now and then. In a couple of minutes you can. Let's hurry along."

"I just thought," cried Rod, "of the most important question in all the worlds!"

"Stop thinking it, then," said C'mell, "until we come to a safe place."

Instead of going straight on through the big aisle between the forgotten crates and packages, she squeezed between two crates and made her way to the edge of the big underground storeroom.

"That package," she said, "is stroon. They lost it. We could help ourselves to it if we wanted to, but we're afraid of it."

Rod looked at the names on the package. It had been shipped by Roderick Frederick Ronald Arnold William MacArthur McBan XXVI to Adaminaby Port and reconsigned to Earthport. "That's one hundred and twenty-five generations ago, shipped from the Station of Doom. My farm. I think it turns poison if you leave it for more than two hundred years. Our own military people have some horrible uses for it, when invaders show up, but ordinary Norstrilians, when they find old stroon, always turn it in to the Commonwealth. We're afraid of it. Not that we often lose it. It's too valuable and we're too greedy, with a twenty million percent import duty on everything . . ."

C'mell led on. They unexpectedly passed a tiny robot, a lamp fixed to his head, who was seated between two enormous piles of books. He was apparently reading them one by one, because he had beside him a pile of notes larger in bulk than he was. He did not look up, nor did they interrupt him.

At the wall, C'mell said, "Now do exactly what you're told. See the dust along the base of this crate?"

"I see it," said Rod.

"That must be left undisturbed. Now watch. I'm going to jump from the top of this crate to the top of that one, without disturbing the dust. Then I want you to jump the same way and go exactly where I point, without even thinking about it, if you can manage. I'll follow. Don't try to be polite or chivalrous, or you'll mess up the whole arrangement."

Rod nodded.

She jumped to a case against the wall. Her red hair did not fly behind her, because she had tied it up in a turban before they started out, when she had obtained coveralls for each of them from the robot-servants of the Lady Frances Oh. They had looked like an ordinary couple of working c'people.

Either she was very strong or the case was very light. Standing on the case, she tipped it very delicately, so that the pattern of dust around its base

would be unchanged, save for microscopic examination. A blue glow came from beyond the case. With
an odd, practiced turn of the wrist she indicated that
Rod should jump from his case to the tipped one,
and from there into the area—whatever it might
be—beyond the case. It seemed easy for him, but he
wondered if she could support both his weight and
hers on the case. He remembered her order not to
talk or think. He tried to think of the salmon steak
he had eaten the day before. That should certainly
be a good cat-thought, if a monitor should catch his
mind at that moment! He jumped, teetered on the
slanting top of the second packing case, and scrambled
into a tiny doorway just big enough for him to crawl
through. It was apparently designed for cables, pipes
and maintenance, not for habitual human use: it was
too low to stand in. He scrambled forward.

There was a slam.

C'mell had jumped in after him, letting the case
fall back into its old and apparently undisturbed
position.

She crawled up to him. "Keep going," she said.

"Can we talk here?"

"Of course! Do you want to? It's not a very sociable
place."

"That question, that big question," said Rod. "I've
got to ask you. You underpeople are taking charge of
people. If you're fixing up their new cultures for them,
you're getting to be the masters of men!"

"Yes," said C'mell, and let the explosive affirmative
hang in the air between them.

He couldn't think of anything to say; it was his big
bright idea for the day, and the fact that she already

knew underpeople were becoming secret masters—that was too much!

She looked at his friendly face and said, more gently, "We underpeople have seen it coming for a long time. Some of the human people do, too. Especially the Lord Jestocost. He's no fool. And, Rod, you fit in."

"I?"

"Not as a person. As an economic change. As a source of unallocated power."

"You mean, C'mell, you're after me, too? I can't believe it. I can recognize a pest or a nuisance or a robber. You don't seem like any of these. You're good, all the way through." His voice faltered. "I meant it this morning, C'mell, when I asked you to marry me."

The delicacy of cat and the tenderness of woman combined in her voice as she answered, "I know you meant it." She stroked a lock of hair away from his forehead, in a caress as restrained as any touch could be. "But it's not for us. And I'm not using you myself, Rod. I want nothing for myself, but I want a good world for underpeople. And for people too. For people too. We cats have loved you people long before we had brains. We've been *your* cats longer than anyone can remember. Do you think our loyalty to the human race would stop just because you changed our shapes and added a lot of thinking power? I love you, Rod, but I love people too. That's why I'm taking you to the Aitch Eye!"

"Can you tell me what that is—now?"

She laughed. "This place is safe. It's the Holy Insurgency. The secret government of the underpeople. This is a silly place to talk about it, Rod. You're going to meet the head of it, right now."

"All of them?" Rod was thinking of the Chiefs of the Instrumentality.

"It's not a them, it's a him. The E'telekeli. The bird beneath the ground. E'ikasus is one of His sons."

"If there's only one, how did you choose him? Is he like the British Queen, whom we lost so long ago?"

C'mell laughed. "We did not choose Him. He *grew* and now He leads us. You people took an eagle's egg and tried to make it into a Daimoni man. When the experiment failed, you threw the fetus out. It lived. It's He. It'll be the strongest mind you've ever met. Come on. This is no place to talk, and we're still talking."

She started crawling down the horizontal shaft, waving at Rod to follow her.

He followed.

As they crawled, he called to her,

"C'mell, stop a minute."

She stopped until he caught up with her. She thought he might ask for a kiss, so worried and lonely did he look. She was ready to be kissed. He surprised her by saying, instead,

"I can't smell, C'mell. Please, I'm so used to smelling that I miss it. What does this place smell like?"

Her eyes widened and then she laughed: "It smells like underground. Electricity burning the air. Animals somewhere far away, a lot of different smells of them. The old, old smell of man, almost gone. Engine oil and bad exhaust. It smells like a headache. It smells like silence, like things untouched. There, is that it?"

He nodded and they went on.

At the end of the horizontal C'mell turned and said:

"All men die here. Come on!"

Rod started to follow and then stopped. "C'mell, are you discoordinated? Why should I die? There's no reason to."

Her laughter was pure happiness. "Silly C'rod! You are a *cat*, cat enough to come where no man has passed for centuries. Come on. Watch out for those skeletons. There're a lot of them around here. We hate to kill real people, but there are some that we can't warn off in time."

They emerged on a balcony, overlooking an even more enormous storeroom than the one before. This had thousands more boxes in it. C'mell paid no attention to it. She went to the end of the balcony and raced down a slender steel ladder.

"More junk from the past!" she said, anticipating Rod's comment. "People have forgotten it up above; we mess around in it."

Though he could not smell the air, at this depth it felt thick, heavy, immobile.

C'mell did not slow down. She threaded her way through the junk and treasures on the floor as though she were an acrobat. On the far side of the old room she stopped. "Take one of these," she commanded.

They looked like enormous umbrellas. He had seen umbrellas in the pictures which his computer had showed him. These seemed oddly large, compared to the ones in the pictures. He looked around for rain. After his memories of Tostig Amaral, he wanted no more indoor rain. C'mell did not understand his suspicions.

"The shaft," she said, "has no magnetic controls, no updraft of air. It's just a shaft twelve meters in diameter. These are parachutes. We jump into the shaft with them and then we float down. Straight down. Four kilometers. It's close to the Moho."

Since he did not pick up one of the big umbrellas, she handed him one. It was surprisingly light.

He blinked at her. "How will we ever get out?"

"One of the bird-men will fly us up the shaft. It's hard work but they can do it. Be sure to hook that thing to your belt. It's a long slow time falling, and we won't be able to talk. And it's terribly dark, too."

He complied.

She opened a big door, beyond which there was the feel of nothing. She gave him a wave, partially opened her "umbrella," stepped over the edge of the door and vanished. He looked over the edge himself. There was nothing to be seen. Nothing of C'mell, no sound except for the slippage of air and an occasional mechanical whisper of metal against metal. He supposed that must be the rib-tips of the umbrella touching the edge of the shaft as she fell.

He sighed. Norstrilia was safe and quiet compared to this.

He opened his umbrella too.

Acting on an odd premonition, he took his little hiering-spieking shell out of his ear and put it carefully in his coverall pocket.

That act saved his life.

# His Own Strange Altar

Rod McBan remembered falling and falling. He shouted into the wet adhesive darkness, but there was no reply. He thought of cutting himself loose from his big umbrella and letting himself drop to the death below him, but then he thought of C'mell and he knew that his body would drop upon her like a bomb. He wondered about his desperation, but could not understand it. (Only later did he find out that he was passing telepathic suicide screens which the underpeople had set up, screens fitted to the human mind, designed to dredge filth and despair from the paleocortex, the smell-bite-mate sequence of the nose-guided animals who first walked Earth; but Rod was cat enough, just barely cat enough, and he was also telepathically subnormal, so that the screens did not do to him what they would have done to any normal man of Earth—delivered a twisted dead body at the bottom. No man had ever gotten that far, but the underpeople resolved that none ever should.) Rod twisted in his harness and at last he fainted.

He awakened in a relatively small room, enormous by Earth standards but still much smaller than the storerooms which he had passed through on the way down.

The lights were bright.

He suspected that the room stank but he could not prove it with his smell gone.

A man was speaking: "The Forbidden Word is never given unless the man who does not know it plainly asks for it."

There was a chorus of voices sighing, "We remember. We remember. We remember what we remember."

The speaker was almost a giant, thin and pale. His face was the face of a dead saint, pale, white as alabaster, with glowing eyes. His body was that of man and bird both, man from the hips up, except that human hands grew out of the elbows of enormous clean white wings. From the hips down his legs were bird-legs, ending in horny, almost translucent bird-feet which stood steadily on the ground.

"I am sorry, Mister and Owner McBan, that you took that risk. I was misinformed. You are a good cat on the outside but still completely a human man on the inside. Our safety devices bruised your mind and they might have killed you."

Rod stared at the man as he stumbled to his feet. He saw that C'mell was one of the people helping him. When he was erect, someone handed him a beaker of very cold water. He drank it thirstily. It was hot down here—hot, stuffy, and with the feel of big engines nearby.

"I," said the great bird-man, "am the E'telekeli." He pronounced it Ee-telly-kelly. "You are the first human being to see me in the flesh."

"Blessed, blessed, blessed, fourfold blessed is the name of our leader, our father, our brother, our son the E'telekeli!" chorused the underpeople.

Rod looked around. There was every kind of under-person imaginable here, including several that he had never even thought of. One was a head on a shelf, with no apparent body. When he looked, somewhat shocked, directly at the head, its face smiled and one eye closed in a deliberate wink. The E'telekeli followed his glance. "Do not let us shock you. Some of us are normal, but many of us down here are the discards of men's laboratories. You know my son."

A tall, very pale young man with no feathers stood up at this point. He was stark naked and completely unembarrassed. He held out a friendly hand to Rod. Rod was sure he had never seen the young man before. The young man sensed Rod's hesitation.

"You knew me as A'gentur. I am the E'ikasus."

"Blessed, blessed, threefold blessed is the name of our leader-to-be, the Yeekasoose!" chanted the underpeople.

Something about the scene caught Rod's rough Norstrilian humor. He spoke to the great underman as he would have spoken to another Mister and Owner back home, friendlily but bluntly.

"Glad you welcome me, Sir!"

"Glad, glad, glad is the stranger from beyond the stars!" sang the chorus.

"Can't you make them shut up?" asked Rod.

"'Shut up, shut up, shut up,' says the stranger from the stars!" chorused the group.

The E'telekeli did not exactly laugh, but his smile was not pure benevolence.

"We can disregard them and talk, or I can blank out your mind every time they repeat what we say. This is a sort of court ceremony."

Rod glanced around. "I'm in your power already," said he, "so it won't matter if you mess around a little with my mind. Blank them out."

The E'telekeli stirred the air in front of him as though he were writing a mathematical equation with his finger; Rod's eyes followed the finger and he suddenly felt the room hush.

"Come over here and sit down," said the E'telekeli. Rod followed.

"What do you want?" he asked as he followed.

The E'telekeli did not even turn around to answer. He merely spoke while walking ahead.

"Your money, Mister and Owner McBan. Almost all of your money."

Rod stopped walking. He heard himself laughing wildly. "Money? You? Here? What could you possibly do with it?"

"That," said the E'telekeli, "is why you should sit down."

"Do sit," said C'mell, who had followed.

Rod sat down.

"We are afraid that Man himself will die and leave us alone in the universe. We need Man, and there is still an immensity of time before we all pour into a common destiny. People have always assumed that the end of things is around the corner, and we have the promise of the First Forbidden One that this will be soon. But it could be hundreds of thousands of years, maybe millions. People are scattered, Mister McBan, so that no weapon will ever kill them all on all planets, but no matter how scattered they are, they are still haunted by themselves. They reach a point of development and then they stop."

"Yes," said Rod, reaching for a carafe of water and helping himself to another drink, "but it's a long way from the philosophy of the universe down to my money. We have plenty of barmy swarmy talk in Old North Australia, but I never heard of anybody asking for another citizen's money, right off the bat."

The eyes of the E'telekeli glowed like cold fire but Rod knew that this was no hypnosis, no trick being played upon himself. It was the sheer force of the personality burning outward from the bird-man.

"Listen carefully, Mister McBan. We are the creatures of Man. You are gods to us. You have made us into people who talk, who worry, who think, who love, who die. Most of our races were the friends of Man before we became underpeople. Like C'mell. How many cats have served and loved Man, and for how long? How many cattle have worked for men, been eaten by men, been milked by men across the ages, and have still followed where men went, even to the stars? And dogs. I do not have to tell you about the love of dogs for men. We call ourselves the Holy Insurgency because we are rebels. We are a government. We are a power almost as big as the Instrumentality. Why do you think Teadrinker did not catch you when you arrived?"

"Who is Teadrinker?"

"An official who wanted to kidnap you. He failed because his underman reported to me, because my son E'ikasus, who joined you in Norstrilia, suggested the remedies to the Doctor Vomact who is on Mars. We love you, Rod, not because you are a rich Norstrilian, but because it is our faith to love the Mankind which created us."

"This is a long slow wicket for my money," said Rod. "Come to the point, sir."

The E'telekeli smiled with sweetness and sadness. Rod immediately knew that it was his own denseness which made the bird-man sad and patient. For the very first time he began to accept the feeling that this person might actually be the superior of any human being he had ever met.

"I'm sorry," said Rod. "I haven't had a minute to enjoy my money since I got it. People have been telling me that everybody is after it. I'm beginning to think that I shall do nothing but run the rest of my life . . ."

The E'telekeli smiled happily, the way a teacher smiles when a student has suddenly turned in a spectacular performance. "Correct. You have learned a lot from the Catmaster, and from your own self. I am offering you something more—the chance to do enormous good. Have you ever heard of Foundations?"

Rod frowned. "The bottoms of buildings?"

"No. Institutions. From the very ancient past."

Rod shook his head. He hadn't.

"If a gift was big enough, it endured and kept on giving, until the culture in which it was set had fallen. If you took most of your money and gave it to some good, wise men, it could be spent over and over again to improve the race of Man. We need that. Better men will give us better lives. Do you think that we don't know how pilots and pinlighters have sometimes died, saving their cats in space?"

"Or how people kill underpeople without a thought?" countered Rod. "Or humiliate them without noticing that they do it? It seems to me that you must have some self-interest, sir."

"I do. Some. But not as much as you think. Men are evil when they are frightened or bored. They are good when they are happy and busy. I want you to give your money to provide games, sports, competitions, shows, music, and a chance for honest hatred."

"Hatred?" said Rod. "I was beginning to think that I had found a Believer bird . . . somebody who mouthed old magic."

"We're not ending time," said the great man-bird. "We are just altering the material conditions of Man's situation for the present historical period. We want to steer mankind away from tragedy and self-defeat. Though the cliffs crumble, we want Man to remain. Do you know Swinburne?"

"Where is it?" said Rod.

"It's not a place. It's a poet, before the age of space. He wrote this. Listen.

> *Till the slow sea rise*
>     *and the sheer cliff crumble,*
> *Till the terrace and meadow*
>     *the deep gulfs drink,*
> *Till the strength of the waves*
>     *of the high tides crumble*
> *The fields that lessen, the rocks that shrink,*
> *Here now in his triumph*
>     *where all things falter,*
> *Stretched out on the spoils*
>     *that his own hand spread,*
> *As a god self-slain on his own strange altar,*
>       *Death lies dead.*

Do you agree with that?"

"It sounds nice, but I don't understand it," said Rod. "Please sir, I'm tireder than I thought. And I have only this one day with C'mell. Can I finish the business with you and have a little time with her?" ·

The great underman lifted his arms. His wings spread like a canopy over Rod.

"So be it!" he said, and the words rang out like a great song.

Rod could see the lips of the underpeople chorusing, but he did not notice the sound.

"I offer you a tangible bargain. Tell me if you find I read your mind correctly."

Rod nodded, somewhat in awe.

"You want your money, but you don't want it. You will keep five hundred thousand credits, FOE money, which will leave you the richest man in Old North Australia for the rest of a very long life. The rest you will give to a foundation which will teach men to hate easily and lightly, as in a game, not sickly and wearily, as in habit. The trustees will be Lords of the Instrumentality whom I know, such as Jestocost, Crudelta, the Lady Johanna Gnade."

"And what do I get?"

"Your heart's desire." The beautiful wise pale face stared down at Rod like a father seeking to fathom the puzzlement of his own child. Rod was a little afraid of the face, but he confided in it, too.

"I want too much. I can't have it all."

"I'll tell you what you want.

"You want to be home right now, and all the trouble done with. I can set you down at the Station of Doom in a single long jump. Look at the floor—I have your books and your postage stamp which you left in Amaral's room. They go too."

"But I want to see Earth!"

"Come back, when you are older and wiser. Some day. See what your money has done."

"Well—" said Rod.

"You want C'mell." The bland wise white face showed no embarrassment, no anger, no condescension. "You shall have her, in a linked dream, her mind to yours, for a happy subjective time of about a thousand years. You will live through all the happy things that you might have done together if you had stayed here and become a c'man. You will see your kitten-children flourish, grow old, and die. That will take about one half-hour."

"It's just a dreamy," said Rod. "You want to take megacredits from me and give me a dreamy!"

*"With two minds? Two living, accelerated minds, thinking into each other? Have you ever heard of that?"*

"No," said Rod.

"Do you trust me?" said the E'telekeli.

Rod stared at the man-bird inquisitively and a great weight fell from him. He did trust this creature more than he had ever trusted the father who did not want him, the mother who gave him up, the neighbors who looked at him and were kind. He sighed, "I trust you."

"I also," added the E'telekeli, "will take care of all the little incidentals through my own network and I will leave the memory of them in your mind. If you trust me that should be enough. You get home, safe. You are protected, off Norstrilia, into which I rarely reach, for as long as you live. You have a separate life right now with C'mell and you will remember most of it. In return, you go to the wall and transfer your fortune, minus one-half FOE megacredit, to the Foundation of Rod McBan."

Rod did not see that the underpeople thronged around him like worshippers. He had to stop when a very pale, tall girl took his hand and held it to her cheek. "You may not be the Promised One, but you are a great and good man. We can take nothing from you. We can only ask. That is the teaching of Joan. And you have given."

"Who are you?" said Rod in a frightened voice, thinking that she might be some lost human girl whom the underpeople had abducted to the guts of the Earth.

"E'lamelanie, daughter of the E'telekeli."

Rod stared at her and went to the wall. He pushed a routine sort of button. What a place to find it! "The Lord Jestocost," he called. "McBan speaking. No, you fool, I own this system."

A handsome, polished plumpish man appeared on the screen. "If I guess right," said the strange man, "you are the first human being ever to get into the depths. Can I serve you, Mister and Owner McBan?"

"Take a note—" said the E'telekeli, out of sight of the machine, beside Rod.

Rod repeated it.

The Lord Jestocost called witnesses at his end.

It was a long dictation, but at last the conveyance was finished. Only at one point did Rod balk. When they tried to call it the McBan Foundation, he said, "Just call it the One Hundred and Fifty Fund."

"One Hundred and Fifty?" asked Jestocost.

"For my father. It's his number in our family. I'm to-the-hundred-and-fifty-first. He was before me. Don't explain the number. Just use it."

"All clear," said Jestocost. "Now we have to get notaries and official witnesses to veridicate our imprints of your eyes, hands and brain. Ask the Person with you to give you a mask, so that the cat-man face will not upset the witnesses. Where is this machine you are using supposed to be located? I know perfectly well where I think it is."

"At the foot of Alpha Ralpha Boulevard, in a forgotten market," said the E'telekeli. "Your servicemen will find it there tomorrow when they come to check the authenticity of the machine." He still stood out of line of sight of the machine, so that Jestocost could hear him but not see him.

"I know the voice," said Jestocost. "It comes to me as in a great dream. But I shall not ask to see the face."

"Your friend down here has gone where only underpeople go," said the E'telekeli, "and we are disposing of his fate in more ways than one, my Lord, subject to your gracious approval."

"My approval does not seem to have been needed much," snorted Jestocost, with a little laugh.

"I would like to talk to you. Do you have any intelligent underperson near you?"

"I can call C'mell. She's always somewhere around."

"This time, my lord, you cannot. She's here."

"There, with *you*? I never knew she went there." The amazement showed on the face of the Lord Jestocost.

"She is here, nevertheless. Do you have some other underperson?"

Rod felt like a dummy, standing in the visiphone while the two voices, unseen by one another, talked past him. But he felt, very truly, that they both wished him well. He was almost nervous in anticipation of the strange happiness which had been offered to him and C'mell, but he was a respectful enough young man to wait until the great ones got through their business.

"Wait a moment," said Jestocost.

On the screen, in the depths, Rod could see the Lord of the Instrumentality work the controls of other, secondary screens. A moment later Jestocost answered:

"B'dank is here. He will enter the room in a few minutes."

"Twenty minutes from now, my Sir and Lord, will you hold hands with your servant B'dank as you once did with C'mell? I have the problem of this young man and his return. There are things which you do not know, and I would rather not put them on the wires."

Jestocost hesitated only for the slightest of moments. "Good, then," he laughed. "I might as well be hanged for a sheep as for a lamb."

The E'telekeli stood aside. Someone handed Rod a mask which hid his cat-man features and still left his eyes and hands exposed. The brain print was gotten through the eyes.

The recordings were made.

Rod went back to the bench and table. He helped himself to another drink of water from the carafe.

Someone threw a wreath of fresh flowers around
his shoulders. Fresh flowers! In such a place . . . He
wondered. Three rather pretty undergirls, two of
them of cat origin and one of them derived from
dogs, were leading a freshly dressed C'mell toward
him. She wore the simplest and most modest of all
possible white dresses. Her waist was cinched by a
broad golden belt. She laughed, stopped laughing, and
then blushed as they led her to Rod.

Two seats were arranged on the bench. Cushions
were disposed so that both of them would be comfortable. Silky metallic caps, like the pleasure caps
used in surgeries, were fitted on their heads. Rod
felt his sense of smell explode within his brain; it
came alive richly and suddenly. He took C'mell by
the hand and began walking through an immemorial
Earth forest, with a temple older than time shining
in the clear soft light cast by Earth's old moon. He
knew that he was already dreaming. C'mell caught
his thought and said,

"Rod, my master and lover, this *is* a dream. But I
am in it with you . . ."

*Who can measure a thousand years of happy
dreaming—the travels, the hunts, the picnics, the
visits to forgotten and empty cities, the discovery
of beautiful views and strange places? And the love,
and the sharing, and the re-reflection of everything
wonderful and strange by two separate, distinct and
utterly harmonious personalities. C'mell the c'girl and
C'roderick the c'man: they seemed happily doomed to
be with one another. Who can live whole centuries
of real bliss and then report it in minutes? Who can*

*tell the full tale of such real lives—happiness, quarrels, reconciliations, problems, solutions and always sharing, happiness, and more sharing . . . ?*

·When they awakened Rod very gently, they let C'mell sleep on. He looked down at himself and expected to find himself old. But he was a young man still, in the deep forgotten underground of the E'telekeli, and he could not even smell. He reached for the thousand wonderful years as he watched C'mell, young again, lying on the bench, but the dream-years had started fading even as he reached for them.

Rod stumbled on his feet. They led him to a chair. The E'telekeli sat in an adjacent chair, at the same table. He seemed weary.

"My Mister and Owner McBan, I monitored your dreamsharing, just to make sure it stayed in the right general direction. I hope you are satisfied."

Rod nodded, very slowly, and reached for the carafe of water, which someone had refilled while he slept.

"While you slept, Mister McBan," said the great E'man, "I had a telepathic conference with the Lord Jestocost, who has been your friend, even though you do not know him. You have heard of the new automatic planoform ships."

"They are experimental," said Rod.

"So they are," said the E'telekeli, "but perfectly safe. And the best 'automatic' ones are not automatic at all. They have snake-men pilots. My pilots. They can outperform any pilots of the Instrumentality."

"Of course," said Rod, "because they are dead."

"No more dead than I," laughed the white calm

bird of the underground. "I put them in cataleptic trances, with the help of my son the doctor E'ikasus, whom you first knew as the monkey-doctor A'gentur. On the ships they wake up. One of them can take you to Norstrilia in a single long fast jump. And my son can work on you right here. We have a good medical workshop in one of those rooms. After all, it was he who restored you under the supervision of Doctor Vomact on Mars. It will seem like a single night to you, though it will be several days in objective time. If you say goodbye to me now, and if you are ready to go, you will wake up in orbit just outside the Old North Australian subspace net. I have no wish for one of my underpeople to tear himself to pieces if he meets Mother Hitton's dreadful little kittens, whatever they may be. Do you happen to know?"

"I don't," said Rod quickly, "and if I did, I couldn't tell you. It's the Queen's secret."

"The Queen?"

"The Absent Queen. We use it to mean the Commonwealth government. Anyhow, Mister Bird, I can't go now. I've got to go back up to the surface of Earth. I want to say goodbye to the Catmaster. And I'm not going to leave this planet and abandon Eleanor. And I want my stamp that the Catmaster gave me. And the books. And maybe I should report about the death of Tostig Amaral."

"Do you trust me, Mister and Owner McBan?" The white giant rose to his feet; his eyes shone like fire.

The underpeople spontaneously chorused, "Put your trust in the joyful lawful, put your trust in the loyal-awful bright blank power of the under-bird!"

"I've trusted you with my life and my fortune, so

far," said Rod, a little sullenly, "but you're not going to make me leave Eleanor. No matter how much I want to get home. And I have an old enemy at home that I want to help. Houghton Syme the Hon. Sec. There might be something on Old Earth which I could take back to him."

"I think you can trust me a little further," said the E'telekeli. "Would it solve the problem of the Hon. Sec. if you gave him a dreamshare with someone he loved, to make up for his having a short life?"

"I don't know. Maybe."

"I can," said the master of the underpeople, "have his prescription made up. It will have to be mixed with plasma from his blood before he takes it. It would be good for about three thousand years of subjective life. We have never let this out of our own undercity before, but you are the Friend of Earth, and you shall have it."

Rod tried to stammer his thanks, but he mumbled something about Eleanor instead: he just *couldn't* leave her.

The white giant took Rod by the arm and led him back to the visiphone, still oddly out of place in this forgotten room, so far underground.

"You know," said the white giant, "that I will not trick you with false messages or anything like that?"

One look at the strong, calm, relaxed face—face so purposeful that it had no fretful or immediate purpose—convinced Rod that there was nothing to fear.

"Tune it, then," said the E'telekeli. "If Eleanor wants to go home we will arrange with the Instrumentality for her passage. As for you, my son E'ikasus will change you back as he changed you over. There is only one detail. Do you want the face you originally had or do you want it to reflect the wisdom and experience I have seen you gain?"

"I'm not posh," said Rod. "The same old face will do. If I am any wiser, my people will find it out soon enough."

"Good. He will get ready. Meanwhile, turn on the visiphone. It is already set to search for your fellow-citizen."

Rod flicked it on. There was a bewildering series of flashes and a kaleidoscopic dazzlement of scenes before the machine seemed to race along the beach at Meeya Meefla and searched out Eleanor. This was a very strange screen indeed: it had no visiphone at the other end. He could see Eleanor, looking exactly like his Norstrilian self, but she could not observe that she was being seen.

The machine focused on Eleanor/Rod McBan's face. She/he was talking to a very pretty woman, oddly mixed Norstrilian and Earthlike in appearance.

"Ruth Not-from-here," murmured the E'telekeli, "the daughter of the Lord William Not-from-here, a Chief of the Instrumentality. He wanted his daughter to marry 'you' so that they could return to Norstrilia. Look at the daughter. She is annoyed at 'you' right now."

Ruth was sitting on the bench, twisting away at her fingers in nervousness and worry, but her fingers and face showed more anger than despair. She was speaking to Eleanor, the "Rod McBan."

"My father just told me!" Ruth cried out. "Why, oh why did you give all your money for a Foundation of some kind? The Instrumentality just told him. I just don't understand. There's no point in us getting married now—"

"Suits me," said Eleanor/Rod McBan.

"Suits you, does it!" shrieked Ruth. "After the advantages you've taken of me!"

The false Rod McBan merely smiled at her friendlily and knowledgeably. The real Rod, watching the picture ten kilometers below, thought that Eleanor seemed to have learned a great deal about how to be a young rich man on Earth.

Ruth's face changed suddenly. She broke from anger to laughter. She showed her bewilderment. "I must admit," she said honestly, "that I didn't really want to go back to the old family home in Old North Australia. The simple, honest life, a little on the stupid side. No oceans. No cities. Just sick, giant sheep and worlds full of money with nothing to spend it on. I like Earth and I suppose I'm decadent . . ."

Rod/Eleanor smiled right back at her. "Maybe I'm decadent too. I'm not poor. I can't help liking you. I don't want to marry anybody. But I have big credits here, and I enjoy being a young man—"

"I should say you do!" said Ruth. "What an odd thing for you to say!"

The false "Rod McBan" gave no sign that he/she noted the interruption. "I've just about decided to stay here and enjoy things. Everybody's rich in Norstrilia, but what good does it do? It had gotten pretty dull for me, I can tell you, or I wouldn't have taken the risk of coming here. Yes, I think I'll stay. I know that Rod—" He/she gasped. "Rod MacArthur, I mean, a sort of relative of mine. Rod can get the tax taken off my personal fortune so that I can stay right here."

("I will, too," said the real Rod McBan, far below the surface of the Earth.)

"You're welcome here, my dear," said Ruth Not-from-here to the false Rod McBan.

Down below, the E'telekeli gestured at the screen. "Seen enough?" he said to Rod.

"Enough," said Rod, "but make sure that she knows I am all right and that I am trying to take care of her. Can you get in touch with the Lord Jestocost or somebody and arrange for Eleanor to stay here and keep her fortune? Tell her to use the name of Roderick Henry McBan the first. I can't let her have the name of the Owners of the Station of Doom, but I don't think Earthpeople will notice the difference anyhow. *She'll* know it's all right with me, and that's all that matters. If she really likes it here in a copy of my body, may the great sheep sit on her!"

"An odd blessing," said the E'telekeli, "but it can all be arranged."

Rod made no move to leave. He had turned off the screen but he just stood there.

"Something else?" said the E'telekeli.

"C'mell," said Rod.

"She's all right," said the lord of the underworld. "She expects nothing from you. She's a good underperson."

"*I* want to do something for her."

"There is nothing she wants. She is happy. You do not need to meddle."

"She won't be a girlygirl forever," Rod insisted. "You underpeople get old. I don't know how you manage without stroon."

"Neither do I," said the E'telekeli. "I just happen to have long life. But you're right about her. She will age soon enough, by your kind of time."

"I'd like to buy the restaurant for her, the one the

bear-man has, and let it become a sort of meeting place open to people and underpeople. She could give it the romantic and interesting touch so that it could be a success."

"A wonderful idea. A perfect project for your Foundation," smiled the E'telekeli. "It shall be done."

"And the Catmaster?" asked Rod. "Is there anything I can do for him?"

"No, do not concern yourself with C'william," said the E'telekeli. "He is under the protection of the Instrumentality and he knows the sign of the Fish." The great underman paused to give Rod a chance to inquire what that sign might be, but Rod did not note the significance of the pause, so the birdlike giant went on. "C'william has already received his reward in the good change which he has made in your life. Now, if you are ready, we will put you to sleep, my son E'ikasus will change you out of your cat-body, and you will wake in orbit around your home."

"C'mell? Can you wake her up so I can say goodbye after that thousand years?"

The master of the underworld took Rod gently by the arm and walked him across the huge underground room, talking as they went. "Would you want to have another goodbye, after that thousand years she remembers with you, if you were she? Let her be. It is kinder this way. You are human. You can afford to be rich with kindness. It is one of the best traits which you human people have."

Rod stopped. "Do you have a recorder of some kind, then? She welcomed me to Earth with a wonderful little song about 'high birds crying' and I want to leave one of our Norstrilian songs for her."

"Sing anything," said the E'telekeli, "and the chorus of my attendants will remember it as long as they live. The others would appreciate it too."

Rod looked around at the underpeople who had followed them. For a moment he was embarrassed at singing to all of them, but when he saw their warm, adoring smiles, he was at ease with them. "Remember this, then, and be sure to sing it to C'mell for me, when she awakens." He lifted his voice a little and sang.

> Run where the ram is dancing, prancing!
> Listen where the ewe is greeting, bleating.
> Rush where the lambs are running, funning.
> Watch where the stroon is growing, flowing.
> See how the men are reaping, heaping
>                Wealth for their world!
>
> Look, where the hills are dipping, ripping.
> Sit where the air is drying, frying.
> Go where the clouds are pacing, racing.
> Stand where the wealth is gleaming, teeming.
> Shout to the top of the singing, ringing
>                Norstrilian power and pride.

The chorus sang it back at him with a wealth and richness which he had never heard in the little song before.

"And now," said the E'telekeli, "the blessing of the First Forbidden One be upon you." The giant bowed a little and kissed Rod McBan on the forehead. Rod thought it strange and started to speak, but the eyes were upon him.

Eyes—like twin fires.

Fire—like friendship, like warmth, like a welcome and a farewell.

Eyes—which became a single fire.

He awakened only when he was in orbit around Old North Australia.

The descent was easy. The ship had a viewer. The snake-pilot said very little. He put Rod down in the Station of Doom, a few hundred meters from his own door. He left two heavy packages. An Old North Australian patrol ship hovered overhead and the air hummed with danger while Norstrilian police floated to the ground and made sure that no one besides Rod McBan got off. The Earth ship whispered and was gone.

"I'll give you a hand, Mister," said one of the police. He clutched Rod with one mechanical claw of his ornithopter, caught the two packages in the other, and flung his machine into the air with a single beat of the giant wings. They coasted into the yard, the wings tipped up, Rod and his packages were deposited deftly, and the machine flapped away in silence.

There was nobody there. He knew that Aunt Doris would come soon. And Lavinia. Lavinia! Here, now, on this dear poor dry earth, he knew how much Lavinia suited him. Now he could spiek, he could hier!

It was strange. Yesterday—or was it yesterday? (for it felt like yesterday)—he had felt very young indeed. And now, since his visit to the Catmaster, he felt somehow grown up, as if he had discovered all his personal ingrown problems and had left them behind on Old Earth. He seemed to know in his deepest mind that C'mell had never been more than nine-tenths his, and that the other tenth—the most valuable and beautiful and most secret tenth of her life—was forever given to some other man or under-man whom he would never know. He felt that C'mell would never give her heart again. And yet he kept for her a special kind of tenderness, which would never recur. It was not marriage which they had had, but it was pure romance.

But here, here waited home itself, and love.

Lavinia was in it, dear Lavinia with her mad lost father and her kindness to a Rod who had not let much kindness into his life.

Suddenly, the words of an old poem rose unbidden to his mind:

*Ever. Never. Forever.*
*Three words. The lever*
*Of life upon time.*
*Never, forever, ever!*

He spieked. He spieked very loud, "Lavinia!"

Beyond the hill the cry came back, right into his mind, "Rod, Rod! Oh, Rod! Rod?"

"Yes," he spieked. "Don't run. I'm home."

He felt her mind coming near, though she must have been beyond one of the nearby hills. When he touched minds with Lavinia, he knew that this was her ground, and his too. Not for them the wet wonders of Earth, the golden-haired beauties of C'mell and Earth people! He knew without doubt that Lavinia would love and recognize the new Rod as she had loved the old.

He waited very quietly and then he laughed to himself under the grey nearby friendly sky of Norstrilia. He had momentarily had the childish impulse to rush across the hills and to kiss his own computer.

He waited for Lavinia instead.

# Counsels, Councils, Consoles and Consuls

## Ten Years Later, Two Earthmen Talking

"You don't believe all the malarkey, do you?"

"What's 'malarkey'?"

"Isn't that a beautiful word? It's ancient. A robot dug it up. It means rubbish, hooey, nonsense, gibberish, phlutt, idle talk or hallucinations—in other words, just what you've been saying."

"You mean about a boy buying the planet Earth?"

"Sure. He couldn't do it, not even with Norstrilian money. There are too many regulations. It was just an economic adjustment."

"What's an 'economic adjustment'?"

"That's another ancient word I found. It's almost as good as malarkey. It does have some meaning, though. It means that the masters rearrange things by changing the volume or the flow or the title to property. The Instrumentality wanted to shake down the Earth Government and get some more free credits to play around with, so between them they invented an imaginary character named Rod McBan. Then, they had him buy the Earth. Then he goes away. It doesn't make sense. No normal boy would have done that. They say he had one million women. What do you think a normal boy would do if somebody gave him one million women?"

"You're not proving anything. Anyhow, I saw Rod McBan myself, two years ago."

"That's the other one, not the one who is supposed to have bought Earth. That's just a rich immigrant who lives down near Meeya Meefla. I could tell you some things about him, too."

"But why shouldn't somebody buy Earth if he corners the Norstrilian stroon market?"

"Who ever cornered it in the first place? I tell you, Rod McBan is just an invention. Have you ever seen a picturebox of him?"

"No."

"Did you ever know anybody who met him?"

"I heard that the Lord Jestocost was mixed up in it, and that expensive girlygirl What's-her-name—you know—the redhead—C'mell."

"That's what *you* heard. Malarkey, pure genuine ancient malarkey. There was no such boy, ever. It's all propaganda."

"You're always that way. Grumbling. Doubting. I'm glad I'm not you."

"Pal, that's real, real reciprocal. 'Better dead than gullible,' that's my motto."

### On a Planoforming Ship, Outbound from Earth, Also Ten Years Later

The Stop-Captain, talking to a passenger, female: "I'm glad to see, ma'am, that you didn't buy any of those Earth fashions. Back home, the air would take them off you in half a minute."

"I'm old-fashioned," she smiled. Then a thought crossed her mind, and she added a question: "You're in the space business, Sir and Stop-Captain. Did you ever hear the story of Rod McBan? I think it's thrilling."

"You mean, the boy who bought Earth?"

"Yes," she gasped. "Is it true?"

"Completely true," he said, "except for one little detail. This 'Rod McBan' wasn't named that at all. He wasn't a Norstrilian. He was a hominid from some other world, and he was buying the Earth with pirate money. They wanted to get his credits away from him, but he may have been a Wet Stinker from Amazonas Triste or he may have been one of those little tiny men, about the size of a walnut, from the Solid Planet. That's why he bought Earth and left it so suddenly. You see, Ma'am and Dame, no Old North Australian ever thinks about anything except his money. They even have one of the ancient forms of government still left on that planet, and they would never let one of their own boys buy Earth. They'd all sit around and talk him into putting it in a savings account, instead. They're clannish people. That's why I don't think it was a Norstrilian at all."

The woman's eyes widened. "You're spoiling a lovely story for me, Mister and Stop-Captain."

"Don't call me 'Mister,' Ma'am. That's a Norstrilian title. I'm just plain 'Sir.'"

They both stared at the little imaginary waterfall on the wall.

Before the Stop-Captain went back to his work, he added, "For my money, it must have been one of those little tiny men from the Solid Planet. Only a fool like that would buy the dower rights to a million women. We're both grown up, Ma'am. I ask you, what would an itty-bitty man from the Solid Planet do with one Earth woman, let alone a million of them?"

She giggled and blushed as the Stop-Captain stamped triumphantly away, having gotten in his last masculine word.

## E'lamelanie, Two Years After Rod's Departure from Earth

"Father, give me hope."

The E'telekeli was gentle. "I can give you almost anything from this world, but you are talking about the world of the sign of the Fish, which none of us controls. You had better go back into the everyday life of our cavern and not spend so much time on your devotional exercises, if they make you unhappy."

She stared at him. "It's not that. It's not that at all. It's just that I know that the robot, the rat and the Copt all agreed that the Promised One would come here to Earth." A desperate note entered her voice. *"Father, could it have been Rod McBan?"*

"What do you mean?"

"Could he have been the Promised One, without my knowing it? Could he have come and gone just to test my faith?"

The bird-giant rarely laughed; he had never laughed at his own daughter before. But this was too absurd: he laughed at her, but a wise part of his mind told him that the laughter, though cruel now, would be good for her later on.

"Rod? A promised speaker of the truth? Oh, no.

Ho—ho—ho. Rod McBan is one of the nicest human beings I ever met. A good young man, almost like a bird. But he's no messenger from eternity."

The daughter bowed and turned away.

She had already composed a tragedy about herself, the mistaken one, who had met "the prince of the word," whom the worlds awaited, and had failed to know him because her faith was too weak. The strain of waiting for something that might happen now or a million years from now was too much. It was easier to accept failure and self-reproach than to endure the timeless torment of undated hope.

She had a little nook in the wall where she spent many of her waiting hours. She took out a little stringed instrument which her father had made for her. It emitted ancient, weeping sounds, and she sang her own little song to it, the song of E'lamelanie who was trying to give up waiting for Rod McBan.

She looked out into the room.

A little girl, wearing nothing but panties, stared at her with fixed eyes. E'lamelanie looked back at the child. It had no expression; it just stared at her. She wondered if it might be one of the turtle-children whom her father had rescued several years earlier.

She looked away from the child and sang her song anyhow:

*Once again, across the years,*
*    I wept for you.*
*I could not stop the bitter tears*
*    I kept for you.*
*The hearthstone of my early life*
*    was swept for you.*

*A different, modulated time*
     *awaits me now.*
*Yet there are moments when the past*
     *asks why and how.*
*The future marches much too fast.*
     *Allow, allow—*
*But no. That's all. Across the years*
     *I wept for you*

When she finished, the turtle-child was still watching. Almost angrily, E'lamelanie put away her little violin.

## What the Turtle-Child Thought, At the Same Moment

I know a lot even if I don't feel like talking about it and I know that the most wonderful real man in all the planets came right down here into this big room and talked to these people because he is the man that the long silly girl is singing about because she does not have him but why should she anyhow and I am really the one who is going to get him because I am a turtle-child and I will be right here waiting when all these people are dead and pushed down into the dissolution vats and someday he will çome back to Earth and I will be all grown up and I will be a turtle-woman, more beautiful than any human woman ever was, and he is going to marry me and take me off to his planet and I will always be happy with him because I will not argue all the time, the way that bird-people and cat-people and dog-people do, so that when Rod McBan is my husband and I rush dinner out of the wall for him, if he tries to argue with me

I will just be shy and sweet and I won't say anything, nothing at all, to him for one hundred years and for two hundred years, and nobody could get mad at a beautiful turtle-woman who never talked back . . .

## The Council of the Guild of Thieves, Under Viola Siderea

The herald called,

"His audacity, the Chief of Thieves, is pleased to report to the Council of Thieves!"

An old man stood, very ceremoniously. "You bring us wealth, Sir and Chief, we trust—from the gullible—from the weak—from the heartless among mankind?"

The Chief of Thieves proclaimed,

"It is the matter of Rod McBan."

A visible stir went through the Council.

The Chief of Thieves went on, with equal formality: "We never did intercept him in space, though we monitored every vehicle which came out of the sticky, sparky space around Norstrilia. Naturally, we did not send anyone down to meet Mother Hitton's Littul Kittons, may the mildew-men find them! whatever those 'kittens' may be. There was a coffin with a woman in it and a small box with a head. Never mind. He got past us. But when he got to Earth, we caught four of him."

"Four?" gasped one old Councilor.

"Yes," said the Chief of Thieves. "Four Rod McBans. There was a human one too, but we could tell that one was a decoy. It had originally been a woman and was enjoying itself hugely after having been transformed into a young man. So we got four Rod McBans. All four of them were Earth-robots, very well made."

"You stole them?" said a Councilor.

"Of course," said the Chief of Thieves, grinning like a human wolf. "And the Earth Government made no objection at all. The Earth Government simply sent us a bill for them when we tried to leave—something like one-fourth megacredit 'for the use of custom-designed robots.'"

"That's a low honest trick!" cried the Chairman of the Guild of Thieves. "What did you do?" His eyes stared wide open and his voice dropped. "You didn't turn honest and charge the bill to us, did you? We're already in debt to those honest rogues!"

The Chief of Thieves squirmed a little. "Not quite that bad, your tricky highnesses! I cheated the Earth some, though I fear it may have bordered on honesty, the way I did it."

"What did you do? Tell us quick, man!"

"Since I did not get the real Rod McBan, I took the robots apart and taught them how to be thieves. They stole enough money to pay all the penalties and recoup the expense of the voyage."

"You show a profit?" cried a Councilor.

"Forty minicredits," said the Chief of Thieves. "But the worst is yet to come. You know what Earth does to real thieves."

A shudder went through the room. They all knew about Earth reconditioners which had changed bold thieves into dull honest rogues.

"But, you see, Sirs and Honored Ones," the Chief of Thieves went on, apologetically, "the Earth authorities caught us at that, too. They liked the thief-robots. They made wonderful pickpockets and they kept the people stirred up. The robots also gave everything back. So," said the Chief of Thieves, blushing, "we have a contract to turn two thousand humanoid robots into pickpockets and sneak-thieves. Just to make life on Earth more fun. The robots are out in orbit, right now."

"You mean," shrilled the chairman, "you signed an *honest* contract? You, the Chief of Thieves!"

The Chief really blushed and choked. "What could I do? Besides, they had me. I got good terms, though. Two hundred and twenty credits for processing each robot into a master thief. We can live well on that for a while."

For a long time there was dead silence.

At last one of the oldest Thieves on the Council began to sob: "I'm old. I can't stand it. The horror of it! Us—*us* doing honest work!"

"We're at least teaching the robots how to be thieves," said the Chief of Thieves, starkly.

No one commented on that.

Even the herald had to step aside and blow his nose.

## At Meeya Meefla, Twenty Years After Rod's Trip Home

Roderick Henry McBan, the former Eleanor, had become only imperceptibly older with the years. He had sent away his favorite, the little dancer, and he wondered why the Instrumentality, not even the Earth government, had sent him official warning to "stay peaceably in the dwelling of the said stated person, there to await an empowered envoy of this Instrumentality and to comply with orders subsequently to be issued by the envoy hereinbefore indicated."

Roderick Henry McBan remembered the long years of virtue, independence and drudgery on Norstrilia with unconcealed loathing. He liked being a rich, wild young man on Earth ever so much better than being a respectable spinster under the grey skies of Old North Australia. When he dreamed, he was sometimes Eleanor again, and he sometimes had long morbid periods in which he was neither Eleanor nor Rod, but a nameless being cast out from some world or time of irrecoverable enchantments. In these gloomy periods, which were few but very intense, and usually cured by getting drunk and staying drunk for a few days, he found himself wondering who he was. What could he be? Was he Eleanor, the honest workwoman from the Station of Doom? Was he an adoptive cousin of Rod McBan, the man who had bought Old Earth itself? What was this self—this Roderick Henry McBan? He maundered about it so much to one of his girl-friends, a calypso singer, that she set his own words, better arranged, to an ancient tune and sang them back to him:

> To be me, is it right, is it good?
> To go on, when the others have stood—
> To the gate, through the door, past the wall,
> Between this and the nothing-at-all.
>
> It is cold, it is me, in the out.
> I am true, I am me, in the lone.
> Such silence leaves room for no doubt.
> It is brightness unbroken by tone.
>
> To be me, it is strange, it is true.
> Shall I lie? To be them, to have peace?

*Will I know, can I tell, when I'm through?*
*Do I stop when my troubles must cease?*

*If the wall isn't glass, isn't there,*
*If it's real but compounded of air,*
*Am I lost if I go where I go*
*Where I'm me? I am yes. Am I no?*

*To be me, is it right, is it so?*
*Can I count on my brain, on my eye?*
*Will I be you or be her by and bye?*
*Are they true, all these things that I know?*

*You are mad, in the wall. On the out,*
*I'm alone and as sane as the grave.*
*Do I fail, do I lose what I save?*
*Am I me, if I echo your shout?*

*I have gone to a season of time . . .*
*Out of thought, out of life, out of rhyme.*
*If I come to be you, do I lose*
*The chance to be me if I choose?*

Rod/Eleanor had moments of desperation, and sometimes wondered if the Earth authorities or the Instrumentality would take him/her away for reconditioning.

The warning today was formal, fierce, serene in its implacable self-assurance.

Against his/her better judgment, Roderick Henry McBan poured out a stiff drink and waited for the inevitable.

Destiny came as three men, all of them strangers,

but one wearing the uniform of an Old North Australia consul. When they got close, she recognized the consul as Lord William Not-from-here, with whose daughter Ruth he/she had disported on these very sands many years before.

The greetings were wearisomely long, but Rod/Eleanor had learned, both on Old North Australia and here on Manhome Earth, never to discount ceremony as the salvager of difficult or painful occasions. It was the Lord William Not-from-here who spoke.

"Hear now, Lord Roderick Eleanor, the message of a plenum of the Instrumentality, lawfully and formally assembled, to wit—

"That you, the Lord Roderick Eleanor, be known to be and be indeed a Chief of the Instrumentality until the day of your death—

"That you have earned this status by survival capacity, and that the strange and difficult lives which you have already led with no thought of suicide have earned you a place in our terrible and dutiful ranks—

"That in being and becoming the Lord Roderick Eleanor, you shall be man or woman, young or old, as the Instrumentality may order—

"That you take power to serve, that you serve to take power, that you come with us, that you look not backward, that you remember to forget, that you forget old remembering, that within the Instrumentality you are not a person but a part of a person—

"That you be made welcome to the oldest servant of mankind, the Instrumentality itself."

Roderick/Eleanor had not a word to say.

Newly appointed Lords of the Instrumentality rarely had anything to say. It was the custom of the

Instrumentality to take new appointees by surprise, after minute examination of their records for intelligence, will, vitality, and again, vitality.

The Lord William was smiling as he held out his hand and speaking in offworldly honest Norstrilian talk:

"Welcome, cousin from the grey rich clouds. Not many of our people have ever been chosen. Let me welcome you."

Roderick/Eleanor took his hand. There was still nothing to say.

## The Palace of the Governor of Night, Twenty Years After Rod's Return

"I turned off the human voice hours ago, Lavinia. Turned it off. We always get a sharper reading with the numbers. It doesn't have a clue on our boys. I've been across this console a hundred times. Come along, old girl. It's no use predicting the future. The future is already here. Our boys will be out of the van, one way or the other, by the time we walk over the hill and down to them." He spoke with his voice, as a little sign of tenderness between them.

Lavinia asked nervously, "Shouldn't we take an ornithopter and fly?"

"No, girl," said Rod tenderly. "What would our neighbors and kinsmen think if they saw the parents flying in like wild offworlders or a pair of crimson pommies who can't keep a steady head when there's a bit of blow-up? After all, our big girl Casheba made it two years ago, and her eyes weren't so good."

"She's a howler, that one," said Lavinia warmly. "She could fight off a space pirate even better than you could before you could spiek."

They walked slowly up the hill.

When they crossed the top of the hill, they got the ominous melody coming right at them.

*Out in the Garden of Death, our young*
*Have tasted the valiant taste of fear.*
*With muscular arm and reckless tongue,*
*They have won, and lost, and escaped us here.*

In one form or another, all Old North Australians knew that tune. It was what the old people hummed when the young ones had to go into the vans to be selected out for survival or non-survival.

They saw the judges come out of the van. The Hon. Sec. Houghton Syme was there, his face bland and his cares erased by the special dreamlives which Rod's medicine had brought from the secret underground of Earth. The Lord Redlady was there. And Doctor Wentworth.

Lavinia started to run downhill toward the people, but Rod grabbed her arm and said with rough affection,

"Steady on, old girl. McBans never run—from nothing, and to nothing!"

She gulped but she joined pace with him.

People began looking up at them as they approached.

Nothing was to be told from the expressions.

It was the Lord Redlady, unconventional to the end, who broke the sign to them.

He held up one finger.

Only one.

Immediately thereafter Rod and Lavinia saw their twins. Ted, the fairer one, sat on a chair while Old Bill tried to give him a drink. Ted wouldn't take it. He looked across the land as though he could not believe what he saw. Rich, the darker twin, stood all alone.

All alone, and laughing.

Laughing.

Rod McBan and his missus walked across the land of Doom to be civil to their neighbors. This was indeed what inexorable custom commanded. She squeezed his hand a little tighter; he held her arm a little more firmly.

After a long time they had done their formal courtesies. Rod pulled Ted to his feet. "Hullo, boy. You made it. You know what you are?"

Mechanically the boy recited, "Roderick Frederick Ronald Arnold William MacArthur McBan to the hundred-and-fifty-second, Sir and Father!"

Then the boy broke, for just a moment. He pointed at Rich, who was still laughing, off by himself, and then plunged for his father's hug:

"Oh, dad! Why me? Why *me*?"

## TIMELINE OF THE INSTRUMENTALITY OF MANKIND

| A.D. | STORIES |
|---|---|
| 1900–2500 | No, No, Not Rogov<br>Mark Elf (prelude only)<br>War No. 81-Q |
| 2500–6500 | How the Dream Lords Died<br>(projected story) |
| 6500–8500 | Mark Elf<br>The Queen of the Afternoon |
| 8500–9500 | Scanners Live in Vain<br>When the People Fell<br>The Lady Who Sailed the Soul<br>Think Blue, Count Two<br>The Colonel Came Back from the<br>Nothing-at-All |
| 9500–12,000 | The Game of Rat and Dragon<br>The Burning of the Brain<br>From Gustible's Planet<br>The Lady Who Sailed the Soul<br>(prologue and epilogue) |

## SURROUNDING EVENTS

More than Ancient times. Forgotten first age of space. War games to settle disputes, Chinese conquer Australia, turning it into vast city state of Aojou Nan Bien. Australians manage to flee to Paradise VII, a hellish planet where they barely remain human.

The Ancient Wars, destruction of civilization and erasure of all ancient nations save Chinesia in the Long Nothing. Survivors include Others in the Earth—saints, morons and the Unforgiven. Beasts and menschenjagers also inhabit the Wild, still plagued by the Kaskaskia Effect.

Saints die off. The Dwellers restore cities, but leave the Wild to remaining Unforgiven, morons and Beasts. Fighting trees and weeds planted to decontaminate land and sea environments. Rule of the Jwindz, ended after return to Earth of the Vomacht (Vomact) sisters.

Return of vitality to history. Founding of the Instrumentality. New age of space begins. The Great Pain of Space and the Scanners. Chinesians conquer Venus. Two hundred worlds settled by sailship, including Norstrilia (from Paradise VII). Standard human lifespan is 160 years. Discovery of planoforming towards the end.

Rapid interstellar flight and commerce by planoforming. Thousands of worlds settled. Adaptation of men to strange worlds like Viola Sideria. Appearances of the Daimoni at Earth and Norstrilia. Development of Norstrilian immortality drug stroon. Instrumentality arbitrarily sets maximum life span for ordinary people at 400 years.

➡

| A.D. | STORIES |
|---|---|
| 12,000–14,000 | No, No, Not Rogov<br>    (prologue and epilogue)<br>Golden the Ship Was, Oh! Oh! Oh!<br>Himself in Anachron (?)<br>The Crime and Glory of<br>    Commander Suzdal |
| 14,000–16,000 | The Dead Lady of Clown Town<br>Under Old Earth<br>Drunkboat<br>Mother Hitton's Littul Kittons<br>The Robot, the Rat and the Copt<br>    (projected story)<br>Alpha Ralpha Boulevard<br>The Ballad of Lost C'Mell<br><br>*Norstrilia*<br>A Planet Named Shayol |
| Post-<br>Rediscovery<br>of Man | On the Gem Planet<br>On the Storm Planet<br>On the Sand Planet<br>Three to a Given Star |

## SURROUNDING EVENTS

Creation of underpeople and robots for ordinary labor. Succession of dynasties on Earth under the Instrumentality, including the Bright, sponsors of dance festivals and other artistic extravaganzas. Bright later create Bright Empire in far reaches of space. Instrumentality suppresses challenges from that empire and any other potential rivals. Creation of Shayol as place of punishment and source of organ transplants.

The pleasure revolution and stagnation of utopia, Martyrdom of D'joan and the development of an underpeople's underground. Rediscovery of Man and liberation of the Underpeople under Lord Jestocost. Discovery of Space$^3$. Rebirth of the Old Strong Religion, based in part of revelations from Space$^3$ by the Robot, the Rat and the Copt.

**Note:**
With most of Smith's own notebooks lost, chronology is largely a matter of guesswork, based on internal evidence. But the order of stories and surrounding events can be fairly well established. "Projected story" indicates stories planned but not written.